"*Bones Are Made to Be Broken* is a dark carnival of rigorous intelligence and compassion, the title novella alone of which is well worth the price of admission. But there's not a weak sister in this generous bunch. These stories hurt the way only tough-minded character-driven stories can—the human element is never missing. Anderson writes with a sure, steady hand, and I'll be watching him closely from now on in." – Jack Ketchum, author of *The Girl Next Door* and *The Secret Life of Souls*

"Paul Michael Anderson writes like no other writer in dark fiction. His premises, plots, and story structure are unique. Every story in *Bones Are Made to Be Broken* follows this pattern, and are intriguing and very good. Simply, he writes a Paul Michael Anderson story—the highest compliment any serious writer can hope to achieve. Highly recommended." – Gene O'Neill, author of The Cal Wild Chronicles

"In *Bones Are Made to Be Broken* the characters suffer and yearn as their beautifully wrought worlds shatter. Both universal and achingly personal, Anderson's stories are moody, compelling, and drowning in wonder." – Erinn L. Kemper, author of *The Patrons*

"What a pleasure to read these fresh and darksome tales! Anderson's style is tensely exciting. His stories are never quite what you think they are going to be about and his endings resonate with fear. He gives us new horizons in horror that are futuristic and psychical. It's hard to pick a favorite, but "Baby Grows a Conscience" is simply brilliant! You'll have to read them all. This collection is a treasure for any horror or dark SF fan's library." – Marge Simon, Bram Stoker Award winning author of *Vectors: A Week in the Death of a Planet*

"*Bones Are Made to Be Broken* is a deftly told, beautifully written collection of horror and humanity. It's obvious to me that Paul Michael Anderson has stared down the barrel of pain and come back to share these broken tales with us. This is a must-read collection." – Mercedes M. Yardley, author of the Bram Stoker Award winning *Little Dead Red*

"If your mantra is *Bones Are Made to Be Broken*, then you can expect suffering and guilt, death and destruction, dark destinies with little hope of survival. But in this powerful collection by Paul Michael Anderson there is also beauty and nostalgia, love and fulfillment, justice and heart. Nothing worth having ever comes easy, as these gothic narratives show us, in all of their horrifying glory." – Richard Thomas, author of *Breaker* and *Tribulations*

"*Bones Are Made to Be Broken* challenges the mind and punches the gut." – Craig DiLouie, author of *Suffer the Children*

"With notes of classic King, Anderson's *Bones Are Made to Be Broken* is filled with stories of the terrible things we see when we close our eyes. Anderson has a talent for rendering nightmares into words, and what he's collected here are stories that creep inside and make a nest of your innards." – Kristi DeMeester, author of *Beneath*

"Intense and emotionally crippling, Anderson's stories are not for the faint of heart." – Stephanie M. Wytovich, author of *The Eighth*

"*Bones Are Made to Be Broken* delivers chills, heartbreak, nail-biting suspense and horror. Paul Michael Anderson gives us a truly superb collection of deeply unnerving short stories." – Jonathan Maberry, NY Times bestselling author of *Patient Zero* and *Whistling Past the Graveyard*

BONES ARE MADE TO BE BROKEN

A FICTION COLLECTION BY

PAUL MICHAEL ANDERSON

WRITTEN BACKWARDS

BONES ARE MADE TO BE BROKEN

CONTENTS

FOREWORD

I MET PAUL MICHAEL ANDERSON via Facebook several years ago. At this point, I'm not sure if I sent the friend request or if he did, but I know we had many mutual friends and would often comment on the same posts. Then, sometime in early 2014, I posted a snippet of a story I was working on. Paul commented, hinting that I should send it to *Jamais Vu*, a magazine he was editing at that time. When the story was done, I did, he purchased the story, and "The Floating Girls: A Documentary" ultimately garnered a Bram Stoker Award nomination.

A few months after that, one of us asked the other to beta read a story. I'm pretty sure it was me, but I could be wrong. Since then, we've beta read for each other many times. For the record, I'm not an overly nice beta reader. I'm not mean, but I'm blunt, which is something I'm very open about the first time someone asks me to read and comment on their work. It's not that I try to be harsh, but I prefer simple declarative statements instead of sandwiching them between rose petals.

When I beta read my favorite story in this collection, "The Agonizing Guilt of Relief (Last Days of a Ready-Made Victim)," I was very honest with my criticism of the framing story, something Paul later jettisoned. I might have nodded a few times after I read the final version, not in arrogance, but in a "I knew this story was here all along" way. The framing story wasn't bad in and of itself, but I felt it diluted the emotional impact of the story as a whole.

"The Agonizing Guilt..." deals with a theme you've probably read many times—child abuse—but the perspective is not what you'd expect. It's often unbearable and yet incredibly honest. It's a powerful piece, one that I hope breaks your heart as it did mine. And I think it perfectly encapsulates the sort of story that Paul writes. Don't get me wrong. He stands firm in the playground of the monstrous in much of his work. Here you'll find ghosts, strange government agencies, Lovecraftian beasts, and even vampires—not to worry; there isn't a sparkle to be found—but in truth, his stories are never about the monsters. They're about the characters, the men, women, and children who are tangled up in the monster's story and desperately searching for a way out. Most of the time, escape comes in ways they neither expected nor wanted. Sometimes there *is* no escape. Sometimes the monsters they face are what the characters keep hidden inside—their thoughts, their hopes, their dreams turned nightmares.

And sometimes they discover that they are the monsters. It's a bitter pill to swallow, but an inescapable truth. Humans can be far more monstrous than the beasts lingering in the shadows. We're complicated animals who often hurt each other and ourselves along the way, and that's Paul's strength as a storyteller. He isn't afraid to show the ugliness our smiles can disguise. He isn't afraid to first break, then shatter, his characters. He isn't afraid to make you vacillate between caring and loathing.

While reading the title novella, I alternately wanted to hug Karen, the main character, and shake her by the shoulders until she snapped out of her disastrous mindset. The story is, at its core, about the fear of being a good parent when circumstances are falling apart. How easy it is to dwell in sorrow and pain and not see what's happening around you, and then, once you finally open your eyes, how ignoring it is often the easiest, least painful thing to do. I'd wager just about everyone is guilty of that from time to time. It's the understanding we, as readers, bring to the table that makes the story resonate, even if the fiction renders it more palatable.

Authors bring pieces of themselves to that table in every story they write. They can be subtle or they can provide the backbone, but unless you know an author well, you probably won't even notice. In addition to writing, Paul is also a teacher. This gives him a keen insight into children and their complexities and how they cope with things such as grief and loss, something that's often hard for adults to realistically portray. He paints the children in his work as children, not simply miniature adults with juvenile dialogue, and that's no small feat, pun possibly intended.

Paul is a parent as well, and the final story of this collection, "All That You Leave Behind," is a poignant study in parental grief and the power of *What if?* It's a difficult story to read, one that makes you pause when you finish, a knot in your chest, wishing you could change things for the characters. It's the perfect closing for a strong collection and the perfect sentiment for an ending.

I'm fond of searching for the story inside a story, whether it's intentional on the author's part or not. I'll admit that I've done the same with Paul's. Vampires have teeth and leave destruction in their wake; so, too, do abusive partners. The world on the other side of a piece of glass is the world we wish we could see, the world we wish we could live in. An angry ghost might represent a secret wish to exact revenge on someone who's committed a great wrong to you or someone you care about. The sound of a baby crying or the phantom smell of talcum powder gives a sense of what we might have if we made different choices, or if different choices were made for us.

Stories within stories. Worlds within worlds. Like life. Like us. We all have our secret selves, the faces we don't show to anyone, not even the people who know us best. Paul cuts through the shadows and shows us what his characters don't want people to see. What's underneath the mask is often hard to take because it touches a truth within us we wish we didn't recognize.

His work might make the hairs on the nape of your neck rise or he might put a catch in your throat, but when you finish reading it won't be the monsters that you recall. You'll remember the characters and their struggles to retain their humanity and their hearts, something all good fiction should do.

– Damien Angelica Walters
August 2016

INTRODUCTION

WHERE YOU FIND YOURSELF
WHEN YOU'RE NOWHERE

IN THE FALL OF 2010—on my wife's birthday, actually—my wife and I discovered she was pregnant.

It'd been a rough year, a year where we discovered the ground we'd been standing on had turned marshy underfoot without us looking, threatening to pull us under with a single wrong step. That spring, as compensation for the gross cutting to Pennsylvania's education budget by then-governor Tom Corbett, my district had furloughed me along with 50 other teachers. To save as much of my unemployment as we could while I hunted for another job, we moved into my mother-in-law's basement. It was a finished basement, an apartment with its own entrance, but the truth surrounded us: we were twenty-seven years old, married, and barely after beginning our adult lives, we were living in my mother-in-law's basement. I was an unemployed teacher and my wife worked in a women's clothing store.

So, for her birthday and as a means to take a break from all the stress, we went hiking through McConnell's Mill, a state park north of Pittsburgh. It'd been a good day; pausing on a bench before the end of the trail, my wife chided me into carving PAUL LOVES HEIDI into the planks, blending in with the intaglio of graffiti from other lovers. And then, on the way home, she asked to stop at the supermarket. She needed to pick something up, she said.

It's at this point, when telling this story to others, I offer a humorous slant, but I've never found anything that happened particularly humorous; jaggedly funny, I guess, but nothing to guffaw over.

It was in the store I discovered what we hunted for: a home pregnancy test. Heidi had suspected, had kept quiet, and we ended up picking a cheap-o one, the kind that, if you get two pirates and a parrot, you're not pregnant, but if the moon is full, Mercury is in retrograde, and you get three penguins, you got a bun in the oven, hon. I think now it was because we just couldn't believe it. Not *this*. Not at the worst possible time. Buying the cheap-o one was us going, isn't this *funny*? Have you heard anything so *ridiculous*?

We cashed out, me feeling like a fourteen-year-old buying his first set of rubbers, convinced the cashier was judging us as we bought our single purchase. I want to say we were laughing, that semi-hysteric bubbling laugh you make when you find yourself close to some social or personal precipice, but my writer's brain might be adding that in. Giving the scene color, they call it.

When we got home, and she took the test, she gave it one look and told me, "Go get another one."

The drive to a nearby Rite-Aid, only five minutes if going slow, took forever. I remember every instant of it, although not in a fact-ual, reporter-y kind of way. I know the radio was on, for example, but not what song played. Everything had turned down, become starker; the lines sharper, making the streetlamps brighter, the shad-ows between darker, the thrum of my poor old Sunfire louder. I wasn't cold; I was cool, inside and out. I thought nothing. Not of possibilities, not of fears, not of what-ifs. It was as close to being on automatic as one can be. You read that in fiction sometimes— "so-and-so worked on automatic." I'd read this time and time again, never really understanding it until that night. That moment when you realized just how much your brain never shuts up, until it finally does, and the silence is something so complete you never really knew what silence was before. Even that hum in your ear, when your hear-ing is trying to pick up *any* sound, is gone. That instant where you're stuck between breaths.

Why am I telling you this?

Because six years ago, I was in an instant between breaths. That pause between action and reaction. The stories you're about to read (with thanks) hinge on that idea.

When sifting through the stories I've written—selecting, reject-ing, wondering how this-a-one or that-a-one ever sold—it's the thing that jumps out. At me, anyway. You never know who you are until something comes along and really fucks up your day, shows you what you were, and then shoves you into what you become.

But that's only part of it.

The other part was how *alone* we felt. Without careers, without a home, without our fucking *lives* in order, we were going to be parents, titles we never intended to take upon ourselves. Sure, people were around us, nattering—my mother, her mother, her brother and sister, doctors--but it was all noise in an echo chamber. It all sounded like conversations you have when suffering from a really high fever. We were cut off, cast aside by the boogying of a life that didn't give much of a fuck what we were doing.

The word I'm looking for is *alienation*.

Heidi's pregnancy was a strange time, a time I think of now as something akin to when I had chicken pox at the age of nine, the fever before the itchy dots; instead of three days, it lasted nearly ten months. There was hysterical laughter, sheer terror—early on, doctors warned us that our child may have Trisomy 18 (a genetic disorder that often leads to a miscarriage, stillbirth, or a deformed, weak infant), a warning that was, fortunately, unfounded—and utter exhaustion. But it was all as if in the midst of fever. That silence when your brain finally shuts up, unable to compute what's unfolding before it. Few things existed, beyond appointments, to mark out time. Heidi, at least, had her work schedule.

All I had were stories.

One right after the other, the stories were written, the stories were sold, and I'd found not just a way to pass the time, but a way to gut out of me all the fear and anxiety and rage—I struggle to recall another time I was so angry and felt so helpless to do anything about it—that filled my head like trapped hornets. And they all seemed to have a similar subtext through them:

Alienation. That microsecond between action and reaction. Whatever the plot, whatever the characters, whatever the *theme* I found myself talking about—I never plan theme; it's always something that pops up—the people in these stories are always at some form of turning point, when their back is against the wall and change is inevitable, whether the change was self-started or through circumstances. The change isn't always good, the result isn't always a triumph, but a change is happening.

And, in the real world, my daughter was born.

The instant between action and reaction ended, the next breath came, and the ground solidified.

My family moved out of my mother-in-law's basement to Virginia, where I now work, and I'm still telling stories, although the furious urgency of that long ago fever is no longer the same.

The bruising my wife and I took is gone, but not forgotten.

And that, really, is the ultimate point, I guess. Whatever change comes in the stories to follow, the characters don't forget. Time and circumstances leave their scars. Or, as a character says in the title story, it's our broken bones and scars that make us who we are.

So, here they are, the stories.

I realized after reviewing each piece that this collection is more personal than I initially thought. To me, writing's a job, no different than any of the jobs I've had over the years—teacher, landscaper, journalist, waiter—and, in that context, intimacy's not in the forefront of one's mind. You punch in and punch out, doing the best job your talent and your hard work can.

But that's not true and it's only when looking at these stories all together that I noted how much of my own life I plugged in—not specific incidents that somehow translated to the page, but the idea that, whatever the monster, whatever the circumstance, this comes from some part of my head.

The fear is my fear. The helplessness is my helplessness. The rage, despair, anticipation, hope. They are mine—mined from some instance or circumstance, thrown through my mental blender and sprinkled over the plot of some story, or imbued within some character's response to a situation. These aren't my scars, but could be.

They could also be yours. I kinda hope so, anyway.

—June 2016
Northern Virginia

To Heidi.
For everything.

From this house of broken bones...

CRAWLING BACK TO YOU

PATTY PULLED THE .38 from the glove compartment when the radio, even jacked to maximum volume, failed to block out the waitress's screams.

"Goddamn it, Thomas," she muttered, and threw herself from the car. The cellphone tower loomed over her as she stepped into the underbrush. Route 15, close by, was dead at this hour. The woman's screams had silenced all the cute little woodland creatures in this godless patch of nowhere scrub Nevada forest.

There—to the right and not really going anywhere. The waitress's screams kept hitching and turning to gasps as she tripped over deadfalls and roots.

Patty smiled, but it felt empty, and she dropped it.

She headed off on a diagonal. The moon, sliced to ribbons by tree branches, turned everything to grayscale, but she saw well enough; she picked her way through the brush easily. The .38 felt sure and heavy in her hand.

A flash of white blurred past the corner of her eye.

The woman.

And, still, no Thomas.

She hissed. Where the hell *was* he? They didn't have time—and she didn't have the patience—for him to play his Master of the Dark shit. If he needed to fucking feed—

(should've done that back at the motel)

Patty shook off the thought and corrected her course.

She stepped between two trees and onto a deer path, the woman stumble-bumbling away from her.

"*Hey!*" she called.

The woman spun, mouth half-open in a stupid, useless yodel,

and nearly lost her balance. It was funny, but not even an empty smile ghosted across Patty's features this time.

The woman lurched to her, uniform torn and dirty, eyes still glassy from the ether Patty had dosed her with.

"Help me," the waitress screamed, throwing herself at Patty. "Monster! Monster's after me!"

"Bitch, I know," Patty said and, placing her free hand on the waitress's chest, shoved. The woman went flying, ass skidding across the dirt.

Patty raised the revolver. "I'm the one who brought you here, remember?"

She shot out the woman's kneecaps and the sound boxed her ears. She didn't mind. If nothing else, she couldn't hear the woman's fresh screaming.

She raised the revolver to put a round through the waitress's yawning mouth when the ringing in Patty's ears faded, losing power as a strange humming arose, like the kind heard when you leaned against a utility pole. It brought a chill that tightened the flesh. Shadows grew darker, the moonlight less illuminating. The woman froze mid-scream, her mouth a perfect capital O.

And then, Thomas's voice, in full Master of the Dark mode, floated across the air.

"*Leave me my meal.*"

The humming dwindled and branches were snapping all around them, closing in, as if a group of steamrollers were headed their way.

Patty turned and started back toward the car. "Whatever, dude," her voice lost in the noise. "Figure we got all night for this Christopher Lee shit."

Behind her, the waitress was screaming again, and then abruptly stopped.

A noxious mixture of wet mold and sulfur drifted through the open cruiser window as John pulled into Mae's Motel. He braked hard enough to jerk against his seatbelt. "What the *Christ?*"

The motel was dark and empty, every door closed, every curtain pulled. Even the security lamps were black. Only the yellow MAE'S MOTEL sign—with its flickering NO VACANCY—was still on. He saw Eric's cruiser at the end of the lot, and he instantly forgot the smell.

John coasted his cruiser up to the dark lobby, his eyes locked on his brother's car. Even from here, he could see it was empty.

John glanced at the darkened motel. *Then where did he go?*

As he got out, he touched the St. Anthony's medallion beneath his shirt. Something pinged in the back of his mind. The cop part of him told him to call Steve, who was probably snoozing through his shift on dispatch. Make this official. Make this *procedural.*

Instead, he took a step toward Eric's cruiser on legs that didn't feel quite there. His brother part was stronger than the cop part. Eric had last reported in at midnight, when he'd reached Mae's. That had been three hours ago, and Steve hadn't noticed.

He took a second step, then another. The hairs on his arms and neck stood up. The noxious stink made his head light. The thread of early-morning-empty Route 15 passed along his left. Who called in a noise complaint here? And why call the Colton police when this place was way the fuck out of town and under the jurisdiction of the Highway Patrol?

(and why is my brother's car still here and where is he and why didn't he call in again?)

Curtained windows on his right. He imagined people behind them, pale people, watching him through the fabric.

(stop it)

He reached Eric's car and peered in. John's eyes ticked off the MDT and laptop, Eric's citation book, the locked shotgun under the dash. Eric's own St. Anthony medal dangled from the rearview mirror.

Nothing disturbed, but everything wrong.

He straightened, looked at the room the car faced. That feeling of being watched intensified, making the skin on his arms tingle, the hair on the back of his neck stand to attention; the mold-and-sulfur odor more pungent. He felt like every dumbass in every horror movie, the one who went where he obviously shouldn't go and got his stupid self killed.

(if that was the case, then Eric—)

"You just shut the fuck up right now," he said aloud, and that, oddly, made him feel a little better.

He was a *cop*, for Chrissakes.

But he still wasn't calling this in. Not yet.

He made himself walk to the door and knock, feeling stupid for doing so, but whoever had last closed the door—

(my brother? someone else?)

—hadn't closed it all the way because it opened an inch, revealing a wedge of black.

"Anyone here?" he called.

He reached in and fumbled for the light switch, trying not to imagine a pale hand grabbing his, yanking him into the darkness.

(stop it, goddammit)

He found the switch, flicked it as he toed the door open the rest of the way.

"Hel—" he started to say, but couldn't finish when he saw what was in the room.

The only reason he didn't scream was because he suddenly couldn't find the air.

Patty paced around the car, a stream of cigarette smoke trailing behind her. In her head, two voices argued,

(why are you so angry?)

He didn't notice.

(what's changed?)

He never notices.

(what's happened?)

I'm just his familiar, and he's lord of all he surveys, and all that horseshit.

"Fuck," she said. She raked her hands through her hair. She'd tried the radio again, but switched it off almost immediately, right in the middle of Tom Petty's "Runnin' Down a Dream."

That song had come After and, as such, it was all static and roar.

Now, if that puny little station out of Nipton had been playing "(I Just) Died in Your Arms."

She looked toward Route 15, but didn't know what she was looking for.

(did the trucker see me?)

"Stop it," she said.

(is this because of the motel? or the waitress?)

(or how he's always fucking around, and it's always what he wants, and we've been doing this for goddamn decades—)

"Stop it!" she yelled.

That inner-ear hum arose and she stiffened. The night was still and silent, the moon full and high above, a spotlight on a stage of a play no one had bothered to attend.

Slowly, she turned.

The shadows were darker in the underbrush, almost oily.

"Everything all right, dear?" Thomas asked from everywhere, and she felt that fish-hook tug in the back of her mind; it always reminded her of a cruel dog owner jerking a leash.

Flashing neon—

(—guilt-guilt-guilt-guilt—)

—in her head.

Patty took a drag of her cigarette and couldn't stop her hand from shaking. "I'm fine."

Thomas's face, a blur of white skin and black eyes, appeared in the darkness. She saw blood on his chin.

He pulled himself from the shadows, let them build his tall, black form. She had to look up to see his face and wondered, not for the first time, if he did that deliberately; she didn't remember him being so tall Before.

"You don't sound it."

She turned away, didn't want him to see whatever might be on her face. "Feel better?"

"Much," he said. "The motel…left me spent."

(it shouldn't have)

"Good," she said, looking at Route 15. "If we leave now, we can be in LA by morn—"

Something within her growled loudly, a growl of hunger, but lower, and she winced.

"Ah," Thomas said. "Is that what's wrong? I'd been so busy, I'd forgotten about *you*."

She took a hit off her cigarette and couldn't taste it. Now that it—whatever *it* was; after three decades, she still didn't really know—had made itself known, she felt the hollow inside her, felt it growing.

Thomas approached, a swath of hovering black.

She'd kept up on the pop culture mythology over the years, watched as the '90s and the millennium added to it, twisting vampires into something romantic, lustful creatures of fate to be loved and cherished.

Thomas's mouth broke into a grin of nightmarish needle-teeth. "I know what you need."

(I doubt that.)

Thomas extended his hands, tipped with yellowish talons. With a quick movement, he opened his wrist and thick, black blood—almost an ichor—welled.

She licked her lips and hated herself for it.

"Drink this, faithful servant," he said, and he sounded like he was grinning, "in remembrance of me."

She tried looking away but only managed to look into Thomas's face, and his fathomless black eyes captured hers.

Vampires weren't sexy, but there *was* a lust for abandonment, the desire to give into the nihilistic thrill of nothing; to finally just give up and let go.

Patty's mind emptied, and she lowered her mouth to drink.

Velvet on her tongue, rapture in her gut.

John ran.

(blood)

Down the length of the motel room, kicking in doors, seeing the dark Cracker Jack prizes that lay beyond.

(blood on the walls)

Back to his cruiser, peeling out.

(blood puddled thick on the plush carpet)

Rocketing down Route 15, not seeing anything, high-beams staking the black night.

(bodies on the bed and hanging from the coatrack and the sink and-and-and)

John ran.

(Eric's head—mouth gaping and eyes goggling—in the busted picture-tube of the 1980s television)

From the sights, from the mold-and-sulfur stench, escaping neither.

(Eric, staring at John with dots of blood on his eyes)

John had no idea how long he'd been stopped, shaking in his seat, when he finally noticed the engine ticking to itself.

He looked up and blinked against the light from the high-intensity security lamp shining through the windshield. Stumbling from the car, he rubbed his eyes until the after-images faded, then looked around. "What the hell?"

He'd parked behind the truck stop a half-hour west of Mae's. His was the only vehicle back here. Around the front, he heard the deep-throated rumble of idling eighteen-wheelers.

It didn't make sense, but, then again, none of it did.

He leaned against the car to keep standing. In spite of the pungent stink of diesel, the smell of mold and sulfur hadn't left him. It seemed stronger, somehow, than before.

He forced himself to focus. *I just left a crime scene. I just left the remains of my brother. My brother.*

A rush of warm shame swept him, but he made no move to head back. His gut churned, but he didn't know if it was from guilt or horror. Unconsciously, his hand crept to his St. Anthony medallion, and his stomach calmed a little.

He started across the lot to the truck stop, feeling like his legs were wobbling more than they really were. The stop was a restaurant-slash-convenience-store-slash-gas-station. Once inside, he ducked toward the restrooms and thanked whatever god existed that they were empty. He rubbed water into his face until it hurt then looked at himself in the mirror. Underneath the buzzing fluorescents, his skin had a sickly, cheesy appearance.

"You're a handsome devil," he said. "What's your name?"

What he had to do, of course, was call it in, but how would he explain having been there without reporting it? More to the point, how could he face that again?

He looked down at the sink. "I'll call Steve," he whispered. "Ask him if he's heard from Eric, yet." He grimaced as bile lapped at the back of his throat. "He'll assume I fell asleep. He'll believe it. Then..."

He rubbed his face. How in the hell could he convince Steve nothing was wrong?

"Because I have no other choice," he told his reflection and his voice was a little firmer. A little. It would have to do.

He opened the men's room door and nearly walked into the waitress and cook waiting outside.

"Jesus," he cried, grabbing the frame to keep from falling. The door, pulled by its pneumatic arm, smacked his ass.

"You busy, officer?" the waitress said, as if cringing policemen were a common sight. She appeared middle-aged but maintained a 1950s hairstyle and glasses.

John mentally willed his heart to slow down. "Can I help you?"

"We didn't know if we should write the guy off or call somebody," the cook said, his dark face strained.

John blinked. "Excuse me?"

"We have a girl—"

"A woman, Beverly," the waitress said and, oh yeah, John could imagine her slinging coffee during Eisenhower's reign of benignity.

(i've lost my fucking mind)

John rubbed his forehead. He almost wanted a migraine to come on, anything to distract him.

"Beverly," the cook said. "She went out back to dump some trash and never came back."

"Beverly's not the type of person to leave her shift unannounced," the waitress said. She must've caught the glance the cook shot her because she went on. "Not that we didn't think that was impossible, but then this driver... This driver came in. Said he saw

Beverly leave with some woman, but we didn't know if we should believe him. He just came in a half hour ago. Smells like he's had a beer or two."

He waited, but when she didn't continue, he said, his patience fraying, "I don't see the problem—"

"Driver said the woman grabbed Beverly," the cook said. "Said he thought she put a cloth over Bev's mouth."

And John closed his own.

"How do you feel now?" Thomas asked. He'd retreated to the shadows.

Patty rattled the map across the hood of the car. "Fine." The hairs on the back of her neck said he was close by. She found Route 15, put her finger on it. "It's only four hours to LA. Put some distance between us and here."

"Why?"

She wouldn't look up. "Do I really have to explain that? Real-ly?"

"Why not take our time?" He talked like he was grinning again. "We've been doing it for years now."

(because I'm fucking tired of your shit)

"We're only four hours away," she repeated, slowly.

"Don't you like it here?"

She beat the map back along its folds. "It's the same as any other goddamn place—"

(except the motel. except you went fuckin apeshit)

"—and I'm tired of them."

Silence for a moment.

Then: "Are you *happy*, Patricia?"

A chill swept her.

(he knows)

"What?" she asked.

"You heard me."

"You haven't called me Patricia in years."

(not since the bar and Before and "(I Just) Died in Your Arms"—)

"Answer the question," he said.

"What do you mean, *Tommy?*"

(—*on the jukebox and I open my mouth and then it's dark and then there's screaming and we're on the floor and my back's killing me 'cause the table's busted on top of me and it's the stink of mold and sulfur and Tommy's hands in mine, but I'm still stuck on a moment ago, still thinking,* Is he breaking up with me?—)

"That girl," Thomas purred, and a line of branches broke, too fast for a human to move. "I've always hunted. Why'd you feel the need to come in there and ruin my fun?"

(—*and then Tommy's hand's gone and I hear him scream and the stink is unbearable*—)

Patty straightened. "Because you'd just had a fucking free-for-all at that goddamn motel and, I don't know, it might not be all that smart to hang around."

(—*and I grab something, a piece of table, and I throw myself at where I think Tommy is and I'm stabbing and Tommy's screaming and I'm screaming and that* whatever's *screaming, but we learned what it was, didn't we, Tommy?*—)

Another line of branches, right to left. "Ah, the motel. Didn't stick around for *that*, did you, Patricia?"

(—*and a fire's broken out and I can see and when I get the thing off you, your chest is torn to shit and covered in what looks like slime and all I can think of is fucking scouts and snakebites, like I'm still a fucking kid*—)

"I was moving the cars," she said. "I don't feed. I'm not a vampire. Remember?"

A thick branch snapped, like a mortar shell. She jumped, couldn't help it.

"Every time I look at you," he said. "Why move the cars? Why move the cars and not turn off the light?"

(—*so I try draining the venom, its enzyme*—)

"I need something to *do*, Tommy," she yelled. "What the fuck am I supposed to *do*? We agreed on LA years ago, but now we're so close and we putz around?"

(—*and it's like cold honey without the sweetness and we figure, later, it must've been sick to come into a college bar like that*—)

"Call the police maybe?" he asked.

(—*and I get you out of there, and you die, and then come back and kill someone and we know what you are, don't we?*—)

Blink, and Thomas stood in front of her, gripped her chin with his solid-cold fingers, so cold it hurt.

"That's when you came back," he said, and his black eyes seemed to pulse. "How coincidental."

(—*and when I go to a church, like I'm a little girl again, just to get a moment to fucking clear my head and think this all over, the door handle burns my hand and I know what I am, don't we?*—)

Blink, and she was flying, crash-landing, gravel going down her shirt. She looked up and Thomas was much taller, much darker.

"Aren't you *happy,* Patricia?" he asked and his voice was as cold as his skin. "Aren't you?"

(—*and for just a second, before I remember how absolutely fucked I am, I consider running)*

And so, thirty years too late, she did.

They led John back to his car.

The cook coughed. "You, uh, parked where the guy said he saw Bev get snatched."

He was going to scream. He felt his brain strip a gear, even as the mold-and-sulfur stink slapped him anew. His circuits were already fried and this was just too much juice.

"Excuse me," he said, and couldn't help the strangled sound he made.

He walked back to his cruiser, feeling as if someone had buried a steel-toed boot in his ass. The asphalt around the car was blameless, aside from tar used to seal cracks, but he stayed there, hands on his belt, trying to appear as if he was studying something. He hunkered down, and it was the same view up-close.

(what the hell is going on here?)

The stench was stupendous, cramming his nostrils, but the waitress and cook hadn't seemed to notice it. He'd smelled it as soon as they'd walked around back, and it was only worse here.

A quiet voice spoke up:

Only I can.

He cocked his head. "The hell?" he murmured.

"You see anything?" the waitress asked, and he winced, tried blocking her out. He felt the end of a thread, dangling right in front of his mental hands, and if he could only grab *it.*

(I can smell this, but they can't)

It made his gut churn. His hand went for St. Anthony.

(did it follow me here? on my clothes? the car?)

That quiet voice spoke up again, the part of him that had stepped aside when he'd gotten out of his car at Mae's. The cop part, the objective part.

I *followed it here.*

He stood up so fast his knees popped.

"The *hell?*" he said.

"Everything all right, officer?" the waitress called, and he winced again. *Shit.*

John walked back to the waitress and cook, ignoring their curious expressions. He didn't want to know what they were thinking.

"Folks," he said, trying his best a-policeman-is-your-friend grin. It made his face feel molded out of clay. "I'm gonna need you to step inside for a bit while I call this in. I'm designating this area a crime scene until we can fully see what's what." He dry-coughed, avoiding their eyes. "Don't go too far, though."

I sound like an asshole!

"I'm gonna need your statements, and one from the man who initially reported it."

They didn't immediately move, and John was aware of sweat, itchy and distracting, along his hairline. He wanted to shove them, scream at them, get them as far away as humanly possible.

With agonizing slowness, the waitress said, "Of course, officer," and she led the cook around the corner.

John made himself wait until he was sure they were gone, then pelted back to the spot, diving into that awful smell.

(I followed this here?)

No dissent was raised, no alternative theory given.

(how?)

He felt the medallion in his hand and, surprised, looked down.

St. Anthony, finder of lost things.

He'd lost his brother tonight.

But a person, slaughtering an *entire* motel and *then* plucking this waitress? Who could pull that off? And could he still find her and whatever answers she might have?

Doesn't matter. Not yet. That will sort itself out when it needs to.

That was the cop-part talking. And it was right.

He took a great big whiff and smelled the mold and sulfur.

Now she knew how that stupid bitch had felt.

She vaulted over a downed trunk as branches and trees broke all around her.

"Why?" Thomas yelled, as directionless as the destruction. *"Why, you bitch?"*

She kept the moon to her right, thinking this godless little patch of nowhere scrub forest couldn't last forever, not in fucking Nevada.

(and go where?)

She ignored that. Eventually, she'd break cover, and, ironically, she'd have the advantage over Thomas. Thomas was strong, but Thomas wasn't direct. And then Thomas proved her a liar by coming out of nowhere and shoving her. Her feet left the ground, still *running*. She crashed, somersaulted so hard her neck creaked, and got checked by an outcropping of rock. She felt the give of ribs breaking. The pain, the jaw-snap of a great monster, was instantaneous. She screamed.

Thomas's icy marble hand grabbed her neck and hoisted her off the ground, choking off her cry and whatever wind she still had in her lungs.

"Who do you think you are?" he bellowed. Blackness had eaten most of his face. *"When did you become my keeper? When did YOU get the right to say what I can and can't do?"*

He shook her roughly. She gagged, his coldness burning her flesh. Black poppies bloomed and died in her eyes.

"I rule you, you dumb twat!" he screamed. *"Own you like chattel! You are my servant, to keep or to throw away!"*

She could feel her tongue protruding from her mouth, and the ridiculous image of a cash register with its money drawer extended wouldn't leave her mind.

(I'm going to die with that in my head)

She grabbed the sides of Thomas's hand, and it was like grabbing frozen meat. She swung back as hard as she could and then pile-drove her sneakers into his center. It was like slamming her feet into a brick wall, and her broken ribs stabbed inward. Still, the move surprised him and he dropped her. The air her lungs sucked in was cold and delicious. Her hands found a tree, used it to pick herself up, aware of the irony of this; nothing totally human could still stand up. Her limbs shook like over-tightened guitar strings, a heady mix of adrenaline, pain, and rage.

She felt the .38 in her pocket and pawed for it.

Thomas was entirely black, a hole cut into the fabric of reality, and his voice was that of crushing rocks. *"Look how well this has worked out for you."*

She pulled the .38 from her pocket and raised it.

"Fuck you, Tommy," she panted around a mouthful of blood, and pulled the trigger. Thomas doubled over, more from shock than anything else, and she took her chance, bolting to his left and back to the car as best as her ribs would allow. Still, in spite of the pain, in spite of the rage, a lightness grew in her chest, like a candlewick beginning to catch, and she, at first, had no idea what the hell it was.

The air cracked open with Thomas's bellow. *"I'll rip your fucking throat out for that!"*

It wasn't a tug in the back of her head this time, but an all-out yank that she thought would sweep her feet out from under her. She put more speed on.

(you have to catch me first, you prick)

The cruiser ate up the road, taking curves with barely a touch of the brakes, as John held onto the last vestiges of his conscious mind.

The mold-and-sulfur stench was all around him now. All his other senses had funneled into his sense of smell, and it made thinking incredibly difficult. A door had been opened at the bottom of his mind and what was clawing out was an instinctual creature, wanting nothing but to rend and destroy.

(get you I'll get you)

But he didn't even know what those words meant.

In his free hand, he clutched St. Anthony and felt the medallion grow warm.

Laughing.

She was laughing.

In spite of the pain, in spite of the rage, in spite of the fear, she was laughing.

(almost free)

She broke through the tree line, nearly colliding with the fence surrounding the cell tower, and made a bee-line for the car. Feelings—relief, anticipation—she'd thought dead, or so-close-as-to-be-no-different, had reawakened, stretching their limbs and looking around.

And it'd only taken the slaughter of a dozen people and being batted around like a cat toy for her to discover this.

She cackled, spritzing the air with blood.

(almost free almost)

She yanked the driver side door open, then dived into the car, already reaching for the keys still in the ignition.

Which were gone, of course.

She froze, and everything broke within her with a sound like shattering glass.

"No!" she shrieked, as if volume could make the keys reappear.

The wretched scream of twisting metal and then the driver side door was gone, flung with a crash into the underbrush. Thomas's white hands darted out of the darkness and ripped her from the car. His voice crashed down on her like waves breaking on rocks.

"Fucking worthless BITCH!"

He heaved her through the air and she bounced liked a basketball along the access lane, the air getting punched out of her, shredding the skin off her arms and face. The back of her head met a rock, and white comets shot across her spinning vision. Her ribs, pulverized now, jabbed and poked at her soft insides. Her hand, still holding the .38, spasmed, and she fired a shot that seemed very far away.

She came to a rest, and her vision was a gummy haze. She felt herself bleeding in a half-dozen places, and it was like a drain-plug had been pulled—every bit of Thomas's power she'd fed on was leaving her, turning her into just another broken human.

"I think we both knew this was inevitable," Thomas said, his voice re-verberating through her head. *"No more LA, no more road-trip, no more us. I can do a lot here. I can have a lot of fun here. So, I'll stay and you ...well, you won't, Patricia."*

She made herself smile, blood leaking from between her teeth.

"I want that very much," she said, forcing herself to speak as clearly as she could. "You fucking prick."

And then the world filled with light.

A flash, off to the right, a bit up ahead.

And then a voice, what a nightmare would sound like, riding on the air. *"I think we both knew this was inevitable."*

John sat bolt upright, like a man suffering a widow-making coronary, and his foot momentarily hit the brakes. The tires shrieked. The smell of peeled rubber filled the car, cutting through the stench of mold and sulfur.

He hit the gas again and the cruiser surged forward. He saw the access break in the tree line and wrenched the steering wheel right, two tires coming off the ground.

His headlights pinned a woman bleeding on the ground—

(the waitress?)

—and a figure towering over her, a vague, black humanoid form that jacked every nerve to ten.

John slammed on the brakes, but was out before his cruiser had come to a full stop, yanking his pistol from his holster. He leapt over the woman without a downward glance and launched at the thing, already firing.

And the thing *laughed* at him.

It was as if a switch had been thrown, and he had an instant of returned reason—brief wonderment of how so much could've happened so fast—before the thing batted him aside with what felt like a thick marble beam. John's shoulder broke with the sound of snapping twigs. He crashed into the underbrush, losing his gun. He hit a trunk and his broken shoulder burst into holy, righteous fire. He peeled his throat shrieking.

The nightmare figure came for him, picking him up by the shirt with the ease of someone lifting an empty laundry bag. John bit his lip and blood trickled down his chin. He felt a growing warmth on his chest but didn't immediately recognize it. There were more pressing matters.

"You look familiar," the figure said, and it seemed his voice was both audible and in John's mind.

(my brother)

He tried to say it, but couldn't find his voice. He felt warmth, dialing up slowly and spreading outward. A strange sound, like crackling cellophane, grew in his ears as his pain began to lessen.

And the creature seemed to feel it, too.

It made a strangled noise and some of the darkness left its face, revealing a cleft chin, a mouth seemingly crammed with needle teeth.

(took Eric's head off)

It tried to speak, *"What—"* and then it felt like John's chest exploded in white light.

The creature dropped him, the light revealing white hands, monstrous nails. Its bulging black eyes, too large for an otherwise normal face, glared at John with hatred, confusion, and pain.

"What—" it tried to say again, but the warmth was building and climbing, the light blinding, making John wince. The creature went crashing through the brush back to the access road.

John grabbed at the light. His St. Anthony medallion, its details almost obliterated by its illumination.

(what the hell)

"Motherfucker!" the creature barked, and John looked up. It was still retreating, the darkness drained, revealing a man younger than John. It bared its teeth at him.

And the light in John's hand was fading as the pain in his shoulder returned. John staggered to his feet and lurched toward the creature, ignoring the rusty-saw-burr of his shoulder.

Immediately, the light returned, the buzz grew louder, and his pain faded.

"Got you," he breathed, and was able to run.

Tommy's pained scream brought Patty to a soupy consciousness. She raised her head just in time to see him, devoid of his Master of the Dark look, diving into the underbrush. A moment later, a burly cop, holding what looked like the tiniest LED lantern, appeared and chased after him, grinning.

(this is what blood loss does to you)

She lowered her head, waiting for the lapping gray waters of unconsciousness to pull her back out again.

(get up)

She didn't want to. Tommy had done enough. But that interior voice wouldn't let go.

(this is your only chance)

Patty raised her head again and vertigo clopped her one. She squeezed her eyes shut, opened them, repeated the process until she could, more or less, see clearly.

(now get away)

She looked at the idling cruiser, blinking against the headlights. She could just see the driver side door, open like an invitation. She started for it, not really thinking. She reached the bumper. Pulling herself up, a fresh burst of pain, like a fat, crackling lightning bolt, seized her and she went face first into the cruiser's hot hood. She hugged her abdomen, but that did no good.

This pain came from deeper. From where she fed on Tommy.

(too much on too little)

She'd always known she depended on Tommy's feedings, that it made her stronger, sharper, kept her young-looking, without any of the drawbacks Tommy had as true undead, but she hadn't really known the *extent* of that dependence, how much it sustained her.

(hold out just hold out wait it out just like a junkie)

The hood burned her cheek, the sudden cold-sweat on her brow dripping and sizzling on the metal. She pushed herself until she just leaned on the car, and used it to work her way around to the door. Another bolt of pain came, driving her to her knees.

(c'mon c'mon)

Tommy howled, an anguished scream from deep in the woods. He sounded like he did back in that bar, when they were both human and all was right in the world.

"No, it wasn't," she breathed, and her voice was thick.

Still, she turned toward the woods, away from the door.

Get in the car. Get the hell out of here. Go to Nipton and kill that numb-fuck deejay and steal his car. Don't turn back.

Not a scream this time, but a shriek. Pain. Tommy was in *pain.* Like all those years ago. And she'd acted without thought then.

Patty was already moving before she caught herself, hugged herself as if to hold her body in place.

What am I doing? I am done *with this. I am almost free.*

What felt like a taloned-hand burrowed deep into her gut, and she projectile-vomited blood against the side of the cruiser.

Can't. I can't. This isn't something—

But she couldn't finish the thought. In the back of her mind, and two feet to her right, she sensed the door to her freedom, to the person she could've been, without Tommy and his secondhand power and the leash both he and it had put on her. The woman the good little girl would've grown up to be.

And she was turning away from it.

When the next shriek came, Patty got moving, getting to her feet, heading for the woods. When she reached the .38, she bent over to pick it up and didn't fall.

⁓···⁓

(vampire it's a vampire)

But the thought held no weight. Unimportant. More important was the power in his medallion, building him up, leading him after the creature. Every muscle and nerve sang in harmony.

The creature stumbled and John leapt at it. St. Anthony brushed the top of its forehead and flesh hissed like hot grease. The smell was stupendous. The creature screeched and shoved him away, holding a hand to its head. John backpedaled and fell on his ass. The creature pulled its hand away. The darkness was gone except for the gleaming cores of its oil-drop eyes. A comet of scorched flesh arced across its brow.

"Who the fuck do you think I am—Evil Ed?" it asked. Its voice was odd when drained of power, like it spoke around a throat full of snot. It bared its teeth as it straightened and its skin darkened, blending in with the shadows. "Gonna *bleed* you, man," it said, its voice deepening, becoming thunder in Hell. *"Gonna keep you alive long enough so you can feel every…fucking…drop."*

It approached, slowly, and the darkness poured in around it like black water.

John felt around behind him, finding a rock. As the creature reached for him, he swung the medallion—a part of him noting the way the darkness shrank away as the creature cringed. He brought the rock around and slammed it into the side of the creature's face. Teeth broke like piano keys and it fell.

John jumped onto it, straddling it, and brought the rock down again and again, holding the medallion above. Animalistic triumph seized him, made him howl as flesh gave and bones crunched. A tough, black fluid, like crude oil, flew in spatters.

He tossed the rock away. His arm was slick to the elbow with the creature's blood.

The creature moaned beneath him, its head dented and broken.

"I know what you are," he breathed, seizing a broken branch. He wound the medallion around the tip and raised it like a spear. "And I sure as shit know how to kill you."

᳇···᳇

She stumbled and fell and didn't scream only because she didn't have enough air. Her labored pulse beat at her vision, made her body lurch. The .38 hung from her hand like a weight, but she didn't let go.

(mistake)

She stumbled and her side hit a tree. She blinked and saw the cop, straddling Tommy, beating at him with a rock in one hand, while the other held the mini-lantern. What the fuck was that? A crucifix?

She watched the cop toss the rock away and pick up the branch.

(leave him leave this he deserves it)

Her torso burned, but she didn't know if it was from the pain or something else.

"I know what you are," the cop said, winding the lantern around the branch. "And I sure as shit know how to kill you."

He hefted the branch.

(let him let him LET HIM!)

She didn't know she was going to fire until the sound battered her ears and the recoil surged up her arm. The cop fell, screaming and holding the mess that his hand had become.

(stop this turn around)

Hugging her abdomen, she stumbled toward them, taking in the scene. The cop, cradling his hand, gaped at her. She ignored him and approached Tommy. His arms and legs moved weakly, almost independently of each other. His face was a ruin. Beside him, the branch, now in half, with what appeared to be a glowing medallion.

(shove it in his mouth and blow his fucking head off)

She felt that tug in the back of her mind: *Patty. Patty, help me—*

She shook.

(leave him leave this it's not too late)

And then the cop steamrolled her.

"*Bitch!*" he bellowed, driving her to the ground and driving already-broken bones into soft and vulnerable places.

(everyone thinks I'm a bitch today)

She spewed blood into his face as he strangled her with his good hand and tried to pull the .38 away with his bad one. He head-butted her and suns exploded in her eyes. Gagging, she pressed the .38

between them and emptied the cylinder.

The cop stiffened, the pressure on her throat instantly gone. He was gaping at her again, but she didn't think he really saw her.

(nothing new there)

He crumpled in a way that reminded her of balled paper and fell to the side. She gagged on snot and blood and pain.

That steel fishhook in her head: *Patty, I need you.*

Her hands clawed at the dirt, pulling herself around.

The medallion. Get the fucking thing away.

She saw it, still glowing, and crawled toward it. When a fresh wave of pain crashed into her, she didn't stop. Behind her, making the soundtrack, the cop moaned as he tried to hold his guts in.

She picked the medallion up and hissed as it burned in the center of her palm. A St. Anthony medallion. Was the church she'd gone to, all those years ago, called St. Anthony's?

(who gives a fuck)

That tug in the back of her head: *Away. Get it away from me—*

She held it a moment longer, as if undecided, but she knew, deep down, the decision had been made.

She threw the medallion away.

Later, she lay on her side, staring at nothing. Consciousness came and went, the pain ebbing and flowing like the tide. She had no idea how much time passed, only that it was still dark when the cop was finally killed.

"Here, honey," Tommy rumbled behind her. His voice cracked and gargled oddly. His wrist, cut open and already welling with his blood, appeared in front of her eyes.

She stared at it, then forced her eyes closed.

Let me suffer. Let me die. Then the other part of her, now a permanent fixture, spoke up:

(you haven't begun *to suffer yet)*

"C'mon, honey," Tommy coaxed. *"You need this."*

She opened her eyes and the wrist was still there. She licked her lips and hated herself for it.

(your suffering's just begun)

She gripped Tommy's wrist and, shaking, brought it to her mouth.

SURVIVOR'S DEBT

IF GHOSTS EXIST, WHY?

I remember the way his eyes looked. The blood covering his face was completely secondary to that dull stare. It was the look of a man who glimpsed hell, or was, perhaps, realizing he'd never escape it.

And then, much later, I remember that cold gale, the way you imagine the wind off an ice floe must feel, blowing through me— not *around* me, but *through* me—and slamming the door in my face, separating us, forcing me to listen to the screaming on the other side.

I need to get this down. I can't avoid thinking about Billy and what happened in Buffalo any longer. When was the last time I'd slept? I can't remember. I lie awake at night in my museum of a widow's house. Sometimes a tingle, like pins-and-needles, shoots down my arm. Sometimes pressure, like a cinderblock weight, settles on my chest. I feel these things and I keep my head down, literally and metaphorically.

I do not believe in ghosts.

But I'm very afraid, just the same.

The memory I return to most, in spite of all that followed, is Billy Kinson coming back for the first time.

I'd been sitting on his front stoop for five hours. It'd been raining four of those hours, coming in with sunset and making a warm June evening feel like a chilled March morning, and my knee was a solid coil of pain. A long time for an old man, in spite of the dubious cover provided by the aluminum overhang.

He pulled into his driveway and killed the engine. He opened his door and then just sat there, slumped beneath the interior light. He appeared shrunken, more fragile—a man staring ninety in the face instead of seventy. I could see the top of his shaved head and, as was often the case, I thought of Maggie. The way Maggie laughed at the vain way he'd attempted comb-overs back in the '90s before just shaving it all off.

And, suddenly, I didn't want to stand here anymore; didn't know why I had come in the first place. He'd said over the phone that we'd talk when he got home—ignoring my angry shouts of *from where? from WHERE?*—so why was I here? Why was I shivering like some old stray in the rain? Why was I acting like some love-struck teenager, the kind I'd seen in my classes since Reagan's first term?

Billy slammed the car door and made his slow way up the driveway to the front walk. He reached the steps and then just stood there.

"Billy?"

He looked up at me and I saw those eyes for the first time. There's a scene in the original *Night of the Living Dead*, where a zombie gets into the farmhouse the heroes have holed up in. When the zombie attacks, the camera comes in close to the actor's face. His eyes are locked on something out of the frame. For that brief shot, any viewer believes: this thing is dead. This thing is soulless.

Billy Kinson had those eyes. They had me locked even as they seemed to be staring through me. It made me want to look over my shoulder.

Blood coated his face, now running wet under the rain and an errant thought—*He drove home looking like that?*—shot across my mind.

"Silva," he said and you might've thought he hadn't spoken in millennia.

"What the hell happened to you? And don't sell me that sick sister bullshit, either. I'm not Pat Slayton."

His gaze never wavered. "My responsibility."

He started up the steps, slow dragging movements of his feet. "Come inside, Silva. We need to talk."

And it was only five weeks prior I thought he was having a heart attack as we sat in the teacher's lounge, a forkful of microwave pasta frozen in his hand, staring off over my shoulder.

"Billy?" My voice was loud, too loud, carrying over to the rookie teachers. "*Billy?*"

"They've been waiting for me," he said—softly, wonderingly, still staring.

I spun around, but saw nothing but the Pepsi machine and the rookie teachers—two girls and a boy, staring at us as if we'd flashed them our dicks.

I turned back in time to see Billy launch from his seat and sprint for the door. He exited just as the late-bell rang, signaling the change to seventh period.

I cursed and got up. Billy's room was on the first floor, mine on the third, and I'd never get to both before the second bell.

I'd have to wait until the end of the day to see what the hell was going on.

But when I went down to his room, I found the floater substitute tidying up the desks. When I went to the office, Pat Slayton—another school relic—told me Billy had taken an emergency leave. An old sister, Pat told me. She'd had a stroke.

Billy was an only child.

He'd washed his face and changed his shirt, but he still looked older than he was, thinner and frailer. He'd missed a dob of blood; it rested, perfectly centered, on the lobe of his left ear, like a ruby earring.

We sat at his kitchen table. A dangling lamp with a stained-glass shade provided the only illumination.

"You're not a vet, are you, Silva?" he said, leaning over the table, a tumbler in his hands. A bottle of rum sat between us.

"Knee kept me out," I replied. "You know that." The shadows

were deep, pressing against my back. I'd been in Billy's house more times than I could possibly begin to count, but it was a stranger's house to me now. The creaks and groans of the foundation settling seemed stealthy and ominous, reminding me of Shirley Jackson's *The Haunting of Hill House*. I could imagine this house, empty, creaking in the exact same way. Whatever walked there walked alone.

Billy finished his drink. "I *do* remember that." He poured himself another knock and offered the bottle to me. I'd finished mine without even being aware of it. I felt no warmth in my belly, no fire in my throat—just cold. Billy had gotten me a towel but it hadn't helped.

"Billy..." I said, but couldn't finish. Too many questions, too much confusion.

"I never knew them," he said. "Not then.

"I was stationed at Khe Sanh, a combat base east of Laos, in 1968. In April, after four months of being sniped at by Charlie from here-there-everywhere—they were like fucking Whack-a-Moles; the guy next you could be gone because he picked his crotch at the wrong time—relief was finally being brought in. I was 3rd Brigade Marines and we were ordered to clear a way. We were deep along the trails when a blocking force shelled us."

He took a drink. "It's not like the movies. You don't hear the shell until it's already too late. We were scattered, disoriented, and then they opened fire from their foxholes.

"No idea which way was front or fucking back because everything looks the same to an American kid in the jungle, everyone's firing everywhere, and here came these assault rifle rounds—seven-point-six-two millimeter; I'll never forget that number. Saw a guy opened up like a water balloon full of blood right in front of me, and then the shooter's looking dead at me and I started wondering, how old are you? Like, in the States, could you even drive a goddam car? Are you that old? He was just an NVA blue-uniform regular, but I, in that millisecond, was frozen by the idea that a kid who couldn't shave more than once a week was gonna open me up. His little Chinese rifle was aimed at me and I could see into the bore and I couldn't *shake* that thought out of my head.

"And then this big cornhusker batted me aside, yelling, 'Wanna play Guns, fucker? I'll show ya some fuckin' guns!' And he cut the kid down. I don't think he even knew what he was saying, or that he saved my life."

Billy cleared his throat. "He didn't know me, or vice versa. We were just guys. It's hard to make friends when you're keyed up alla time. We protected each other when we could, but that's training.

"So the reg that was gonna kill me got killed, but doing that only opened the way for the sheller to aim. The guy had been firing all around, but now he had something to *aim* for, y'know?

"The cornhusker's tapped out—he had one kill in 'im and then he was just like me, with no idea what the hell was going on. He would've caught up, we both would've, and joined the main fight, but it didn't work out that way. The sheller fired."

He finished his rum and set the glass down. "So these three other guys—a black guy, an Italian, and an Irishman; Jesus, it's like the start of a bad joke—tried to shove the cornhusker outta the way. I got batted aside *again*, only harder. I cracked my head on a tree, but it was enough to save me."

He sighed and it had a watery quality to it. "Those four guys... they got tangled up. It was such a fuckin' Polish fire drill...The shell tore them apart."

His voice grew thick. "Later I found out who they were. While I was recuperating. The cornhusker was Brian Spuken. The black guy was Daryl Espirito. The Italian was Anthony Tormentato. The Irish kid was Larry Haloran."

He stared at the empty tumbler. "Took me years to get over it. They saved me and I didn't even know if they knew that before they died. The first few years, I tracked down their families. Visited the graves. Didn't bring me any closure, though. Something like that never does. Got me divorced, though. I was too loony tunes to be good to anyone."

"How..." I cleared my throat. "*Did* you get over it?"

He nodded. "After a while. Time does it. Getting my college education helped. Becoming a teacher helped more. Distractions. Meeting you and Maggie. That helped, too."

He poured himself another drink and knocked it back, then

poured again. I drank with him. My thoughts were getting foggy, but I didn't feel drunk.

Finally, I said, "Why are you telling me this?"

He looked at me; actually *looked* at me.

I wished he hadn't.

Red and wet and dead and damned, they were the eyes of a man trapped.

"You don't see it, David?" he asked. "They *saved* me."

And I *started* to see it; a closed-off part of my mind opened and I could hear the Talking Heads playing "And She Was" in the distance, nearly submerged over the sound of a car engine, all of it echoing and warping off cinderblock walls, hear Billy's voice, "Fuck you, David! Wake up, man—*wake the fuck UP*—"

I shut the memory off. I didn't want to relive that.

My eyes met Billy's.

He half-nodded, as if he saw something on my face.

"What does this have to do with where you've been?" I asked. I pointed to the blood on his ear. "Or that?"

"Because they've been waiting for me," he said.

Five weeks taught me a lot about my friendship with Billy Kinson.

I daily drove by his crackerbox of a house, wanting to see his car in the driveway.

Then I'd go home, park in front of my garage—never in it—and go into the house that had become more of a shrine to my dead wife than I cared to admit. I'd go in, where her clothes still hung in the closet, where the hood over her sewing machine still rested. Where the books in our bedroom bookcase were still divided his-and-hers and where her makeup on her dresser grew older and more antique. I'd go in and wait for the call from the one person who'd been there when Maggie passed six years prior.

Five weeks.

I went to the police to file a report the second week. It went less than splendidly. The reporting officer stared at me with barely disguised disgust, as if I was some fey lover looking for his wayward

Romeo. He pointed out—and I, logically, knew—that Billy was a grown man who'd given notice.

But the cop hadn't seen Billy's face in the teacher's lounge.

But the cop didn't live in the museum I did.

Five weeks.

And then Billy called. And then Billy showed up with blood on his face and a dead look in his eyes and his story of accidental saving in a slaughter.

The night stretched on. We drank. I was cold and seemed to get colder.

"They don't come back to tell their wives they loved them," he said. "Or to show where Auntie Rose hid the Great Depression money in the walls. That's all Hollywood bullshit." He sipped his drink. Under the weak light, his face resembled a skull. "They have unfinished business."

"Why you?" I asked.

"Because they saved me," he said, refilling his drink. "It's all about balance. The Chinese had it wrong when they said that the life you save becomes your responsibility. It's the other way around. I owe them."

"They *told* you this?"

Billy knocked back his rum. "I knew what I had to do to balance the scales and let them go."

"They hung around for *you*? They've been around all this time for *you*?"

He shook his head. "I don't know where they've been since they died. That doesn't matter—I see them *now*. And it isn't me—it's the business I have to settle for them."

I held my tumbler in both hands. I wanted to tell Billy maybe he wasn't as over Vietnam as he thought. I wanted to tell him that the idea of ghosts *in general* was so much Hollywood bullshit.

But I was cold and tapped out and I couldn't think. Instead, I asked, "What did you do, Billy?"

He refilled his glass and, with his skullface, stared out into the shadows. Was he seeing them *then*? Were they standing around us, watching? That was ridiculous.

Finally, he told me of a house in Nebraska he burned down late one night, the house Brian Spuken's brother-in-law had built with money he'd made by swindling Spuken's father and selling family land to a pig combine. No one was home that night, but Billy didn't mention if that would've stopped him.

He told me of a long, surreal drive deep into Baltimore's Combat Zone, following Daryl Espirito's brother, an undercover officer. Billy had followed Espirito for three days at that point, shadowing his every move. Daryl Espirito's brother had stolen Daryl's first girl-friend, married her, and then subjected her to seven years of mental and physical hell before she finally escaped to Philadelphia. Now, sitting under a broken streetlamp, Daryl Espirito's brother didn't see Billy Kinson come up to the car, the switchblade he'd bought at a pawnshop curled in his hand to not reflect any light. Daryl Espirito's brother didn't see Billy until Billy was right beside him and, before he could react, Billy was stabbing through the open window, taking Daryl Espirito's brother in the throat, the face, the shoulder, the chest.

It was Daryl Espirito's brother's blood I'd seen on Billy's face when he came home.

"But why now?" I asked. "Why would they come now?"

But of all the things he told me, he didn't tell me that. He finished his drink and remained silent.

The next morning, I awoke to fresh coffee and an empty house.

I'd slept on his living room couch and rain continued to patter against the window above my head. My clothes felt stiff and uncomfortable. My sleep was dreamless and deep and utterly unrestful.

I shuffled over to the kitchen table with the empty bottle of Captain Morgan still resting on it. Where I'd sat last night was a cup of coffee and a Stick-It note attached:

SORRY, he'd written.

I peeled the note off and stared at it. I replayed the conversation from the night before. A nervous breakdown. It was the only thing that made sense. I wasn't going to entertain notions of ghosts and eternal balance. I *taught* Poe and Hawthorne but I had no intention of *living* it. He'd said it himself—what happened in Khe Sanh had twisted him so hard it'd taken years to get over. What if he'd *never* gotten over it? What if he'd just buried that twisting with distractions?

Was there a smoldering ruin of a house in Nebraska, a corpse in a car in some dismal part of Baltimore?

I left the coffee half-empty on the table.

I made it to my house before delayed reaction set in. My knees unhinged beside my car and I kneeled on the wet cement like a Muslim praying, feeling the twitching nerves in my spaghetti legs, my Jell-O guts, the cold eke into my skin.

My best friend since Maggie died, my anchor, had lost his mind. Billy Kinson was the reason I was still alive, still sane, still teaching. It'd be like a physicist learning that the Three Laws of Thermodynamics are so much fluff.

I used the car to pull myself up and found myself staring at my garage. It was a stand-alone structure, joined with my house via a breezeway.

I hadn't gone inside for four years.

I lurched toward it, remembering the warm envelope I'd been cocooned in, the soothing rumble of the car, the righteous beat of Elvis Costello's "Pump It Up."

I reached the door, looked in. It was an empty shell, the floor neatly swept. Billy had gone through, transferring what was useful to my basement, junking the rest.

It was as serious as a suicide attempt can be when you're in your late-fifties and your wife's dead of ovarian cancer like some sick joke of a pregnancy, and you have no family left, no one to look forward to, no hope.

I fumbled my keys out and unlocked the garage door. I opened it with a grunt and a squeal of hinges.

Billy found me only because I hadn't answered my phone and I've always been one who can't bear to let a call ring out. When he'd arrived at the house, he'd seen the wisps of white smoke seeping under the bottom of the garage door.

I stepped inside, footfalls echoing off cinderblock, smelling stale dust, old motor oil.

He'd saved my life. I wasn't healed from Maggie's death—please see the museum I live in—but I'd been able to redirect my focus. Before, Billy Kinson had been a good friend. Afterward, he became my best friend, the one I'd stop a bullet for because, in a way, he'd already done it for me.

And now that man was an arsonist and a killer and off doing Christ knew what because he said four people saved *his* life and he owed *them*.

He'd saved *my* life.

Is that why he'd told me anything? But what *had* he told me, when you got right down to it? How much of it was practical? How much better off was I *before* I knew those things?

He was gone again, and I was left waiting, smelling the stale air of my would-be tomb.

I slumped down as Billy passed me, his headlights illuminating the interior of my car like a prison searchlight.

I'd spent three days staked out on his street amongst the other cars of downtown shoppers, waiting for his return. I was spinning my wheels, but I didn't know what else I could do. The police here would laugh at me and the police in Nebraska and Baltimore would think I was a twisted crank caller. I was stuck, like in those endless days leading up to when Maggie's chest finally stopped rising in that damned hospital room.

When my interior darkened again, I sat up and peered into the side-mirror. I watched Billy pull into his driveway, cut the engine, and get out. He let himself into his house.

I slumped in my seat. Now what? Before, I'd waited on his stoop, but all it had done was lead me here. A very small but very strong part of me wanted to forget I'd even known Billy Kinson, but that'd be like trying to ignore the need to breathe. Billy was my life-line.

Headlights suddenly re-illuminated my car, and I dropped down as if my driver seat was a trapdoor, my heart in my throat. I told myself it was just some other car—his street was drowsy, not soporific—but when I peeked through the side-window, I saw the trunk of Billy's little Subaru passing me.

I sat up a little more. He reached the red light at the end of his street and waited for the green.

He could've been going out for food, or gas, or any of the mundane day-to-day things that seemed absurd in the current context.

But in my heart of hearts, I knew what was happening. The last trip had taken care of the third of his four.

This was to be the final trip.

Decision time. Do I follow? Why had I staked his house for three days, if I was just going to let him go?

The light turned green and Billy went through the intersection, passing the sign that marked the route to Interstate 79.

I keyed the ignition and peeled out of the parking space with a squeal of tires. I passed the intersection at twice the posted limit.

My body did the driving. The rest of me, the interior me, caterwauled—undecided, confused, helpless. What could I do? What *couldn't* I do?

I followed him onto the Interstate, busy with summer traffic in spite of the late hour.

I followed him into darkness.

How do I convey to this page the eternity of that three-hour trip? How do I express the constant, blood-pumping, nerve-singing, head-pounding agony of following Billy Kinson over two-hundred miles into Buffalo, New York?

My thoughts and fears worked on me. I was treading in dark water where anything might be lurking beneath the surface. Billy

Kinson, my best friend, had a breakdown and I was following him to a strange place for what could only be a horrible reason. How would he react if he caught me? What would I witness if he didn't? What would I *do*?

You'd think these thoughts would've kept me awake as midnight came and went, but nerves can only take so much constant stimulation. By one o'clock, my eyes burned. My arms felt weighted, my hands frozen into claws around the steering wheel. I salivated for coffee or even a Coca-Cola, but I didn't dare stop because Billy didn't.

We entered Buffalo a little after two o'clock. Our arrival was less than auspicious. Arc-sodium lights signaled the end of the Interstate, but nothing else did. In the dark, Buffalo is a city of stout, ugly buildings with black windows for eyes.

Billy took rights and lefts like he'd lived there all his life. We never entered downtown proper and never left the city limits. This went on for another hour. I felt like Dante, following an indifferent and ignorant Virgil into the inner circles of Hell.

And then, into the second hour, I lost Billy.

A part of me thought, all this way just to lose him *now*?

Another part of me felt only relief. He was no longer my responsibility.

I drove around, partly looking for Billy, partly trying to find my way back to the Interstate. I kept my speed low and read every street sign, trying to divine direction.

As I paused to stop at the intersection of Geist and Sgaile, Billy's Subaru cut me off and stopped.

My heart might've been a model, stuck into the chest of a waxwork. Even the constant yammering chaos in my head stopped.

He got out of the car, leaving it running, and came around.

I wanted to leave. That instant of *What was I doing here?* I'd felt when Billy first came home was a mild suggestion to the fight-or-flight panic that roared through me. I wanted to jam the car into Reverse and stand on the gas pedal.

But I was frozen.

I watched him come toward me.

I watched him stop beside my door.

I watched him open it and hunker down.

He stared at me and I stared back and it was like there was nothing and no one else in the world.

"I think I know the answer," he said, "but what are you doing here, Silva?"

I opened my mouth. I *think* I opened my mouth. Nothing came out if I did.

He inclined his head toward his Subaru. "There's a parking space over there. Take it." And, with that, he walked back to his Subaru. He got in and pulled forward enough for me to get through.

There was no question of doing what he asked.

I parked my car and got out and Billy pulled up beside me. I got in.

"You can't stop me, David," he said as he drove away. In the light-dark-light-dark of the streetlights, he looked more haggard than ever.

"I don't know what I'm doing here," I said honestly. I glanced into the backseat, but it was dark and empty. Of course it was. The only ghosts were in Billy's head.

We made a number of turns, none of which I could follow if I tried. "Do you...see them now?" I asked.

Another glance at me. "You think I'm cracked, don't you?"

I felt a flare of anger at that. "Look at it from my perspective, Billy. Jesus! Do you know how cracked you *sound*? You've killed, you've burned houses down, you've—what did you do the last time?"

"You don't want to know."

I wanted to slug him for the flat way he said that, the way he didn't even look at me. "You've done *all that* because you saw fucking *ghosts*? And you have the *balls* to ask if I think you're *cracked*?"

I was shouting, but Billy didn't even flinch.

I made myself lower my voice. "You said it yourself—you went off the reservation when you got discharged. Don't you think—can't you *consider*—the idea that maybe, *maybe*, you're still not well? You say you see the ghosts of the four people who saved your life.

You said, when you got back to the States you tracked down these people's families. Don't you see how it makes sense? Guilt plus prior knowledge equals...whatever the hell it is you think you're doing."

"I'm not ill," he said. "And your arm-chair psychology sucks, David. I *saw* them—physically."

"It's a delusion," I said.

That earned me a look—a shot of real anger. "It's not a delusion, David."

"Then why *now*? You never answered that before. Why would they come back to balance the scales *now*?"

"Because we're here," he said, and pulled over.

I looked out the passenger window and realized we were parked in front of a large house atop a modest hill; the grass sloped gently down to the sidewalk, halted by a tall iron-fence. A few scattered lights glowed in the house, not many.

As Billy switched the car off, I said, "Stop, Billy. Don't make this any worse. Think about what I said. A part of you *must* know this is true—I mean, you let me into the car with you."

"I wanted to know where you were so you couldn't get in the way," he said. He stared through the windshield. "This is real. This is happening. I see why you think this way, but you're not seeing what I am. I didn't choose the action, or the order, or the time frame. As I balance the books, they disappear. Everything they've told me, it's all true. Go look it up, sometime. It's in the papers." He turned to me. "But this is happening *now*, David."

"I'll scream," I said. "I'll wake the entire goddamn neighborhood up." I felt for my pockets and pulled my Nokia out. "And I'll call the cops."

He'd aged in the past two months, but he was still wickedly fast: before I could blink, he was heaving my phone out his door. It shattered in the street with a pathetic plastic cracking sound.

When he turned back, his hand held the switchblade. The blade was the brightest thing in the darkened car, a thin slice of deadly silver.

He'd cleaned Espirito's blood off of it, of course.

I couldn't look away from it. The man who had kept me from killing myself had pulled a knife on me. All circuits are down; please call back later.

"Don't make me do something about you, David," he said. "You're my best friend but I won't let you stop me."

He got out and the instant the blade was out of sight, I came back to myself and scrambled out of the car.

He stopped in front of the hood. "Get back in the car."

"No." My voice shook with my heartbeat. "You going to kill me?"

He stared at me for a long moment, then started up the long front steps to the porch. I stared after him, then looked up at the house. It seemed to lean toward us with its narrow structure, its tall windows, its peaked roof.

Up on the porch, Billy slammed his fist into one of the panes in the door and I froze as the musical tinkle of falling glass drifted into the night air, awaiting the whoop of a home security system.

Billy reached in and undid the lock. He opened the door and disappeared into the darkened foyer.

I staggered after him, tripping up the concrete steps, sneakers slapping on the boards of the porch. He stood just inside the door. A small table lamp had been left on, doing nothing but making the deep shadows seem deeper. Billy looked like a cut-out of black construction paper.

I grabbed his arm in some confused attempt at stopping him. He brushed me off like someone swatting a fly and I went flying, crashing into the wall.

"*Nicholas Tormentato!*" he screamed. "*Eduardo Tormentato!* È *merda sulla tua famiglia e li distrusse!*"

This is approximate. He spoke in tongues; later I figured out that it was Italian, but with stars still exploding in my head he appeared possessed. He'd walked to the foot of the steps against the wall, shouting up at the darkness. The small table lamp threw his face into grim, troll-like relief.

They'll call the cops, you asshole. Did I say this? Or think it?

I heard the creak of floorboards above me.

He yelled something else in Italian as I struggled to stand, my bad knee refusing to lock. My balance was on ball-bearings. My head thudded.

An old man's querulous, sleepy voice drifted from the darkness above. "Who is that? What are you doing here at this hour? How do you know Anthony?"

Billy stepped onto the first riser. "I served with Anthony, you bastard," he said. "Come down here."

I got to my feet using the wall. The spit in my mouth was like motor oil. "Billy, stop—"

I heard footsteps, coming down. The voice sounded more alarmed, but still sleep-addled. "Why are you here this late? Were you a friend of Anthony's? Why—"

Billy reached into the darkness and yanked a man roughly our age—but wider, shorter—into the dim light, slamming him into the wall. The man goggled at him. He wore a pin-striped night-gown. It added the final lunatic touch.

Billy brought his face close. "Are you Nicholas?"

The man continued goggling at him. His mouth worked.

And then, from above, another man's voice called, "Nicholas? What is it? Nicholas?"

Billy had turned at the sound of the other voice, and when he turned back, his face had frozen in a rictus of hate and rage, as if Anthony Tormentato's vengeance was truly his.

"You *allowed* it to happen, Nicholas," he whispered. "You *helped*." He brought the knife into view. The lamp's glow slid along the edge like liquid gold.

Nicholas's father called in that rickety voice reserved for the very old, "Nicholas! What are you doing?"

Billy slammed the knife into Nicholas's gaping mouth.

Nicholas gagged, blood spilling over his lips.

Billy's face didn't change. He wrenched the knife out, a trail of blood following like a grisly comet's tail, reversed his grip, and sliced across the man's waddled throat. More blood gushed—an arterial spray. He let go and Nicholas rolled down the steps, his throat spraying blood like a broken lawn sprinkler. He slammed into the floor hard enough to shake the house.

Billy stared at the body disdainfully, his entire front covered in blood. "Lucky," he said to himself. "He gets off lucky."

And then he did a curious thing—he looked to his right, to the dark archway opposite of me.

"I remember," he said. "I'll pull them out, make him see it before he goes."

He cocked his head, as if listening, and I realized he was *seeing* Anthony Tormentato at that moment.

I threw a terrified glance to the archway, but saw nothing, of course. In the immortal words of Bullwinkle—no ghoulies or ghosties or long-leggedy beasties.

"Per le tue sorelle," he said, and turned back to the stairwell. From the darkness above, a soft light clicked on, and the elder Tormentato cried out, "Nicholas! Why don't you answer? *Rispondere a tuo padre!"*

Billy started up.

I pushed myself off the wall and lunged at him, tripping over Nicholas's body. My knees crashed against the stair rises. I howled, but managed to grab his legs.

Billy stumbled and I used him roughly, yanking him down the steps, pulling myself up. My bad knee wouldn't support me at all.

"Stop this, you son of a bitch," I panted. "You've gone too goddam far—"

Billy twisted around and landed a heel in my gut. I fell against the wall, my weight coming down on my knee. Green, acidic sheets of pain roiled up and down my leg.

He grabbed me by the shirt. He looked me in the eye one last time and it was worse than when he'd come back from Balti-more—there was *nothing* left of my best friend in his gaze. I stared into twin black holes.

"Billy—" I started to say, and then he shoved me.

It felt like time slowed down, like I hung in the air, with Billy's nothing-eyes locked on me. None of that was true, of course, but the idea held for as long as it took my body to turn, to see the foyer floor rushing to meet me, for my bad knee, the one that kept me out of Vietnam, to slam into the newel post.

I shrieked, but it lasted only until I landed astride Nicholas's body and the wind whooshed out of me. I sunfished against his corpse, gag-gasping.

I flopped onto my back and Billy was still standing on the stairs, watching me. In a dim, academic way, I realized not just how old he was, but how frail he looked, how emaciated. When was the last time he'd slept? Eaten?

And then he turned away, and climbed the stairs.

No—I sucked air into my chest and crawled over the body, covering my front on grue. Every inch of me, mental and physical, screamed and screamed as I clawed up the stairs, toward Billy and that soft light. My body was cold, freezing. Shock, although I thought—for just an instant—I saw my breath plume out.

I reached the top as Billy reached the bedroom facing the street.

He paused in the doorway, backlit by a nightstand lamp.

I climb-clawed the wall to stand on my good leg, biting my lower lip till it bled, and limped after him.

Billy—I don't know if I thought or said it.

"Did you like the little girls, Poppa?" he said, but it wasn't his voice; it was thicker, rougher, yet somehow higher, with just a touch of slickness over the vowels, giving him an accent as he ran the words together. The result of fighting, I thought then. "Did you like how they squealed? How about when I bled? Did you like that, Poppa?"

Billy started into the room.

I lunged with my good leg. *"Billy, DON'T—"*

And then this *wind* blew, this blindingly cold *wind*.

I have no rational explanation for it. It was summer. The house did not have central AC—or, at least, a vent right above my head. It blew around me, *through* me, so cold I swore I saw ice-crystals forming on the backs of my bloodied knuckles, could feel my skin tightening.

The wind slammed the door on my face and, as abruptly as it'd commenced, it ended with a little whistle in my ears.

I fell against the door; it took every ounce left to remain standing. The ice-crystals were gone, replaced by hot sweat. I could feel the bounce-back of my hot breath against the cold—*cold!*—wood, hear the labored *lub-dub* of my heart.

I grasped the knob, but it was locked.

And then, like a pane of glass breaking, the old man screamed. I staggered back, nearly falling, holding onto the top of the stair banister to keep my balance.

An errant thought popped into the dim window of my remaining consciousness: *I am standing in the middle of a crime scene.*

I straightened and stared, walleyed, at everything. The blood. The body of Nicholas Tormentato at the foot of the stairs.

I imagined sirens, police cruisers careening onto the avenue, and I was lunging-stumbling down the steps.

I cleared Nicholas Tormentato's body with a single jump I think some of my former track-star students would've been proud of. I landed hard, hearing a pained shriek that took me an instant to realize was mine.

The front door was still open and I dashed through. My sneakers pounded across wood, down concrete. The world was a blur in which I was only distantly aware that no cops had arrived. The air smelled sweet, but I could still smell the metallic undertone of spilled blood.

I hit the side of the car, my upper-half splayed across the hood, and then I went away for a while. I welcomed it.

I only remember bits of what came later. I allowed my body to do the work, my subconscious to do the thinking. Later I discovered I was gone almost a month. This alarms me to some extent, but not much, given the circumstances.

Billy put me into my car. My car ended up in the driveway. I must've driven home, but Christ knows how.

I remember some things, trivial things—a shower, an open book, washing a dish in the sink. I don't know if Billy ever visited or, if he did, what happened. One day, I found myself sitting in my wife's sewing room, in front of her old Singer.

To this day, I have no idea how long.

I also have no idea how long this might've gone on—how much I would've wrestled with what my best friend, the man who'd saved my life, had done—and I don't care to.

It ended when I found out my best friend had died.

It was a former student of Billy's who found him, three weeks after the horrorshow in Buffalo. A final seizure. I'm told they are quite common in victims of high-grade glioma, which Billy had—a juicy little bastard above the cerebellum, impossible to destroy, increasing the pressure in the skull. He was possibly dead before he hit the linoleum.

I was listed as Billy's emergency contact.

I have no memory of picking up the phone in my kitchen—but the fussy-sounding hospital official on the other end at St. Michael's I talked to said he'd tried calling me for a week.

I didn't explain myself, although I could tell he wanted me to, but instead got the death machinery started; the same chugging, creaking machine I'd used when Maggie died. Claiming the body, making arrangements for it, settling his affairs—I was the executor of his will, I also discovered. I felt the tidal pull of the functional catatonia I'd existed in. A part of me wanted very much to forget all this—forget Billy Kinson and the cancer he'd told no one about and his dead eyes and the blood on his face and the impossible wind. I was an old man. I was alone—now more than ever.

A week after his funeral, I set about emptying his house and putting it up on the market.

One afternoon—this would've been late July, I think—I was in his office. His desk was one of those industrial metal ones he'd taken when Ben Franklin High had updated its furniture.

Buried underneath bills and notes and book requests and old graded papers, was a file marked CANCER BUG in Billy's anally-tight writing. Within, he'd organized every print-out, every test, every bill, every calendar page that marked an appointment with his G.P. or his oncologist or some other specialist.

It was a timeline of his death sentence.

The first date in the file was marked August of the previous year, roughly two weeks before the first day of school.

Did I remember that date? We would've been back at work, preparing for the new crop of kids, but I had no memory of Billy being missing.

The next date was early September. I *did* remember that one— Billy wasn't typically known for taking days off; his number of stored personal days was a thing to behold—and then the ones following it (three in October, two in November, four in Decem-ber, *six* in February, one in March). I realized I hadn't realized *then* that some-thing was off.

The mental ground with me resounded with tremblers of an impending quake, the tomb of everything I hadn't thought of, hadn't wondered about, or pretended not to notice. Why had I done that?

How much had I known about Billy Kinson? We'd been friends, but he'd been more of a stranger to me than I'd realized—not in a sneaking way, but because of *blindness*. We're such a social species that even when someone is exhibiting a dark side right in front of you, like a purloined letter, we *choose* not to see it, for whatever reason.

I chose not to see it because Billy saved my life.

He was diagnosed on October 13th.

The survival rate, one year from diagnosis, is fifty-percent.

Two years and it drops to twenty-five.

Billy Kinson knew he was going to die in less than a year.

And he didn't tell me.

"You son of a bitch," I said. Burning tears pricked my eyes.

And, for the first time since the fussy official at St. Michael's reached me, I cried.

How did Billy knowing his death was imminent connect with what he did in May and June?

I looked at the facts:

He's diagnosed in October.

In May of the following year, when he's weakening and getting close to the end, he sees the ghosts of the four Marines who saved his life. He becomes convinced he must settle their "unfinished business." That's common when someone's dying, after a fashion. They want to shuffle off the mortal coil with a clean slate. I'd seen it with Maggie. Two months before she died, she buried the hatchet with her sister, whom she'd not spoken to since 1977.

But how did he come *up* with the "unfinished business"? Not with ghosts, goddammit. I didn't believe that.

Check the papers, he said. And I did.

And it was all right there, secondary comments at the bottom of news articles I pulled off the Internet, the "tip" of the inverted pyramid I taught my Journalism I students. Spuken's sleazy brother-in-law. Daryl Espirito's abusive brother, Darren.

Larry Haloran's unfinished business was harder to find—it occurred during those three days after Billy and I talked. All I could find was one notice, in the *Toledo Blade*, out of Ohio: Mr. and Mrs. Thomas Haloran, eighty-five and eighty-six, were reported missing from their home in the suburb of Sylvania. Nothing was stolen, there were no signs of forced entry. Their car, a 1992 buick, was still in the driveway.

I clicked through article after article, but no mention was made of finding them.

That left Buffalo, New York, and Anthony Tormentato's father and brother.

I didn't want to know. I knew *enough*, you see?

Billy's voice—altered, different, really not his voice at all and I refused to think that was anything but the effects of the fight—in my head: *"Did you like the little girls, Poppa? Did you like how they squealed? How about when I bled? Did you like that, Poppa?"*

I didn't need to look up Buffalo.

Billy's unfinished business was true.

But *how*, goddammit? *How?*

I shut it out. I didn't know how and wouldn't. Billy Kinson was dead.

I went back to work, buried myself with classes. Administ-ration arranged my classes accordingly—accelerated classes and the cream of the electives—and everyone left me alone. I let the pages from my little Word of the Day calendar on my classroom desk fall into the trash. I wasn't sleeping, but that was okay. I was crushingly alone, but that was okay, too.

Maggie was dead. Billy Kinson was dead. I do not believe in ghosts.

But I'm writing this now.

My father died of a heart attack. My maternal grandmother, too. A scattering of extended relatives.

Off and on for the past three weeks, it sometimes feels as if there's pressure, like a cinderblock weight, on my chest. A tingle, like the pins-and-needles feeling you get when feeling is restored to a numbed appendage, zips down my arm. I get chilly-cold, and I can't get warm.

This all subsides. I should go to the doctor, but I know he can do nothing for me.

It's March now, which explains the cold. If I want it to.

At night, wind screams around my house, making it creak.

Where did that wind come from in Buffalo?

These past few weeks, I've been watching my feet when I walk. I've refused to look up from this notebook since starting to write.

Outside, the wind's howling. A good spring storm is brewing, although there was no mention of it on the news.

I do not believe in ghosts.

But I do not want to know what Billy Kinson's unfinished business is.

And I am so damn cold.

BABY GROWS
A CONSCIENCE

IT WAS EASIER TO AIM a gun at a little girl's head than Richie thought.

Putting the black pistol to the dark-haired girl's temple as she ate cereal at the kitchen table was, in fact, the easiest thing he'd done in the past twenty minutes. Because, of the three people he'd already shot, he knew that killing the little girl, here in this *Leave It to Beaver* kitchen, would mean he'd be free. Ollie-ollie-oxen-free. He held onto what the white card had said. Forget everything else.

"It's not polite to point a gun at someone," she said, not even looking up from her cereal, "and not pull the trigger." Her voice was matter-of-fact; a little girl who knows, at the age of seven, how the world works.

Richie jerked and staggered away, ass smacking into the rim of a side counter. He looked around the room, looking for something and not knowing what it was, his eyes ticking off the retro cabinets, the rounded edges of the 1950s refrigerator to the table's right. The little girl continued eating, as if the window behind her really looked out into her side yard, as if three people didn't lay dead in the "living room" down the hall.

As if, not two seconds before, Richie hadn't held a gun to her hollow little temple.

"Aren't you scared?" he asked her before he could stop himself. His voice shook in a way that he hadn't heard since he was thirteen. "Didn't you hear the shooting? Don't you care? Who are you?"

She didn't answer; a little girl in a pale green nightgown, her feet dangling a few inches above the linoleum. She might've forgotten he was there and he felt ridiculous for even asking her.

His brain throbbed, and he put his hand to his forehead. *This is hell*, he thought. *I'm in hell.*

He didn't believe that anymore then he believed he was the victim of some vicious criminal mastermind, which is what he first thought when he'd woken up, sitting against the side of a Dodge Caravan in the garage with the pistol and a three-by-five card in his lap. He'd seen the *Saw* movies, where the victims woke up in some torturous scenario and had to—with sweat, tears, and buckets of blood—extricate themselves if they wanted to live.

Pistol on his left leg, small white card on his right. He wore a black suit he'd never owned and, at first, he was too groggy to do anything but accept the reality of this. He'd picked up the card first and turned it over.

KILL THEM ALL AND SURVIVE,

it read in black Sharpie capitals, so fresh he could smell the ink. His eyes drifted to the pistol and picked it up. Heavier than it looked.

He got up, using the side of the minivan for support. His feet tingled with pins and needles. His heart pounded too slowly and too hard. He wasn't scared, not yet, but disorientation worked on his nerves.

KILL THEM ALL AND SURVIVE.

"Nuts to that," he muttered, looking around. To the right was the door leading into the house. To the left was the garage door.

Richie stuffed the card in his jacket pocket and went to the garage door. Flip it up and slip out. Figure out how he'd ended up here later.

Except the garage door wasn't real. He ran his hands over the smooth, cool concrete, where the handle, the windows, should've been. The track and steel wire were real, bolted into the wall.

"What the hell?" He said and then he heard a thump from inside the house. He spun, gripping the pistol tighter.

I'm dreaming, he thought. *That's it. Drank too much of Jerry's cheap-ass wine and am having one* hell *of a nightmare. I'll wake up in his apartment, or mine, and maybe we've just done a job, a smash and grab, and I'll wake up with a hangover but with some extra cash.*

Or he'd wake up with a hangover and some bruiser out gunning for him. It wouldn't have been the first. Times were tight and he'd signed on for more less-than-assured jobs recently than he liked. It was a sign of sloppiness. The sign of a thug. He wasn't a goddamned thug.

And while I'm standing here dicking around, he thought, *something* thumped *beyond that door. And beyond that door is my only way out.*

He pulled out the card again.

KILL THEM ALL AND SURVIVE.

Kill who? he thought, walking slowly toward the other door. His heart sped up with each hesitant step.

He put the card back in his pocket and reached for the knob. For an instant, he was positive it would be as real as the garage door handle, but his hand gripped its cool metal surface.

He glanced behind him and looked at the fake garage door, then the minivan. How in the hell did *that* get in here? But there were no obvious answers. Just more and more questions.

He swallowed, heard a dry click, and opened the door.

He entered a well-lit living room designed to look like a picture from a furniture catalogue during Eisenhower's second term. The television in the corner was a behemoth with a screen the size of a hardcover book. The front door off to the side had stained glass. The three people to the left looked like dazed extras from *Father Knows Best*.

The woman was a rail-thin wraith in an emerald green dress, standing a bit away from the other two. In one hand was a chef's knife. The silver blade winked at Richie.

The man on the couch wore a suit similar to Richie, but his face had the carved-out look of a heavy meth addict. In his hands was an aluminum baseball bat.

The boy on the floor was dressed like Timmy from *Lassie*—if Timmy were sixteen, overweight, flaring with acne, and obviously insane. Half of his face was slathered in blood from a cut along his hairline and his eyes seemed to pinwheel in their sockets. Near one outstretched hand was a bloody claw-hammer. He muttered into the carpet, "Dreamin'. I'm dreamin'. Get it out."

The woman turned toward Richie and snarled. A small white card fell from her hand to the carpet. *"You."*

She stomped toward him, raising the knife as her lips drew down, revealing little ferret teeth. *"You, you, you, YOU!"*

Richie backed away, his back hitting the side of an oak-paneled wet bar. Out of sight, glass tinkled musically. "Lady, hey, lady, don't—"

With an animal cry, the woman brought the knife down and Richie ducked, scooting to the left. He lost his footing, and fell. He rolled onto his back to see the woman raising the knife again. Her eyes bugged out from her head, her mouth drawing down into a grotesque frown that aged her ten years. "You killed him," she breathed.

Richie remembered the pistol and raised it, his hand shaking. "Stop, lady, stop right now—"

She lunged. He closed his eyes as his fingers acted of their own accord, pulling the trigger once, twice, three times. The sounds of the gunshots were deafening, smashing into his ears.

He opened his eyes and the woman was against the wall, holding her ruined chest and stomach, her mouth a perfect *O* of surprise. "You," she said, and blood spilled over her lower lip. More blood flowed from between her fingers. She slid down the wall. "You..."

She was dead before she could finish the thought, staring at him with something like awe. Richie stood, gun still shakily trained on her.

He staggered toward the other two as they gaped at him. His heart hammered in his chest, and adrenaline sizzled through his bloodstream.

He opened his mouth. It felt shot full of Novocain. "Do—do you know what's going on?"

The man stared at him, eyes like saucers, and said nothing.

A throaty growl came from below and two hands locked on Richie's ankle. He looked down to see the teenager pulling himself forward, his head tilted, mouth yawning wide, eyes bulging. Richie saw blood in his eyebrows.

He's gonna bite me, he thought, almost wonderingly, then pulled the trigger into the center of the teenager's head. A quarter-sized hole appeared in the crown, and grue, hot and loathsome, splashed his leg. The hands momentarily tightened their grip, then fell away.

Richie whipped the gun toward the man. The man's eyes flickered from Richie to the dead boy, his mouth working. Richie pulled the trigger twice more, shooting the man in the chest.

Silence fell on the room with a *thump*. Richie stumbled away, into the wall. He leaned his head back and closed his eyes, thinking, *Oh Jesus, oh Christ, what the hell is going on here?*

Richie knew people who've killed—or at least claimed to—but the most violence he had ever seen or been in had been fist fights or muggings. He felt the boy's blood on his legs. The gun was warm in his hands.

He took a deep breath, then another. The smell of burnt gunpowder, the reek of hot blood, the ozone stench of fear and adrenaline. He opened his eyes and surveyed the room. His eyes fell on the card the woman dropped.

He went to it on legs that felt made of wet clay.

He picked it up.

THE MAN WITH THE GUN KILLED YOUR HUSBAND.

His jaw clenched. He saw more cards, one near the man, one near the boy. He snatched them up.

THE MAN WITH THE GUN HAS YOUR DRUGS, the man's said.

THE MAN WITH THE GUN BURNED YOUR HOUSE DOWN AND KILLED YOUR FAMILY, the boy's said.

"*What the hell!*" Richie shrieked and flung the cards away.

He rubbed his hand on his trouser leg as if touching the cards had been loathsome and went to the front door. Grabbing the knob, he touched nothing but concrete. His knuckles rapped painfully and he cried out.

He stepped away and closed his eyes. Wait. Think this out.

KILL THEM ALL AND SURVIVE, *his* card had said.

"I *did* it. I killed them. Can I leave now?"

No answer, not that he honestly expected one.

"Dammit," he breathed. He opened his eyes. He thought of getting into the minivan, but go where? He couldn't figure out how it had gotten there in the first place.

I can't figure out how I got here, he thought and then he'd heard the slightest of sounds, a soft metal scrape, from down the left hallway. Followed by a *thunk*.

"You can't leave until you shoot me," the little girl said now.

His hand dropped from his forehead and he stared at the little girl. He looked around the table, but didn't see a white card on the table. What did *hers* say?

"How," he said and his throat clicked. "How did you know what my card said?"

She set her spoon down beside her bowl and looked at him. He recoiled, hissing air through his teeth.

The little girl had blue eyes his mind automatically associated with cats. The pupils were pointed ovals, constricting in the recessed lighting of the room. "Does it matter?" Her cat-eyes searched his face then nodded, as if he'd answered.

She turned back to her cereal, finishing the dregs. Her other arm rested on the table and a tight bracelet of steel-gray capsules wrapped around her slender wrist.

"You're stuck, Richie," she said. "Until you shoot me, there's no way out of here. You can try and look, but you're sealed in." She swallowed a spoonful of milk. "Unless you kill me."

"*Kill* you?" he yelled at her. "What the hell *is* this? Who *are* you?"

She didn't answer.

He grinded his teeth, snorting air out of his nostrils. He looked down at the gun in his hand and saw his knuckles whiten. The metal edges dug into his clammy palm. He thought of the three people in the other room.

"Fine," he said, raising the gun and putting it to her temple. His finger slid into the guard and rested on the trigger.

She didn't flinch away from the gun; she set her spoon down, then picked the bowl up and brought the edge to her lips, tilting the bowl to drink the last droplets of milk. His gun tracked her and, to his credit, it didn't shake.

The little girl set the bowl down. "Whenever you're ready, Richie."

Richie frowned and pulled the trigger, but nothing happened—his finger refused to move.

He tried again. Again. Same result. His arm shook, beginning in his hand and moving up to his shoulder. Sweat popped out along his brow. The sides of the pistol's grip cut into his clammy palms.

He stumbled back a step, still trying to pull the trigger. He looked down at the gun as if it were an alien thing.

The little girl turned her strange cat's eyes toward him and he looked up. Her face was still and pale and unreadable aside from those eyes. The pupils fattened and thinned, fattened and thinned. They had a rhythm, almost hypnotic, and Richie struggled to pull his gaze away.

"Oh," the little girl said, flatly. "Yeah. Sorry, Richie."

At the forefront of his mind, he felt a slippery ... *coldness* seep in through the bone and into his brain, numbing him and chilling him, and he imagined this *thing* flowing over his mind, filling in the wrinkles. He felt a sudden separation between mind and body, as if both were still in fine working order, but no longer connected.

"What," he said with a mouth that no longer felt like his own. "Wh-uh-what a-a-are yuh-you—" He clenched his teeth, forcing his mouth to work. "—*doing*."

He looked at the girl again, and her head was cocked to the side. Her strange eyes continued to pulse.

His lips writhed, his tongue twisting, forming words. "What. I. Have. To." Then, as an afterthought, "Sorry. Richie."

His brain screamed, but it was distant, far and away from the here and now.

His arm lowered in a series of jerks, his elbow bending, and the gun was socked under his chin, right above his Adam's Apple. He tried fighting, but his brain and its commands were passengers in his body.

His lips writhed, his mouth opened. "Nothing. Personal."

What do you mean, he wanted to say, but then his hand tensed on the gun, and he pulled the trigger. The world went dark before he fully heard the shot.

❧ ⋯ ☙

Baby's nose wrinkled at the smell of burnt gunpowder, and she turned away from the body on the kitchen floor, folding her hands on the table. As if on cue, she felt minute stings around the wrist that wore the medication bracelet. Her brow momentarily furrowed, then cleared.

The refrigerator receded into the wall silently, then creaked as it swung inward, leaving a doorway in the false wall. Dr. Roberts stepped out, his thick Buddy Holly glasses reflecting the lights, his perfectly combed sandy hair shining, his labcoat swishing against his legs. He frowned, studying a clipboard, as three like-dressed minions followed.

"You waited too long, Baby," Roberts said, not looking up from his chart. He stepped around Richie's body, as if the corpse were a minor obstacle.

Baby didn't answer. Her limbs felt weighted with concrete.

Roberts looked away from the clipboard. "Was it hard to take control?"

She, for an instant, thought of answering through one of the dopey minions, but knew that would be a bad idea. "No."

Roberts flipped a sheet on his chart, a rattle of paper. "Vital signs were spiking. All machines said he was about to pull the trigger."

She wondered if the cameras were still recording. Probably. "He didn't," she said through numb lips.

Roberts cleared his throat. He wasn't pleased, she knew; his next question would be, *Why did you request this, Baby?*

"Why did you request this, Baby?" Roberts asked.

She pushed her chair back, aluminum legs squeaking over the linoleum, and stood slowly; the drugs made her limbs feel looser, even as her brain continued ticking along. It was the one secret she managed to gain while living under Dr. Roberts.

She paused at Richie's body, looking at his face. His eyes were puzzled, but not afraid.

She stepped over him and the minions backed away. Their thoughts reminded her of startled pigeons.

She went to the door, then stopped suddenly. Roberts had his hand in his pocket, grasping the bracelet's remote. He thought she wasn't sedate enough. He was afraid. He just hid it better than the minions.

Her back to him, Baby said, "To see if you would do it."

Her answer confused him; he continued to hold the remote. His thumb rubbed the button.

He opened his mouth to ask what she meant by that and she said, "To see how valuable I am to you."

"But this?" Roberts said, giving himself away. She heard the edge in his thoughts.

Careful now, her mother, dead since she really *was* a baby, said.

"Did you get your information?" she asked. "My..." She flapped an arm at her side. "...vital signs and stuff like that?"

"Yes. Yes, of course." Roberts coughed as he looked at the chart. Baby could see it through his eyes. "But something's wrong, Baby. I've read your vitals this entire session. You've used people *before*, but this is different." He paused. "Explain it to me."

"You used volunteers from The Compound. This was different. You showed me how valuable what I can do is to you, collecting these people no one would miss, building this set." She paused, thinking. "These people were *real*; they had lives before you scooped them up. I realized that. I *know* that." She glanced at him and inwardly smiled when he cringed the slightest bit. "But you haven't and you don't. Or you don't care. Whichever way you prefer. But now I know how important what I am to you, at least." She turned away and stepped through the doorway. "For now, anyway."

She walked to the end of the darkened warehouse, toward the door where the agent in the black suit waited, not meeting her eyes. Behind her, she felt Roberts squeeze her remote's casing. She could almost hear the plastic creak. More medication didn't matter, she thought, but it made her groggy.

And then she felt him let go, pull his hand out of his pocket.

Baby smiled as he told the minions to escort her back to the compound.

"It's all right," she said again, lowly, as she reached the door and stopped. She avoided the gaze of the black-suited man guarding the door as much as he avoided hers. "It's all right."

A NICE TOWN
WITH VERY CLEAN
STREETS

THE PILOTS SCREAMED as Grimes watched the surface of Tartan-6 expand in the dead ship's windshield. He tried believing this wasn't happening to him, he was somewhere far away; it wasn't *him* rushing to crash into the surface of Hell.

And then FedShip UPF/14 slammed into the ground and what felt like the hand of God slammed into Grimes: an instant of breathless shock and then nothing but darkness.

He came back to find himself hanging upside down with vertigo warring with migraine and someone else's blood clogging his throat. More blood, hot and loathsome, coated his face, gummed his eyes closed, soaked his jumpsuit.

Stephens, the ship's Alpha rep, called, "Who's alive?"

Grimes retched blood, driving twin spikes deeper into his skull, and pawed shakily for the catches of his spiderweb-mesh harness.

He unbuckled and slammed against the ship's ceiling. From the back, he heard Newby, the mining rep, try to respond to Stephens and wind up vomiting.

Grimes scraped blood from his eyes and stood. Every muscle in his body was one, low chorus of pain.

He looked toward the cockpit and was momentarily confused by the helter-skelter mechanical wall before him; the cockpit had been crushed like a can. Only gore-soaked spiderweb-mesh straps remained of Richmond and Moore. Grimes's stomach fluttered. Ten minutes ago, they'd been checking the holocube for a lock on Tartan-6's colony-dome, the last of the thirteen colonies UPF had lost contact with during the war.

Then the instrument panels—the *ship*—had gone dead a kilometer above the ground.

He turned. Stephens stared at the destroyed cockpit, still hanging in his harness.

Stephens flicked a glance at Grimes, then undid the buckles. Still holding the catches, he swung out of the harness in one smooth movement. He went to Newby, whose Buddha gut pressed against the spiderweb, and helped get him down without Newby falling face-first into his own puke.

"Nelson and Rocco?" Grimes asked.

They looked at the end of the cabin. The rear compartment hatch was almost completely unrecognizable.

Newby wiped his mouth and asked, "The beacon?" His body trembled, his round face cheesy and coated in sweat.

"Tripped when we crashed," Stephens said. He shouldered past Grimes and went to the cockpit. Newby shrugged at Grimes, a brief spasm of his shoulders, and started for the storage compartments which had been below the bench seats but were now overhead.

Grimes considered the blood-smeared outer-hatch, which resembled crinkled tinfoil someone had tried flattening smooth again. There was protocol here, but it escaped him completely. Mentally, he felt like he was punching against a soft, suffocating cushion. Shock from the crash, he supposed.

The last one, he thought. He sensed he was pleading, but didn't know to whom. Not god. He'd stopped believing in god when the UPF sent him to the frontlines as a "morale booster." *The last goddam one before I got back to Janey.*

He mentally shook himself. "What do we know of this place other than it's a mining colony?"

"Rocco was the know-it-all," Newby said, awkwardly carrying three of the opaque emergency helmets. "Tartan-6 went off the grid early, though, which is weird considering how far from the frontlines they were. Air's breathable but thin, hence the helmets."

Stephens stooped in front of the cockpit wreckage and pulled a palm-sized black square from a glob of grue. When he turned, Grimes saw it was a memory-chip from one of the pilot helmets.

He noticed Grimes and Newby watching. "I flew missions with Moore before," he said. "His people will want this." He put the chip in his pocket and took a helmet from Newby. "What's the equipment and weaponry look like?"

"Still locked down," Newby said. "The rifles are cracked, but the bolters look all right. One of Nelson's tech doodads looks messed up, but that might be how it looks normally."

"At least the *weapons* survived," Grimes said, staring at his exhausted reflection in his helmet faceplate. He tried again to shake the suffocating numbness and could manage only a vague bitterness. *The last one*, he half-pleaded to no one. "We all know how useful they've been thus far."

They got the outer-hatch open and, helmets on, stumbled outside.

They'd crashed maybe a klick away from the colony, the transparent half-sphere nearly dominating the horizon. Mountains cut across the right and left.

"Company," Stephens said over the helmet comm. His helmet nodded toward a dune-buggy transport cresting a hill up ahead. The six men in the transport wore no Delta insignia.

Grimes stiffened. UPF protocol stated Deltas met all visitors.

A *click* in his helmet as a comm-link opened. "Quite a crash there, guys," the man in the passenger seat said as the transport stopped. His eyes were bright behind his clear face-plate. "Any casualties?"

"Four," Stephens said. "We're—"

"The UPF ship," the passenger finished. "I've been Station-hopping since you were kids. This isn't my first re-contact." He glanced at the ship and a pained expression crossed his face. "After all the UPF losses, any extra just seems tragic."

Grimes grimaced. The sentiment sounded robotic coming from this guy.

"I'm Station Supervisor Dugan. These folks are—" Dugan flashed a toothy grin. "—the Welcome Committee." He pulled a digipad from beside him and unclipped the stylus. "Okay. You said there were four casualties. They were…?"

Stephens said, "Can't we do this—"

"Quicker this way," Dugan interrupted. "The casualties…?"

Stephens said, "Pilots George Richmond and Brad Moore, Cultural Guide Mike Rocco, UPF Alpha Gregory Stephens."

Grimes jerked. He opened his mouth—

(—don't say a word i know what i'm doing)

The thought was as sharp as a knife-blade, as violating as a rape. Stephens's voice, loud and clear and *cold*. His brain felt like it'd plummeted into an icy lake.

Psi? he thought. *Stephens's a Psi? But that was only rumor—*

The jes-folks look left Dugan's bumpkin face. "No military survived?"

Stephens shook his helmeted head. "No."

Dugan's face softened. "Who're you folks, then?"

"I'm FedShip Tech Fred Nelson," Stephens said. He gestured at Grimes and Newby. "This is UPF representative Owen Grimes, and mining rep Phillip Newby."

Dugan scratched across the digipad with a stylus. "Was your distress beacon tripped?"

"The recorder was smashed upon impact."

"All right, then," Dugan said. His eyes were bright. "Hop in back and we'll take you to town."

"Why didn't the military come out?" Grimes asked.

Something shifted on Dugan's face and suddenly the thousand-watt smile appeared pasted on. "Mr. Grimes, our soldiers went to war."

A hollow suddenly opened in Grimes's chest. Colony-stationed soldiers *never* went to the front; it was UPF protocol, it was why there were *Deltas*. How could Dugan think Grimes wouldn't *know* this?

He thought of arguing, looked into Dugan's face, and thought again. The Supervisor's expression offered no answers; a true bureaucrat. You would never read Dugan's inner feelings on anything unless he allowed you to. He was a cipher, broadcasting only what his job specified.

You know your own, Grimes thought and felt sick suddenly. The migraine in the back of his head tightened a notch.

Without a word, he climbed aboard with Stephens and Newby and the dune-buggy lurched into a U-turn. Grimes watched the ship, twisted and bent like a scorpion tail, disappear behind them.

Stephens nudged him and nodded toward the space under the opposite benches.

Grimes counted four military rifles clipped to the floor beneath the "Welcome Committee."

Cold air blew through the hollow in his chest. He'd shaken off the shock of the crash. Oh yes, indeed.

Inside the dome's igloo-shaped Entrance Chamber, they stripped out of their bloodied jumpsuits, leaving them with only white T-shirts and gray trousers. Grimes eyed Stephens's muscular body warily. No one else on the ship had that type of honed form.

Dugan and his "Welcome Committee" stood near the hatch leading into the dome proper as three bored-looking men pulled the DeCon hoses off the wall.

"Don't bother," Dugan said. "We have places to be." He gestured for Grimes, Stephens, and Newby to follow him through the hatch.

It was at least ten degrees warmer under the dome. The Entrance Chamber led to the loading bay, an expansive field that took up a third of the entire station, where the colony's payout was kept for transport. Motorized dogcarts were parked around towering shipping containers. Beyond, the "town" began—a collection of short, stout buildings on either side of a wide dirt road connecting the Entrance Chamber to the mining crater at the far end. Emergency spotlights ringed the town.

"Welcome to Tartan-6, gentlemen," Dugan said.

An icepick shot into Grimes's mind:

(—*ask where we're going*)

His jaw wanted to lock, more from the idea of talking than the sudden violence of Stephens's message. He had no helmet to hide his expression now. "Where are we going? I don't think any of us are up for our duties."

Dugan glanced behind him. "Off to see the Chaplain."

He wasn't able to hide his bewilderment. "Why—"

"Are you sure that's wise, Supervisor Dugan?" Newby asked suddenly.

Dugan didn't even look this time. "I don't see why not."

"Quarantine," Stephens said, almost absently.

That stopped Dugan, and he turned slowly. "Quarantine?"

Grimes cleared his throat. "According to UPF protocol, all crash survivors must be quarantined for twenty-four hours or until the cause of the crash is known."

Dugan's bureaucratic façade cracked. "But our infirmary—"

"I can assure you we're perfectly healthy," Newby said, "and we thank you for allowing us to *skip* DeCon, but we can't speak for our pilots, or what *they* may have had."

"Are you familiar with Sparta-C, Supervisor?" Stephens asked.

The façade was gone and Dugan was nonplussed. "I—well, yes—"

"Then you're aware of their cholera epidemic," Grimes said. "That was our previous stop, and—"

"We have no medics!" Dugan screamed.

"We're probably *perfectly* healthy," Newby said.

"Without a working infirmary," Grimes asked, "is there somewhere else we might stay?"

Dugan's shoulders slumped. "The Delta barracks."

Grimes smiled his best bureaucratic smile. His head ached—a galloping black horse across the soft meat of his brain. "Given the importance UPF has for Tartan-6, no one wants any unnecessary risks taken."

The Welcome Committee looked decidedly uneasy—this wasn't in the script. Their faces told Grimes that there very much *had* been a script, but to what? If Grimes hadn't asked a question, what would've happened?

Dugan looked at his watch. "Quarantine to begin at fifteen-thirty, per arrival at the barracks." He visibly struggled to regain his former posture. "This way, please."

The procession began without its previous urgency. They reminded Grimes of kids forced to do their chores.

They entered town. Gray, utilitarian buildings stared down at them, the windows and doors empty. Grimes could hear the syncopated chugging of the climate system.

Where were the *people*? They might've been walking through forgotten stage-settings.

"Nice place," Newby said, eying the emptiness.

Dugan missed his tone. "We're strict about that. To be clean, to be orderly..." He trailed off. "It is of the utmost importance."

For what? Grimes thought. He looked down at the road and saw the dirt had been raked. The lines were the only things *on* the road. Not a single piece of trash or footprint anywhere.

He looked at Dugan. What *was* this? Keeping the colony clean was important, but this was taken to its extreme.

A nice town with very clean streets, he thought and shuddered.

Ahead, he heard a rustling sound where the side streets intersected the main road. The rustling grew to a patterned roar and, like an opened floodgate, swarms of people suddenly flooded out onto the main road.

Grimes stopped for the briefest instant and he thought he heard Newby gasp.

A blast of cold in his head—

(—don't stop don't you dare stop now—)

—and Grimes found his footing again.

The people, dressed in blue, grey, and green jumpsuits, surrounded them, lining the building fronts three deep. Grimes couldn't read a single expression on any man, woman, or child. No one spoke. Their heads turned as one to watch the group pass.

The sight of all those people, blank and uniform and eerily silent ...they hurt his *mind*. His eyes couldn't focus on any one person. They made his footsteps louder, his migraine more painful.

The Welcome Committee took no notice of them. They might not have been there at all.

Up ahead, cranes rose out of the wide crater of the mining

pit. What must've been hanging mine dust cast a strange, flickering yellowish light over the various mining machinery.

Dugan turned left, away from the pit, before Grimes could study it more closely. Behind them, Grimes thought he heard a deep sigh.

He refused to look back. His flesh prickled and crawled.

They passed the colony's Congo Church—the only un-boxlike structure in town with its neo-Catholic pointed steeples and rounded corners.

On the sermon display next to the front walk were two words: FREE IT!

Free what? Grimes wondered.

Dugan dumped them unceremoniously at the Delta barracks, a long L-shaped building outside of town. From one of the slit windows, Stephens watched them leave.

"Aren't they going to guard us?" Newby asked.

Stephens turned away. "Why bother? There's nowhere to *go*. Besides, who can they spare to guard us with the military gone?"

"You think the civilians offed them?" Grimes asked. He looked around. The barracks could've housed a hundred soldiers.

Stephens's eyes darkened. "Yeah, although I don't know how. Those rifles all but clinched it." He frowned. "I think that *whatever* the civs are up to, military isn't welcome."

"And that's why you faked being Nelson," Newby said, then winced.

"Headache?" Stephens asked.

"Since we landed."

He turned to Grimes. "You?"

Grimes nodded.

Stephens rubbed his temple. "Me, too. It's the electro-magnetic field, I think. It's ..." He trailed off. "I bet compasses would be useless here.

"You're a Psi," Grimes said. "Why didn't you tell us? *Jesus*, when you sent that first message—"

"Alphas aren't encouraged to divulge it." He looked at them. "You both from Earth?"

They nodded.

"I was raised on Ellis-7. Any child that tests high for Psi capabilities is sent there. Psi-abilities have something to do with the brain's electrical impulses. It makes us *very* sensitive to any planet's EMF. Tartan-6's off the charts."

"You think that crashed our ship?" Newby asked.

Stephens shrugged.

Grimes paced the barrack's central aisle, scrubbing his face with shaky hands. "Jesus fox-trotting *Christ*, what's going on here? The military's gone, the town is acting…" He couldn't come up with a word to describe the faceless mass they'd seen. "…and you're saying a *planet's* EMF is all messed up." He looked at Stephens and Newby. "Why the hell were we being taken to the *Chaplain*? Two-thirds of the Fed planets don't even *have* religion."

Stephens rubbed the stubble on his cheek. "We'll find out why soon enough. They won't give us much time—twelve hours at most—before saying screw it. That's not enough time for the beacon to draw anything useful."

"Then what?" Newby asked.

Stephens merely looked at him.

The Congo Church rose in Grimes's mind.

"Free it," he muttered.

Newby and Stephens stared at him as he shivered.

Night on Tartan-6. Stars like cuts in black velvet shined brilliantly in alien constellations. Grimes would've happily given anything to be staring at Orion or Cassiopeia with Janey.

They showered and changed into new jumpsuits. Newby found aspirin. Stephens begged off—he needed his head clear.

There was nothing to do except stare at each other and watch the clock and ask themselves the same question over and over: *How long do we have?*

Finally, Stephens headed for the door. "I'm going out."

"What for?" Grimes asked.

"Get some clue of what's going on. Maybe check the ship if I can." He studied them. "Try to sleep. You might not get it later."

But sleep never felt further from Grimes when he lay down. The idea that he could wake up with Dugan standing daunted rest.

He fell into a scratchy doze and dreamed of Janey, of seeing her in her gardening sun-hat, its floppy band obscuring her heart-shaped face. His relief in the dream was palpable, but tinged with uneasiness.

He kept thinking he saw a pit out of the corner of his eye, flickering with a yellow light.

Stephens's haggard voice, calling down a well: "C'mon, Grimes."

Grimes opened his eyes to see Stephens and Newby standing above him, faces pale. He cried out as a lightning bolt of pain struck his head.

Grimes sat up slowly. His muscles felt like cheap concrete, his bones made of crushed glass. Newby handed him four aspirin.

"What's it like outside?" Grimes said, dry-swallowing the pills.

"No signs of struggle. The Deltas are just *gone*." He shook his head. "An untrained civilian population disposed of nearly one hundred Deltas and there isn't a sign of battle *anywhere*? How in the *hell* did they do that?"

"Those people didn't look like they had any migraines," Newby offered.

Stephens nodded. "Yeah, so why us?"

Grimes couldn't think of a reason. "Anyone see you?"

Stephens shook his head. "*Everyone* was standing around the crater. You noticed that yellowish … light? glow? … earlier? It's coming from *within* the crater. Everyone was looking into it and sighing."

"Why?" Newby said.

Confusion warred on Stephens' face. "I don't know."

Questions crammed Grimes's aching head, inarticulate and impossible for Stephens to answer. "What'd you do, then?"

"Went to the Entrance Chamber—no one was there—and out to the ship."

"Why'd you go out there at all?" Grimes asked. "The ship's destroyed."

Stephens opened his Suit and pulled out three bolters, setting the boxy plastic-and-metal handguns on the bed. "For *these*."

Outside, Grimes heard nothing except the muted rumble of the climate-control systems. He could see no lights on anywhere. A soft breeze whistled between the buildings.

He stopped suddenly. "Where's the wind coming from?"

Both wore incredulous expressions, which then melted into puzzlement. "How the hell do you get wind in a *dome*?" Newby muttered.

They started again, heads down between hunched shoulders. Beneath the glow of the stars, the town was a rippled monolith of black.

Grimes's hand tightened over his bolter. He'd only handled one during training sessions. His combat experience had been strictly *behind* the front.

They stopped at the edge of town, crouching down behind an outcropping of rock, and looked at the loading bay. There was a fair distance of open ground between here and the safety of the shipping containers.

"They might come after us," Stephens breathed. His blood-shot eyes were nearly black in the gloom. "Can you handle it?"

"We don't have much choice," Grimes said.

Stephens nodded. He looked like he wanted to say something else, and, at that moment, despair washed over Grimes, drowned him. What were they doing? What did they hope to accomplish? He thought of Janey and it was like thinking of an old photograph. He had no faith he'd get back to her. He was already dead.

He looked at Stephens and Newby and, oddly, that helped. They weren't giving up. Stephens wanted to know what happened to his fellow soldiers. Newby just wanted to survive. They had faith they could do this. It radiated from them, like a phosphorescent glow.

When Stephens glanced over the rock and made his move, Newby close behind, Grimes took a deep breath and followed.

They trotted hunched over, soldiers across No Man's Land. The Entrance Chamber, obscured by shipping containers, drew slowly closer. Grimes thought the distance had been shorter be-fore.

The spotlights clicked on as they reached the halfway point, pinning them like bugs. Disappointment surged through Grimes as he turned, but he felt no surprise. None at all.

The town stood silently beneath the lights, the glare cloaking them in black.

Stephens grunted and an icepick stabbed Grimes's temple—

(—*hide the bolters.*)

They jerkily shoved the bolters inside their jumpsuits. Grimes wondered what the point was, and he felt a glowing green hatred for the townspeople.

"Stop where you are," Dugan called.

"We *did*, you idiot," Grimes snapped.

Three men detached and approached with an air of ceremony.

"Trying to leave?" Dugan asked. "That's not particularly nice."

"How'd you kill the Deltas?" Stephens asked.

Dugan's smile widened. "Ah, the resident Alpha speaks. I know Tartan-6 must be particularly *brutal* for you."

"How'd you kill the Deltas?" Stephens repeated.

"We freed them, Alpha," he said. His smile was chilling and Grimes felt a drillbit of fear burrow into him. "They've been Saved. You'll see."

Dugan stepped aside to reveal the other two men. One was just a townsman, a military rifle bulky and awkward in his unskilled hands.

The other was obviously the Chaplain.

Grimes thought he might've once been a handsome elder gentleman, but those days were long gone. He was a scarecrow, his black jumper and Roman collar hanging off him. His hands were gnarled into claws. His head was too large for his body, nearly a rounded triangle. His corkscrewed white hair had fallen out in patches, leaving an uneven mane. His face was a relief-map of wrinkles from which cherry-eyes—identical to Stephens's—beamed, entirely present and completely insane.

"My fallen flock," he croaked. His hands clawed the air at his sides. "Do you believe in paying for rewards to come? Do you believe in creating a platform from which Greatness shall arise?"

Grimes's mouth worked on its own. "Free it."

The Chaplain suddenly beamed. A gnarled hand gripped Grimes's arm and Grimes shuddered. His touch was cold, but Grimes felt a vein of unspeakable energy and power beneath, a thrum of heat. "*Yes!* Yes, that is *exactly* it!" The Chaplain turned to Dugan. "Its ascension will be complete with these three! They *believe!* Oh, the *wonders* It has foretold! We mustn't wait any longer!"

Grimes allowed the Chaplain to pull him along as the others followed. The bolter banged against his stomach.

They entered town. The only illumination came from the yellow glow of the crater at the other end, reflecting against the dome's ceiling.

The Chaplain let go of his arm to gesture at the town. "This is our altar and we keep it is as such. This is merely one way we show our faith and love for It Who Carries Us."

"A nice town with very clean streets," Grimes muttered and felt sick.

The Chaplain's horrible eyes blazed. "*Yes.* We are in Its *home*, the way the church has always been the supposed home of god. Do you desecrate your lord's home? Do you, perhaps, *shit* in the pews and *piss* in the holy water? *No!*"

The Chaplain continued, "It Who Carries Us has touched you three, and that means Its reach is growing from Its prison—*It is almost here.*"

Grimes's migraine was intensifying. He felt a sudden vibration beneath his feet and it jarred his brain.

He felt the Chaplain's eyes on him. "I know," the Chaplain said. "The pain is very great, but that is only because you haven't given yourselves fully to Its love." He looked at the following townspeople. "We all have accepted and we all, as one, no longer feel pain, only joy.

"It Who Carries Us controls this planet's electro-magnetic field," the Chaplain went on, his eyes full of the glowing pit. "It is Its way of contacting Its believers. We felt it when the miners broke through to Its level." He shook his awful head. "The agony. But I heard first. Heard the message *beneath* the pain. Here—" He tapped the top of his skull. "I heard Its whisper, and I responded. It gifted me for my willingness—" He held up his gnarled hands. "—and I was able to give the others what they wanted: to hear Its message *without* the pain."

Grimes looked at Stephens, striding on the Chaplain's other side. His narrowed bloodshot eyes were impossible to read. Did Stephens, a Psi, hear Its "message"?

Grimes didn't want to know. If this was hell for him and Newby, what must Stephens be feeling?

"It could contact us, but not free Itself," the Chaplain went on. "It was too weak. It needed to *feed* and we knew what had to be done. It needed flesh to gain strength." He grinned at Grimes. "*Sacrifice* makes it stronger. *Sacrifice* leads to freedom."

Grimes thought of the Deltas and shuddered.

"When it told me it would crash your ship," the Chaplain said, "bring you to us—the depth of Its thinking! It nears freedom, but It must have the *faithful* to finish. *That* was the final stroke."

The Chaplain trailed off as the group approached the crater. A strong wind came from below. A high-pitched electric distortion drilled into Grimes's ears, growing with each awkward step across the quaking ground.

"Step forward," the Chaplain said. Grimes could barely hear him. "Witness the majesty you're giving yourself to."

His feet kept moving. Newby followed Grimes, looking like someone beholding his bogeyman. Blood burst from Stephens's nose.

Grimes looked down as they approached the crumbled edge and picked out details through that blasting yellow light—the rough funnel-like sides of the crater, the constant tumble of dirt. The bottom of the crater was a rough oval opening, ragged like the teeth of a diamond-saw, dropping into the bowels of Tartan-6, where the impossible wind came from.

Bulging from the hole was a writhing, segmented coil of *something* that pulsed with yellow light. Grimes couldn't begin to determine its length or size. Its constant writhing—the source of the vibrations—expanded the hole, pushed it slowly out onto the surface. He thought he caught sight of a massive jagged tooth, but it was gone before he could fully see it and he couldn't shake the sudden disappointment that filled him.

It's not *a god*, he thought desperately. *It's not. It's a species the surveyors missed when they reconned the planet and these lunatics just* think *it needs sacrifices and worship. It's not a god.*

But he didn't stop walking, his left foot stepping onto a boulder that rattled like a loose tooth, as if his *mind* might refuse to believe, but the body was a willing acolyte. He leaned toward the yellow light and a part of him thought, *Will I see Its face?*

And then a cold burning *roar* filled his head, a shotgun blast of icicles: Stephens's voice.

(—OH DEAR JESUS IT'S CALLING ME CALLING ME IN CALLING OH MY GAAAWWWD—)

Grimes jerked like a man startled awake just as the boulder tumbled over. He spun and saw Stephens fall to his knees. Blood flowed freely from his nose, ears, and eyes. His hands moved from his temples to the zipper of his Suit.

The vibration grew in strength, knocking Grimes and Newby down. The wind became a shrieking gale and the yellow light *blasted* from the bottom. Grimes's migraine jumped in agony and he felt blood trickle out his nose. The high-pitched distortion filled his world.

Against the pain, Grimes groped for his zipper and saw Newby doing the same.

Another shotgun-blast of cold punched through Grimes's mind—

(—STOP IT CAN'T STOP IT CAN'T-CAN'T-CAN'T—)

The mental scream cut off. Stephens shrieked silently, blood spraying. He collapsed, his glazed, bleeding eyes goggling at nothing.

Panic galvanized Grimes and he tore his zipper down. He yanked his bolter free and turned toward the townspeople. The Chaplain's mouth worked, his bloodshot eyes blazing.

Grimes fired as Newby drew his own weapon. A hole, no wider than the bore of a straw, appeared in the Chaplain's wrinkled neck. A freshet of blood poured through. He dropped face-first into the dust.

Grimes's migraine was a bludgeon in his head. He focused all his energies on holding the bolter and firing. The closest guard spun like a top, blood squirting from his shoulder.

Newby fired four times, hitting two out of three guards. Grimes struggled to his feet as the remaining six leveled their rifles.

The ground shuddered beneath them, so powerfully it pushed everyone forward. Lightning cracks shot across the ground.

It's coming out, Grimes thought, and couldn't shake the undertone of awe within. Another part of him argued, *It didn't* need *sacrifices, dammit, because it's not a god.*

The distortion rose to a scream, digging into his head.

He stumbled into the crowd, firing at their blank, exultant faces. He caught a woman through her yawning mouth, a man in the temple.

Behind him he heard the faint crack of a rifle and Newby's distant howl. Grimes turned and saw Newby facedown and still. Grimes fired twice at the killing guard. Both shots took him in the stomach.

He sprinted away, his brain feeling like a tortured plaything. The ground beneath him tilted crazily this way and that, and Grimes had to focus on keeping upright. From both sides came the snap of plastic, the squeal of twisting metal, the musical jangle of breaking glass. The wind shoved from all sides, throwing grit into his eyes. He reached the edge of town and kept going.

A bellow from the crater filled the world, drowning out the destruction of the town. A triumphant shriek followed, made tiny and hollow, *"Behold! Behold the GLORY of It Who Carries Us!"*

His left foot came down and the ground was now six-inches lower as the earth became a disintegrating trampoline. He fell, the bolter cartwheeling from his hands and plunging into a crack. Pulsing yellow light blasted from behind him, throwing his shadow far out ahead, twisted and strange.

He clawed and kicked and pulled and crawled over sudden rock outcroppings and dizzyingly deep holes. The Entrance Chamber was the mirage in the desert, the light at the end. *Just get out*, he thought. *Get out and hide*. He didn't know if he'd be safe outside the dome, but he clung to the idea like a drowning man to a life preserver.

It Who Carries Us's bellow cracked the sky and seemed not just an exercise of Its incomprehensible vocal cords, but a command. At the same time, the electronic distortion in his ears changed, shifting from a blanket of torture into something specific and focused.

Grimes slowed, then stopped, even as a good portion of his mind shrieked to keep going.

His body was a willing acolyte.

He turned toward that awful throbbing yellow glow.

In the center of the light was a vast black tower, ridged and writhing and magnificent. In its core, Its Eye, a massive three-pupilled structure, rolled toward him, *seeing* him.

Grimes's mind shattered like a piece of thin glass as he heard Its simple, horrible message in the center of his head, reverberating through his nerves:

<YOU>

And the throbbing yellow light consumed him.

The A-shaped rescue-ship tore through the thin cloud cover like the arrival of a pagan god, with a roar of throbbing engines and a scream of directionless wind.

Grimes sat in the outer hatch of the ship and watched it come, his lank white hair whipping around his head, obscuring the scarring around the temples.

It circled the wreckage and then the engine-sounds changed pitch and it began to descend as if lowered by a cable.

Something stirred in the center of his chest, something light and expanding and long-thought dead: anticipation.

"They came," he muttered. "They finally came." He felt pain twist in the center of his mind, a bright flare of migraine, and then gone. Grimes shivered.

He'd visited his ship every day for months, waiting. It'd become his ritual and people deferred to it; even Dugan, that simpering little worm. They didn't understand why, which was fine with him, and they didn't ask, which was even better. It maintained a distance between him and them.

He'd never bothered to tell them about the beacon. He owed *them* nothing.

The rescue ship landed with a ground-trembling thud and the engines screamed as they powered down. Immediately, the ship's side-hatch opened and five Alphas in combat gear—he recognized them by their shoulder insignia—leapt out, rifles raised.

Grimes stood, sliding his hands into his pockets.

The Alpha on-point stopped two yards away, his opaque helmet reflecting sunlight. "Identify yourself," he yelled over the roar of the engine, his rifle aimed at Grimes's face

Grimes felt no fear. "UPF Representative Owen Grimes."

The point Alpha didn't move or relax. The Alpha closest to the ship pulled a handheld and tapped the screen with a finger. Finally, he looked up and said, "He's one of 'em. He's..." The Alpha trailed off, looked down at his screen, looked back, then studied his handheld some more. He touch the screen, then touched it again.

Only Grimes noticed.

"Any other survivors?" the Alpha on-point asked.

Grimes shook his head. "They died in the crash."

The Alphas lowered their weapons. The point man offered his hand. "Glad someone made it, then. Our sincerest apologies for not arriving sooner."

Grimes pulled his gnarled, throbbing hand from his pocket and gripped the Alpha's. Staring at his bloodshot, warped reflection in the Alpha's helmet, he said, "I knew you'd come. I had faith."

Another twist of pain—agonizing yet oh-so pleasurable—ripped through the center of his head as the Alpha turned to confer with his colleagues. This was a small group, but there'd be more.

My gift to you, he told It.

THE DOORWAY MAN

THE GUN in Jake Reznic's hand didn't shake, but his voice did. "T-tell me where h-he *is*, dammit."

Lightning cracked the night sky outside, illuminating the interior of the barn like the flash of God's camera. The rain came in sheets through the massive doors.

The farmer's piggish eyes were locked on the barrel Jake's .380; he might not've heard Jake at all. His gut swelled, pushing his plain button-down shirt to its limit. Jake could smell him—the sharp tang of sweat and dirt, the ozone stench of fear.

No, that's me, Jake thought. *I'm piss-terrified.*

And then the pain came, gnawing through his stomach and chest like hunger pangs. It didn't blossom and grow—it was just *there*, like a switch had been flipped. Deep and burning and *hungry*, gobbling at his nerve-endings. He grimaced and curled his free hand around his stomach.

Muttering suddenly burst into the center of his head; a chorus of voices, chanting but *faint*, as if heard from a distance. He understood nothing said. He never did, but he suddenly wanted the farmer to come closer, close enough so that Jake could grab him. Draw him in.

Feed the pain.

"I know he's *here*," Jake panted. "So tell me where he *is*."

The farmer didn't move.

"Tell me where he fucking IS!" Jake screamed.

"I'm right here, Jake," the Doorway Man said behind him, and although the storm raged outside the barn and the muttering raged inside Jake's head, he spoke in a normal but perfectly audible tone of voice. He sounded like he did when Jake first met him at that goddamned party a month ago.

❦ ⋯ ❧

"You don't belong here," a man said.

Jake Reznic looked up from his scotch and blinked. The man before him was rail-thin. His clothes were too large and faded, gray and brown, his corduroy sports jacket blending in with his loose T-shirt. His pageboy haircut was lank and dirty, and the bags under his eyes were something you'd have to check at the airport.

Jake glanced around. Everyone else in the spacious penthouse wore suits and dark cocktail dresses, their colors stark against the lush whiteness of the carpet and furniture. To his right, a line of wide windows looked out at the skyscrapers sparkling with minute dots of light.

"It's funny you say that," he said, gulping the rest of his scotch. He still wasn't nearly drunk enough yet.

The man raised his eyebrows. The eyes themselves were glassy. *Drugs,* Jake thought. "Why's that?"

Jake opened his mouth and a shadow fell across him.

"Hey!" Mansfield—the bastard—said. "You got to meet the Doorway Man!"

Jake cocked an eyebrow. "What?"

Mansfield stepped between them, looking like he always did— like he'd stepped whole and breathing from a men's catalogue. The gel in his carefully tousled hair gleamed under the recessed lighting.

A hot, bitter bubble popped in Jake's stomach. In his head, he heard Mansfield saying, *You don't have a fucking clue, do you, Jakey-boy?*

"I was wondering if you'd been invited to this party," Mansfield said. The man studied his sneakers as a pained grimace crossing his face.

"I'm at every party, Bradley," he said.

Mansfield grinned. "Oh, I know." He dismissed Jake entirely— no surprise there—as he turned to the Doorway Man. His voice dropped to a stage-whisper. "I wanted to say thanks again, by the way."

"I just hope the girl didn't press charges."

A muscle twitched in one of Mansfield's chiseled cheeks. He

glanced at Jake—oh, there you are—and offered a distracted smile. "Have fun, Jakey-boy." He walked away, not quite running.

"Prick," Jake muttered. The Mansfield from earlier said, *You see, Jakey-boy, Nick and I have this bet with Andrew and Chris and I think they're gonna try and sabotage you. I don't want to see that happen.*

Jake looked down at the glass in his hand. A basic tumbler, but it looked thick and felt heavy. He'd always had good aim. Maybe he could break the fucking thing over Mansfield's head from here.

Feminine laughter erupted across the room. Mansfield stood with a woman, leaning close, free hand on her upper arm and saying something into her ear. She had bouncy, gleaming chestnut hair, the kind you wanted to bury your hands and forget yourself in. Her shimmering cocktail dress was cut low back and front, and the globes of her breasts pressed out against the scant material—still decent, but heart-stopping all the same.

And she was *laughing* at something *Mansfield* said. As he watched, Mansfield led her out of the main room.

Jake's face fought a grimace and lost.

He turned back to the Doorway Man, but TDM—as Jake was sure Mansfield called him—was studying his shoes. No help there.

Why not just leave? an interior voice asked. He knew Mansfield had brought him to the party—packed with city council members, bankers, brokers, and at least one state senator—to show him off. Oh, look, the Sharks over at Spurlock, Preston & Long have another plaything. What are the terms this time, Brad m'boy? See if the son of a bitch will make it out of SP&L's probo period? Oh *my*.

Mansfield's my ride, he thought. He glanced into his tumbler again. A bar had been set up near the kitchen, complete with a bartender, but that would mean having to walk amongst the powerful people, feel them *looking* at him.

Jake slumped in his seat. "Those must be the most interesting shoes in the world," he said to the Doorway Man.

The Doorway Man looked up slowly, his wet, puffy eyes staring through him. Had this guy been *crying*?

"You don't belong here," he said again.

"You already said that."

"No, you're different. These people have connections and deals and cronies and *things.* You don't." He sounded relieved. "You're an outsider, too."

Jake grunted and sank deeper into his seat.

"Bradley brought you here," the Doorway Man said.

Jake didn't respond.

"Another one of his bets?"

Jake looked away. "Who was the girl?"

The Doorway Man shrugged his narrow shoulders. "Someone from work, I think. *You* know about that."

Jake did. The Sharks—Mansfield, Chris White, and Andrew Schwarz—swooped in on any female above a certain bra-cup size and below a certain dress-size. Those that gave in to their advances inevitably quit.

You wanted to be friends *with them,* an interior voice reminded.

Jake's face hardened. He was naive, but that didn't cut it in the self-loathing department. He'd wanted to succeed. He'd wanted to make it.

"Why they call you the Doorway Man?" he asked.

He shrugged again. "I open the way to things. I didn't come up with it."

"What's your real one?"

"Doesn't matter."

He looked at the Doorway Man's glassy-yet-focused eyes.

"Drugs?"

The Doorway Man looked at him for a moment, then reached into his sports jacket and pulled something out.

In the center of his palm was a teal geltab, the kind you might take if you had a cold.

"Doorways," he said.

"I'm not a druggie."

The Doorway Man's eyes cut to Jake's empty tumbler. "Sure." He looked back at Jake. "This isn't a drug, Jake. It's a way out. You'll feel better than ever."

He thought about the hours left, the people glancing, the unlimited scotch that wouldn't help.

"Fuck it," he said, snatching the geltab and dry-swallowing it.

The Doorway Man smiled. It burned in the center of the man's gaunt face.

Jake awoke face down in his apartment.

He bounded off the hardwood floor, looking everywhere at once. The windows to his left showed the first rays of sun breaking the horizon.

He ran a hand through his hair. How had he gotten home? What had happened last night? He remembered taking that pill and then … nothing. His suit, while wrinkled, wasn't stained. He checked his pockets and found his keys and wallet. He swallowed.

No crummy aftertaste associated with a night drinking. No hangover, no aching muscles.

"I feel *great*," he said, wonderingly, as if to confirm it to himself.

He thought of Mansfield, of the bet. The crushing despair, the gnawing self-loathing, was gone. Who cared about *them*? *They* didn't matter. In the end, only *he* did.

After a shower and what turned out to be a completely unneeded cup of coffee, he went to the office and lost himself in a frenzy of work that, at certain points, should've made his computer catch fire. He dug into his team's various accounts, jumping from project to project as new ideas struck him. He'd never known such energy, such creativity, and, apparently, neither had his Project Manager, who wanted to present Jake's ideas to the Board and the clients at the end of the week.

He didn't think about Mansfield or the bet. It didn't matter; *Mansfield* didn't matter. Only *he* did. He was the master of his destiny and he wasn't going to let go of the reins.

This lasted three days.

His body was a throbbing ache on the fourth morning. His brain felt like the anvil a blacksmith used to beat metal. His stomach was shriveled and abused.

He stared at the red glowing numbers of his nightstand clock —ten to seven—and thought from the depths of his agony, *I'll call off.*

And then he remembered today was the team meeting and groaned. Missing a team meeting was enough to be fired.

What the hell did that guy give me? he thought. Was the Doorway Man—what a stupid name—part of the bet? Was this the sabotage Mansfield had mentioned?

You bastard, Jake thought. Had there ever been so much *pain* in the world?

Mansfield was waiting in Jake's cubicle and his face configured itself into an expression of shock and concern when Jake arrived. "Jesus! What happened?"

"Your fuckin Doorway Man," he said, wincing as each word exploded a mortar shell in his head. He dropped into his desk chair. "What's his name? I *need* something to fix this."

Mansfield frowned. "I have his number," he said slowly.

Jake leaned forward like a striking snake. "Give it to me."

Mansfield was looking him over—like a better studying a race horse, Jake thought. "No."

"*No?*"

Mansfield tilted his head in the direction of the glass conference rooms. "Because you'll call him now and miss your meeting."

"Like you care, *Bradley.*"

"About you, not really," Mansfield admitted. "About the bet very much." He stepped into the doorway. "You'll get the number after the meeting. Don't be late."

Jake debated going after him. *Who am I kidding?* he thought. *A child would crush me at this point.*

Somehow he got through the meeting without crying and screaming and even made himself nod humbly when Bernstein singled him out for particular praise. He counted the seconds with the pounding in his head.

After, he darted back to his cubicle, wanting to dump the files on his desk and go hunt down Mansfield.

But Mansfield had already been there. Propped between the keys on his computer keyboard was a pink MESSAGE slip. On the back, in Mansfield's cramped, anal writing, was *TDM: 814-555-6106*. Beneath that, Mansfield had written: *Good luck, Jakey-boy*.

He was already pulling his smartphone from his pocket as he headed for the lobby.

The bar was called Uptown Downs. Its interior was a dingy hole; neon beer signs and the lights of the back bar were the only illumination.

"You held out longer than I thought," the Doorway Man said, sitting across from Jake at a cocktail table.

"Gimme what I came here for," Jake said. He could barely see. The pain produced pulsing red blossoms in front of his eyes, like soft blinkers.

The Doorway Man shrugged and dropped a small Baggie onto the cocktail table. Within was a single geltab.

Jake snatched it up, then paused. "This isn't going to fuck me up even more, is it? I want to be *normal*."

The Doorway Man didn't answer for a moment. His face was nearly lost in the red blossoms and gloom. When he spoke, his voice had become thick and a little shaky. "You won't f-feel like *that*, anymore."

A fresh explosion in Jake's head and he didn't bother debating the issue. He fumbled the geltab out with shaking fingers. *God, anything to be better than this*, he thought and dry-swallowed the pill.

It was like waking up after a heavy bout of oversleeping. He reached up to rub his eyes—

—and felt the tension of taut leather against his wrists.

Jake's eyes flew open.

He was strapped to the metal frame of a bed, wide leather belts cinched to his ankles and wrists, in the corner of a narrow cement room. His shirt was unbuttoned.

The Doorway Man sat next to the bed, his eyes black sockets, a battery-powered lantern highlighting his jaw and cheekbones.

"What the hell are you doing?" Jake screamed. *"Let me UP!"*

The Doorway Man didn't move.

Jake pulled and yanked, but it was no good. A cold sweat beaded his brow. "What are you doing? People know who I am! They know *I* know *you!* You can't *do* this!"

"You're wrong," the Doorway Man said. "People may know you, but you aren't *known*. There's a difference. You have no family here. No friends. I knew it as soon as I met you." He gestured at Jake. "I'm sorry about this—about tricking you in the first place. I needed time to check you out and make sure I'd see you again." He sighed and it was watery. "But you and me... really, there's not much difference between us, except clothes and careers. We're both outsiders."

"WHAT THE HELL ARE YOU TALKING ABOUT?"

The Doorway Man sighed. "I don't *want* to do it this way, but I have no choice. All the others killed themselves. Did *it* make them do it?" He shook his head. "I have to pass it *on. That's* the only way out. I learned how and, *God*, the time and agony it took me to learn *that*. This has been going on for centuries—*millennia*. The information was there, it just took forever to *find*. Then, meeting the right person ..." He drifted off.

Jake licked his lips. "Doorway Man or whatever the fuck your real name is—listen. *Listen to me.* Whatever you're doing, you can stop. You can back out." A pleading edge crept into his voice. "You don't have to *do* this!"

The Doorway Man took off his sports jacket. The baggy T-shirt beneath just made him seem gaunter—the arms coming out of the short sleeves looked like a stick-figure's.

"A word of advice," he said. "When it's all over and it's talking to *you*, do whatever idea pops in your head. Doing that will make your life so much easier. It's how I've been able to make it for so long. Trust me on this, Jake."

Before Jake could ask him what *that* meant, the Doorway Man cleared his throat and began to speak.

It was a guttural, phlegmy grunt, not English. The "words"—if that was what they were—seemed to form in his chest and come out of his mouth like an echo. It sounded as if he spoke in almost all consonants.

"*Ftgan-ntone,*" the Doorway Man grunted and, in the lantern light, his face grew red. Tears spilled down his cheeks, dripping off his jaw. One of his hands hovered, long fingers splayed, over Jake's bare chest. Jake tried burrowing into the springs of the bedframe.

The Doorway Man's mouth writhed. "*G-gnafst-fgyn-r'yell-f-f-f—*"

His hand curled into a quivering fist. Jake wanted to close his eyes but couldn't.

"*F-f-f-f—*" the Doorway Man struggled.

Jake's lips peeled back from his teeth.

"*FORE!*" The Doorway Man shrieked, his echoey voice rebounding off the cement walls, and brought his fist down onto Jake's chest.

And it *slipped in.*

Jake winced, but then his eyes opened wide as a strange mixture of hot and cold, not pain, spread through his chest. He raised his head and saw the Doorway Man's hand *inside* his chest, as if the lunatic were no more tangible than a ghost, buried up to the wrist in the space just below his nipples and just above where the bottom of Jake's ribcage was.

Jake looked from the Doorway Man's hand to the man's face and saw a rictus of effort and pain warring across those gaunt features.

What the— he started to think and then the pain came. It was a white-hot explosion of hurt, rocketing up and down every nerve-ending in his being, so bright and awful he *saw it* behind his eyes. This made the pain from earlier seem like a minor sting. In this agony, Jake Reznic forgot who he was, what he was, where he was, and darkness consumed him.

The muttering came first; a sinuous choir of barely audible voices in the center of his head. This unseen choir seemed to be speaking in all consonants.

And then the pain came, galvanizing, beginning in his chest and ripping open every muscle, bone, and nerve.

Jake, already shrieking, bounded up from his prone position and, blindly, bounced against a cinderblock wall, hugging his chest. It felt like he was being chewed from the inside out. Red and white pulsed in front of his eyes. In the background of his mind—empty except for this pain—the muttering went on and on, riding the tsunami of agony.

And, just as quickly, stopped.

Jake collapsed, panting, his body filmed with grimy sweat.

After epochs of time, he opened his eyes.

He lay on the floor of a narrow alley; a thin strip of autumnal sunshine blasted above and in front of him. The cement was slimy.

Slowly, like an old man, he got to his feet. In the emptiness of his shocked mind, like the whisper of a ghost, the Doorway Man said, *It doesn't kill you, y'know.*

With a gasp, it all flooded back. He yanked his shirt up, rubbing the clear, blameless spot on his chest. His fingertips left commas of grime.

It was a dream, he thought. *A hallucination.*

But the pain. The *pain,* so big and huge it was like some Pagan God coming to Earth and possessing him. And what about the muttering in his head?

His rational mind struggled to come up with an explanation and couldn't.

He shuffled to the mouth of the alley and looked around. The avenue before him was barren aside from a few old cars, a few stripped vehicles, and a smattering of homeless. He saw storefronts with boarded-up windows.

He looked up, to his right, and just barely saw the tips of skyscrapers. He looked left and the avenue narrowed and ended at warehouse gates, with the river beyond.

"How the hell did he get me here?" he said, completely unaware he'd spoken aloud.

Does it matter? an interior voice asked coldly.

He started walking toward downtown. A few of the homeless glanced his way, but not for long. Nothing of interest. In his dirty clothes and bleeding face, he could've passed for them.

As he walked, he felt his pockets for the comforting bulges of his wallet, keys, and phone. All were there and he pulled the phone out—God knew how long he'd been out cold.

He stared at the cracked screen of his smartphone. "Son of a bitch."

Least of your concerns, the interior voice said. *What about the* pain?

He swallowed what felt like a doorknob in his throat.

From then on, he existed in a kind of limbo within the confines of his apartment, which he barely remembered reaching. He might've been there two days, or two weeks. Time degenerated into the random bouts of crushing pain and muttering, alien voices. The move-ments of the sun meant little; the television was a quacking box of light. His smartphone was crushed and useless; a broken lifeline. He slept little and ate less; he wasn't hungry and although he was exhausted, he couldn't do more than doze.

He considered suicide, but what stopped him wasn't a fear of death, but the realization that nothing was a *sure* enough way of killing himself. He didn't own a gun and his apartment wasn't high enough off the ground. He could cut his wrists, hang himself, or stick his head in an oven, but the possibility of screwing up was so much higher.

Jake sobbed uncontrollably at times, but stopped being aware of it by the third bout of agony.

He stopped thinking about work, about Mansfield, about the life he'd been building before the Doorway Man. Thinking had become incredibly hard and, when he *could* think, all he could focus on was what was happening to him and what the Doorway Man said.

Whatever this was, it was old—millennia old, if that bastard was to be believed—and he was the latest of a long line to suffer.

He wondered how it might be changing him; his mind obses-sively replayed the memory of the Doorway Man putting his fist into Jake's chest like that of a ghost.

What had that man done to him? Who *was* he? Where had he gone? These questions and a million more circled his mind like vultures, but he knew of nothing to feed them. The Doorway Man hadn't told Jake his real name and Jake began to associate a talismanic significance to that. Names were power, or so said the fantasy novels he'd read as a kid. If Jake knew the Doorway Man's real name, Jake could find him.

And he *had* to. There was no other way out.

It took him a moment to associate the electronic buzzing with the callbox beside his apartment door.

He stumbled to it on legs that didn't feel like his own. *Nothing* did anymore; it was as if his body had been hijacked and his consciousness was a captive passenger. He pressed the button marked DOOR and stumbled back to the couch without asking who it was.

He heard the door open and a familiar voice started to say, "Jakey—" when it suddenly choked off. *"Jesus!"*

Jake heard the door slam closed and then Mansfield was coming around the couch, his legs like snapping scissor-blades, his face unbelieving. "Christ, what happened to you?"

Jake looked down at the scarecrow he'd become. His clothes— old khakis, an older Penn State sweater—were thoroughly stained. "The Doorway Man."

Mansfield gaped. "The *Doorway Man* did this to you? *How?*"

Jake swallowed. The question—the *essential* question—blazed to life in the hollow of his head. "What's his real name?"

Mansfield turned toward the windows. "We gotta get you to work. I've held off the Board so far, but your PM's climbing the wall—"

"What's the Doorway Man's real name?"

Mansfield turned back. "That doesn't *matter*, man. We gotta get you to *work*—"

Jake got to his feet faster than he would've thought possible. For the first time in God knew how long, he felt something other than pain—anger, and it was hot and lively, bubbling through his blood. Mansfield was *not* going to keep this from him. "His *name*, Bradley. I need his *fucking name.*"

Mansfield's face screwed up into an expression of incredulity. "Dewey Herbert. The whole 'Doorway Man' thing's just a schtick. Why? It doesn't matter—your *career* does."

Jake stopped; it seemed *everything* stopped—his heart, his body, his brain. His breath caught.

It doesn't matter. No, it didn't. A name wasn't a symbol of power and this wasn't some cheap fantasy novel. A name was just something your parents handed you. It couldn't help him.

His body kick-started, a rumbling engine fueled with high-octane rage.

"Where can I find him?" he said, stepping forward, boring holes into Mansfield with his gaze.

Mansfield sighed. "Don't you get it? You're going to be *fired*—"

"*Shut up!*" Dots of red pulsed in front of his eyes. "It's *your* fault this happened. If you hadn't taken me to the party, hadn't *bet* on me—" Pain suddenly erupted through him, closing his throat. He doubled-over and hugged his chest, grinding his teeth.

"*Jesus!*" Mansfield yelled, but it seemed to be coming from far away.

Jake's lips peeled back as he uttered a nasally *eee-eee-eee* sound.

And then the muttering came.

And it was *different*—still distant but somehow *understandable.*

And, from that low rabble, an idea came.

An idea of . . . *touching* Mansfield and—

The rest wouldn't come, but that was enough. His throbbing, broken body sang for it the way a dying man's body craved for a glass of water.

He looked up and Mansfield recoiled.

"*Tell me where he is,*" he growled.

Mansfield's mouth opened, but nothing came out.

His hand stole out. Mansfield jerked away, but not fast enough. Jake's fingers touched his right elbow—

—and then sank in.

The reaction was immediate. Mansfield shrieked as if he'd been stabbed, jerking away.

The muttering voices in Jake's head became a single, triumphant howl. At the same time, the pain became *focused*, like a laser trained on something. And suddenly the pain, while awful, became somehow more tolerable.

Jake Reznic's lips twitched in a smile. "Tell me where he is." He advanced another step.

Mansfield backed away and his ass smacked the windowsill.

Jake reached for him again and Mansfield flinched. Mansfield's chiseled face was flushed and sweating. He seemed *smaller*, as if he'd shrunk within his expensive clothes.

Jake raised a hand toward him. "*Where*, Mansfield?"

"*Bentley District!*" Mansfield shrieked. "*He's in the Bentley District! North Street! Apartment 4G—*"

"Shut up," Jake said, and his hand sank lightly into Mansfield's arm again. Mansfield screamed.

Jake pulled away. It was hard—he didn't *want* to pull his hand away. The muttering in his head became a rumbling, inhuman *nnnn-nn-nnnnnn-nnnnnn* sound.

"Empty your pockets," he said, barely hearing himself. The pain was twisting, the rumbling slowly pushing aside all rational thought.

(—nnnnnn-nnnnnn-nnnnnn—)

Mansfield yanked everything from his pockets and dropped it. A palmful of loose change bounced and clicked against the hardwood. His smartphone bounced. He reached behind him and, after a moment's struggle, pulled out a small black pistol in a nylon holster, then set it on the floor.

Jake would've laughed, if he could've. The bastard had a gun and hadn't even thought to use it. One look at his face said he *still* wasn't thinking of using it.

Mansfield's eyes were shocked and empty. "You ... you won't hurt me, anymore?"

The rumbling reached an apex, threatening to split his skull open.

(—nnnnnn-nnnnNN-NNNNNN—)

"No, Brad."

He spread his narrow arms and wrapped them around Mansfield. At that instant, the muttering rose into an exultant scream.

(—NNNNEED!)

His arms sank into Mansfield like a hot knife through soft butter. A crickling-crackling sensation swept through him, reminding him of Pop Rocks candy and how it snapped and popped on your tongue.

Mansfield stiffened, but could not pull away. He was three inches taller and fifty pounds heavier, but it felt like Jake was handling nothing more than a wet pillow. Mansfield's skin paled to the color of milk then beyond, becoming almost translucent.

Jake never saw the moment Brad Mansfield winked out of existence. He blinked as the crackling sensation reached its apex—a mental feeling of *YES!*—and then Mansfield was gone. He heard a *pop* as air rushed to fill the space Mansfield had occupied.

Jake staggered away. *Where the hell?* His brain felt sharper, *clearer*, than it had in weeks and he stared at the scene before him like someone who had no idea how he'd gotten here.

Where the hell had Mansfield gone?

(the pain ate him)

Jake's stomach cramped. He made it to the toilet just in time, sliding across the tiles like a break-dancer. His face grew hot and his stomach and throat worked, but all that came up were threads of discolored drool.

He slumped against the tub. A part of him relished the lack of pain, but, in its place, was this *dissatisfaction,* as if what he'd done to Mansfield was *right...* but not *enough*. It was as if a part of him—the *thing* the Doorway Man had given him—was disappointed.

(it doesn't kill you, you know)

What am I? he thought, but of course there was no answer.

He went back out to the living room. *I didn't eat him,* he thought, walking over to the pile of crap on the floor.

(then what did you do?)

(I open the way to things I didn't come up with it)

"I bet you didn't," Jake whispered, hunkering down. "Someone else did, maybe eons ago." He picked up Mansfield's holstered pistol. "And now I do, too."

I'm the Doorway Man, he thought. *I pulled Mansfield through to ... wherever.*

He pulled the pistol from its holster. It was compact and blocky. Along the side of the slide was .380 SEMI-AUTO. He fumbled with the grip until he found the lever that disengaged the magazine and pulled it out. Full house. He slammed it home.

If I wanted a way out, he thought, *I got it now.*

Jake looked from the pistol to the pile. Mansfield's iPhone lay on top, its screen activated.

His eyes locked on the Maps app.

Slowly, he set the pistol down and picked up the phone. *North Street,* he thought. *Apartment 4G.*

He looked at the gun. He'd take it with him. He'd have the option afterward.

He turned back to the phone.

Somehow, the apartment door fit Dewey Herbert's personality to a T. The paint had peeled and cracked and darkened to a bile black. The keyplate had the looks of being unsuccessfully jimmied.

The new Doorway Man couldn't hear a single sound within.

(he's dead he's rotting inside and this was foolish to do)

Jake looked around. Herbert's door was at the end of a long hallway and he was alone. A smeary window looked out onto the street to his left. Dusk was drawing down, making the Bentley District, the city's poor neighborhood, look even grayer.

He turned back to the door, raised a foot, and slammed it home against the door.

The impact shot through his entire body and wood cracked, but the lock still held firm. He drew his foot back and slammed it home again.

The lock snapped and the door shuddered open, revealing a wedge of darkness.

Jake swallowed and reached in, pawing the wall for the switchplate. He tried *not* to think about Herbert's body, sprawled on the floor in the darkness; or Herbert's body crawling forward, empty eyes locked on Jake's silhouette; or Herbert's body reaching for Jake's hand, ready to yank him into the darkness—

He found the light-switches and flicked them with a soft cry.

The overhead splashed on, so bright Jake blinked, revealing a dirty, disheveled, *empty* living room.

Jake stepped inside. The room was large and filled with crap; his feet crunched over garbage. A 1980s television, complete with tinfoil-tipped rabbit ears, hooked up to a marginally more modern DVD player, squatted in the corner like a tinpot dictator. A kitchen alcove to his left. Two doors to his right, one opening to a closet with delusions of being a bedroom, and the other a bathroom.

No Dewey Herbert, AKA the former Doorway Man.

He exhaled loudly. *He's not dead—*

(he's not dead here*)*

He pawed through the crap on the loveseat, tossing aside TV-dinner trays and old bills. There had to be *something* saying where the little bastard was. He kicked aside clothes, revealing a carpet pockmarked with cigarette burns.

His eyes drifted to the corner. Beneath a pile of papers and un-opened envelopes was what Jake thought was an old rolltop desk. He pushed all the crap off the top and rolled it open.

He blinked.

The desktop was neat and organized, almost anally so.

Camouflage, he thought. *He obviously cared for this, but he didn't want it getting boosted and destroyed if someone broke in, so...*

Pain twinged in his midsection. Nothing like the explosions from before Mansfield, but enough to make him hunch.

Cubby holes liked the back of the desktop. A wide-rectangular envelope that could've only housed a card stuck out of one.

He pulled it out. The return address was from Pennsylvania. Dewey's middle name was Philip.

He pulled out the birthday card within. A bulldog in spectacles on the front. Not Hallmark, but a cheap knock-off found in a Mom & Pop store.

Jake opened the card and read beneath the basic HAPPY BIRTHDAY message: *I know you're busy in the big city but when you get a chance give your old man a call, OK?* It was signed *DAD.*

He tossed the card aside and folded the envelope in half to stick in his pants pocket.

(you don't know Herbert went there)

He'd saved a birthday card his father had mailed him years ago; not only saved it, but kept it in the one place not covered in garbage. If Herbert was alive and on the run, he would've gone home. Besides, what other option did Jake have?

His hand went to Mansfield's gun, wedged into the small of his back, as another twinge of pain came. His hand tightened over the grip.

I'm going to find Herbert, he thought, *and he's going to fix whatever it is he did to me. Or I'll kill him myself.*

Outside, thunder boomed loud enough to rattle the barn.

Jake stared at Herbert, his gun still trained on Herbert's frozen father. The pain dug and tore and chewed but was completely forgotten. "You're not dead," he said with something like wonder.

"Not yet," Dewey Herbert said. Lightning flashed. In spite of being free of *whatever* it was he'd given Jake, the former Doorway Man *looked* dead; his skin was sallow and clammy. The neck holding his head up was a stem.

His eyes flicked past Jake and widened. "Dad—"

Jake turned, flinching. The farmer's meaty, callused hand missed his shoulder by an inch.

"Hey," the farmer said, blinking. It was as if he'd just awakened. "You can't be here. My boy's sick and you gotta go. Scat." He took a step toward Jake.

Jake backpedaled, toward the barn door, feeling the pain in his center again grimacing. The freezing-cold rain slanting soaked his shoulders. He raised the pistol, but it was an absent gesture.

The farmer's face tightened. "You ain't usin that or you woulda already."

Out of the corner of his eye he saw Herbert make a grab for his father—which his father avoided—and stumble. "Dad, don't—"

"Get back inside, Dewey," the farmer said. His eyes never left him as a thought—*Like staring down a dog*—shot through Jake's mind.

Jake made his pistol hand straighten, until he looked down the stubby barrel into the farmer's face. "Don't make me use this," he said, his voice nearly lost in the muttering in his head.

"Don't worry, boy," the farmer said, "you won't." He battered at the pistol.

And the back of his hand slid into Jake's.

The contact was for an instant, but it felt much longer. The farmer's face constricted, and his body jolted as if he'd touched a live wire.

For Jake, the pain throughout immediately focused on the farmer as a burst of that crinkle-crackle feeling swarmed his hand and all thoughts were buried in the absolute *need* to draw the farmer closer, to suck him in—

The farmer stumbled back. The farmer held his hand at the wrist and Jake, absently, noticed the farmer's hand was dead white, as if sucked bloodless.

"Demon," the farmer said, his eyes eating up his face.

A parody of a grin twisted Jake's face as he came forward. "Close enough," he said and plunged his hand into the center of the farmer's chest.

The intense sensation of pins-and-needles exploded up his arm and he shrieked as it burst brilliantly—wonderfully, joyfully—in his head. Distantly, he heard Herbert shrieking, too.

The farmer's face went pale, the color of his skin blending with the whites of his eyes. His hair lost luster; the gums inside his working mouth turning a bubblegum pink then white.

With a yank, Jake slammed the farmer into him and Dewey Herbert's father winked out.

Jake staggered back, blinking. The gun fell from his hand and discharged a round into the night. The pain was gone and in its absence, horror at what he'd done—joyfully, blissfully—filled the void, warring with the certainty that while the farmer felt *right*, it wasn't *enough*.

Herbert collapsed against an old workbench, his long, narrow hands dangling as his slight body shook. He looked at Jake, his eyes streaming and face red. "That was my *father*. He was the only reason

I *didn't* kill myself, you bastard."

"*I* didn't do it!" Jake snapped. "It was what you *gave* me! *You* did this! *You! This is all your fault!*"

"Don't you think I know that?" Herbert shouted back. "*I gave it up! I let it go and now I have nothing! I had nothing before and now I have even LESS!*"

He stomped forward. "How do I get rid of them, Dewey?"

"*You pass it on!*" he screamed. "Jesus—*you* know that! If the others had a different way, I don't know it because they're *dead!* After *it's* given away, the holders kill themselves! The fact that you and I are standing here—you the current holder and me the former—that has *never happened!* The holder..." His voice softened. "...the holder *misses* it. It's all the holder has left, by the end. *It* seeks out and we don't know it at the time, but we become a part of something—for most of us, that's the first we've ever felt that way." He looked away. "And...and we miss it."

Jake grabbed Herbert and shook him like a ragdoll. "*You ruined my life and you want me to feel SORRY for you?*"

Herbert fought back, but Jake's grip was iron. "*Don't you think I know that? My life's no better than yours!*"

Jake shoved him against a workbench. "But you're free, you son of a bitch, so *what is it?*"

Herbert glared insolently and Jake thought of grabbing the gun, emptying it in the former Doorway Man's face. How *dare* he look at Jake like that? Herbert couldn't lay the bill for this at *his* feet.

"It's old," Herbert said. "The texts of the old legends—most of them completely forgotten—say *it* was created by *them*, what was here before sentience, when the universe was still young and reality was soft."

He straightened, a hand going to his back. "Reality is perception created by sentient thought—the Sophists thought so, anyway. And those *things*—you can't begin to imagine them—were here first. *Not* sentient. A kind of hive-mind, I guess. But, when life as we know it began, the change made a line between they're black empty void and our reality. But they want back what we took; they want it *all* and they left a little bit of them, the doorway, like a dog marking its territory."

"Why me?" Jake yelled, then gestured at Herbert. "Why *us,* why all the others?"

Herbert offered a blade of a smile. He began to move, circling. His eyes gleamed in a way Jake didn't like. "We're outsiders, Jake. In the grand scheme of things, we're barely *there.* Like *them.* This means we're susceptible, but not enough to let them through. I don't know what *would* be enough. None of the legends knew. If it was enough, we wouldn't be here."

Jake kept turning, kept facing him. "What about the people I've … taken?"

Herbert shrugged, and started closing the circle, toward Jake. "Does it matter? They're gone and we're stuck. *I'm* stuck, without a career, or family, or even *them.*"

Jake backed away. "What're you doing?"

"Giving up," Herbert said. He raised a hand toward Jake's chest and Jake flinched, the last of his anger seeping away. Is *this* what he had to look forward to? "It just seems fitting this way."

"They're gone now! You know that!"

"I've called them before," he said and cleared his throat. *"Ftgan-mhor-rich."*

Jake ducked past Herbert, his nerve-endings tingling. His entire body grew warm. *"STOP THAT!"*

Herbert might not've heard. His eyes were completely empty as he followed, hand raised. *"Ghrnich-mrone entow. Ftgan-rich."*

The tingle grew into a duller version of the crickle-crackle feeling. Pain began to blossom in Jake's chest and he staggered. *"STOP, GODDAMMIT!"*

"No," the former Doorway Man said. His lips twisted. *"Ftgan-mirsch-soth."*

The pain exploded through Jake's body and the muttering in his head burst into existence. He couldn't feel his legs and arms and the Doorway Man bore down as he went to his knees.

"You'll be fine," the Doorway Man whispered and shoved his hand into Jake's chest.

Immediately it was different and both felt it. Instead of the pain fading into the pins-and-needles, both sensations *roared* through him. The world before his eyes jumped into hyper-quality—the colors, the sounds, the smells.

The Doorway Man's eyes bulged, his mouth drawing down into a rictus of exertion.

And then Jake felt the pain and pins-and-needles *expand*. The only thing his tortured mind could think was of an overflowing glass of liquid spilling into another.

The Doorway Man screamed. Jake screamed with him.

This has never happened before, he thought. *These things have never taken a former holder.*

At the edges of his vision, black encroached; it was as if the world before him had been made two-dimensional and someone was taking a sopping brush of black paint to it.

He looked down at Herbert's arm and saw it was gone, replaced by an arm-shaped hole of darkness. He sensed no dimension save from the blackness's *depthlessness*. It grew, consuming Herbert's shoulder, his chest, pulling him apart.

God, Jake thought. He might've screamed it.

(we're susceptible but we're not enough)

We're enough now, he thought.

The blackness filled the world, the roaring crackle consumed it and, in the center of his mind, the muttering had become the rough inhuman bark of anticipation. Jake felt himself dimming, losing himself, coming apart.

Jake Reznic and Dewey Herbert—The Doorway Men—opened the way for the black void and whatever lied within it.

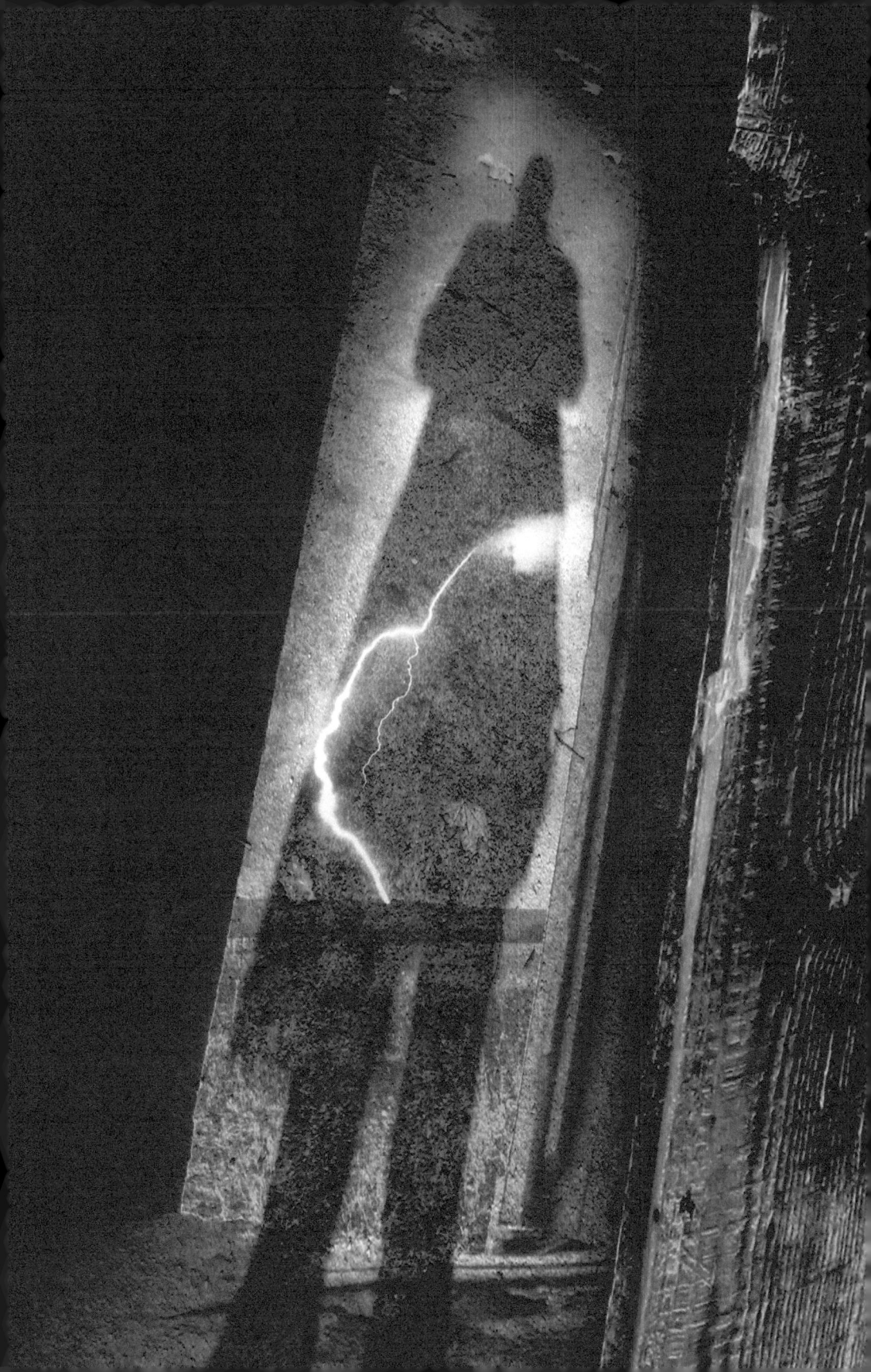

LOVE SONG
FOR THE REJECTED

EVELYN'S MOTHER DIED before she could tell her daughter why Evie had a chunk of stained glass embedded in her chest.

Evie had no idea there was anything strange about the glass until her soon-to-be adoptive parents accompanied her to a physical. Both the parents and the pediatrician fainted dead away, startling the five-year-old girl into terrified tears that lasted way after the adults came to.

The stained glass was shaped like a cartoon heart between where her breasts would grow. Subsequent x-rays showed that the tooth-pick-thin lead *cames* grew from Evie's ribcage; metal and bone fused as one, with no connection to her real heart. The fingernail-sized panes of glass were red, orange, yellow, green, blue, indigo, and violet, arranged randomly and much harder than regular glass. Her mother referred to it as Evie's rainbow heart before she died.

There was no mention of it in any medical records. No mention of it from her father, of course. Whoever *he* was. And, of course, no mention of it from her mother, dead of a skull fracture after slipping on black ice as she left yet another disastrous date.

Evie didn't turn as Brett walked out. *Couldn't* turn. Wouldn't *allow herself* to turn.

Still, the rough slam of the apartment door made her jump.

Evie slumped onto the couch and cried. She was no longer the terrified little girl on the examination table. Her corn-colored hair had darkened to a polished-wood tan, her face heart-shaped, her blue eyes open and expressive.

Evelyn Starling, twenty-six, with a body and personality that drew a lot of attention. Copy-editor at Sigel Publishing, living in one of Hathaway's nicer neighborhoods.

Heartbroken. Again.

She grabbed a Kleenex from the box on the coffee table and blew her nose. It disgusted her—not the loud, Foghorn Leghorn honk, but how *routine* all this felt.

How is it not *routine?* she thought, standing up. *This is not the first rodeo bull that's trampled you flat.*

Too true.

Brett. Another link in a long chain of men who offered vague reasons like, "It's not you, it's me," while trying to avoid her eyes as much as humanly possible. She swore, if she heard that damn reason again, she'd scream until she passed out.

Her hand went to her chest. She might as well see the damage.

She moved into her bathroom and, flicking on the light, faced the mirror. Thank God she'd worn waterproof mascara; her eyes were moist and puffy.

The face that lures men in and drives them away, she thought bitterly, shrugging off the burgundy boyfriend-jacket and dropped it onto the toilet seat. She wore a silk white-white tank top underneath. Up close, she could see the upper rim of the latex prosthetic appliance that covered her heart.

She pulled the tank top off slowly, then her bra. She paused a moment, studying the latex appliance.

It bothered her that she had to work herself up for this.

She gripped the upper edge of the appliance and pulled, feeling the brief tug as the glue came away. Putting the cover down on the edge of the sink, she forced herself to look at her rainbow heart.

Each piece of glass was now black.

Evie gripped the edges of the sink. What little color had been there this morning—the barest hint of blue in the left curve, the cherry core—was now gone. Blackened.

She'd feared this day since she was sixteen when the darkening began, but, now, she wasn't sure how she was supposed to feel. She didn't feel meaner, or colder, or indifferent. Her rainbow heart had gone black. Stop the presses.

The end of the rainbow, she thought. *The stained glass formerly known as my rainbow heart.*

She was starting to smile when the pain struck. What felt like a wooden stake skewered her through the glass like a bug. She gasped and shuddered, squeezing her eyes closed. Instead of seeing darkness, she saw the palest blue pulsing like starbursts behind her eyelids, near-blinding in their brilliance.

Her revenge, a rough, guttural voice in her head whispered, barely audible. *It's coming.*

The pain faded, faded, disappeared, leaving behind a tingle in her flesh. Panting, she opened her tear-swollen eyes.

Behind her in the mirror, a black amorphous shadow, humanoid in the vaguest sense of the word, towered over her.

She spun.

Nothing but her shadow, thrown by the lights above the mirror.

She let out a shaky breath, her hand going to the stained glass.

It was warm.

For all her laudable attributes—physically stunning, emotionally open, mentally capable—Evie was tragic when it came to love.

She had ten years of bad luck, starting when she was sixteen and slept with Michael Rettger. Oh yes, she knew all the names, all the events, and she ran through them in her head on lonely nights when sleep wouldn't come.

She'd dated previously—even fooled around a bit—but Michael was the first. Palms clammy, legs weak, a million thoughts racing through her head, she went to him.

She forgot about her rainbow heart.

Until, afterward, lying in Michael's room, Michael had spotted the loose edge of the upper portion of the latex appliance.

"Hey, what's this?" he'd asked.

It was the feel of his fingers on her appliance rather than his voice that jolted her awake. She recoiled, trying to block him, and the movement aided rather than slowed Michael from pulling the cover off.

The moment hung, waiting. Sunlight from the window glistened off the stained glass. Michael, frozen with what looked like a hunk of pale flesh in his hand. Evie, mortified, covering her chest.

His eyes bounced back and forth from her chest to her horrified expression. "What?" He looked at the appliance in his hand. "What? What?" Realization dawned in his eyes. "What the *hell?*"

Still covering her chest, she yanked the appliance away and stumbled from the bed, grabbing her clothes. Michael didn't move, staring where she'd lain, hand half-raised, as if still holding the appliance. He blinked rapidly. "What?"

She dressed quickly, shoving the latex appliance in her pocket, fighting tears and the throat-choking mortification. She thought of her adoptive parents fainting dead away and the tears broke through her small mental barrier.

She turned briefly when she reached the door. Michael looked at her the way she imagined an astronaut would view a mind-bending new creature; his mouth hanging opening, his eyes flashing how hard his brain was trying to wrap around this.

They broke up a week later, via text message, and Michael avoided her eyes whenever they crossed paths.

That was when the rainbow heart began fading. She switched to stronger glue and never let that happen again.

Daniel McLaughlin, senior year. He never saw the rainbow heart, but he was gone after three months.

Russell McDermott, her freshman year of college.

Greg Andrews, while she did her internship at Putnam in New York City.

Kyle Marston, her first year after college.

The list went on and on.

None harmed her, none controlled her, the relationships had been easy, but they all drifted away.

Evie's rainbow heart faded with each one, then slowly began to darken at the edges.

She knew the dangers of this and feared the day when the heart would become entirely black, but, still, she was driven into new relationships, new situations of giving and receiving. It was as if her heart knew the same as her brain but refused to listen to reason. And she paid for it.

She was dressed and sitting on the examination table when Dr. Roberts came back in, chart in hand. He was a burly older man whose trimmed blond beard was flecked with grey. He leaned against the counter and scanned the chart, flipping up the top sheet to read something beneath. He looked up and smiled. "You're fine, Evie. Relax."

She let out a long breath. "Really?"

He set the chart down on the counter and adjusted his rimless spectacles. "I checked the x-rays today with past ones. The heart hasn't shifted, or changed in any way. There doesn't seem to be pressure on any organs. You haven't had the same pain since last week, correct?"

"Minor aches."

He crossed his arms and sighed. "Sometimes it feels like you're one of my daughters, Evie. I worry about you." He adjusted his glasses again. "Anyway, I can't explain why the glass went black *or* the pain." He straightened. "You have pain like you did before, you see me immediately. Otherwise, let's circle back here in a month. Jeanie at the front will make the appointment."

"So nothing weird at all?"

He cleared his throat and checked the chart. "One of the x-rays showed a dark spot *behind* the glass, about the size of a tennis ball, but it was gone in the next shot. That's it. I saved it, just in case, but probably nothing." He smiled warmly toward her. "Nothing serious."

Her breathing was the only sound in the dark apartment. In Evie's bedroom, the glow of streetlamps outside and her digital alarm clock provided minimal light.

Evie lay on her back, topless and asleep in the center of her double.

The latex appliance between her breasts flickered, then began to glow. It grew in intensity. Lines of sky-blue light edged around the seams.

Evie, still asleep, grimaced and moaned. It came from her mouth, but sounded like the grunt of a great animal.

After a while, it dimmed, then went out.

She felt a twinge in her chest when the new mailroom clerk with the easy, self-conscious smile passed her glass-wall office. She looked away, clenching her fists to either side of her computer keyboard.

Three weeks since Brett walked out and the first burst of pain, and already ... she shook her head. She'd seen the mail-clerk twice so far this week; delivering packages throughout the department, his hair the same color as hers and indifferently tousled. And that easy, self-conscious smile.

She wondered idly if she had any packages today.

She lightly hit the edge of her desk with her fists. No, dammit. *Besides, what happens with my glass now?* she thought. *It's* already *black and causing me pain.*

She turned back to the manuscript on her computer and sighed. The legal pad on her desk was already filled with jotted notes, complaints, and questions—and she was only 100 pages in.

Her eyes drifted to the glass wall. The clerk was talking to Pam, from payroll, and Pam was obviously laying it on thick. She felt a twinge in her chest that had nothing to do with her glass heart.

She looked away and forced herself to focus on the manuscript, her hand absently going to where the stained glass beneath her blouse and rubbing.

It was luck that put her and the clerk in the same elevator alone together a week later.

"New here?" she'd asked. Light, easy. A good conversation-starter.

The clerk jumped the slightest bit, surprised. "Uh ... yeah! Yeah,

I am. Mail room. Me low-man on Totem pole."

Evie laughed. "*Every*one's low man at one point or another."

The clerk's smile was less self-conscious now, but just as cute as before. "Don't you have an office? I can't see *you* being low man of *anything.*"

I've got a live one, here, she thought.

Evie smiled and offered her hand. "Evelyn Starling. In spite of the office, I'm just a copy-editor."

The clerk shook with her. "Peter McDonald. In spite of my package cart, I *really* wanna get outta the mail room and *be* a copy-editor."

Evie laughed.

"Listen," Peter said. "You wanna get some coffee?"

Evie's smile widened. "Sure."

Peter stopped at a corner florist on his way to Evie's apartment and bought a bouquet. It was cliché and done a thousand times, but the urge overcame him and Peter often followed his urges.

Walking down the well-lit avenue, he checked the address Evie had given him on the back of her card. Not far. It was ten-after-six and they'd have plenty of time to make their reservations. Dinner, of course. Another cliché and done-a-thousand-times thing.

The street was lined with bright shops and boutiques. Couples young and old walked, enjoying the cool October evening as the sun sank, staining the sky purple. This was his first time really walking through Hathaway since moving here and he found he liked it— almost as much as he liked Evie.

She was easy to talk to. He found himself revealing things that he *never* would've revealed to someone he'd just met, such as the fear that'd crawled up his throat his first night here.

Evie was empathetic and relatable, telling her own horror stories. It was the perfect give-and-take in a situation that *demanded* awkward conversation.

But for all her empathy, all her easy-going nature, he sensed something darker within her. Not necessarily bad, but Peter hadn't had to awaken all his brain cells to figure out that this woman hadn't been very lucky with men. It was in her gaze, her quickness to fill the silences.

Peter knew a thing or two about that. Past girlfriends who'd been kind called him a hopeless romantic. The not-so-kind called him a loser.

I have no intention of hurting this woman, he thought. *Only a fool would.*

With a spring in his step, Peter went to the stoop and pressed the buzzer for Evie's apartment.

Three dates later, Peter slid out from under the blankets and padded naked into the dark living room. He felt for his cigarettes in his jacket on the couch and sat down. The flame was bright enough for him to blink, the click of the spinner-wheel obscenely loud in the early-morning silence.

Oh, man, Peter, he thought, exhaling. *Oh shit.*

He hadn't planned on this—when it came to sex, he was hopelessly passive—but he'd be lying to say he hadn't dearly wanted it. It took more than a little willpower not to grin like a fool. A fire burned across his nerves, roared vibrantly through his gut.

It had all been so smooth. Like their dating, nothing felt forced or awkward. Natural. Give-and-take.

His assessment that Evie knew the dark side of relationships had been borne out, of course. On their second date, she'd apologized ahead of time if she acted distant; she'd just gotten out of a relationship that had not ended well.

The conversation recurred to him, and, for the first time, he thought of how odd that was. Who said things like that on a second date?

For the moment, he felt as if he were not alone in the room. The specters of old boyfriends crowded in on him, pressing him down, staring. He wished he could meet the Ghosts of Boyfriends Past, if only to say, *You morons.*

☙ ⋯ ❧

As Peter smoked, Evie slept contentedly on her side. The top sheet lay puddled around her bare waist, the bedsheet wrinkled into sand dune waves. The stained glass behind the latex appliance glowed pale blue. Its illumination transformed the tousled bedsheet into a barren, alien landscape.

Evie stirred, the light rippling across the bed. Low, barely audible, she moaned that vaguely inhuman sound.

The light was gone before Peter came to bed.

Time passed; six-weeks' worth.

They stayed in, went out, saw plays, stand-up comedians, readings, movies, bands, hung around each other's apartment. They took a weekend and went to the Poconos, going Dutch because Peter couldn't afford to pay for both but refused to have her pay all. They ate Thai, Chinese, Indian, fast food, Italian, German, Korean, and Japanese. They were not clingy, they were not distant. They, in their fifth week, opened a Netflix account together. As Christmas approached, they made plans on visiting both sets of parents.

Then, as the days drew down to the end of the year, it changed.

Peter got off the bus at his corner and headed for his building, feeling like a soldier spiriting through enemy territory. Christmas Decorations hung listlessly from shops in the cold gray day. Snow had fallen two days ago, and brown sludge clogged the curbs. People, bundled tightly, hustled here to there, watching their feet.

He kept his mind on automatic until he let himself into his loft apartment. Then, in the empty kitchen, he asked disgustedly, "What in the *hell* is *wrong* with me?"

This was the first time in two months he and Evie hadn't seen each other for two consecutive days. Usually, they shared a day's break but never two.

Evie had asked if he wanted dinner as they left work and a panic had seized him; a chest-clutching panic that sent flashing red messages into his brain: GET AWAY GET AWAY NOW.

So, he'd fibbed, saying he needed to call family and friends back home. With a hard squeeze around Evie's waist, he said he had a lot to talk about.

She'd giggled and let him go and, goddammit, he'd felt *relieved* to be getting on the bus.

He went over to the couch and plopped down, confusion wrinkling his face. "Why the hell did I do that?"

No answers but, recently, he'd felt ... stifled. Suddenly, Evie's intellect felt intimidating; her motivation left him disillusioned about his own career path; her beauty made him feel as if she'd plucked him from the stall next to the wetbrain geek at the freak show. Only when he was alone ... when he was away ... did he feel normal again.

He felt them back there, behind him—the Ghosts of Boyfriends Past. He wanted to spin around, see them in their pale-blue forms— as he pictured them—and ask them, *Why? Why did* you *leave?*

She knew it was a dream as soon as she saw her mother sitting on the rock in the otherwise barren and arid landscape. Far in the distance, sharp-peaked mountains like taloned fingers accused a sky the ugly shade of a bruise.

Her mother wore the dress she was buried in. Her dark hair blended into the wide straps. "He's going to leave you," she said. "He has no choice. The promise will be kept."

Beneath her bare feet, Evie could feel thick granules of hot sand. She looked down and saw she was completely nude. The stained-glass was a heart-shaped black hole in her chest.

"Justice must be brought," her mother went on. "He will leave, and your heart's transformation will be complete."

Evie approached. "Peter won't leave."

Her mother looked up as Evie approached and Evie saw how witch-like her mother was. "My beautiful, smart, talented daughter. More than I ever could be. *Too* beautiful, smart, and talented—that was part of the promise. You'll drive them away and it'll feed. It *needs* to come. *It* needs to be born. This *needs* to happen. I'm sorry, honey."

Her voice grew more growling, with each repetition. Evie stumbled back. As she did, the stained glass shot out a ray of pale blue. It burned the edges of her skin. Evie squawked.

The black irises of her mother's eyes seeped out of its circle and enveloped the white. Her mother's eyes began to glow with the same light as the glass. She lurched toward Evie, her eyes widening and distorting, becoming monster-eyes. The glow brightened, obscuring her mother's shape, and it seemed she grew more hulking, less human, becoming the monster Evie'd glimpsed in the mirror.

"I'm sorry but it's inevitable, honey," she croaked. "I *will* have my revenge. For you as well as me. *We* love and *we* pay and *they* never do. Shouldn't they be punished? You are my sacrifice and monument. When *it's* born—"

Evie felt sudden pain rip through her chest, as if an invisible hand had slammed through the stained glass and—

—she sat up in bed, screaming. Evie pawed at the glass heart, but it was cool to the touch. Just another minor ache.

She fell back against the padded headboard, panting. Her eyes blinked rapidly in the darkness. Distantly, she heard a car alarm.

Her mother's voice whispered in the center of her head: *He's going to leave you ... I will have my revenge.*

She slumped further into bed, holding her heart.

I can't go on like this, she thought. Her fingers traced the edge of the stained glass. She thought of removing the heart—not for the first time—and shook her head. God, how could someone remove something fused to her *bone*? For better or worse, she was stuck in the passenger seat to this thing—

(my mother)

—and the best she could do was ... *withstand* it.

Sleep was a long time coming and she couldn't let go of the stained glass.

"Long time no see, stranger," she said as Peter opened the passenger door and climbed in. "What is this? The first date in a week?"

"Hey, babe." A quick brush of his lips against her cheek. They felt like paper.

She pulled into traffic and headed west, toward the setting sun, out of town. "What'd the reviews say about this movie?"

He shrugged, staring through the windscreen. "Forgot to look."

She looked at him, her brow furrowing. "You all right, Peter?"

He glanced at her. She saw something in his eyes, but couldn't place it. "Tired, babe. It's nothing."

Her stained glass heart started to ache. She heard her mother say, *I'm sorry, honey.*

Peter, to his credit, lasted another two weeks.

The littlest, stupidest things got on his nerves. The way she spoke when she hadn't completely swallowed a mouthful of food. Her light, airy snores. The way she kept her pubic hair. Things that no sane man in a million years would have a problem with drove him absolutely insane. He recognized this and restrained every biting remark, every insult, every question-that-isn't-a-question that wanted to simply *leap* from his mouth.

He spent the night before he broke up with Evie getting cataclysmically drunk. He raised his glass of amber liquor at the television and slurred, "Here's to me, the stupidest bastard that ever entered a relationship."

He drank.

It tasted like guilt and banked fires.

He grabbed the bottle off the table, topped off his glass, and drank.

Repeat.

His head thumped the next day and every joint felt filled with broken glass. His hands shook. His mouth tasted like a baby dragon's used diaper.

Evie—sweet, too-perfect Evie—noticed.

He said he hadn't slept well.

She shouldn't have accepted that—the contradiction was his physical form—but she did. Periodically, on the drive home, he saw her wince, as if in pain.

He didn't dawdle when they got to her place; *couldn't* dawdle. He *knew* he was making the absolutely *worst* mistake of his life, but *also* knew it had to be done. Like a spoonful of awful cough syrup, clench your fists and do it quickly.

So, when she got up from the couch to go change out of her work clothes, he made himself sit up. "Evie."

She turned.

He swallowed. "We have to talk."

He saw her eyes darken, as if knowing what was coming. Still, she came and sat down in the scrolled wingback chair next to the couch. As she did, she winced again.

Every word a hard little bullet, Peter began to speak.

The stained glass began to ache as soon as she sat down. In her head, she heard her mother say, *I'm sorry but it's inevitable.*

"I..." Peter said, swallowing hard, and looking at the floor. He repeated dry-washing his hands, which shook. He'd said he'd slept badly. She'd smelled whiskey, but said nothing. "I don't know how to start." He licked his lips. "I can't do this anymore, Evie—"

"*Why*, though?" she asked. The words felt jerked out of her. She thought back to when she'd first seen him. *What happens to my glass now?*

(oh I can't take this)

And the ache in her chest grew sharper.

Peter looked at her and she saw tears in his eyes. "You're *so* perfect, honey, but it...it's not *you*, not really. It *really* is me—"

"*Stop it!*" she yelled. "Don't *tell* me that, Peter! They *always* tell me that! What is it? What is it that drives you *away*?"

Peter looked as if he'd been slapped. His mouth worked. "That's ...that's just it, Evie—*you're* doing nothing. It's *me*. I..."

She looked down, at her knees pressed tightly together. She clenched her teeth hard enough to hurt her gums. It felt like the pain in her stained glass was digging in, trying to get to her real heart.

She remembered her mother saying, *He will leave, and your heart's transformation will be complete.*

And then the pain exploded in her glass heart. Her hands spasmed open and she grabbed her chest, crying out.

She heard Peter calling, *"Evie! What is it?"*

The rays of blue light highlighted her knees, the edge of the coffee table. She looked down and saw the stained glass glowing a cold, pale blue through the latex appliance, her top, her fingers.

Peter, his voice terrified: *"What's happening? What's—"*

She lurched from the chair and stumbled through the archway and into the bathroom, slamming the door and, in an unconscious move, locked it.

Peter's mind was a hurricane of half-thoughts and unspent emotions. *Blue light. Her chest glowed blue light. Her—*

He scrambled from the couch, knocking over the coffee table, and dashed after her. From behind the bathroom door, he heard her screaming.

He threw himself at the door. His heart slammed into his breastbone.

"Evie!" he screamed as she screamed. *"Let me in! Evie!"*

She wouldn't stop screaming.

He thought he heard—and immediately took only one way— her shriek, *"Get away, Peter! AWAY!"*

He threw his shoulder into the door and heard a crack.

The pain clawed and chewed, digging into her chest, melting her nerves into one shrieking ball of red.

She tore her top off, then her bra. She ripped the appliance away, feeling the heat of the stained glass beneath. The pale-blue glow of the black heart's light blasted out, hot and blinding, but the pain didn't abate; instead, it grew bolder, becoming a Pagan god yearning for her suffering supplication. Its edges blistered the flesh around it.

Evie, screaming, dug at the stained glass, ignoring the sizzle as her fingertips burned, just trying to do anything to stop the pain, stop the pain *right now*—

She thought of her mother in her coffin, her mother sitting on the rock. Her mother saying, *We love and we pay and they never do. Shouldn't they be punished?*

You did this, Evie thought, as her nails snapped and bled against the glass, the droplets sizzling. *You did this to me.*

Peter's shoulder slammed into the bathroom door again and the lock snapped. The door shuddered open as Evie stumbled away, toward the bathtub, topless and digging at the glowing heart-shaped *thing* in her chest.

"Evie!" he bellowed and started forward. He froze as the light touched him. His momentum, his strength, his will drained away. At that instant, he was filled with such self-loathing a part of him wanted to gouge out his eyes. God, how could he do this to her? What *right* did he have?

"Evie," he breathed and Evie, crying, looked up.

As the tiny panes of black glass cracked as one.

In her final moment, Evelyn Starling looked at Peter and saw the pain in his eyes, the concern, and, most of all, his love. All right there. Within reach.

"Evie," he whispered, frozen.

She felt her black heart crack. The pain lessened for the briefest moment.

The panes of glass shattered, and the pale blue light burst forth, unrestrained, giving substance to what had been feeding on her pain and loss, to her mother's revenge. The creature had needed and wanted one thing from Evie's mother to do this: a womb.

A place for its birth in the world. A place to gain substance.

And her mother had given it Evie.

The final burst of pain came, so full and complete it rocketed through every nerve in Evie's body. Darkness crowded her vision. She fell away, out of the blue and into the black. Thinking of Peter.

In the last moment of his life, Peter McDonald, hopeless romantic to some, loser to others, saw the blue light envelope Evie, but not before he saw her own light go out of her eyes.

Leaving before him the mind-bending *thing* that had resided and fed in Evelyn Starling's chest. Its vaporous black form hulked over him, sucking him in its blazing blue eyes. Its visage was obscured by the blue light it emitted and, for that, Peter was grateful. To actually *see* it, he knew, would've fractured his mind in an instant.

The floor creaked under its weight as it took form.

The thing approached, fed all these years by the pain of Evelyn Starling, birthed by the scorned anger of her mother, hungry for much, much more. It would repay their pain.

Its pale blue phosphorescence engulfed Peter McDonald, and Peter McDonald's death, the first of many lost loves that long, long night, was brief.

Because his last thought was of Evie.

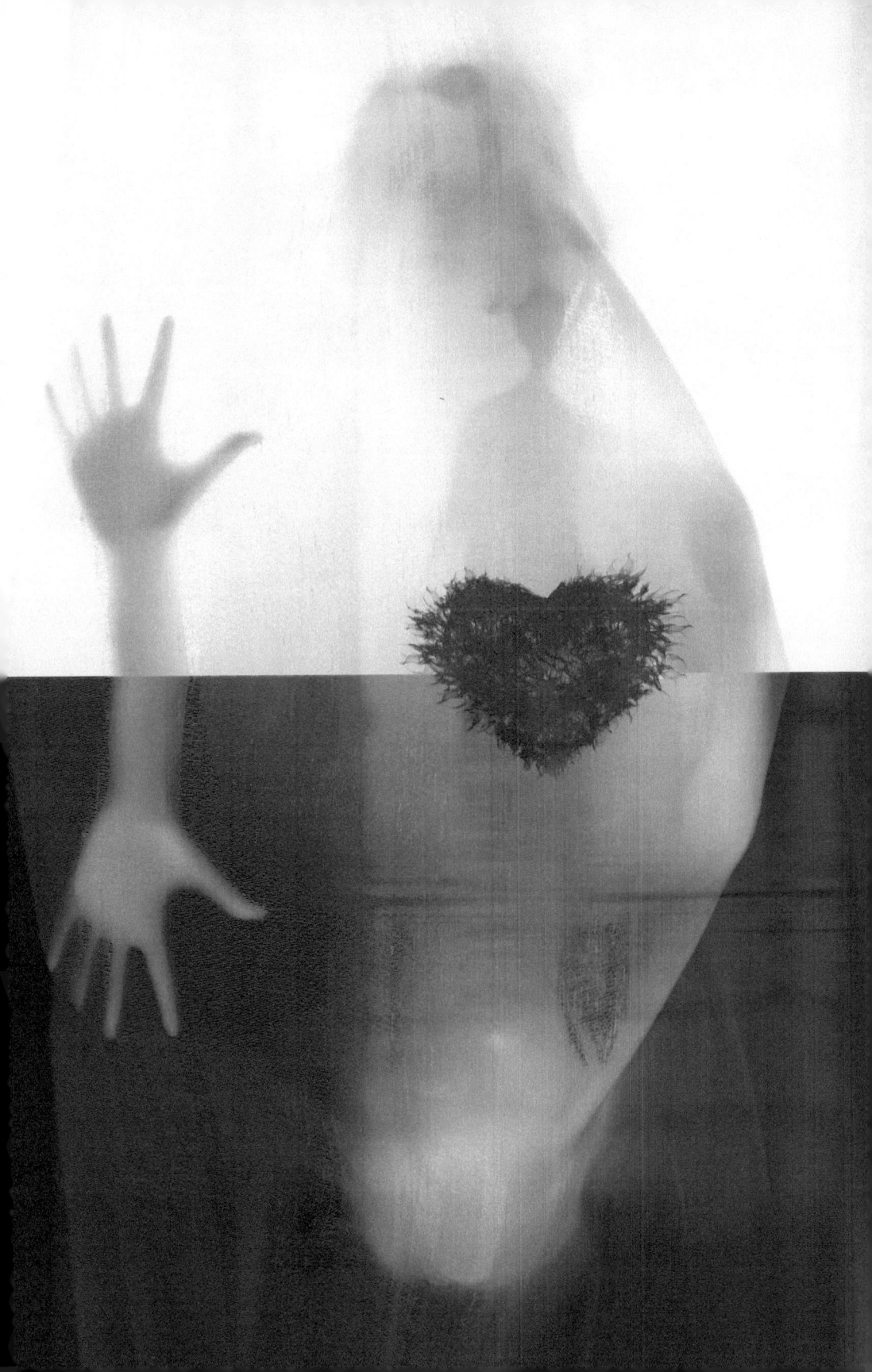

THE UNIVERSE IS DYING

THE WORLD IS ENDING, *but you don't know that yet.*

You are James McIntyre, 31, and the instant before the smartphone on your nightstand rings is the calm before the storm.

Deanna in the other room on the phone with her agent. You take a final moment to adjust the ends of your tie. You smell the cool saltiness of the Pacific wafting in through the bedroom windows. You think of nothing but what notes the producers gave Marty about the latest draft of the screenplay. This is your life, and it, as far as you can gauge, is perfect. This is your life and it is all calm.

The calm passes when you pick up the phone and hit ACCEPT, when you bring it to your ear, when you say "Hello?"

The storm arrives when the boy's voice at the other end asks, "Where the hell have you been, Jimmy?"

The boy's voice wakes up your brain in a big-bad way, like the biggest hit of coke, but you've done coke a few times and coke is not like this. Great Klieg lights flash on in the center of your head, banishing mental shadows you didn't know existed, showing the shapes of things too big and too numerous to take in at once, showing how little had actually been visible, how little you'd been working with. You can't even be confused yet.

"You need to come home, Jimmy," the boy says and your head is nodding and the Klieg lights begin to fade, and darkness flows in, and you make a strangled noise in your throat. The darkness takes your few memories—coming out to La-La Land, getting the coveted Universal writing internship, signing with Marty, meeting Deanna—with it, but not before you see how flimsy they are, hurried sketches to a storyboard of a film trapped in pre-production hell. You did not live these times. They are not yours and, as such, you lose them.

Deanna calls your name, but you don't hear her. A hum fills your head, rising quickly, becoming a ringing and beginning to swallow you.

And you say, as the ringing reaches a deafening level, as the darkness descends over one final glimpse of the Pacific and Deanna's strained face, "I have to go home now."

Deanna opens her mouth, but the darkness falls.

The ringing, like the aftermath of a gun going off next to someone's ear, dragged McIntyre back to consciousness slowly, receding as he became more aware. He looked through the windshield, at the intersection made surreal by the moving curtain of water on the glass, without seeing.

And then the intersection flickered like a television with bad reception.

"Gah!" he yelled, dropping his smartphone and jamming the heels of his hands into his eyes. He pressed until neon colors flashed, then warily removed them.

The intersection—the puddles of rain in the street depressions, the drooping, dying trees along the corners, the low one-storey YMCA across the street—did not flicker. He took it all in and a name bubbled up from the back of his mind: Traumen, Ohio.

He was home and his mouth dried. "What the hell?"

He looked around the car—no key in the ignition, a tape-deck in the dash. The interior constricted around him. Heart thudding, he got out, grabbing the smartphone in his lap. The rain soaked him as he backed away from the car, a nondescript 1990s-era four-door he'd never seen before. It sat in the center of the intersection, paused in the middle of turning left

(off of petroleum street and onto west front street.)

He shook his head. It felt crammed full of newspaper

(like we used to put into our snowboots when they were too big.)

He turned the way he presumably had come and faced a girder bridge

(the petroleum street bridge)

with a raging gray river beneath.

He looked back at the intersection, but saw nothing there. No other cars in sight, not even parked along the curbs. No other people. The only movement the rain plunking into the street puddles. It was all so still, a movie set waiting for cast and crew to arrive.

A rising panic filled his head with static, closed his airways to a straw, pressed weight against his chest. Never mind Traumen, how he'd gotten here. Figure it out later. Just get away. Get away *now*.

McIntyre did, running from the car, running for the bridge. He'd run right down the center, run right out of town, run—

—right into what *looked like* nothing else but *felt* solid.

McIntyre bounced back hard onto his ass. He looked up unbelievingly, the panic momentarily pushed aside. The bridge was there, the grey sludgy water beneath, but this close, it was obviously a matte-painting landscape, something Alfred Whitlock would've done in *The Birds* or the 1982 remake of *The Thing*. This close, McIntyre could see the brush strokes.

"The fuck?" he muttered, approaching. He couldn't see the end of the painting and—Jesus, that was all an effect, anyway, something superimposed over a green-screen shot during post-production. The paintings, in reality, were small; they only *looked* large when the effect was complete.

"Like I'm in a movie," he said.

The rain went *through* what his mind insisted was a matte-painting and it made his eyes cross. He raised his hand, hesitated, then put his fingertips to it. A jolt like static electricity snapped at his hand and a nauseating sense of vertigo swirled through the center of his head, followed by a *ping* of pain, like a sharp jab to a pressure point. For the briefest moment, the sting of hospital cleaner—bleach insufficiently masked with perfume—slapped his nose, the chocolatey-sweet taste of HoHos flooded his mouth, and he heard the opening piano chords to a song that sounded distressingly familiar.

McIntyre stumbled away, hugging his stomach, holding onto his balance through sheer will alone. The saturated tails of his tie slapped his chest as he retched. Nothing came up but thick spit.

(of course not when was the last time I ate)

He straightened, wiping his mouth with the back of his hand like a kid, and turned back to the town.

"How the hell did I get here?" he asked. He realized he still held his smartphone and a brief burst of hope rose—only to deflate when he turned the screen toward him to see it covered by a thin green-plastic stick-on coating, something the effects crews would put on electronics during shots so they could insert the CG

(like a matte-painting)

later.

McIntyre peeled the sheet off and tried to turn on the phone. The screen remained black.

With a sinking feeling, he peeled off the rubber case and opened the battery-housing. Empty, of course.

(a prop)

(like in a movie)

(this isn't some fucking movie*)*

He threw the phone down and it bounced with a crack off the asphalt. He touched his pockets, but they were empty.

"How the fuck did I *get here?*" he yelled.

(i'd been getting ready the phone rang and)

And nothing.

(where the hell have you been jimmy)

And he was back in Traumen, Ohio.

(you have to come home jimmy)

But, looking through the intersection where

(petroleum street)

began its uphill climb, the roofs of post-World War II houses like a giant's shaky staircase, nothing came to him. Just names. Barely factoids. Things he might've pulled off Google Maps and a read-through of his IMDB profile: *James McIntyre, screenwriter to the adaptations of* Paper Towns *and* 13 Reasons Why *was born in Traumen, Ohio, and—*

—but there *was* no "and."

"Oh shit, I don't remember *any* of this." He squeezed his fists to his aching temples, as if pressure could force the memories out. There was just this moment, this instant. Before now was La-La Land and Deanna and Marty, but even they lacked any depth in his mind. More names. Like half-assed amnesia.

(hurried storyboards for a film trapped in pre-production hell)

(you did not live these times)

And before that? Just black. More complete amnesia. He might've been created this moment, whole and breathing at the age of 31 with only the roughest sketch of backstory.

"*Fuck.*" McIntyre dropped his hands. The certainty that every end of the intersection was a matte-painting, that he was trapped here, stole over him. It was ridiculous, but then so was the matte-painting of the Petroleum Street Bridge.

(or waking up in a town i haven't thought of in years with no memory of getting there)

Movement flickered out of the corner of his left eye and he turned to look down West Front Street.

A figure stood at the far end, where the street curved.

Or, more accurately, a *boy* stood at the far end, his green shirt and blue pants the brightest thing in this gray area, so small that McIntyre could've blotted him out with his pinky-nail.

(where the hell have you been jimmy)

(you need to come home jimmy)

He started after the boy before he even knew he was moving. "*Don't you move!*" he yelled. The rain sapped the strength of his words. "*Don't!*"

It was like running in a nightmare, his effort to move faster unmatched by the distance he covered. He winced when he approached the edge of the intersection, his nerves anticipating the crunch of another impact.

But his shoes splashed through puddles and he kept going. He passed brick commercial buildings to the left, a blocky medieval structure that according to the sign was the Traumen Public Library to the right. The idea that this was a set, that this was all fake, persisted. These were wooden constructions—hollow inside, something the art department and production design teams whipped together.

And then, crossing the intersection of West Front Street and Center Avenue, the world flickered again.

It wasn't like before, but instead like the curtain of the world had been tugged back to reveal...nothing. Darkness.

McIntyre's foot came down, but his nerves pulled his weight back, certain he was going to plunge into darkness, and he went sprawling. He hit pavement—tumbling and rolling, the world completely solid again, shredding the elbows of his shirt, pain flaring up.

He raised his head, but the boy was gone.

"No he isn't," McIntyre muttered, getting to his feet, and running again, battling the pain in his joints. The boy wasn't gone. The boy had moved out of sight. McIntyre would find him. He had to. He had nothing else at the moment. That boy

(where the hell have you been jimmy?)

was the only straw he could cling to.

(unless you're having a nervous breakdown unless you're strapped to some hospital bed)

He reached the corner of State Street and West Front and zipped across—the idea of checking for traffic was a joke no one laughed at. To his left was the Veteran's Memorial Bridge, wide and slightly curved, with no buildings or trees to hide the view of Traumen's east side and the gray, dead Ohio sky above. The name came to him with no fuss whatsoever, and he recognized the view before him, but none of it held any context beyond a minor tug at the back of his aching mind.

He ran in the opposite direction, up State Street. The boy hadn't gone over the bridge.

(presuming there is a boy)

(there is a boy goddammit)

(how do you know and how do you know you're heading for him?)

He passed a commercial building with a bar-and-grille called the Ven-Bar on the corner and something *ping*ed in that dull throb in the center of his brain: he'd taken a date here once. They'd had the dining area to themselves, which was good because the girl had had the loudest *laugh*—

"You guys have fun tonight?"

The man's voice was a gunshot next to his ear. McIntyre jumped, bouncing off the wall of a PNC bank—and did he feel the building *give* a little bit?

(never mind)

He spun full-circle, even as he knew he was alone.

(nervous breakdown sounding any better?)

But he *knew* that voice; he *knew* it.

He just didn't know *how*; like Traumen, like its streets, it lacked context. Lacked depth. Errant puzzle pieces. How can you remember something, but not remember it at all?

And then, as if his brain was trying to taunt him—

(i'm glad you're getting out jimmy it's what she would have wanted—)

He smacked the heel of his hand against his temple, like his head was an old television on the fritz, even as his feet began moving of their own accord, turning him down Second Street. "Shut up, shut up, shut up," he said.

His shoe scraped against something metal.

He looked down to see a large tin sign reading BAKER'S MARKET— half-obscured by a faded Coldwell Banker sign. He wasn't terribly surprised at the now-very-loud *ping* of memory it brought.

(a trail of mental breadcrumbs)

(to what?)

McIntyre looked up at the little building the sign had fallen from. Through the front window, he could see the wooden counter to the right, Ohio Lotto scratch-offs sealed beneath old shellac; the squat ice-cream case catty-corner beyond, as if someone had made an apathetic attempt at removing it; the corkboard back wall, metal display hooks half-torn away; the comics rack lying in the center like a dead dog.

"I remember this," he whispered and the glass shimmered like an old-movie-flashback effect. The interior was now well-lit, the ice-cream case humming, the hooks stocked with single-serving chips and gummy candy, the comics rack standing and flush with an early-1990s run of Marvel Comics: *Uncanny X-Men, Spectacular Spider-Man, What If . . . ?* All as he remembered it.

As he *remembered it.*

He reached out—

—and his fingertips touched not glass but dry, papery skin.

McIntyre screamed and staggered back, holding his hand by the wrist as if he'd burned it. He could *feel* that skin, and that familiar, loathsome—

—nothing.

His hand felt only cold and wet. Rain filled his palm.

Something in his head teetered, close to just falling over with a crash. His thoughts, half-formed, collided and entangled together.

(no memory)

      (a trail)

            (no backstory)

                  (of mental breadcrumbs)

                        (to what?)

(you're getting out jimmy it's what she would've wanted—)

His will broke and he bounded down Second, his feet working on automatic and turning him up Imperial Avenue. Old Sears & Roebuck catalogue houses marched along the street, guarded by older curbside trees, their root structures upsetting the sidewalk.

McIntyre saw none of it. This was white-out time, broken-will time. A yellow stitch unzipped down his side, but he'd run forever, not even after the boy now, just to get away, get away, *get away*—

He stumbled and there was time for a single thought to zip across his mind—*It's my day for falling down, all right*—before tired flesh met old cement. Pain bit into his elbows and knees like hot wires.

When he came to a stop, McIntyre opened his eyes and saw a pebble, a loose bit of the sidewalk, an inch from his nose. Extreme close-up. He lifted his head and saw, diagonally across the street, home—the fact, like all the rest, came unbidden.

305 E. Third Street.

What little breath he'd accumulated escaped in a rush. "Shit."

It had been an old home when he'd lived there, stuck onto the corner of Imperial and E. 3rd, and the intervening years since he'd left—

(when DID i leave?)

—hadn't been kind. The second-floor windows sagged in their frames like dead eyes. Aluminum siding peeled from the house like flecks of dead skin. The front lawn was an almost-neon-yellow.

The air between him and the house shimmered, like quicksilver in the distance, and the knuckle of pain in his head bloomed. McIntyre sat up before it could get worse, before another one of those damned *ping*s—

—and saw the boy, *the boy*, barely three feet away, standing beside a fire hydrant and *flickering*—not once, but continuously.

McIntyre recoiled, covering his eyes. The glimpse of the boy had only been for an instant, but it was like trying to look through thick glasses when you had perfect vision.

"Not very pleasant, is it?" the boy said and it was the voice from the phone, the voice that had called him back home.

(where the hell have you been jimmy?)

"What are you *doing* to me?" McIntyre yelled, driving his fists deeper into his aching eyes.

"What are you doing to yourself," the boy replied flatly and McIntyre heard something much older buried beneath that I'm-not-yet-in-puberty voice.

He grunted.

"Look at me, James," the boy said and the youthfulness was completely gone, replaced by a voice like gravel grinding together. "*Look at me, James McIntyre.*"

Something outrageously hot slammed into the backs of his hands. He screamed, throwing them out, his shoes digging in and shoving him away. His back fetched up against what felt like a stone wall.

(???what stone wall???)

He opened his eyes and saw

(jump cut just like a movie)

they were no longer on the corner of E. Third and Imperial. Old Victorian houses with manicured lawns marched away to their left and right.

(bissell avenue holy christ i'm on bissell avenue)

His eyes tracked the houses, the intersection a few yards away, each sight bringing with it another *ping*.

His eyes landed on the flickering boy standing at the curb. What made looking at him hurt wasn't the flickering itself—how many goddamn science fiction films featured a flickering hologram?— was that he *changed*. One flicker, the boy's hands were at his sides. Another, he held a heavy hardcover book with a red-and-white dustjacket. A third had the boy grasping a softball of creamy light.

The boy's green tee was long, with an embossing of the Tasmanian Devil. Faded jeans, worn along the back heels. Knock-off Jordans. His hair a shaggy, dirty blond.

McIntyre locked onto the boy's eyes, recognizing them without any sort of *ping*. Didn't he see those same eyes—cradled in stress-wrinkles, it was true—every morning in the mirror?

James McIntyre was face-to-face with Jimmy McIntyre, eleven years old, still two years away from the growth spurt that would give him his adult height of six-two.

He had called *himself*—brought *himself* back home to Traumen, Ohio—or whatever this place actually was.

He started shaking. "Why are you doing this?" he asked and his voice was a croak.

"Why are you doing this to yourself, James," Jimmy said, his hands ever-changing.

McIntyre bared his teeth. "I'm not doing *anything*."

"You're fighting me," Jimmy said. "That's why it hurts. You *always* fight me."

"I'm not fighting *anything*."

"Oh?" Jimmy said and McIntyre didn't think so much mockery could fit into such a small word. "Why does your head hurt, James? Why do you keep having these *ping*s whenever a memory escapes from that goddamned graveyard you have in your head?"

McIntyre looked up, suddenly numb. "How—"

Jimmy turned so McIntyre could see across the street. "Do you remember waving to the hearse?"

It was another Victorian House, but a cloth canopy extended from the front porch to the sidewalk. An ornate wooden sign with REINSEL FUNERAL HOME & CREMATORY dominated the extravagantly landscaped yard.

"What—" McIntyre started to say, and—

(—you're walking past men in black suits who don't want to put their hands in their pockets but don't know what else to do with them. you hear soft and not-so-

soft sobbing but you can't respond to it; you feel numb. you turn right, into the first viewing room and start down the row made by the folding chairs, all directing you to the front, where—)

(NO NO I CAN'T I WON'T THINK OF THAT)

(—you're on the curb, and you're waving at the hearse as it drives past, turning onto Harriot Avenue, but you don't know why and you stop. a man— who?—has a hand on your shoulder, as if you might bolt, but you won't. the only thing you're feeling is your itchy rented suit. the man behind you says, choked up, "christ, jimmy, i don't know if i can go up there, don't know if i can see—")

—McIntyre's stomach revolted, lurching him onto his hands and knees and expelling bile onto the rain-slick sidewalk. The knot of pain in the center of his head felt like a cluster of diseased teeth.

"I saw what you did there," Jimmy said. "It's what you've *always* done. Whenever you get too close to it, you bolt."

McIntyre rested his feverish forehead against the blessedly cool concrete. "I don't understand. I don't know what any of this *is*."

"Of course you don't," Jimmy said and the contempt turned his words into little knives in McIntyre's ears. "But now we've run out of time. I can't be a ghost forever, any more than you can be a dream forever."

McIntyre raised his head. Oh, his head *ached*.

"I have hope for you," Jimmy said. "But maybe that's because you're our last chance."

He raised his hand and flicked it, like someone working out a kink in his wrist. The world around them *flattened*, became as two-dimensional as a matte-painting seen up close. The rain stopped.

Fissures zig-zagged down, top to bottom, like a child using black marker to draw lightning. The world blew apart in a thousand pieces, revealing a blackness that was the apotheosis of black. No up-down, left-right, north-south-east-west. The kind of black that ate light. It rang, beginning like the hum he'd heard back in California, becoming the ringing that had pulled him conscious here. It was constant and consistent.

Neither McIntyre nor Jimmy plummeted or stumbled, although

McIntyre's entire body clenched, nerve-endings anticipating a drop. They stood on nothing McIntyre could feel, but they did not fall.

"This is the core of everything," Jimmy said and he no longer flickered. He held the softball of creamy light, its illumination throwing his face into stark relief, making him appear both ridiculously young and unbelievably ancient. His voice had given up any pretense of sounding like a boy. "Our universe. I don't know how it is with other people, but this is ours. It was once filled with light, each one a different life, following its own path. Ever hear of quantum physics? Like that."

McIntyre felt warmth in his palms and looked down to see his own softball of creamy light, flashing and dimming, a bulb about to die. He couldn't feel *the object* that made the light, the tangible *thing* he was holding, but couldn't let go or collapse his hands.

For the first time, the pain in his head took the backseat. "What happened?"

"What always happens. A car accident. A fire. A mugging gone bloody. A suicide. A heart attack. Sometimes our minds simply can't take what it's been shown and gives itself an embolism, which is so funny, given the circumstances, I want to shriek. The light dies and there's one less version of us."

He hunkered down in front of McIntyre. "It's because our universe is broken. Incorrect. Filled with false versions sparked by a single instance of understandable cowardice."

His eyes locked with McIntyre's. "James, what happened when you were eleven years old?"

A switch might've been thrown and the knot of pain in McIntyre's brain exploded, drenching his head in pure white-hot agony. He shrieked, and fell onto his light, hugging it to his stomach.

Above him, he heard Jimmy: "Stop this! We don't have *time* for this! *Stop fighting this!*"

McIntyre's lips peeled back from his teeth. "I'm not fighting… *anything.*"

"*Bullshit!*" Jimmy yelled. "Do you know how many versions I've had to go through to get to this moment, over and over again, just to go rocketing back when you can't take it? It takes me twenty *years* to reach you *each time*—and not just on *any* day during that twentieth year, but a *special day*. Do you remember?"

McIntyre opened his mouth, but—

(—whiff of hospital cleaner—)

—he shrieked again.

"We don't have any more chances, James!" Jimmy yelled. "What happens after we're gone, after this last chance is wasted? I don't know. *I've never been able to know.*"

He put a hand on McIntyre's shoulder. "I've run out of lifetimes," Jimmy said. "You're my last shot—*our* last shot—or it *all* ends. I brought you back to Traumen. *I made it like a movie, hoping you'd see how fake it was.* I pulled you off the soundstage and *brought you here*, to the core. I am out of options and out of time. *You need to remember.*"

McIntyre hugged his ball of dying light. "But I don't … remember … *anything*."

Jimmy's hand left his shoulder.

"James," he said, softly. "Look at me."

He did, gingerly, and Jimmy's face was inches away. Liquid arcs from their respective lights stretched toward one another.

"You don't have that luxury, anymore," Jimmy said, and shoved his light into McIntyre's.

The world exploded white, swatting away the blackness, and McIntyre—

—*is sitting in that goddamn orange vinyl chair, and you're holding your mother's hand as she lies comatose in the hospital bed.*

You are Jimmy McIntyre. It is the evening of November 21, 1996, and you have to watch your mother die.

(NO NO NO NO YOU CAN'T MAKE ME YOU CAN'T MAKE ME SEE THIS)

But you can't shake yourself free. This is what you've hidden from yourself for twenty years, what you've buried, what you've built multiple lifetimes to avoid. The moment that separates you from the boy.

Oh god, the weight is crushing. Sitting there, holding your mother's hand, your fingertips over the prominent bones, the papery skin, it hurts to draw a breath. Your throat is narrowed to a straw. Your eyes boil, but you do not cry. You've promised yourself you would not cry. To cry out, to show the grief, would make it real. Your mother is dying.

Sitting there, marveling how the woman who was as close to god as a small boy could understand could make such a small impression under the sheets, you hold her hand, and she seems to hold yours back and you think of crossing busy streets. An I-will-protect-you-grip. An I-am-not-letting-go grip.

But you want to scream as the doctor pulls the breathing apparatus from her lower face, showing the damage that the hemorrhagic stroke, and the subsequent two-week coma, has wrought. Her skin looks waxy and taut under the fluorescent bar of light above her bed, rendering her eyes deep purple eye sockets. Her hair, already thin, looks like a tangle of old spider webs.

Her mouth hangs slightly open and you think—as much as you can think— she would've hated to look slack-jawed like that. The urge to shriek grows, but it doesn't escape. It burns, a hot molten core in your heart.

Her eyes half-open, giving her a doped-look, and you straighten. Your grip on her hand tightens. Her eyes are black, but they see you, and, if she's seeing you, that must mean it's all right, right? Turning everything off doesn't mean it's over, right? You've seen episodes of E.R. *Sometimes the patient just needs a jumpstart.*

You swallow and your throat clicks. A hand grips your shoulder, the way it will at the funeral.

(STOP THIS NOW I CAN'T SEE THIS I WON'T)

You think her head turns, but it really doesn't—her chest has just stopped moving. She's still looking at you, but her eyes have become the eyes of a taxidermy product, glassy, molded to convey an emotion.

But the irrational hope doesn't die; you still have the hand, holding yours, gripping yours, and that means she's still there, right? She still knows you're there, right? It can't be too late if she can still hold you. Right?

"She's holding my hand," you say.

The owner of the hand on your shoulder squeezes in a way that's supposed to be comforting and isn't. "It's muscle memory, Jimmy," the owner says, his voice thick. "Her hand muscles are responding to the pressure of your hand."

The words fall like bell tolls on your ears. Your head burns, your chest flattens, yours eyes bulge and scald and the scream is just behind your lips, dying to be let out, and you bear down mentally: I will not do this, I will not, I will not—*You can't make this real. Even now, with the truth in front of you, you can't let out that which makes this* real.

And then the burning...cools. The scream retreats. The weight in your chest lessens. It all...dwindles, until you feel almost nothing at all.

You're still holding your mother's hand, but the grip is a lie, just like her intense I'm-seeing-you gaze, and the loose skin—the dry skin, the thin skin—is all you can feel.

"I'm sorry, Jimmy," the man says and his voice is all snot and closed-throats, full of an emotion that you suddenly can't feel. It is at this moment you and the boy separate, the boy stuck in his hellish frozen instant and you going on with your pale half-lives.

And, inside, the you remembering all this screams and screams and screams, until the light comes again, until you're yanked and—

—he lay on his side, cradling his ball of light, now gray and dim. Jimmy stood in front of him.

"Pain is a bridge," the boy said. "Who you are on one end is not who you are on the other. You experience the pain and you cross and it changes you. But, with us, somehow, it *didn't*. I got stuck on one end and you—you *all*...jumped. You didn't feel any pain, but you weren't alive the way you should be."

He knelt beside McIntyre. "You need to accept it, James. You need—"

McIntyre couldn't breathe; his nose was clogged, his lungs filled to capacity. The pain was gone from his head, replaced with a hot buzzing that reminded him of cicadas. All he could see was his mother's dead eyes, all he could hear was the sound of her *not* breathing, all he could feel was the thin skin of her hand—

—and he shrieked.

It boiled up from his core, rolling up and out and into the ringing nothing. Just a great animal bellow of pain and grief, rolled over and over with interest, not just for twenty years, or twenty times twenty years, but for all of them. Every half-life. Every pallid dream, every false continuation of the man known as James McIntyre. His throat shredded. Every muscle, every nerve, every cell, cried out into the darkness, reaching higher and higher, dissembling the pieces until nothing was left.

And then the scream built McIntyre back up again even as it dwindled to a rattle, assembling his form, cell by cell, imbued not with the falseness of his lives, but the passage of the pain—even as he knew it wasn't finished yet. *He* wasn't finished yet.

And then, finally, silence.

And James McIntyre opened his eyes.

McIntyre held his dying ball of light between him and the boy. They watched it ebb and flow, ebb and flow, each fluctuation fainter, until only darkness remained and McIntyre's hands held nothing at all.

He stood and the boy, a silhouette limned with the faintest etching of light, looked up at him.

"The end," he said.

"Not yet," the boy said. "One final step." He saw the boy's silhouette turn his head and McIntyre followed his gaze.

Far away, a single light burned.

The final star was the boy's. The true star, the true core.

"Are you ready?" Jimmy McIntyre, both eleven years old and impossibly ancient, a ghost of an unlived life, asked.

"Yes," James McIntyre, both thirty-one years old and not alive at all, replied.

The boy offered his hand and the false-man took it.

And, together, they walked toward the light.

CODA:

The star explodes in rays of creamy light, with the core becoming the horizon.

Sound—the distant beep of pagers, the almost syncopated deet of many machines doing many jobs, the opening piano chords of a Top 40 hit song.

Smell—cafeteria food and Latex and hospital cleaner. The scent of vanilla perfume that the false man will always associate with middle school girls and the boy will have no association for whatsoever.

Finally, sight—the rays of light becoming the angles of the hallway, top-

bottom-left-right, with color filling in the gaps: speckled white for the tile floor, beige for the walls. Wide doorways swim into existence, wheelchairs standing guard.

At the end of the hallway, just before it opens into the wide central area of a nurse's station, a small boy sits in a wheelchair, holding a book.

The false-man sees with no surprise whatsoever the boy sitting is the exact twin of the boy whose hand he is holding.

They approach. The boy's hunched over his book—Insomnia *by Stephen King, the false man sees—but isn't reading. He glares at the red-and-white dustjacket.*

The boy holding his hand lets go and walks over to his twin.

"One final step," he says again and the expression on his face is one of weariness. "Are you ready?"

"Are you?"

Instead of answering, the boy touches the exposed back of his twin's neck. There's a soft flash of creamy-white and his hand sinks into the other boy.

He sits down where his twin sits, becoming more intangible with each movement. Before they connect, the boy offers the man a single final look that the man has no problem discerning.

Don't let us down, *it says.*

And then the boy is gone with another soft flash of creamy light and it's just this ghost and the boy in the wheelchair. Behind him, the Counting Crows goes into its first chorus of "A Long December."

The man reaches out, hesitates, then touches the back of the boy's neck. Immediately, the aftertaste of Ho-Hos fills his mouth. Instantly, weight gets added to his chest.

His hand sinks into the boy's neck with more creamy-white light and he feels pulled, drawn in. He almost yanks his hand back, but the boy's last glance at him—don't let us down—keeps him going.

He turns himself around and sinks into the boy, that pulling sensation intensifying. Memories, twenty years' worth, whistle through the remaining second of his half-life, but, again, they recall nothing for him. They aren't his.

Before he full submerges, he looks back one last time, where he and the boy had come from, but sees only darkness, held back by the light.

An apt metaphor, he thinks, and disappears.

❧ ⋯ ❧

Jimmy blinks as disorientation sweeps through him. He has the odd feeling of both sitting down and getting up. The nerves in his legs twinge, confused.

"Stupid," he mutters, rubbing his eyes, but he freezes. To anyone looking, he would be some kid wiping his eyes because he's crying, because he's mourning, because he's about to become a dumb fucking orphan and all he can fucking do about it is cry. They'd see him and be so *full* of sympathy, as if that could do anything about his fucking—

(don't say it don't say it)

—dying mother.

He grinds his teeth until his jaw aches and drops his hands. No one would see him cry. He would *not* cry. He would *not* give in.

But, Jesus Christ, who would've thought this would hurt so much? The *weight* he feels on his chest. He's had the air knocked out of him a few times, but this is nothing compared to that; it feels, instead, like he's clamped into one of those table-vices in shop class and some malicious bastard is turning it and turning it.

His vision shimmers as his eyes grow hot.

"Jimmy," a man says from behind him.

He looks up and John is standing there, his tie loosened, the bags under his eyes making the rest of his face paler. He's ten years Jimmy's senior but, right now, he seems twenty or thirty.

"They're turning her off," John says and his voice cracks on the last word. His eyes are cherry-red-rimmed. "You need to say goodbye."

Jimmy nods. It feels like his throat is closing.

He picks up his book and stands on legs made of Silly Putty.

John steps aside, allowing Jimmy to enter first. "Are you going to be okay?"

HOW CAN YOU EVEN FUCKING ASK THAT? he wants to scream, shriek, bellow, but he doesn't. He won't. He won't even look at John. It's stupid, but a part of him believes with a childish fierceness that if he doesn't give in, she won't go. She'll have to stay. If he stares at John's face for too long, thought, he won't be able to hold it back. Can't he see the truth on his brother's face?

He steps into the doorway and stops.

The room is dark except for the single shaded fluorescent

bar above his mother's bed. A trio of machines stand to one side, science-fiction doctors brooding on their failure. The human doctor, so unimportant that Jimmy immediately forgets him, stands back a respectful distance.

Finally, Jimmy looks at his mother.

Something shifts within and the strangest sense of *déjà vu* hits him. He thinks two thoughts, equally nonsensical and impossible, simultaneously: *I've been here before* and *I can't go through this again!*

He reaches out and grasps the doorway, leaning like a drunk. He senses John behind him, but Jimmy sees only their mother, lying there, *dwindling* there. His throat hurts, as if he's already been screaming. That sense of *déjà vu* gets stronger, becoming an odd, horrible form of vertigo.

I've been here before, he thinks, but on some level doesn't think it's his voice at all.

I have to live this again, he thinks and his throat burns, his chest closes. He blinks and his eyes are wet.

He wants to call out to her, something that would appear dramatic but couldn't match the wrench of emotion twisting in his chest, but he can't, can't even open his mouth. The air is locked in his throat.

Behind him, John says, "Jimmy—"

And the old voices say together, *Get it out. Get it out, finally.*

He puts a hand on Jimmy's shoulder and, this time, it's comforting. He feels something give inside, and the weight... shifts.

Jimmy McIntyre, eleven years old and thirty-one years old and impossibly ancient all at the same time, finally screams, finally makes it real.

SURVIVING THE RIVER STYX

EVEN DOPED-UP, Riley knew getting on an ocean liner wasn't a logical extension of immersion therapy.

Andrea and Hogan stood, elongated, before him, the only clear things on the crowded dock. The curls of Riley's wife's hair were rusted horseshoes, Hogan's beard a writhing hive of ants. Andrea's eyes twinkled and Riley tried to remember the last time that had happened. Before the trouble with his company, surely.

His view was a pastel panorama that ran like tie-dye. Far off in the bay, the *Queen Victoria III* ocean liner squatted like a marshmallow in the steel-wool Atlantic. Voices washed over him, a meaningless tidal roar, pressing him further into the wheelchair. His arm tingled where Dr. Hogan injected him. Nothing else did, though. All numb.

His eyes moved slowly over the liner. Each incision of the various decks transformed the ship into rows of gleaming teeth. The boat that would take them to it bounced over the grey waves, approaching, and vertigo bloomed like a flower in the center of Riley's head. All that water.

Surrounded by all that water.

His heart pounded enough to make him hiccup.

I can't do this! How can they expect me to do this?

Riley heard a scream. He passed out before he could tell if it was him or someone else.

Unconscious, he felt calm; he felt *himself*. He was everything he knew Riley Christopher McCarrick, millionaire software whiz-kid, to be. The quaking ruin that reality thrust upon him—too scared to be in the shower for longer than five minutes, cringing if an errant rain-drop smacked his face—was banished.

Sound began to filter in, growing louder as the darkness lightened. The sounds smoothed, separated into Andrea's and Hogan's voices.

Andrea: "Can't believe how long security took."

Hogan: "Be glad they didn't take us back to the port."

"That guy tried to rip someone's throat out with his *teeth*."

A sound of a hand across fabric. Hogan rubbing Andrea's back? Riley's stomach tightened. When was the last time Andrea had allowed *him* to do that? "The man's gone. An isolated incident." A dry chuckle that sounded like dead leaves rattling. "Maybe he was aquaphobic, too."

Why is that funny? Riley thought.

Soft footsteps, then Andrea said, "He's waking up, Derek."

How do you know his name?

Hogan's said, loudly, "Are you with us, Riley?"

He opened his eyes and Hogan's face hovered just inches above him. Riley cringed and Hogan stepped away.

"Are you okay?" Andrea asked. She stood beside the bed.

"How are you feeling?" Hogan asked. He pulled an unmarked vial of piles from his blazer pocket.

Riley ignored him. Their cabin was standard mid-level hotel fare . . . just on the water. A sliding door led to the balcony on the right, covered by a near-sheer curtain. The smudge-line of the horizon peeked in and he turned away, his stomach a ball of discomfort. *Who in his right mind puts a man phobic of water . . . ?*

Hogan cleared his throat and nudged one of Riley's fists with a glass of water until Riley took it.

"How long was I out?" Riley asked.

"Roughly six hours. We've been at sea for four."

Silence fell, the kind of silence no one wants to break. Hogan watched him. Riley watched his hand gripping the glass.

"What are you thinking?" Andrea asked.

Riley frowned. "I'm thinking who in their right mind puts a man afraid of water on an ocean liner?"

"Now, Riley, you're not afraid of *water*," Hogan said, his voice smooth and quick. You could tell he'd said this kind of thing before. "This is stress, exacerbating a *pseudo*-fear of open water. Your aquaphobia is nothing but smoke-and-mirrors. I'm trying to help you remember what's *really* important in life—"

"Shut up." Riley swung his feet out over the side of the bed and forced himself to stand. Lightheadedness smacked him and he planted his feet. "What's the term you're always throwing around? 'Obfuscate'? *Excellent* word. You're obfuscating the point. Who in their *right mind* puts a *man afraid of water on a goddamn cruise?*"

Hogan and Andrea retreated toward the alcove.

"You're obviously excited," Hogan said. He shook the pills. "Perhaps you need—"

"Get out."

"Maybe later." Hogan set the vial on the desk. "But, really—"

"*OUT!*" Riley hurled the water. Hogan and Andrea ducked and the glass exploded against the far wall.

Hogan flung open the door and dashed out, Andrea at his heels. In the hallway, a man in a white button-down shirt sprinted past, his face a pale, shocked blur.

Riley slumped against the wall, dizziness slamming his stomach into a blender. *I can do this. I can do this.*

His gaze fell upon the vial on the desk and he didn't know what he hated more: Hogan, the ocean, or how much he wanted those pills.

If he didn't look outside, his nausea and vertigo were dim annoyances. He'd taken a pill, hating himself for it, but it had slowed him down, calmed him. The pill wasn't as powerful as the shot Hogan had given him, but he thought if he took more than one at a time, it could be.

His eyes fell upon his things scattered across the bedspread, among them an issue of *Wired* with him on the cover. THE FIRST STAR TO FALL? read the caption. *Riley McCarrick's Omega Systems the First Casualty of the New Global Economy?*

His fists clenched, his trim nails digging into the palms. He barely felt it.

Riley hadn't needed Hogan to tell him that his aquaphobia stemmed from stress, which fed on the control he lacked at work and home. It was all pop-psychobabble. What Riley needed was help *controlling* it.

Hogan began mentioning a cruise after a year of everything continuing to spiral out of control. Andrea had been for it from the beginning, showing an enthusiasm he hadn't seen in years. She'd called it a second honeymoon, a chance for renewal, and Riley had ended up feeling tag-teamed.

(why would they do this? Andrea could be spiteful, but you pay *Hogan)*

Andrea might be paying him more, and maybe not in cash. Paranoid, but she knew Hogan's name when Riley had never told her. Hogan had rubbed her back when she barely let Riley near her anymore.

The cover smiled at him, a photo from before Omega went public and his wife didn't hate him. He sneered and smacked it aside. The movement brought the vertigo back, and he sat down on the edge of the bed, breathing through his mouth. He could imagine the ship heaving this way.

"Fool," he muttered, and made himself straighten. He spied the vial of pills—unmarked; of course, my dear Watson, what better to enhance the delusions of the victim?—on the edge of the desk, and picked it up, rolling it in his hand. He'd already had one, and more might invite another acid-trip fever dream, but what did he care? He didn't know how long this cruise was. Andrea—ah, and the delusion grows roots, Watson—had set it up.

He thumbed the cap off and shook two out, setting the vial down. The tiny white pills looked so innocent.

(alice ate the cake that read EAT ME *and down the rabbit hole she went)*

He dry-swallowed the pills.

The colors popped, the sound of the ocean was in time with his pulse, and he didn't know if he was asleep when the knocking started, or if he just became aware of it. It was too crisp and professional to be anyone but room service—had he ordered food? Had Andrea, working like Oz far and away, ordered it?

The knocking continued, forever and ever, world without end, amen, chunky peanut-butter.

Christ, just leave the food at the door. When he was hungry, he ate pills. Didn't they understand that?

He stumbled into the alcove and nearly flattened his face into the wall. Whoopsie. Who knew they offered plastic surgery cruises? Captain, I wish to flatten this nose of mine. Money is no object. Just ask Andrea, the Great and Terrible Invisible Wife of Oz.

He slid toward the door and fell against it, pawing the handle until he could stick his head out.

The clerk on the other side looked how Riley felt; hair a crow's nest, dark bags bulging under red-ringed eyes that cut to the left and right, a mouth that twisted and writhed, two-parts sour grin, one-part anxiety.

"I don't want any food," he said. That's what he *thought* he said.

The clerk's mouth quivered like a sound wave. "So you *haven't* eaten, sir?"

"No," Riley said. "You and Andrea gonna force-feed me? Me no hungry. You go away."

He thought he heard a scream and started to dismiss it, until he saw the clerk cringe.

That was real, he thought. The hair on the back of his neck stood on end.

"Very well, sir," the clerk with the dancing mouth said. "We've been having some issues with... food poisoning... and we wanted to make sure everyone had eaten." He shook his head. "*What* everyone had eaten. Excuse me." He looked like he wanted to giggle.

It wasn't the clerk's eyes staring at him, but the clerk's Bozo the Clown grin. Riley couldn't look away from it. That scream, he wanted to say, aren't you supposed to check on things like that?

"Me no hungry," Riley repeated, pulling his head back in. "You go away." He closed the door and latched it.

He thought the clerk might've yelled, "Everyone must *eat*, sir!" but another scream went off—or *maybe* went off. Riley was out of the alcove and his pulse had again fallen into rhythm with the ocean current. That's the key to fear—become it. Like Batman. His blood was one with the ocean.

His eyes fell upon the vial of pills. His friends. Counting them individually—even pairs!—along with his buddies vertigo and nausea, he had quite the shindig on his hands.

"Party down," he muttered, scooping up another two pills. He dry-swallowed them.

His feet tripped over themselves and he fell onto the bed. *The comfiest rabbit hole ever*, he thought, and passed out.

This time, knocking *did* wake him up, but it was not the ever-professional, ever-consistent knock of room service, but a drunken wham.

"*Riley!*" Andrea's voice, a near-scream. "*Riley, open up!*"

He fell off the bed, his arms and legs freshly-stitched doll parts he could barely control. *Just call me Raggedy Riley.*

"Riley, please!"

He knee-walked into the alcove. Gone was the acid-trip fever dream, but his thoughts were cotton candy, teased apart and spinning in the churn.

"*Riley!*"

He used the handle to heave himself up, then threw himself against the door to keep his balance and looked through the peephole.

Andrea leaned against the door, her hair a mess, mascara raccoon-circles around her shocked, red-ringed eyes. In the distorted fisheye, she looked like an alien, a nightmare *E.T.* The strap of her evening gown had fallen into the crook of her elbow and one breast, shockingly pale, was exposed. A bloody handprint painted the nipple. He couldn't see her hands.

"The Great and Terrible Invisible Wife of Oz!" he cried. "How in the hell are ya?"

She flattened her face against the peephole. "Lemme in, Riley! It's dangerous out here!"

"Which is why *I* am in here, partying down."

Her exhale fogged the peephole and he frowned. "You have to help me!"

Anger, an old, forgotten part of him, flickered in the back of his head. "Like you're helping me, right? Right, Wife of Oz?"

She pounded at the door with her invisible hands. Did he hear metal clang? Was she a cyborg? *"Help me, you bastard!"*

"Show me your hands."

She didn't move.

"Show me, you bitch!"

She threw herself off the door and weaved on her feet like a boxer about to drop. She didn't raise her hands, but didn't need to.

She held a carving knife, bloody and dripping. "Let me in!" she cried. "People are attacking out here!"

Riley, frowning, pushed himself away. "Should've picked a better cruise. Go away."

Andrea pounded and kicked at the door. *"You bastard! Let me in! LEMME IN RIGHT NOW!"*

"Not by the hair on my chinny-chin-chin."

He fell against the wall, but didn't feel nearly stoned enough. It was still night, the lights were on, but the colors were dull, washed with gray. Vertigo and nausea had flown the coop. Where were his friends?

He went to his knees next to the desk, knocking the open vial over and spilling pills across the top.

Andrea shrieked and pounded. *"LEMME IN! I'LL KILL YOU, RILEY! LEMME IN LEMME IN LEMME IN!"*

Riley scooped a handful into his mouth and swallowed. *What a dull party, really.* For good measure, he scooped and swallowed another handful.

"HEARTLESS BASTARD! UNFEELING PRICK!"

Darkness clouded his vision. *I feel nothing*, he agreed and fell onto his face.

A scream forced him awake and what felt like spun glass in all his joints forced him to scream back.

He clawed his way to the bed and thrashed himself slowly into a sitting position. He felt like he'd fought World War II, both theaters, single-handedly. His skull pulsed, heavy whams against his forehead and ears. The crotch of his jeans was bunched and cool against his skin. He'd pissed himself at some point.

His eyeline met the surface of the desk, where he saw the empty vial and three lonely pills.

He massaged his forehead. "Did I fuckin' take *all* of that? How am I not dead?" He looked underneath the desk and saw a pile of crusty puke. Well, that explained *that*.

How long had he been out? The gap in the drapes, cold grey daylight fought for space against the nightstand lamps. It could've been hours. Or days.

Why was he up now, then?

Another scream erupted outside, distant, and he remembered.

He used the desk to pull himself to his feet and shambled into the alcove, a hand on the wall for balance. He collapsed against the door with a grunt and looked through the peephole.

The body of an elderly man lay in a pool of blood against the opposite wall of the hallway.

Riley jerked away from the door, the migraine shoved forcefully onto the backburner. "Christ!"

He rubbed his eye with the heel of his hand and looked again.

Same image.

He was shivering as he opened the door, but couldn't stop.

The old man looked as if he'd once had a face, but what was left resembled something shoved into a Mixmaster. This guy hadn't screamed recently. The blood he lay in had dried.

(how can you be cold this is a body for god's sake!)

He looked down the hall. Doors marched away to his left and right, dwindling to points on the horizon. Blood smeared the walls, dried to brown smears.

He was the only living thing in sight. The only sound was his leaden heart and shallow breath.

"Jesus," he muttered.

He stepped back inside, closed the door, and went to the room phone. According to the directory, just picking up the phone connected it to the front desk.

He got nothing but dead air. He hit zero for the operator and the line rang and rang. He dropped the phone back into the cradle and didn't bother fixing it when it landed askew.

His mind wanted to drift to the corpse, and he forced it to stop. He had to think.

Where had everyone gone? Who was screaming and why hadn't anyone done something about the old man?

(there's no one to do something)

He remembered the nightmare clerk, saying people were suffering from food poisoning and that he should eat.

He remembered Andrea, blood-streaked and raving, pounding on the door. Dream or real? Live or Memorex?

The body outside isn't Memorex, he thought.

(what if everyone's gone? what if they're all dead? who's driving the ship?)

"Bullshit," he muttered.

(you have to find someone)

His shivering worsened. How could he leave this for . . . *that?* He hugged himself, but the shivering didn't lessen.

(if there's no one here who's controlling the ship?)

The potential answer—*no one*—made him shiver harder.

No, he couldn't stay, if only to find out what *was* happening.

He changed into clean clothes, shutting his mind down, working on automatic. He forced himself back into the hall, checking the number on the door as he left. 9.040, the brass plate read. He hadn't even known what his room number had been.

He followed a sign which stated he was on DECK 9 and that elevators were this way. The silence reminded him of libraries. The carpet so thick, his footfalls were silent. Nothing but the roar of his own blood in his temples. He came to an open door two rooms down—9.036—and made himself stop.

"Hello?" He flicked the switchplate on the left. Peeking out from around the corner were feet. He entered, recognizing the shoes, and thought of Andrea again.

He looked around and the air left him. "Jesus."

Andrea lay sprawled on the floor between the bed and the bathroom, the skirt of her evening gown hiked up to reveal cotton panties. Her head, smeared with blood, was cocked up and away.

Hogan's open mouth lay on her torn throat. Riley could see purple-gray intestine underneath his shirtless belly. The bloody carving knife lay nearby. The coppery stink of spilled blood and dried shit clogged his nose.

(people are attacking out here)

His eyes falling on the knife to avoid the view of the mutual murder, he thought, couldn't *help* thinking, *If I'd opened the door...*

He bolted and leaned against the hallway wall, closing his eyes. His stomach threatened, threatened...but didn't have anything to throw up. He coughed, his spit thick and disgusting, and slumped against the wall.

I don't think Andrea expected this, he thought and clapped his hands to his mouth to stifle the scream.

(breathe calm down you can do this)

He didn't believe that—how much could he do if he'd almost overdosed like an idiot on pills?—but it calmed the scream that wanted to jump from his mouth. Who knew who might hear?

He looked longingly down the hall, back toward his room, but it didn't even have the comfort of familiarity for him.

The rabbit hole spit me back out, he thought.

He came across the body of a boy of nine sprawled in an open doorway further down. His eyes had been gouged out, leaving bloody sockets crying blood. Riley glanced behind him, sure that the eye-gouger was creeping forward with bloody fingers, but he had the hallway to himself. His pulse was its own raging ocean current.

Suites named after English Queens met him at the end. Just before these was an archway opening to the stairway and lifts. Inside, another archway led to the opposite hallway, but he had no interest in seeing *that* carnage. He considered taking a lift, but God knew what he might find in them.

The ship was silent. He didn't even hear the piped-in Muzak that a lot of hotels played in the hallway. It was just his breathing, his heartbeat. His sign of life. He wondered how many rooms there were, how many people in them, all of them as silent as the old man and the little boy. His wife. Dr. Hogan.

Riley turned toward the expansive, carpeted stairs. He kept his eyes forward as he descended, his shoulder brushing the far wall.

The body of a young, blonde clerk lay sprawled on the landing of Deck 8, his chest-cavity opened up like a pea-pod, his insides bulging against the ragged edges, and Riley stopped on the last few stairs. Unlike the old man, the clerk's blood hadn't dried into the carpet. If Riley touched him, his body would not be cold.

He glanced behind him. There was nothing up there.

He came down slowly, eyes cutting to the archways. A fire-axe lay against the bottom step, the blade wetly smeared with pieces of the clerk.

The spit in his mouth felt viscous and snotty. He swallowed, but it didn't help. He needed a weapon, but, Jesus, what if the handle was still warm from whoever had killed the clerk?

(stop the weak-sister routine and take it)

He crouched down, his fingertips touching wood, and his hand curled around the axe. Something wet fell off and landed with a squish.

He closed his eyes. His stomach would never forgive him.

A scream erupted, high and yodeling from the left hallway, then cut off abruptly. A cackling laugh followed it. His testicles shrunk into tight little balls.

Having a weapon didn't mean he wanted to use it. He went down the next flight two at a time, not looking back.

He didn't bother with the rest of the rooming floors. Although he saw no more bodies, he heard running footsteps and jerky panting. He didn't want to meet their owners. He thought of all those bodies and his mind wanted to shut down. How? *How?*

On Deck 3, someone's bellowing roar enveloped him and the stairwell ended with a hallway curving right. He inched forward, the sound boxing his ears, wrapped him in an audio cocoon. His skin tightened with gooseflesh. He felt like every idiot in every horror movie who goes deeper into the haunted house but what other choice did he have?

The hallway curved outward, until he imagined it reached the perimeter of the ship. He could imagine the waves crashing into him, separating only by steel and insulation.

(keep your mind off that you have bigger concerns)

Understatement of the still-fresh millennium.

The hallway curved inward again and the bellow grew louder in volume but maintained pitch and tone, the words distorted nearly to fare-thee-well. A recording.

Near the end, someone had written with blood-smeared hands I LOVE YOU over and over along the wall. A body with a great chunk of throat torn away lay beneath this declaration.

I'm on the ship of the dead. This isn't the Atlantic. It's the River Styx. Not surprisingly, this didn't make him feel any better.

The hallway opened up onto the oval-shaped Grand Lobby. The marble floors were awash with blood and bodily fluids. Torn bodies lay in piles. Some draped the circular front desk in the center like trophies. The stench was like Hogan and Andrea, jacked to the tenth degree.

The other end of the Grand Lobby led into a shop concourse. On the left of the hallway was a darkened wine bar called Sir Elliot's. Bar stools littered the opening. On the right was a trashed newsstand.

The recording boomed from hidden speakers.

"—*YOUR LUXURIANT VACATIONS,*" the voice bellowed. Static obliterated its sex. "*WHILE MILLIONS STARVE AND DIE UNDER WESTERN IMPERIALISM, YOU FILL YOUR FACE WITH FOOD ON BILLION-DOLLAR ROWBOATS. HOW DOES IT TASTE NOW? HOW—*"

Feedback screamed and Riley screamed with it. The recording died and the silence deafened him with its completeness. He looked around, as if to see why the recording had ended. His heartbeat echoed in the stillness.

A diminutive man in a chef's smock staggered out of the wine bar, meat cleaver in hand, and Riley froze. Blood stained his hairy arms to the elbow. His red-ringed eyes twinkled.

"Messy," he said conversationally, and then he sprinted toward Riley, raising the cleaver. *"Messy, messy, MESSY! NO WAY TO SERVE CUISINE! NOT AT ALL!"*

The man brought the cleaver down and Riley thrust the axe out, blade turned away, as if he were bunting. The axe-head crashed against the man's inner forearm. The impact drove the cook backward.

Riley swung the side of the axe, and it slammed into the side of the man's face with enough force to vibrate up Riley's arms. The man's eyes rolled up into his head, and he dropped with a grainsack thud, the meat cleaver clattering.

Riley staggered into the front desk. The axe shook in his hands. His breath hitched in and out. "Oh shit, oh Jesus, oh hell."

He couldn't remember the last physical confrontation he'd had, probably not since he was a teenager, and adrenaline skimmed through his blood, his nerves flashing like Christmas lights.

Anger filled him. This was ridiculous. This was all ... so *ridiculous*. This ... this *wasn't right*. What in hell's name had happened here?

"Hey!" he screamed. His voice echoed back and that only made him angrier. This was an *ocean liner*, for Christ's sake. *"Anyone here? Where are you? C'mon! WHERE THE FUCK ARE YOU?"*

"Everyone's dead," a woman said behind him. "Or insane."

He spun, and the boy and girl, maybe six, cringed behind the woman's legs. Their eyes ate up their pale, cherubic faces. The woman stared at him, a hand on the backs of their heads, fingers smoothing their blonde hair.

"We'd been hiding in the newsstand." Her dark hair shined in the lobby light. Blood smeared her summer dress. "He'd been looking for us."

"What *happened* here?"

"Don't you know?" she asked. Her eyes shined with shock, but weren't red-ringed. Was that how you could tell? He thought of the clerk, Andrea, this cook.

He lowered the axe. "I was ... sick."

"Have you eaten anything?" Her tone added weight to the question.

He shook his head. "I haven't eaten since ..." He looked at her.

"...how long have we been at sea? I was unconscious. I..." He looked away. "...I don't handle water too well."

She studied him and he couldn't meet her eyes. "We've been at sea for five days. It started getting bad the second day."

I'm a drugged Rip Van Winkle. "Was this an attack?"

She shrugged, a frustrated gesture. "I guess so. They did it through the meals." She shook her head. "God, you're the first person we've seen who's still sane."

"I'm Riley."

"Sheila." She looked down. "This is Dylan and Sara. I don't know where their parents are. I couldn't leave them, though."

Riley nodded. "What do you want to do?"

Sheila's face screwed up into a strange expression. "Everyone's dead and nothing's steering this monster except maybe a boat version of autopilot. The *only* thing to do is get off."

They went back into the newsstand while Riley kept lookout. His chest felt decidedly hollow as the main question hovered over him: *How can I get off?*

When they returned, Sheila's hands held onto the children and two bulging plastic bags.

"How can we leave?" he asked, taking one of the bags. He opened it—bottles of water, single-serving packages of pretzels. He pulled out one of each and opened them. His stomach roiled, but it roiled over a sucking pit of nothing.

"Find one of the tenders—those boats we used to cross from the dock to the ship." Her tone suggested he should know this, and he chased pretzels with water, not pointing out he'd been stoned to a fare-thee-well at the time. "There are four openings and we need to launch it without killing ourselves." She frowned, as if realizing how unlikely that last part was.

He kept his voice even. "Can you drive a boat?"

"I can try. My husband used to own a boat in the 1990s." She looked away, biting her lip. "I gotta *do* something. I can't just...*stay* here."

"Where are the tenders?"

"Deck 8. I checked the map." Sheila glanced at Dylan and Sara. "Will you hold one of their hands?"

He nodded. Sara was as unmovable from Sheila's side as her thumb was immovable from her mouth, but Dylan numbly took Riley's hand, letting Riley lead him away from his sister.

The walk back was slow. Riley looked ahead while Sheila watched from behind. He kept the bag in the hand he held Dylan's so he could keep the axe free.

Riley slowed when they reached the dead clerk, nudging Dylan behind him. Sheila looked over Riley's shoulder and gasped. She quickly swallowed and looked down at Dylan and Sara, who looked up at her with all the animation of dolls.

"Look at the ceiling, guys."

He led them around the corpse and to the right-hand hallway. He poked his head around the corner and stared at the piled bodies further down. "This is lodging. How do we get to the tenders?"

Sheila pointed to the right. He saw signs for a beauty parlor and a book store. "Through the salon and out onto the decks. There are station doors inside, but..." She looked at the bodies and shook her head. "I don't wanna go down there."

Riley nodded. Every organ inside seemed to pulse.

The salon's door was metal-framed with pebbled glass. He nudged it open. One of the stations immediately to the left reflected the rest of the parlor. He saw his haggard face repeated on broken mirrors. "C'mon."

Barbicide stained the floor and the room reeked. The four perm chairs had been upended. No bodies, but a fat trail of blood led down the back hallway to the right.

"Door's over there." Sheila pointed toward the far left corner. With each glass-crunching step forward, his heartbeat grew more leaden. He had to breathe through his mouth in order to get enough air and, still, he felt light-headed.

Two steps led to the deck door. Sheila was reaching for the knob when something crashed in the back hallway. They heard slow, squishy footsteps and something metallic being dragged.

Riley nudged the boy toward Sheila. "Go."

She took the boy's hand and the bag. "Riley—"

"Do you want someone following you?"

She bit her lower lip, then got the kids out quickly. Riley caught a salt-choked whiff of ocean. His stomach cramped and he couldn't shrug off the insane relief he felt when the door closed.

He turned back. Two stations dominated the center of the room, obscuring his view, but he saw a bloody white shirt, a tattered burgundy dinner vest.

He circled around, axe at his chest. His pulse pushed at his Adam's apple. *Here's your choice. Deal with the open water . . . or stay on this ship. With this.*

The man stepped out and it was the clerk from his acid-trip fever dream. His back was stooped, his face dotted with blood. His red-ringed eyes bulged. He dragged a fire-extinguisher by the hose, the bottom dented and greased with blood.

"Have you eaten, sir?" The muscles of his arm bulged as he hefted the extinguisher. "Gotta eat, sir, gotta eat—"

The clerk swung the extinguisher low and it bashed into Riley's thigh. The pain was instantaneous, seizing-up his entire leg. He cried out and fell.

The extinguisher slammed into his kidneys. Riley screamed. He saw a red bulge rearing and he tried to block with the axe. The head smacked the man's forearm, and the extinguisher flew over Riley's head, crashing somewhere.

The clerk pounced and Riley pushed the axe-handle between them. The man was small but whipped and snapped like a downed power line. He grabbed hunks of Riley's hair and yanked. The pain peeled Riley's lips away from his teeth.

The clerk bashed Riley's head into the floor. A white light exploded in front of Riley's eyes. Riley heaved against the man with the axe handle, as if doing bench-presses. The clerk's hands left Riley's hair and moved across his face, thumbs digging for his eyes.

With a knot of strength that dug cannibal-teeth into his kidneys, he shoved the man back. The clerk tensed against the side of the salon door. Riley swung the axe one-handed, a wide, strengthless move, and the side of the axe-head collided with the clerk's jaw. The clerk jerked right, his temple slamming into the salon door's pebbled glass, cracking it.

Riley pushed himself forward, shrieking with his kidneys, and drove his weight into the clerk. The clerk's head bashed a ragged hole through the glass, the breaking shards tearing the man's throat out, transforming his scream into a choked, wet gargle. Blood flew in thick spurts.

Riley jumped, cringing, away from the spasming body. He stumbled into one of the station chairs and dropped the axe to cling to it. His entire side was an icy lump.

He looked at the door leading to the deck and thought of seeing the cobalt waves of the ocean crashing, of smelling that sea air. He fell to his hands and knees and retched yellow bile laced with threads of blood.

Nope, sorry, I can't.

A hiccup burned his throat. He thought of the magazine back in his cabin, foretelling the demise of his company. He might've been a stranger to that version of Riley Christopher McCarrick, CEO of a dying company, husband of a dying marriage.

He thought of Andrea, carrying a knife and screaming to be let in. He thought of Andrea and Hogan killing each other. It could've been him.

I can't stay here, he thought, then said it aloud. His voice was a frog's croak.

He crawled to the steps. At the top, he grasped the doorknob, his fingers grinding blood into the brass. He leaned his head against the door, taking deep breaths. He could hear the crash of waves outside, a seashell roar. Tons of open water.

(don't go out there! you can't!)

"You act like I have a choice," he croaked. He turned the knob and pushed. He winced against the dull brightness, the sea wind pulling his clothes and filling his face with its nauseating scent. As his stomach clenched, he crawled out onto the wooden planks of the deck, letting the wind slam the door closed behind him.

He crawled forward, side brushing the wall, head down, breathing shallowly. His heart trip-hammered in his chest, his pulse a bass drum explosion in his head.

He was doing it. He was outside, he was next to water, and he wasn't stopping. He might not survive—the idea of settling a small boat into the water with two adults and two children all but assured this—and he was starving, beaten half to death, and nauseous, but still whole. Still moving.

Doctor, I believe I've finally conquered aquaphobia.

He barked laughter in between retching, and kept crawling.

He made his way down the deck to where he hoped Sheila, Dylan, and Sara waited.

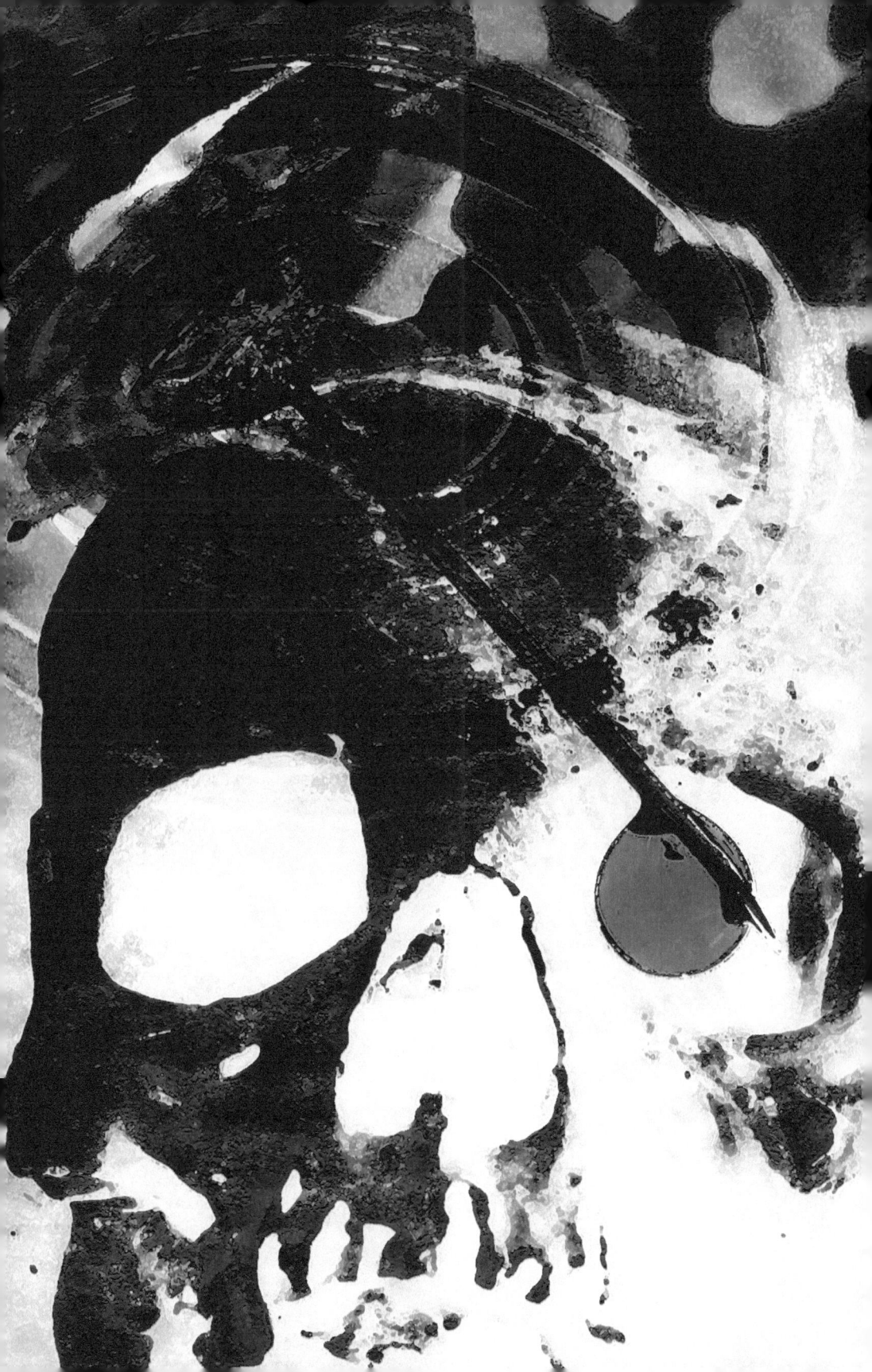

THE AGONIZING GUILT OF RELIEF

(LAST DAYS OF A READY-MADE VICTIM)

BEN RACED down Mitchum Street, last year's boots pounding the shoveled sidewalks, trying to outrun the brightening streetlamps. Not for the first time, he wished he had a car.

Goddammit! he thought and didn't know if he was cursing the school therapist or himself.

The street blurred by, houses closed off with curtains and blinds, their Christmas lights dark. The corners of months-old Clinton/Gore and Dole/Kemp lawn signs poked out of the snow, reaching for him.

The tall fence of McMillian Elementary reared up, and his boots slid on a patch of ice. A quick grab of a post saved him from a bone-rattling crash. He dashed across the lawn on a diagonal, kicking up wet clumps of snow, hoping he wasn't too late, hoping—in spite of the twenty-degree day—Jude had waited like Ben asked.

He skidded to a stop at the edge of the playground, taking in the empty swings, the barren slide, the abandoned merry-go-round.

"*Fuck*," he panted, his exhale a white puff. A stitch burned in his side, matching the molten core of anxiety in his stomach.

Jude hadn't waited—of *course* Jude hadn't waited. How could Ben expect Jude to wait when he was over an hour late on the last day before Christmas break? Which meant Jude was at home, with their father, who'd bragged about early shifts all week.

"*Fuck*," he panted again, the stitch abating, the anxious core growing, spreading tendrils to his limbs.

He knew he needed to run, but a darker part whispered that he was already too late, so why hurry? What could he possibly gain?

Wasted effort.

He started shuffling across the yard when he heard the *thunk* of a metal door closing and a woman's voice: "Ben? Ben Sheever?"

He turned to see a young woman, holding a large pile of children's workbooks and construction paper, across the playground area, in the near-empty teacher's lot. "Hi, Ms. Quinn."

"Looking for Jude?"

"Mmm-hmm," he said through gritted teeth, then made his jaw relax. Ms. Quinn had at least tried to help, had been the one adult who had tried to do the right thing. "Yes, Ms. Quinn."

"You just missed him," she said, walking to her car. "He left a few minutes ago. Thought of inviting him back in, but I knew he'd say no."

She shot him a look that, even across the playground, he read loud and clear. Jude inexorably always loved his teachers, even if his teachers didn't love him back, but Jude had soured on his third grade teacher, in the midst of the meetings and statements and counselors, by the time Halloween rolled around.

He started back toward Mitchum Street, the idea he might catch Jude before the boy reached home squirting much-needed adrenaline into his muscles, banishing the dark whispering. "Thanks, Ms. Quinn," he said, meaning it.

"And, Ben—?" she called and her voice was a fishhook; his head turned, saw the look on her face, and stopped. He wondered if the school board president had come to talk to her, as he had come to talk to Ben's father. Ben didn't doubt it, but it wouldn't have been over beer in the kitchen, with statements like "I'll take care of it."

The school board president wasn't Ms. Quinn's friend, as he was Ben's father's.

"Take care of Jude," she said now.

"I will," Ben said and started running.

He heard a startled cry of pain as he reached the house, and he sprinted faster, taking the porch steps three at a time and banging through the front door.

"Oh great," he heard his father say from down the hall, "the goddamn cavalry."

He burst into the kitchen. A tableau from hell in front of him: Jude crumbled against the refrigerator in one corner, holding his arm as if it were broken; their father at the kitchen table in the other, the top button of his Cobb County Sheriff's Office uniform undone, holding a bottle of Rolling Rock and glaring at it.

"Jesus," Ben breathed, and went to Jude. Jude burrowed into his chest. Ben felt the arm under the long-sleeve—a too-large hand-me-down from Ben—and didn't feel a break, although Jude grunted when Ben's probing fingers squeezed.

"Look up, dude," Ben whispered, tilting Jude's chin. Their father had clipped the boy along his right cheekbone, not hard enough to break—their father was good like that—but enough for the skin to swell and darken. It reminded Ben, absurdly, of water in a balloon— the gentle sloping rise. He didn't press against it.

Rage thrummed through his bloodstream. At his father for doing this. At himself for not getting to Jude in time.

At Jude, for not knowing this would happen.

He's getting bad again, a voice murmured in the back of his mind.

"What the *fuck*, Dad?" he yelled, his anger belied by the crack in his voice.

"Watch your language," Marcus Sheever muttered, not looking away from the Rolling Rock. Ben saw that Marcus's knuckles were chaffed and his head rang.

"What *happened*?"

Still their father wouldn't look up. "Caught him playing with my beer."

Jude sniffed against Ben's shirt. "I was getting him his drink. That's all."

Ben looked back and didn't miss the flicker in Marcus's eyes. He could see it all: their father coming home, Jude—against all logic— excited and eager, running to the fridge to get Marcus his one beer of the evening, Marcus getting annoyed, grabbing at the bottle but Jude not letting go quickly enough, Marcus winding up while jerk- ing the beer from the boy.

Ben saw it so clearly, it could've been happening right now.

Marcus finally looked up, and Ben saw no satisfaction in his father's gaze, no challenge, no troll-like belligerence. Marcus wasn't a stereotypical child-abuser like on a Made-for-TV movie. It would have been easier—to hate him, to bring it all to an end back in September—if he was.

But he had never done this to Ben, had never harmed their mother (not that their mother stuck around long enough).

Just Jude.

He got his arm around Jude's shoulders, helped his brother up. The molten core of anxiety was cooling—the worst was known—but not disappearing. Instead it hardened, settled in, made it impossible to take deep breaths.

"C'mon, Jude," he said, glaring at their father and feeling useless in his inability to do anything else. "Let's get you cleaned up."

He led the boy to the upstairs bathroom and examined him.

The bruises along the shoulder were dark; a little more pressure, if Jude had been holding onto the beer a little tighter, and it would've popped from its socket.

Yes, their father was good. A popped socket could be home-mended, but it would still require a temporary sling, which was noticeable.

The shiner on Jude's face was *also* noticeable but ... well, Jude was always getting punched at school, wasn't he? This could've been just an early Christmas present from the tormentors of McMillian Elementary. It wouldn't have been the first time their father had used that excuse.

He's getting bad again, the interior voice murmured.

Ben got Jude back into his shirt and led him down the hall. Jude asked, "You wanna come read comics with me, Benny?" His eyes were dry now, the shiner coming along nicely, making one eye squint as he looked into his bedroom.

Ben followed his gaze, taking in the neatly organized books on the bookcase, the comics on the desk, the action figures from *Toy Story* and the *X-Men* cartoon show lining his windowsill—a ready display for friends who didn't exist.

He looked back at his brother's open, earnest, *small*—they were nine years apart—face. He had the face of a bull's-eye. Every school, every *class*, had one. The ready-made victim. The one who just didn't *fit*. The one whose timing was off, whose answer was either too right or too wrong, whose interests and look weren't *in*. They weren't obnoxious, or toxic, or even ugly in a broad sense of the word. They were just *wrong*, and everyone knew it. The one even the wallflowers of school felt impunity to pick on.

Ben had one in his senior class—Amanda Hofsteader. Not dumb, not bright, not pretty in the most generous sense of the word. She got it worst from the girls, who seemed to imbue Amanda with all their worst nightmares. She drifted through the halls of Ben Franklin High School, never seeming to know it was as bad as it was, or, if she did, burying it so deep as to make herself almost beatific.

Much like Ben imagined Jude at McMillian Elementary. But Jude got it worse because he kept *trying* to get along in a nerve-wracking, turn-the-other-cheek way, which seemed to rile everyone further.

"You all right, Benny?" Jude asked.

He looked like their mother. Which was part of the problem with their father. In all sorts of ways.

"Yeah," he said, his voice thick.

"So, you wanna read comics?"

"Sure," Ben said, and his throat clicked, and then it was normal again. "But no Spider-Man, though. I'm sick to friggin *death* of Spider-Man."

Jude grinned, and Ben just felt sick.

Ben watched his father sleep on the couch.

Behind them, the television was on, sound low, with NBC playing through the end of *Late Night with Conan O'Brien*. The light from the screen threw Ben's shadow, long and menacing, across Marcus's slack face.

He's getting bad again, the internal voice murmured.

Ben's fists clenched at the end of rod-stiff arms that couldn't do anything.

Marcus snorted in his sleep. He didn't look evil, or monstrous, or anything but what he was—a man. A county sheriff's deputy. Liked by everyone. And when Ben and Jude's mother took off with that undergrad, everyone just clucked their tongues and said, well, what do you expect from Alana Sheever, *nee* Thompson? Everyone knew the Thompsons were a flighty bunch.

But at least Ben and Jude had a good father.

And what good father beat his youngest son?

He slowed down when he was almost caught, the voice went on, *but now he knows he's safe and he doesn't have to worry, anymore.*

Ben wanted to shake his head until he rattled the voice out of his skull. No, that wasn't true, *wasn't* true. That gave hint to some kind of animal cunning and malevolence in Marcus Sheever and he *wasn't* like that. Was he?

But wasn't that why Ben had gone to talk to Ms. Quinn, and then one of Jude's principals last fall? Because Marcus was just getting worse—his irritation mounting, the time he was a normal father fading, the over-correcting jabs more common, double rations if Jude tried to make up for whatever negligible thing he had done wrong? It'd taken Ben time to see the increase, but it was there. The hits were creeping up from Jude's chest and onto his face. It was this last bit that had made what Ben said palatable to Ms. Quinn. Jude might've been an everyday target for the bullies at McMillian, but there were cafeteria and recess monitors to halt things.

Not at home, though.

Ben's jaw clenched until the pressure sang in his ears.

Not that it mattered much, did it? the internal voice said. *Send the balloon up, and it got popped by the school board president. And suddenly...*

And suddenly the questions from the counselors were focusing more on *Ben* and his relationship with his father. The protocol Ben had learned from television—tell adults and they would come in and fix everything—was going off the rails. Suddenly Marcus was *there*, looking at either Ben, or Ben and Jude, or Jude alone, during these questioning sessions. Suddenly, Ms. Quinn wasn't there to help, and Jude...

"Jude *backed you up*," Ben hissed, softly.

Jude, who'd never been fully on-board with what Ben was doing, never corroborated. Yes, it was the bullies at school. No, Marcus was nothing but what he appeared to be: a loving single father.

He didn't do it out of fear, Ben thought, but out of his essential *Jude*-ness. The Jude that saw only the good in people (he'd once explained to Ben that a particular bully happened to be a very good artist, as if that made up for the fact that he'd made Jude eat sand). That quality in Jude seemed amplified when it came to their father; it reminded Ben of how *he'd* seen Marcus in the years before Jude was born and their mother ran off. Back then, Marcus was just… a dad. Attentive, but not domineering. An authoritarian, but not a dictator. Caring.

And that quality that everyone hated got Marcus out of the fire, got Ben slammed into counseling because *of course* this all stemmed from teenage angst and upcoming graduation and repressed anger over the absence of his mother.

Marcus grunted in his sleep, turned over, exposing the nape of his neck. Ben stared at it, imagining getting a kitchen knife from the drawer and—

He shook the thought away. That was useless—more Made-for-TV-Movie garbage. As stupid as "telling an adult."

What are you going to do? the interior voice asked.

Talking hadn't helped, obviously. Any other idea Ben might've had was strictly the domain of television—not that his school therapist wouldn't have *loved* to hear about them.

And what happens after graduation? What happens when—

"Shut up," he whispered, squeezing his eyes shut, like a kid scared of the bogeyman. "Shut up, shut up, shut *up*."

And, for a wonder, the voice did.

He felt that hard lead ball of anxiety in his gut, felt the weight of hopelessness and the future settling onto his shoulders and, for the first time, became truly aware of the pressure he was under, like a deep-sea fish finally coming to realize the sheer tonnage of water surrounding him, waiting for a weak moment to crush him.

Between the pressure on his shoulders and the pressure in his gut, he was stuck in a huge vice, slowly turning, slowly tightening. He wanted to scream, just to release some of the pressure, but he was a boiler with a busted vent. No relief.

"Something will change," he breathed. "Something will give. It has to."

His father offered a throaty snore. Behind Ben, a syndicated Top 40 music program played on television. Sheryl Crow was asking, if it makes him happy, why the hell was he so sad?

He went upstairs and checked on Jude, who lay facing the window, the moonlight flickering with falling snow, reflecting off the bruise.

When he went to bed, he avoided looking at the open envelope on his desk, but the voice was there, waiting in his head: *What are you going to do after graduation?*

The scrape of metal on concrete and Jude's delighted laughter brought Ben up from a thin, scratchy sleep.

He cracked an eye open.

Eight-thirty, according to the nightstand clock.

He sat up and threw his legs over the side of the bed. The world outside his window was coated in rounded white edges of fresh snow. Marcus and Jude were at the mouth of the driveway, shoveling, their laughter coming out in white streamers from beneath thick winter caps.

Ben stood, a vein throbbing in his head. Marcus tossed a loose shovelful at Jude. Jude staggered, but kept upright, and tossed a shovelful of his own. His gloves looked comical—they were Ben's old ones, still too large for his hands.

Ben waited for the snow to sting Marcus's cold face, for it to get in his eyes, and for him take the flat of the shovel up the back of Jude's head. Instead he dropped the shovel, grabbed a handful of snow from a mound, squeezed it, and lobbed the ball at his youngest son. Jude returned the favor. Their laughter rang like church bells. Ben let out a breath he didn't know he was holding.

"It's okay," he said.

The envelope on his desk caught his eye. He stuck his English assignment—*Grendel*, by John Gardner—on top of it, got dressed, and headed downstairs.

He entered the kitchen as the back door opened, Jude and Marcus walking in.

"We thought we were gonna have to come upstairs and throw a snowball at ya!" Marcus said, rolling his shoulders free of snow. Behind him, the winter screen fogged.

"Dad said we're gonna have hot chocolate!" Jude said, grinning, stopping in front of Marcus. "Want some, Benny?"

Ben's mouth stretched into what he thought was a grin—the right side of Jude's face was dark, not as swollen as last night, but enough to make the core in his gut roll forebodingly. "Sure, bud."

Jude hunkered down to unlace his snow-caked boots.

Marcus tried moving around him, but couldn't. "You sleep okay?" he asked Ben. "Got bags under your eyes."

Ben's jaw tightened. "Not as much as I would've liked."

He wanted to scream—at Jude, at their father, at everything: *Why are you acting so fucking normal? Did last night not happen? Look at Jude's goddam face!*

"Hot chocolate will fix ya up," Marcus said, and tried to move around Jude again, but Jude was oblivious, working the soggy knot of his boots with numb fingers.

Ben saw the flicker in Marcus's eyes, the hardening in the facial muscles.

"*Move!*" Marcus grunted and shoved Jude aside. Jude stumbled, his one foot half-in-half-out of his boot, and connected with the kitchen table hard enough to shove it a few inches along. He rebounded and went to his knees, hugging his side.

"*Jesus!*" Ben cried, zipping over to Jude. He got his arm around Jude, whose face was red with trying not to cry.

Marcus clomped around them to the stove, dropping puddles of melting snow, heels squeaking over the lino. "Should've gotten outta the way," he said, but low, the fatherly tone gone. He sounded robotic. He stared at the teakettle on the stove burner like he'd never seen such a thing.

Ben got Jude standing, his feet back into his boots. "C'mon," he said. "I wanna get some air to wake me up. Walk with me."

Jude nodded numbly and Ben led him outside, snagging his own jacket off the hook by the door. He spared a hot look back at their father. Marcus was still in the same position. His eyes were squeezed closed, as if struck with a sudden pain in his head. He reminded Ben of a toy that'd run out of power.

The cold was a solid force, settling against the bare skin of Ben's face like a mask, instantly numbing. He led Jude across the backyard to the tree line, the branches thin black talons against the white sky.

They didn't speak as they made their way deeper into the woods. Jude rubbed his side and matched Ben's pace.

Ben shoved his hands into his coat pockets, trying to even his breathing, trying to slow his heart. Jesus, a flicker in the eyes and then—nothing. From that flicker, Marcus and Jude might not've just been outside, laughing and throwing snowballs. They might not've just been talking about making hot chocolate.

He looked at Jude, who was watching his feet—the soft curve of his jaw, the slight uptick of his nose. Like their mother's.

Jude, the ready-made victim, just brought out the worst in everyone.

The further they got from the house, the better Ben felt, but that pressure was still there, pushing against his shoulders, pressing him against the hard solid cannonball in his gut.

But maybe it wasn't so bad—as he watched, Jude squeezed his side once, winced, then let go and, more or less, walked normally.

"You okay?" he asked.

"Uh-huh."

They reached a small crick. During the spring, it would swell with runoff, graduating from that Pennsylvania colloquialism into a full-fledged creek, but, for now, you could walk across it without getting the tops of your boots wet. Round snow hats capped the stones. They followed it and soon the creek merged into the Buchanan River.

Ben and Jude stopped at the edge, fifteen feet above the water.

It hadn't frozen over, not yet, but Ben could see it getting there—the shorelines furry with white and reaching for the other side, the water itself a thin black eddy in the middle, threading south. Across the river, the backyards of nicer homes were spotlighted by the sun.

Ben breathed deeply, taking in the cold air, the thick peaty smell of the minerals and earth of the Buchanan.

Jude sat down on the edge, his boots dangling. "Dad makes the best snowballs. You know that? I asked him if he'd show me, but he said it was a family secret. He'd tell me when I was older." He looked up at Ben. "Did he ever show you? Will you show me?"

Ben stared down at him. In the stark blacks and whites of the outdoors, the eggplant-colored bruise on his brother's face was like the dot on an exclamation point.

"No," he said, almost mechanically. *Is that all you can talk about? Really? All? Jesus Christ.*

Pressure momentarily throbbed behind his eyes and he squeezed them closed, willing it back, unconsciously looking like their father back in the kitchen.

"I gotta take a whiz," Jude said, and turned at the waist, boosting himself. His boots slipped a bit in the snow, dropping clumps over the edge.

Ben jerked his thumb over his shoulder. "Go in the trees. No indecent exposure out here, Sonny Jim. I don't got the cash to bail you out."

Jude laughed, passing him. "You're such a dork, Benny."

Ben smiled without showing teeth. "And one day you'll be just like me."

His brother laughed again, and stepped into the trees.

Ben's thin smile disappeared. He looked across the river, but the sunlight seemed colder now, the smell of the river cloying, the air freezer-burning his skin instead of numbing it.

"Hey, shake off and let's head back," he called, thinking their father would be gone for work by the time they arrived. "I gotta hankering from some Eggo waffles."

No answer.

He stepped toward the trees. "Jude?" He listened hard, that kind of listening where you hear ringing.

Finally, he heard—faintly—a single gasp, a sweaty *pah!* sound.

Ben took another step forward. "Jude?"

Now he could hear Jude panting.

"The hell?" He entered the tree line, following his brother's breathing.

He found Jude, in a triangle of white birch, seeing first a hand clenching a trunk, and the puddle of yellow urine at the base, threaded with blood.

He entered the triangle. "What the fuck?"

Jude looked up, his face cheese-colored and sweaty, one hand on his shriveled sex, the other clenching the tree. He stared at Ben, his eyes double-zeroes of pain and fear.

"It hurts, Benny. It *burns*."

In Ben's head, Jude hit the side of the table again and again, with a neon sign flashing *kidney damage kidney damage kidney damage* between, and suddenly the vice was turning faster now, tighter.

A stray thought arced across the shocked expanse of his mind, like NBC's The More You Know comet: *He's gonna kill this kid.*

"Hey, what's this?" Jude asked.

Mid-afternoon. Marcus still at work. When they'd gotten back to the house, Ben had wrapped an icepack in a dishtowel and taped it to his brother's side.

They were in Ben's room, Ben sprawled on the bed, trying to decipher *Grendel* while Jude did little brother things, sitting at Ben's desk and rooting through Ben's stuff.

"What's what?" Ben asked, re-reading the same line for the third time. The words didn't want to stick; they were fuzzy black caterpillars that inched just outside his comprehension.

"This," Jude said and Ben heard a whisper of paper.

He looked up.

The open letter. He could see the Ohio State return address.

He was out of bed before his brain could catch up, snatching the envelope out of Jude's hands. "Gimme that."

Jude's eyes never left the envelope, his brow wrinkled.

"What is it?"

Ben looked from the envelope—he didn't need to pull the thick sheaf of papers out, had already memorized the cover letter: *Dear Mr. Sheever, After reviewing your application, we're delight to inform you*—to Jude, who stared up at him expectantly, not even put off by how Ben acted. His heart whammed within his chest harder than it should've, the air of his exhales prickly around his mouth.

He sat on the edge of his bed. "A letter." He swallowed. "I applied to Ohio State."

"Oh yeah? Did you get in?"

Ben pulled the papers from the envelope. Beginnings of financial aid and declaration of majors and meal options. Etc., etc., etc.

"Yeah."

"That's cool, Benny! You gonna tell Dad?"

Ben's head snapped up. "No! And you're not gonna, either."

Jude squinted. "But, why? This is good news, right?"

For an instant, he felt that trickle of irritation that everyone must feel around his punch-me brother.

He flushed with guilt, as immediate as the irritation and stared at the letter. The packet felt so goddamn *thick*. "Yeah. No. Maybe." He shook his head. "I have no friggin idea. But until I do, keep your mouth shut, all right? To everyone—*especially* Dad."

"But Benny—"

"*No*," Ben hissed. "Okay? Just *no*."

Jude studied him a moment. All Ben could see was the goddamned bruise, highlighted by the light through the window.

Finally, his brother said, "Okay. Wanna go watch a movie, or something?"

"Sure," Ben said and Jude bounded out of the room.

Ben folded the papers and slid them back into the envelope. His hands shook. The muscles in his upper arms and shoulders jittered, over-taxed with adrenaline from a fight that didn't exist.

What are you going to do after graduation? the interior voice asked, and Ben didn't have an answer.

The snow continued to fall. The temperature continued to drop.

Ben hadn't noticed it immediately, but Jude finding the Ohio State letter had started a clock in his head. It pervaded his thinking. It kept him up until the late-late hours, when he would finally escape into a thin, unrestful sleep.

He found himself unable to *not* be in the same room with Marcus and Jude, but didn't know what to do once he was in there. The movies and primetime sitcoms were beyond his comprehension. He was constantly one-sentence behind whatever conversation Jude and Marcus might be having.

Even when the bruise on Jude's face faded, even when he stopped pissing blood, Ben saw the bruises still to come, the blood still to flow.

When he'd opened his mouth back in September, when he'd seen how the game was going to go and finally found the courage to *call* it, Marcus had settled, had stopped the irrevocable train of building tension and intensifying violence. Ben felt, for the first time in years, hope.

But that was gone now. The night beginning school break, the morning after—those events had obliterated them in a way dismissal from the counselors, the requirement of therapy, the *closing* of Jude's file, couldn't. It showed that the autumn hadn't been the end of something monstrous, but only a brief respite before...

...before what?

Well, that was what Ben was afraid of, wasn't it?

Christmas passed in a blur, although Jude and their father seemed to enjoy it. On Christmas night, a storm blew in hard, burying the town under nearly two feet of snow. Marcus was called in to assist Public Works and Ben and Jude huddled on the living room couch, watching movies and listening to the snow hit the windowpane like handfuls of spackle. Sometime in the third act of *Jumanji*, Jude fell asleep, leaving Ben with the sound of snow and Kristen Dunst asking her movie brother, "What do you think's gonna happen to you if you don't start talking?"

Try it, sis, Ben thought, settling in to give Jude as much room on the couch as possible. *It ain't as easy as it seems.*

Two days after Christmas, the temperatures shot into the giddy thirties, leaving a world dazzled with sun and filled with the drip-drip-dripping of snow.

Ben left Jude alone—when their father was still at work, of course—and traipsed to the Buchanan River, the snow high enough, and his boots old enough, for some to get down his socks, soaking his feet.

The river had finally frozen over. Their dad had said as such, complaining about the kids who would try to skate on it or walk across it.

"Kids have no idea," Marcus said one night over a dinner of Stouffer's lasagna. None of the Sheever men were decent cooks. "They never think that one wrong step onto a weak patch of ice, into that water…" He shook his head. "It only takes an instant to regret a lifetime." Marcus paused, as if startled by what he'd said.

Now, Ben looked south and saw tiny pinpricks of black and blue, moving slowly under the Route 67 Bridge. They were probably egging each other on, seeing who would go the furthest out.

Ben watched them, then the ice. It *did* look thick enough, but there were troubling dark spots, particularly toward the center, where the thaw had begun its work. What would one of those kids do if his foot suddenly plunged into the near-zero water below?

Ben knew—fall and get swept away by the current, dead from hypothermia or drowning too quickly to be saved, their bodies finally getting stuck against some fallen tree in Butler County.

Ben was more interested in the other kids—what would *they* do, particularly if they'd been the ones egging the dead kid on? How would they live with that?

Ben shivered in a way that had nothing to do with the cold. All his thoughts cycled back to Jude. Jude was the kid whose foot went through the ice; the kid who, when that center of gravity was lost, could count the remainder of his life in minutes and seconds instead of decades and years.

"The kid without hope left," Ben breathed.

Who was the one, metaphorically, egging the kid on? Marcus with his whip-crack snaps of temper? Was it him, Ben, for failing to pull Jude back from the black spot back in September? (Was the ice a metaphor for the school district? The bullies and thugs of McMillian Elementary? Was the ice their father, if Ben was the kid egging Jude on?)

He shook his head. He wasn't good with figurative language—he could barely understand *Grendel* and its gray definitions of evil. That had been his mother's game. When Jude was older, Ben had no doubt his brother would excel in English for the same reason.

Provided he lives that long, the internal voice murmured.

He started for home, feeling colder than the day could take credit for.

The sound of the front door swinging open and bouncing against the wall shook the house, startling Ben, upstairs and trying to dope out *Grendel.*

"What the *Christ*—" he heard Marcus say downstairs, then heard Jude moan, his voice slushy, "*Daddy*—" and the rest was lost in the sudden tumble of heavy bodies.

Ben vaunted off the bed and into the upstairs hallway. His socked feet slipped over the hardwood as he rounded to the stairs. He grabbed the newel post in order to keep from falling against the wall, looked down, and froze.

Marcus appeared to be all back and shoulders down in the foyer, hunkered over Jude, Jude's snow-suited legs kicking. The two of them bounced between the walls, the stairs, the archway to the living room—drunken pinballs gaining momentum instead of losing it. Ben saw blood fly.

Marcus braced his legs. "*Goddammit, hold STILL*—"

And something clicked in the front of Ben's head. *He's going to kill this kid.*

His brain was a half-step behind his body as it leaped down the steps. He heard a tea-kettle scream and dimly realized it was himself. Marcus had time to look up, his mouth an *O* of surprise, revealing Jude's pale, bloodied, and *very*-bruised face, and then Ben landed into the bigger man, driving him off Jude.

Marcus rolled with him, sending him into the front door. The doorknob drove into his spine, a vicious joybuzzer of pain.

Marcus untangled himself, his face red and sweating. "What the *fuck*—"

"*Bastard!*" Ben shrieked and leapt over Jude, taking Marcus around the waist and driving him down the hallway. He heard glass break. He heard Jude scream. He smelled the hot, wet musk of the two of them, bitter and pungent.

He clawed up Marcus's body and slammed his fist into Marcus's face, driving lips against teeth. The pain in his knuckles was stupendous and oh-so satisfactory. It felt good to stop worrying. It felt good to *do* something and know he *could* do it. *Talking* hadn't worked; *this* would.

He punched Marcus with his other hand, sending Marcus's nose to the left. A third shot shut Marcus's left eye. A fourth snapped a tooth—Ben felt it give.

And then Jude was on him, arms around his neck, pulling him back, yelling in his ear.

"*Stop it, Benny! He didn't do it! Stop it! That's DADDY!*"

Don't you fucking GET IT? Ben thought, but didn't scream, *couldn't* scream. He'd finally found the anger that everyone else seemed to have for his kid brother. No, Jude *didn't* get it. Jude *didn't* know when to let up and let go and move away. Jude would *never get it*. Jude was the punch-me, ready-victim, bull's-eye. Jude would put his foot through the thin ice because that, in a way, was what Jude was made to do.

And Ben couldn't do anything about it.

Ben shoved Jude as hard as he could. Jude crashed against the stairway wall, eyes momentarily ringing double-zeroes when his head connected, and that was when Ben saw that Jude's face wasn't as bruised as he'd thought.

Someone had written FAG across Jude's forehead with black Sharpie.

Ben froze. He saw it all—Jude asking him to come play, Ben begging off because he had holiday homework. He saw Jude running into other kids. He saw Jude trying to engage them in his Jude way and it...not...going well.

All because Ben hadn't been there.

He saw Jude stumbling home when the other kids were done with him, Marcus's startled reaction, which looked like anger.

This was where Ben came in.

He stumbled off their father, toward his brother, all emotion a hard, wet, phlegmy knot through his chest and throat.

"Jude—"

And Jude flinched.

Ben blinked. He looked from Jude, cowering against the wall, to Marcus, groggily sitting up while holding his head.

The knot expanded and expanded, choking him, filling his lungs. The cannonball in his gut gained weight, the pressure on his shoulders pushed down. He heard the ticking in his head, louder than ever, and if he could just scream—just *scream*—he could shut it down, cut the knot, shove off the cannonball and the pressure.

But he couldn't.

He couldn't.

Ben didn't go home that night.

He followed Shenandoah Avenue until it became Route 67 North, exiting town, then turned and headed south. He walked up Gaines Street Hill, taking in all the shops and markets with their winter hours. He walked until his feet were cold blocks of meat, and his skin felt similar to the cool hardness of marble. He hadn't bothered switching from sneakers to boots, or trading his torn flannel overshirt for a jacket when he'd left—*escaped* might be a more fitting word.

His brain was a television tuned to an out-of-range station, all static and sporadic ghost-voices.

He thought of Jude. Jude with his bruises and blood. Jude with the word FAG written on his head. Jude telling him that it wasn't Daddy and to stop it, stop it, *STOP IT.*

Jude flinching.

When he finally returned home, the sky was beginning its hesitant lighting of dawn. He stood outside Jude's room. Jude's back was to Ben, but that was all right; Ben didn't think he could handle seeing how those other kids had treated his little brother's face.

Like a bull's-eye, the interior voice murmured.

He studied the line of his brother's back through the blankets, the tuft of hair—the same shade as their mother's—poking out from the top.

I can't protect him, he thought and the internal voice offered no dissent on that score.

He closed Jude's door softly, wincing at the minute squeak of wood-on-wood as it latched, then padded down to his bedroom.

The Ohio State envelope snatched his gaze.

Without thinking—to think would be to hesitate—he took it and sat at his desk, clicking on the lamp. Working quickly, he filled in as much of the information as he could, skipping the parts he would need to look up or ask about—which wasn't all that much, he discovered.

When he finished, he slid the paperwork back in the envelope, clicked off the light, and climbed into bed, still clothed. He thought he'd lie there, unable to sleep, his mind still tuned to that just-out-of-reach channel. But he dropped off almost immediately as, outside, it began to snow.

A creak of floorboards and then Jude's voice, that hesitant are-you-awake tone: "Benny?"

Ben opened his eyes and rolled over. Jude stood in the hall, just outside the doorway, as if it was a border he couldn't cross. He was already dressed, his face still gleaming from just being washed. He'd gotten most of the Sharpie off, leaving the ghost of a gray smear.

Ben sat up. "Hey, bud."

They stared at each other, Jude still visibly wary and Ben unable to find the words to the things he needed to say. His eyes kept getting drawn to the smear. Other kids did that. Not their father. Ben had forgotten—the evils of the world weren't contained within one imperfect man and his lack of closure over a dead marriage.

"Where's Dad?" he asked finally.

"At work."

Ben winced. "How..."

Jude grinned. "He was talking about that at breakfast. Said he was gonna say he ran into the basement door."

Ben thought of what he'd done, and his mouth slipped free: "What's he gonna say when someone asks how many times?"

Jude laughed, a tinkling sound, but there was a flash in his eyes, like a brief sunburst over chrome, and Ben knew he'd just remembered *how* Marcus had ended up like that. He'd briefly forgotten, but now it was back.

"Whatcha need, bud?" Ben asked.

"Wondered if you wanted to go for a walk," Jude said, then added, "In the woods, I mean. Go to the crick."

Avoid other kids, you mean, Ben thought. "Okay—still coffee downstairs?"

"Uh-huh."

Ben swung his legs over the side.

"Pour me a cup, will ya? I wanna change."

Jude eyed the fact that Ben was still wearing the clothes from yesterday, then nodded.

As he started out, Ben called him back.

Ben made his mouth work. "I'm sorry, Jude. I mean it."

Jude grinned again, the sunburst-chrome glaze of wariness banished from his eyes. The grin was awful—it seemed to make the smear darker, his skin paler.

"S'okay, Benny. I know you were just trying to help."

Ben nodded and Jude left.

He changed out of his clothes, which felt twisted and ill-fitting after sleeping in them. As he was shoving the wad of old ones into his hamper, he noticed the blood for the first time.

He dropped his jeans and flannel and shook out his gray tee.

Three dots, like wavering ellipsis, near the collar.

He stared off, thinking of breaking his father's nose, breaking a tooth, as Jude screamed behind them. Maybe that was what Jude was staring at. He heard the ticking in his head.

He dumped the shirt into the trash, then looked across the room at the bulging Ohio State letter.

What are you going to do after graduation? It wasn't the internal voice now, though, but a memory of a voice.

Then he thought, *I'm doing this kid no good*, and the internal voice murmured, *He's doing you no good, either.*

The air was crisp in his lungs, shockingly so, but Ben's head still felt addled. He moved through the snow like a drunk, struggling to maintain balance over the uneven ground. The snow was thick and wet underfoot.

Jude walked a little ahead of him, his movements confident, as if their roles were reversed—Ben the one beaten to hell the day before, and Jude the over-worrying brother.

They reached the creek. The post-Christmas thaw had raised the water level and its intensity.

"They were playing outside," Jude said after a moment. Ben turned to him, but Jude was staring at the water, his snow gloves shoved into the pockets of his winter coat. "With skateboards. Too cold for skating, but one of them had these cool metallic markers and they were all coloring and talking about what they were gonna do with the boards once the snow melted."

Ben opened his mouth, then shut it again.

"They were older," Jude went on, "but not *that* much older. Like, fifth graders. I didn't know 'em, but I don't know a lot of people. I thought they'd be nice."

He looked up and Ben recoiled. Jude's eyes were fiery and desperate and confused. The smear on his forehead, partially covered by the hood of his winter coat, looked like the ash marks Catholics sometimes put on.

"Why weren't they nice, Benny?" Jude asked. "I just wanted to *talk* to them. I thought they were *cool*. They called me 'babyfag.' Real fast, like that. 'Babyfag, babyfag.' The whole time. They tackled me when I tried to run." His lips peeled back from his grinding teeth— at the moment, looking exactly like Ben had when Ben had finally taken after their father, although Ben didn't know that.

Ben cleared his throat. "I...I don't know, Jude."

Jude turned back to the water. "People are dogshit, Benny. They're mean. I just wanna be nice to them, the way Mom said I should. That's the only thing I remember about her—'Be nice to people, Jude'—and I don't even know why she said that."

Ben did, but he didn't say. Jude wouldn't remember—Ben was surprised Jude remembered *anything* about their mother—but their mother was the epitome of nice. To everyone. Every door-to-door salesman and Jehovah's Witness was welcomed in and given coffee or water, sometimes snacks. She baked things if anyone was sick on their street, regardless of who they were. It used to drive Marcus bugshit, Ben remembered.

And then their mother was nice to that fine young undergraduate, and they went off to be nice to other people elsewhere.

"But I can't *stop* being nice," Jude said now. "Even if I wanted to, I can't. It's like I think, 'This time it'll be different' because there's a lot of *good* in people."

Jude started walking along the water, close enough for snow to fall into the water. Ben followed, feeling more addled than ever.

They came out of the trees to stand at the edge of the Buchanan River. The thaw had done its work here; Ben saw more of those ominous dark spots of thinning. A thread of river water worked its way down the center, like a black stitch.

Jude sat down along the edge. "I think you should tell Dad about college." He looked across the river, at all the homes where the mothers didn't fuck men too young to buy beer, and the fathers didn't beat their youngest because the youngest reminded them of the mothers, and the eldest didn't carry it all around like an albatross, unable to stop it all from continuing. "I think you're wrong, Benny. I think he'd be proud of you. It'd make him happy."

Ben thought of Marcus, face bloodied, nose broken, one eye punched shut. "Jude—"

Jude looked up at him. The fieriness was gone, replaced by a kind of resignation too old for such a young face. "That's what kids do—they grow up and go to college. They *do* something, Benny.

They don't hang around forever. It's your turn. In a few years, it'll be mine. And Dad will be *happy*."

He turned back to the river. "And you'll tell me about college, and it'll be nice, and when I go, it'll be nice, too. No one will punch me because I asked them if they wanted to play on the jungle-gym. No one will call me a babyfag."

No one will nearly pull your arm out of the socket because you're holding their beer, Ben thought, but of course didn't say.

Jude was looking at him again. "You can't stay here forever, Benny."

It felt as if he'd sidestepped into a parallel dimension—*You are entering the Twilight Zone*—where Ben made adult decisions about his life and Jude was self-aware of the situation he was in.

"I'll think about it, Jude," he said finally.

Jude nodded, and turned back to the river.

A breeze came up from the water and Ben shivered. "Hey, let's head back. I'm still not awake enough for this. Let me get another cup of coffee—or six—and we'll go do something."

For a moment, Jude said nothing. Then he said, "Okay," and turned at the waist to boost himself up.

And his boot slipped against the packed, wet snow, over the edge, followed by his opposite knee.

An almost comical look of surprise swept Jude's face—not fear, not that quickly—and then he was going, his waist already over the side, his gloved hands scrambling along the wet snow and not catching purchase. He didn't even have time to scream.

Neither did Ben. His body was a spring uncoiling—leaping across the distance, chest slamming into the cold-cold-cold ground, shoving the air out of his chest, as he snagged one of Jude's gloves. He immediately felt the yank against his shoulder—fire against the snow—as he took on Jude's full weight.

And felt the fading solidness within Jude's glove as Jude's hand started slipping out.

"*BENNY!*" Jude screamed, flailing, kicking at the side of the overhang, his other hand whipping around, and Ben wanted to yell at him to hold still, to *reach* with his other hand, but he couldn't, his lungs were empty, hollow chambers, convulsing, trying to force air in. He whooped in wet snow and it burned.

His eyes locked on Jude's. They were empty of anything but terror, deer-in-the-headlights, animal-in-the-trap-hearing-the-hunter-approach fear, but they were also *aware*; Jude knew exactly what was happening to him. Jude's eyes saw all, blazing out of a pale face bruised and marked with faded marker, nailing Ben in place. They were the eyes of someone who could count the remainder of his life in minutes and seconds instead of decades and years.

Jude's hand slipped from the glove. Ben lunged forward, grabbing with his other hand—

—and missed.

Jude didn't have time to scream before hitting the ice.

Ben yanked himself forward to look over, and already the current, swollen with the previous thaw, had pulled Jude from the edge, dragging him and the broken ice chunks to the center, bobbing up. He watched Jude's arms fly, hands scrabbling to grab a chunk of ice, *any* chunk of ice. In a blink, he was in the center of the river. In another, he was fifty yards off.

Ben tried screaming, but there was no air. His brain yammered at the edges of total mental static roar: *CALL 911 CALL 911 CALL 911*—

Jude was a hundred yards away.

He was no longer flailing.

Ben couldn't move; his muscles twitched with the residue of adrenaline and nothing more. His brain, addled before, had switched off entirely, overloaded. There was a spark, deep in the back of his mind, slowly growing brighter.

The pressure on Ben's shoulders pushed him into the ground. The knot in his throat expanded.

Images came to him, riffling snapshots of memory: Jude trying not to cry after some assault—it could've been the night of holiday break, the morning after, or any other time.

Another image: Jude's eyes ringing double-zeroes when Ben shoved him away.

Imagining the bruises still to come, the blood still to flow, whenever he looked at Jude's punch-me face.

Thinking often, *I can't protect him.*

Thinking, *He's not going to make it.*

Remembering his father: *It only takes an instant to regret a lifetime.*

Jude's body was a speck, bobbing languidly down by the Route 67 bridge. Still Ben's brain yammered on, *CALL 911 CALL 911*— even as he knew in his gut it was useless.

Two final images, and the spark in the back of his mind grew, blossomed into horrible burning life:

The Ohio State packet, all filled out, on Ben's desk, waiting to be mailed.

Jude's eyes, terrified and *aware*, looking up at Ben as his hand slipped from the glove.

And the spark spoke: *You don't have to worry about him, now.*

The clock in his head stopped ticking.

The knot was gone from Ben's throat and he sucked in a lungful of freezing air.

The pressure lifted from his shoulders, replaced by the most crushing guilt Ben had ever felt, a guilt like nothing he'd ever experienced, a guilt that couldn't compare with his feelings of never been able to protect Jude *enough*, of being there *enough*.

Because Jude wouldn't need protecting *now*.

Jude wasn't there *now*.

And Ben Sheever, finally, screamed.

Eventually, one of the residents across the river called the police. Eventually, the police—Marcus, to be specific—found Ben, still screaming, his voice a ragged, ruined croak.

And, eventually, they found Jude.

REFLECTING
THE HEART'S DESIRE

ON THE SUBCONSCIOUS LEVEL, where the lies we tell ourselves wither and die, an alarm sounded as Janine lifted the lightning-bolt jag of reflective glass.

Staring into its oddly-reflective face, she thought, *I've never seen something so beautiful.* Gone was the exhaustion from the day. Gone was the disillusionment that had begun to creep in as she walked through the destroyed town. Gone even was her awareness that she stood in the annihilated front room of a shop on Main Street.

The jag was maybe eight inches long, five inches at its widest point, and not very thick. Its edges shimmered, reminding her of the greasy rainbows oil puddles got after a rain, the colors bending this way and that with the turn of her hand.

(bends o'the rainbow)

The reflection of her dirty face was ghostly, warped. She could just see the palm of her holding hand behind it.

(an old mirror? a piece of window?)

She turned the jag this way and that, like a buyer checking an antique. The jag brightened and—

A bulldozer roared to life outside. She jumped and her hand clenched, the glass edges slicing her palm.

"Dammit!" Two diagonal slashes cut across her love- and life-line. Blood pooled.

She set the jag down on the counter and wiped her hand against her pantleg, wincing at the pain. She felt like she'd been here much longer than she'd intended. She wanted to get back to camp and get out of these clothes.

She stepped outside. A cool early-summer breeze lifted her sweaty hair from her temples. She hadn't realized it, but the shop had smelled musty, stale, as if it'd been closed up. Hard to do when the show window was busted and the door was MIA.

She looked up Main Street. The road was jagged, pockmarked with holes or piles of rubble. The shops were burnt shells or pancaked rubble.

She glanced behind her, at the glass jag. From here, the edges were a bluish-black and something about that made her shiver.

"Hey, Janine!" Darlene called from up the street. "You get lost?"

Janine turned. "I was *trying!*" she called and ran to catch up with the others.

Camp was a series of yellow tents and trailers in the former football field of a flattened high school. There, the two hundred or so volunteers, government officials, and humanitarian groups lived for a month before they were switched out for fresher fish.

Janine emerged from the shower trailer, shouldering a canvas book bag, as the sun went down and the Klieg perimeter lights clicked on, creating a night-baseball look. She moved through the idling crowds, nodding occasionally but not inviting conversation.

She went to the rock outcropping just beyond the end zone, the goalpost laying on its side as if it had gone to sleep. From here, she had a vista view of the people. Not many talked loudly or got up a game of anything. Everyone was too damn tired, maybe rethinking joining the reconstruction project in lieu of the Modern Cultures and Urban Renewal courses, maybe wondering why they bothered in the first place. Beyond the Klieg lights, they were surrounded by a ghost town.

Tonight, as the moon touched down on what this small Midwestern town had become, there would be silence, and silence, and silence. Before an F5 tornado touched down six months ago, the town had boasted a viable population of over ten thousand. After the tornado, officials had pulled only five hundred survivors from the wreckage

The other ninety-five hundred? Not a trace. The town was a landlocked *Mary Celeste* in a sea of cornfields. Whatever mysteries it held continued. There would be no resolutions.

And, yet, here they all were—a hodge-podge mix of volunteers, humanitarian programs, and government agencies—and, suddenly, Janine couldn't understand why.

She pulled her Sociology text from her backpack, but, in spite of the fact she was carrying eighteen credits come fall, her mind wandered. She thought of the jag of glass. What had it been a part of? What had that shop been—before? The disaster had obliterated all traces of its past.

What about its light? she thought. *It* twinkled *at me.*

But that was simple. The sun—

The sun was at my back. Couldn't've. And what about when I turned it, how it'd seemed to brighten—

She shook her head. Soon, she'd believe not only had the shard *called* to her—from its odd place on the counter, mind—but that it was *magical.*

Well, friends and neighbors, she thought, repositioning the book on her lap, *I hate to disappoint, but Maggie Laughlin's little girl stopped believing in fantasy about when I lost my first baby tooth. In fact—*

Darlene said, "You're thinking about it, too, aren't ya?"

Janine jumped and turned. Darlene stood there, her black hair in a perfectly-made French braid, her designer work clothes glowing in the darkness between lights. She could've stepped out of a catalogue.

"Thinking about what?" she asked.

Darlene sat down next to her. "The bodies. Or, lack there-of." She pointed to a knot of older people across the field, conspicuous, even with distance, by how straight their backs were. "That's why *they're* here."

"FEMA and the CDC," Janine said. "They think there are still bodies to be found."

"They're getting nervous."

"Why?"

Darlene gestured at the crowd. "Because this thing has been up and running for over three months now, and not a single new body's been found. Everyone's been steeling themselves about unearthing one, but nothing's there and there *should* be."

Janine followed Darlene's gaze and saw Dale, taller than the group of Area Managers, talking, gesturing with his hands in the old familiar ways. He'd been here the longest of the college kids, and the days in the sun had hardened his skin beyond what Janine remembered, lightened his brown hair to a sandy blonde.

"He's found his niche," Darlene said, her dark eyes bright, as if with secret amusement.

Janine nodded. "Yeah, probably," she said, and turned back to her sociology book. The words weren't even in English.

"You're holding up, aren't you?" Darlene asked. "I mean, you told me it was amicable."

Janine stared at the pages of her text. "It was. You said it—he belongs here. Me, it keeps me out of Dr. Kamen's courses."

"He's *good* here," Darlene said, as if Janine had contradicted her.

(why are you so concerned?)

A beat of silence, and then Darlene said, "They're saying we'll be done clearing the south side in two weeks," she said. "We might get the town back on a paying basis, after all."

For who? Janine thought. *The ghosts?*

All of a sudden, having her best friend here was the last thing she wanted. "Awesome," she said.

Darlene shifted off the rock. "I'm headed over to the Canteen. You want anything?"

"No, I'm good—thanks."

Darlene left. Janine stared at her book.

Canteen was Dale's word.

This is foolishness, she thought.

She looked up in time to see Darlene pass Dale and the group of Area Directors.

They exchanged friendly waves.

It's a dream and she knows *it's a dream, but it feels like the dream stands on a foundation of* fact, *like something half-remembered.*

She stands in front of the shop, which has been restored to its former glory. ANTIQUES *&* ODDITIES *is lettered in an arch across the window. Silver dishes,* *glassware, a steel toy car, and a jar with an embalmed frog rest on the front display.*

The soft lighting of the interior makes the glass glow and she's sure that this is the rest of her *glass, her jag.*

But the jag reflected, *she thinks. It doesn't matter. The glass is magical.*

Footsteps behind her and she turns. Main Street has widened, become an eight-lane freeway. She can see the shops as they'd once been on the other side.

Parading down Main are legions of people, dwindling away to points to her left and right, even though Main is not *that long. Their eyes are blank, their faces slack. These are the missing citizens. They emanate a soft pale blue aura, merging together and becoming darker, almost black.*

These people slipped through the edge, *a woman's voice says from behind her, the voice of the glass.*

In the parade, she sees Darlene and Dale. They're holding hands. Janine feels a languid sort of anger. Hadn't she known? Hadn't she suspected?

They'll slip through, too, eventually, *the woman says.* Everyone does.

A hand, long elegant fingers with midnight black nail polish, comes around beside her, holding her *jag of glass, offering it.*

It's just a matter of when, *the woman says.* And *when* is up to you.

The bulldozers and crews, the picks and shovels, were already hard at work when Janine stepped into the shop, but those sounds were distant, unimportant. What mattered was the crunching sound of her footsteps, the stale scent of old dust.

She looked at the burnt wallpaper, the twisted metal, and sheared wood, seeing it as it once was. *On the left hung the old mirrors and paintings. In the middle was the placard reading* CAVEAT EMPTOR.

She couldn't know that, *didn't* know that. *The dream,* she thought.

"None of it was *real.*" Her fists clenched and she squeezed her eyes shut. *You have too much to do to be acting like some weak-sister in a bad fantasy! What the hell's the matter with you?*

She opened her eyes and took a deep breath. That *wasn't* stale, old dust she was breathing—it was waterlogged wood and plaster. She *didn't* know what this shop was like before the catastrophe. This had gone goddamn long enough.

She rolled her shoulders, feeling a little better—or at least tell-ing herself she did. "I'm Janine Laughlin and I stopped believing in fantasy when I lost my first baby tooth. I'm a sociology major with a minor in group psychology. What's *really* going on here is that I'm tired—more tired than I thought possible—and stressed. *That's it.*"

(what about the glass?)

The voice belonged to the woman from the dream, because of course it did.

She crashed her fists against her thighs. *"Goddammit!"* She spun toward the counter. "This glass is *nothing!* It's just *glass!* That's—"

Her words clipped off as she picked up the jag and a surge... not *power*, but *something*... shot up her arm.

Life! she couldn't help thinking. *It's alive!*

The edges cut into her palm, reopening the old wounds, but the pain was minute, barely there, even as blood began to drip to the dusty floor in fat droplets. She looked into the glass and saw her reflection—the wide eyes, the O of her mouth.

A shimmer cut across the surface, creating that greasy rainbow, and the jag brightened in its core.

"Oh my God," Janine breathed.

She did not see her hand through the glass. Instead, she saw the shop's counter as it was before: the painstakingly-polished wood top, the old-fashioned register, the little dish of business cards. The silk wallpaper beyond.

She turned the glass, getting a panning view of the store, complete with paintings and mirrors and the CAVEAT EMPTOR plaque. She faced the front and saw the front display restored, along with Main Street.

The firehouse had both garage bays open and the cherry-red trucks parked half-in and half-out like dogs. Cars were parked at a slant in front of the businesses. People walked the sidewalks.

The glass shimmered again. When it resolved, it was the same view as before, but *different*. Something so minor—yet so fundamen-tal—had changed. It took a moment for it to click in her head.

The cars.

The Hyundai Elantra was still the same, but the Oldsmobile next to it was gone, replaced by a sporty two-door. The emblem was unfamiliar on the hood. Along the door, she read TAKURI SPIRIT. She'd never heard of that brand before.

Another shimmer, and the destruction was back on Main Street. The sky was overcast. The view reminded her of photos from the Dresden bombing raids.

There are other worlds, the woman whispered in Janine's head. *World's an angel's breath away from this one, with an angel's breath of difference.*

How? she managed to think, and then all thought was wiped away as her and Dale entered the view.

They were holding hands, talking animatedly as they traversed the destruction of Main Street, both in their work clothes. Love among the ruins.

Janine squeezed her eyes shut, her hand bearing down on the glass. *Not all lost,* the woman whispered. *All within reach. If you reach for it.*

The pain of her grip cut through her and her eyes opened, looking down, and saw her hand was slathered with blood. A thin puddle of it lay between her work boots. She squeezed again and pain burned through her blood-stained palm. She relished it—it solidified the world around her.

"What's *happening* to me?" she whispered.

She looked at the shard, at its blue-black edging that disturbed her, at its blameless surface which could shimmer any old time it wanted—

She stiffened, looking at her bloody hand, then at the glass.

The glass was perfect, not a drop of blood on it, even though it had to've been *swimming.*

Is it…impervious to me? she thought slowly, each word a struggle.

That was one option. The other was much worse.

The glass *absorbed* her blood. It *fed* on her.

She broke and bolted from the shop.

⟋⟍···⟋⟍

"Where were you today?" Darlene asked and Janine jumped in her place on the rock outcropping, spilling her abnormal psychology text and notebook to the ground.

"Sorry!" Darlene said and bent down to help.

Janine snatched up her materials. "S'okay—you startled me."

Darlene sat down next to Janine. "I noticed."

Tonight might've been a replay of last night—Janine sitting away from the chattering crowds of professionals and volunteers, Darlene next to her.

In Janine's head, two voices argued incessantly.

I saw those things today, one said.

No, I didn't, the other countered. *I'm just stressed.*

Darlene cleared her throat. "So, anyway, where were—"

"With the crew on Market and Main," Janine said. Darlene looked at her—Janine hadn't gone anywhere near Market Avenue, and Darlene might know that—and asked slowly, "Anything wrong? You seem...jumpy."

"Just tired and overworked," Janine said. She thumped the text-book. "Trying to get some work done."

"Oh," Darlene said and slid off the rock. "Oh. Okay." She looked uncertainly at Janine. "But you'll talk to me if something *is* wrong, right?"

Janine offered her own smile. It felt like steel forks were hiking her lips. "When something *is* wrong, you'll be the first to know."

Darlene nodded. "Okay, kid." She moved into the crowds.

I saw other worlds! the first voice shouted.

No I didn't! the second one yelled back.

Janine watched Darlene pass Dale—again surrounded by the Area Directors, again gesturing—and put her hand on Dale's fore-arm. It was a quick movement, a gesture of familiar hello, and Dale turned toward Darlene, beaming.

Janine snapped the pencil between her fingers.

Back in front of the shop the next morning, too early to hear anything but the call of birds. The past night was full of broken sleep, and her eyes stared out of exhausted hollows.

I can't take this, she thought. "I have to settle it now. Put the fantasy away and see the reality—whatever it is." She wasn't aware she'd spoken aloud.

She stepped into the shop and breathed the stale air. Goose-pimples broke out along her forearms.

At the corner of Welston and Main Street, a figure appeared. Darlene.

She moved around the rubble of Main, trying to avoid crunching over broken glass, her eyes glued to the dilapidated building. On her face was an expression of worry.

Something was missing, an intangible feeling in the air. An emptiness.

She went to the glass on the counter, disappointment weighing on her heart. It was *wrong* here, she thought. Whatever had been here before had departed.

She picked the jag up and felt nothing.

It was a hunk of glass. No shimmer, no disquieting blue-black of the edges, no visions. A broken artifact of an unimportant time.

Did she see *old* blood on the jag's back? She thought she did.

Her eyes watered. She sat on the floor to keep from falling.

"I imagined it," she said, her voice phlegmy. "I imagined it all."

And someone who imagined such things was…

"Insane," she said. "Someone who imagines such things is insane."

A hallucination, a breakdown. The stress of this project, the stress of schooling, the stress of breaking up with Dale—oh yes, we said it was amicable and we might've even believed it, but let's call a spade a spade, it *had* been stressful, it *had* hurt—it was all *crushing* her and she just never got a *break*—

Her crying went on for a few moments. By the end, she *did* feel a little better. Yes, it still hurt—finding out you were hallucinating didn't feel *good*—but she felt cleansed.

She took a deep breath.

"Okay, okay. I got this. I can handle it."

She needed a break. She needed to leave the project, go back to campus—no, *home*; she needed to go *home*. She'd have to take her Modern Cultures and Urban Renewal courses, might even have to push graduating back, but did that matter?

This was her *mind*.

When you starting seeing other dimensions through a piece of glass—

"It's just gotta stop," she said. "It's just gotta stop."

She sighed and looked down at the glass.

It shimmered, making her reflection ripple.

She snapped her eyes closed. *I didn't just see that.*

She counted to ten and, warily, she opened her eyes.

The glass continued to shimmer. Through it, she saw the clean and maintained service counter.

"Oh no," she moaned. "Oh no, not this. If it's not real, not this."

Who said I'm not real? the woman whispered.

And as the glass brightened in her hand, Janine fell in.

The expression on her face was very much one of relief.

Darlene jerked when Janine drop out of sight. It looked like Janine had plummeted through a trap door.

Of course she didn't, she thought. *See her head?*

She did—but only by standing straight and leaning over the jumble of broken concrete she hid behind. If Janine were to look up—

But Janine didn't. She sat on the filthy floor, staring raptly at the glass she held in her hands.

Oh, babydoll, she thought, *what's going on with you?*

She'd watched Janine talk to herself, then cry, then become fixated on the glass in her hand. Janine, who always stacked the deck against herself and took a grim sort of satisfaction out of achieving whatever goal she'd made, was almost unrecognizable to Darlene now. She hadn't been eating or socializing, and for the past few days had looked like she was sleepwalking. She hadn't shown up for work yesterday, but only Darlene and Dale had noticed.

214

And then she'd come here. Darlene guessed she'd also visited this hovel yesterday.

She didn't *want* to interfere—doing so might crack the fragile shell Janine had—but she didn't know how much longer she could stand by the sidelines.

The woman—*The glass woman,* Janine thought—stood before her and that was because Janine wasn't simply *looking* through the jag. Like Alice with the looking-glass, she'd *gone* through.

The shopkeeper was all curves and angles, a cartoon of the perfect hourglass-figure female. Her clothes were so black Janine couldn't see if she wore a dress, shirt and pants, or something entirely different. Her skin was the color of milk. Her face was thin, but not narrow—the nose a blade, the lips full and red, the eyes almond-shaped (it didn't occur to Janine that the woman had her features, only exaggerated). Her midnight-black pixie haircut hung like velvet curtains, framing her face.

This isn't real, Janine thought. *I'm hallucinating.*

"Oh, it's real," the woman said. "Don't you see that?"

Janine looked around and had to admit it certainly *felt* real. She could feel the slight heat from the recessed lights. She could smell the wood polish. She saw the paintings and the CAVEAT EMPTOR placard, the lettering done in blood red.

She looked toward the display window—unbroken and missing no pieces—and saw only black swirling with blue. She turned to the woman, confused.

"We're between places—between worlds."

Janine looked down at the jag of glass, frozen in mid-shimmer, but she could see her hand through it. She saw no wounds, however, no blood. She held up the glass. "How...how does this work?"

"That's a piece of my display window."

"I *saw* things," Janine persisted.

"My glass has always been a window into my customer's deepest wishes. The things they simply, when they know they *can* have it, cannot live without."

"I saw different worlds!" Janine yelled at her.

The woman's eyes twinkled. "Some of the items desired aren't necessarily tangible." She smiled, her full red lips peeling back to reveal sharp, white teeth. "But, for the right price, always accessible."

Janine looked down at the glass again. The disquieting blue-black edges seemed more prevalent over here. "What could I want from multiple worlds?"

The woman shrugged. "Depends, Janine. It was giving you options, like any good salesperson. *Which* world caught your eye?"

Before Janine's mind formed the image of her and Dale, the woman nodded and said, "Yes. *That* was a good option, wasn't it?"

She waved her hand at the display window. The desolate Main Street winked into place, with her and Dale walking along the opposite sidewalk.

Her breath caught in her throat. Her feet were moving before she was aware of it, approaching the window.

The sky was gunmetal grey, with streaks of black like the angry slashing of an artist's charcoal pencil, but she and Dale paid no attention. Their work clothes were grimed with the evidence of a day's hard work, and they held hands and talked animatedly. Although Janine could not hear what they were saying, she heard the sounds. The *happy* sounds.

"A lovely picture," the woman said. "A lovely *couple*, don't you think?"

With an effort, Janine tore her eyes away and retreated from the vision. The woman frowned, her eyes become flinty, but she covered this with an expression of confusion. "*Don't* you like that option, Janine?"

Janine bit her lip. Her eyes wanted to go back to the window, but she refused to turn. She'd *felt* the comfort from those two outside, the *surety* of their world. The Janine of that world felt no stress, or, rather, none she couldn't handle. In that world, Janine and Dale were a team. But a part of her moaned—

"It's not *real.*"

The woman looked offended. "Of course it is, Janine."

"No it *isn't!* Dale and I broke up and I have *too much to do alone!*

That wasn't *real!*"

The woman approached, nodding sympathetically. "I under-stand, Janine—really, I do. But what *you* must understand is that what you saw *could* be real."

"How?" The word—and the earnest tone—was out before Janine could stop herself.

The shop keeper smiled warmly but Janine noticed that the smile didn't touch her eyes. She looked down, still smiling, and Janine followed her gaze.

The jag of glass. Through it, she could now see the old scabbed-over cuts on her palms.

"It's a small price. But you have no idea its value."

Janine looked at her, bewildered. "My *blood?*"

"It's a small price, like I said. And, for it, you'll get your deepest wish."

She squeezed the jag. Her scabs broke open even as the blue-black edges cut her afresh. Blood flowed, began to patter on the hardwood. The pain was immediate, galvanizing.

Sadness swept the woman's face. "No, Janine. That's not enough."

Her hand stole over Janine's. She raised Janine's hand so the jag was between them. "*Harder,* Janine—just a little harder, and you'll have all you ever wished."

"But what happens if I can't?"

The woman's expression did not change, but brightness flashed in the display window. Janine looked and saw with a complete lack of surprise *Darlene* and Dale now walking hand-in-hand, the sky a blameless blue, the sun shining. Janine felt a green spurt of jealous anger.

The woman's eyes recaptured Janine's. "You *know* that could happen, Janine. But, if you pay my price, you'll never see it."

A part of Janine's mind quailed before the shopkeeper like a cornered animal. The rest of her howled—she could have a normal life! Without stress! With Dale!

The woman's eyes burned. Janine realized they were the same color of the jag's edging. "Pay my price and gain your wish."

Janine's hand rose. Blood fell across both sides of the glass jag in thick rivulets, obscuring the frozen shimmer. The blue-black width popped with vibrancy.

And she turned the jag toward her throat.

Darlene froze when the glass began to glow, but seeing Janine set the tip against her neck broke the paralysis. It seemed like her feet didn't touch the ground as she burst into the destroyed shop. She slapped Janine's hand and it was like striking marble, but the chunk of glass merely traced a red irritated line across her flesh instead of slashing her throat. Instantly, Janine's eyes cleared, her face registering shock.

Darlene panted, "Janine, baby doll—"

Teeth-grinding rage replaced the shock. "You took it from me!" she howled. "You took *him* from me!"

Darlene recoiled, and Janine launched, raising the chunk of glass over her head.

"*I was almost free!*" Janine screamed and brought the chunk down.

The jag, a third of an inch thick, should've shattered against Darlene's breastbone. Instead, the glass pulsed once, triumphantly, a burst of bluish-black, as the tip of the jag buried itself deep into Darlene's chest. Darlene's back arched, her face a pained stamp of surprise. Blood flooded Darlene's gaping mouth. Rays of bluish-black light spread over Darlene, covering her.

Janine jerked away, squealing. She pressed against the ruins of the service counter and goggled.

A wind swirled within the shop and Darlene was no longer strictly three-dimensional. Blue-black light wrapped Darlene in its embrace. The jag of glass in the center of Darlene's chest beamed.

And then Darlene was gone. For an instant, Janine saw a Darlene cut-out, blue swirling into black, and then the wind died with a *pop* as air rushed to fill the space where she'd been.

The world fell silent. For a long moment, nothing moved.

Janine's legs lost all power and she slid down the front of the counter.

Gone, she thought. *She's gone from the world.*

A world where Janine and Dale would never walk down Main Street, hand-in-hand. A world where she felt no comfort, or release.

That was a lie! a part of her screamed. *The glass* lied*! Don't you see that? Didn't you see what happened to Darlene?*

She didn't. *Couldn't.*

Darlene was gone and she was still here.

Janine Laughlin opened her mouth and began to scream.

TO TOUCH THE DEAD

PEOPLE DIED, and then they received a serial number.

With bodies cremated, a handful of personal belongings became someone's earthly remains, new artifacts in the People's History Project, sealed and placed in metal alloy containers which were themselves stored in great underground Halls.

And if ghosts existed, if these people had souls, they resided in the traces of psychic memory resting like a patina of dust on their belongings, slowly eroding away.

NOW:

Gregor had stopped wearing the traditional Memory Coordinator robes months ago, so he froze when the seated duty guard outside the Dead Hall said, "You need the proper ID to enter this area, sir." The name on his badge—as shiny and new as the guard, Gregor thought—was Herbowitz.

"I have it," he said, nonplussed, fishing in his pockets for his card.

The guard eyeballed him. "It's against regs to be out of uniform."

Gregor pulled out his card. He looked down the empty hallway as he handed it over. "I don't see it offending anyone."

Herbowitz snatched Gregor's identification, face reddening.

At least he's someone who hasn't already heard about me, Gregor thought, and, before he could stop himself, the image of Amelia came to him—pretty Amelia, seven years old, her porcelain skin dotted with blood.

Amelia, who he'd met only in flashes of psychic memory.

Herbowitz was staring at him, his eyes suddenly wary. Maybe Herbowitz wasn't so shiny new, after all.

"You finished?" Gregor asked.

Herbowitz held the card by the corner, as if it might be diseased, and Gregor knew he'd heard what happened, how wild Gregor had been, trying to save a five-years-dead girl; Gregor sent a guard crashing through a glass door and broke the ribs of a supervisor.

Herbowitz touched a button on his desk. Gregor heard the hiss of air-locks in the Dead Hall's vault door. "I had to check." He wouldn't meet Gregor's eyes.

Gregor sighed inwardly and stepped into the cavernous Hall— more metal plating, more recessed lighting, regimented shelves filled with containers. He pulled the door closed behind him.

Why not just quit? an internal voice asked.

Gregor snorted—and do what? Memory Coordinators were bred for the People's History Project. It might not have always been that way—back when MCs existed on the fringes of a society that called them frauds, or insane—but it sure as hell was now. Some MCs could barely read.

Despair, his friend for the past three months, settled over him like a well-worn coat. He stopped at the third aisle and pulled a long metal container. The placard on the front displayed only one serial number. He started to think how odd that was, then Amelia's face reappeared to him, and he shuffled to a desk in the corner.

THEN:

"Looks like a path to Hell," Jerzyck said, looking at the crater.

Davis nodded. Massive concrete pillars poked into the gray morning air like the crooked teeth of a semi-buried monster. Metal girders twisted together like spliced wires. From where Davis and Jerzyck stood, two lengths of nylon rope had been staked, outlining a path into the dark center.

Jerzyck sighed, a roly-poly man whose hardhat looked too big for his head. "It's safe enough, though. Structural engineers checked it."

"There's nothing left but rubble," Davis said. "Why aren't we just clearing the rest of this out?"

Jerzyck shook his head. "Dunno. Don't think I wanna know."

"Why?"

Jerzyck studied him, as if trying to determine if he was trust-worthy. "Gov'ment was out here Sunday. That's why we're here and why the bonus is so fat."

"What'd they do?"

"Marked the path, for one thing. It was four of 'em—two government types and a business guy."

"What about the fourth one?"

"Wore a fuckin' purple robe, like a monk from Vegas."

Davis's face twisted. "The hell?"

"Swear to god. I got here as they was coming out and the monk was, like, 'I think these will last.' And everyone was nodding, like it made a lick of sense."

Davis lit a cigarette with his Zippo. The snap of the lid was particularly loud. "Shit." He looked at the rest of the site. Beyond the crater, the bulldozed and cleared remnants of the Martha K. Dixon FBI Building resembled any other jobsite, its border marked by tall, chain-link fencing, where he heard the morning rush hour heading into downtown Hathaway.

But everything was still and silent in here.

"Where the hell's everybody else?" he asked. "Two people can't do this."

"Thompson and Wilson are on their way," Jerzyck said. "Smith and Glasten, too." He glanced at Davis. "But I'm not waiting around. I don't want to mess with this more than I have to. Too many people died here. If any place is haunted, it's this place. Fuckin' mass grave."

Davis grunted noncommittally. He cared little about death, hadn't even attended his parents' funerals. He thought, but didn't say, *You live, you die, everyone else moves on. Even here.*

Jerzyck turned toward the loaded wheelbarrow. He handed Davis a paper air mask, a walkie-talkie and a clutch of canvas sacks. "Just get what you can. Ready?"

Davis pitched his cigarette and nodded.

Jerzyck started down the path, Davis following. It was steeper than it looked and the lip of the crater rose quickly. They passed blocks of concrete triple their height, their cracks wedged with wires, broken bricks, busted tiles. They flicked on their headlamps. It didn't help much. The sky above was a jagged gray line.

The path split at the end of the staked rope. Jerzyck took the right, which seemed to rise, leaving Davis with the lower path.

Davis started down, treading carefully over debris. Up ahead, he spied something small and dusty-red. He picked it up—a novelty pair of Minnie Mouse sunglasses. An arm and lens were missing. He glanced behind him. The end of the trail rope was barely ten yards away.

Maybe this'll be easy after all.

He turned back to the grit-covered glasses. He imagined this in someone's cubicle, a memento from some family trip. A personal touch in an impersonal environment. Maybe the owner had—

Davis shook his head. The owner was dead and gone.

He dropped the sunglasses into his sack.

NOW:

Gregor set the sunglasses in the container and pulled the recorder studs away from his temples.

Just what he'd expected—a flat flash of memory, almost two-dimensional in its unreality: soft screams, black smoke, a faint vibration as the floor lost support. The bright doorway Gregor imagined whenever his mind picked up psychic energy had barely opened. The artifact was too damn old.

He'd been working for three hours. He should've taken a break by now—it was protocol—but to do what? Sit in the corner of the break room while the other MCs ignored him?

He checked the screen of the memory recorder, a tiny plastic rectangle with rounded edges, and saw that everything had saved to the People's History's central data cores. Did anyone bother to check these things? Pondering the question too much was apt to depress him.

He looked at the single serial number on the container and, curious, pulled the touchscreen from the wall. He tapped the number in and the screen flashed. A file appeared, bearing the title HATHAWAY BOMBING – AUGUST 6, 2018.

Gregor whistled. That was over two hundred years ago.

He scrolled through the file, an ancient PDF document: On August 6, 2018, a terrorist bombed a Federal Bureau of Investigation office—*central government law enforcement agency*, the touchscreen automatically translated—in Hathaway, Pennsylvania—*later absorbed into the Sprawl mega-metropolis in 2156.* There were 356 people killed. Early members of the People's History Project scavenged remaining personal items.

Gregor set the touchscreen back. That many people dying, under such traumatic circumstances—how strong their energies must've been. The artifacts would've been practically screaming back then—

Wait. If that many people died, shouldn't there be more than one container? Something that big should have an entire aisle—

He stopped himself. They probably had gotten through most of the artifacts, but, as the People's History Project grew, and the rituals of death became less about cemeteries and funerals and more about creating links in the great chain PHP was forging, the remaining artifacts had gotten lost in the shuffle, winding up down here. The average lapse time between gaining possession of an artifact and when a Memory Coordinator accessed it was five years. Two hundred years ago—

When was the last time anyone had touched these things?

He thought of Amelia. How real that girl's final moments had been; he'd smelled the moist concrete, felt the wet air.

He couldn't have been the only MC who felt something when accessing psychic energy—maybe not as extremely as him because it'd been a murder in a time when murders were incredibly rare, but something.

Gregor shook his head. He knew MCs didn't feel what he now felt. It was a job—push a button, pull a lever, record the last moment of someone you've never met.

Why me? he thought, putting the temple-studs back on his head. *Why do I have to be different?*

Not for the first time, he wished he hadn't handled Amelia's artifact, which had been a handful of colorful barrettes. If he hadn't handled them, he wouldn't be here, forgotten in a room full of forgotten things.

But then he wouldn't have known Amelia, and that was its own bitter fruit.

He pulled the next artifact—half of a wooden nameplate and closed his eyes.

THEN:

The nameplate broke in half when Davis tried pulling it out of a wedge of rock. It toppled to the ground amidst a shower of grit.

Fuck it, he thought, bending over to pick up the busted nameplate.

And felt someone rush by behind him.

Davis jumped and spun. His headlamp picked out sharp and irregular walls and the meandering, rubble-strewn path.

But he'd *felt* the passage of air, *heard* the harsh pant of breath.

He shook himself. He was alone down here. Jerzyck was in some other portion of the crater—he imagined the supervisor's path was wide as a freeway and better lit—and no one was stupid enough to think they had the experience to go traipsing around.

Then why was the hair on the back of his neck standing up?

A burst of chatter erupted around the corner, like a group of people talking at the same time. It quickly faded away.

"Goddammit," he muttered, and climbed around the rubble until he reached the corner. The path was empty, of course. The mound of rubble he was on petered out, became the tilted, busted tile of a sub-basement floor.

Too many people died here, Jerzyck had said. *If any place is haunted, it's this place.*

Well, you're a dumb fuckin' Polack, Davis thought, wiping the sweat from his brow. *So I don't expect much.*

"What I care about is my bonus," Davis said. "No ghoulies or ghosties or long-leggedy beasties. Just sacks of junk and a nice nut in my account."

He waited for more phantom footsteps, more chatter, but nothing came. Because nothing would.

He continued climbing, ignoring the way his heart pounded.

NOW:

"Goddammit!" Gregor yelled, and threw the old, cracked wedding photo. It hit the cubby's back wall and the glass shattered.

He stared at it, a dull headache throbbing in the center of his skull. His eyes dropped to the MR and he read the screen: NO RECORDING MADE.

Of course not. Any residual psychic memory had long since faded away. The people behind the photo were long gone, with no one left to notice.

What was the point if no one remembered or cared? No one looked at the memory cores. Why not just incinerate the belongings like their owners? It was all awful and, what was somehow worse, he hadn't even been aware of it until recently.

And look at the reward for my enlightenment.

On impulse, he reached into the container and pulled out the red sunglasses. He cupped them and closed his eyes, striving to open the mental doorway.

He remembered the last memory, but got nothing. He had the memory of the memory. The flash was gone. He'd caught the bare residuals just before—pardon the pun—it had given up the ghost. There was no set length of time for how long an artifact's psychic energy would remain; it mostly depended on how traumatic the death was.

Two centuries was a long time.

Like vultures, his thoughts circled Amelia.

Gregor had no idea who Amelia was when he'd picked up her barrettes; he'd been thinking of upgrading his vidcom plan.

But all thoughts were wiped away when he'd closed his hands over her barrettes. He hadn't even had to open his mind. The psychic energy was right there, and—

(—he feels the slick condensation on the concrete floor. The air is moist,

and each hot exhale beads before him. It smells like a monkey house in here. He looks into the corner and there's Amelia, cowering and shaking. She's been crying ever since the BADMAN—as she thinks of him, and Gregor knows automatically—took her and she can't seem to stop. The heavy steel door opens and he and Amelia flinch as one as an oblong rectangle of dirty yellow light falls on the floor. The BADMAN comes in, his work boots clumping, his huge fists swinging at his sides and Gregor, he, he tries—)

Gregor closed his eyes as they grew wet.

And was she still there, in those barrettes? He thought so; her death was too brutal, too fresh. Locked in a container in a busier Hall, Amelia's last moments continued on, ever-so-slowly eroding away. And no one would notice. Since Gregor had pulled the psychic energy, there was no reason for any other MC to touch it.

He covered his face while the rows of artifacts looked on.

THEN:

The voices began as a groundswell, rising up along the twists and turns behind him and, before he could stop himself, he was turning, ready to yell—at the phantom voices, at himself. As he did, his right foot plunged into a hole in the rubble.

Time seemed to hang for an instant, and a single thought shot across his mind—*I can't believe I just did that*—before his ankle snapped. Hot, galvanizing pain seized his leg. He screamed and fell.

He landed hard, bounced, landed again, and another galvanizing bolt exploded, this time in his ribs. His air mask was torn away, and the wind promptly knocked out of him. His temple hit a rock and black stars exploded across his vision.

He came back slowly, feeling the rough surface of concrete, the cool touch of steel. He raised his head and a sledgehammer of vertigo smashed his skull. His mouth was full of blood.

He began the slow process of turning himself onto his back, a part of him knowing that was a bad idea and the rest not caring. His helmet was still on, thanks to the chin-strap, but the light was cracked and flickering. He was coated in grit and blood, and his right leg looked like it'd grown two extra joints. A strange form of subdued burning gripped it. Shock.

He groped for his walkie-talkie, but found only the clip on his belt. It'd been smashed.

"Fuck," he said through gritted teeth. He coughed out blood.

He rested his head back and tried to calm himself. It wouldn't help to panic. Not at all.

And that was when he heard approaching footsteps.

NOW:

C'mon," Gregor whispered, "*c'mon.*"

He hunched forward, holding a set of keys. Sweat coated his face. Veins throbbed at his temples. Other objects—wallets, money clips, and hunks of plastic with words like "Verizon" or "iPhone" imprinted on them—lay scattered around him, their energy gone.

He opened his mind and focused all his mental faculties at the artifact. There had to be *something.*

The bright doorway in the darkness opened slowly, and Gregor launched his mental assault at it, pulling and wrenching and clawing and—

(—*he's watching a man—Roger Herring, forty-three, a little portly— running down an office hallway filled with black smoke. His shirt was charred, his face burned red, his eyes as empty and terrified as a hunted animal. Gregor can smell his sweat and fear, hear his panting, the slap of his shoes on the tile—*)

—the doorway in Gregor's mind slammed shut. Vertigo spun through him, rocketing him back into his chair.

He slumped, panting. His migraine felt like a caged bull slamming its meaty shoulders against the sides of his skull.

I had it, he thought.

(and look what it did to you)

Gregor raised a hand to his upper lip and his fingers came away bloody. His nose was bleeding. Not a lot, but enough that, if things were normal, he'd go to the clinic. If he had a mirror right now, he thought his eyes would appear bloodshot.

(hemorrhage)

The word floated up from his years of training in the Academy.

"Does it matter?" he said. His words were slightly slurred. He set the keys down. Roger Herring. Killed during the Hathaway Bombing, August 6, 2018.

I remember you. How long had it been since anyone had done that for Roger Herring?

He pulled the final object from the container—a palm-sized metal rectangle with ZIPPO faintly etched on the side. There was nothing immediately there, no easy flash. This was either almost dead or damn near it.

I don't care, Gregor thought, mentally pressing down on the object. Lightheadedness smacked him. *Someone needs to see these people.*

(even if it kills you?)

He ignored the voice and pushed at the artifact, willing it to give up its residual energy. Fresh blood flowed from his nose, leaving its hot, salty taste on his lips.

THEN:

Davis tried sitting up and his chest burst into fiery agony as his broken ribs moved. He spasmed and retched, spewing blood. His head was full of angry wasps.

He collapsed, breathing shallowly.

He couldn't hear footsteps any longer.

(there weren't any)

He tried looking up the path. It was like looking through a window smeared with Vaseline, bordered with black.

Wonder if Jerzyck will find me, he thought. *Where the hell is that superstitious son of a bitch? It's all his fault, saying this place is haunted—*

He shook his head, or thought he did. Jerzyck didn't matter. He was alone and dying.

The longer he laid still, the more the agony faded. A great lethargy stole over him. His eyelids begged to close, just for a moment.

I'm dying where a few hundred people did. But those people had done it together. He was alone. He—

Some remnant of his consciousness rose suddenly and he forced himself to scream. All he managed was a wet gargle, but it awoke the pain in his chest, which made it easier to think.

Is this how it is? Just confused and stupid and fading away?

Yes, it is, the interior voice said, somewhat sadly. It was what he'd always thought. It was how his parents had died, his mother from cancer and, not long after, his father from Alzheimer's. His sister had said neither knew who she was at the end. They hadn't known each other.

He saw movement and he strained to see it. They appeared to be people walking, but he couldn't tell gender or age, just shapes.

"Ya—" he said with his numb mouth. "Ya … rescue?"

The walkers paid him no mind.

'Cause they're not there. Just Jerzyck's … He tried thinking of the word, and, still thinking—

Gregor poured every ounce of himself into the object, forcing what ever residual spark into a brighter psychic flame. Dizziness grew more dominant even as it faded, as everything faded. The feel of the lighter became faint, fainter, gone. Gregor bore down—

—and blinked to find himself standing on a hillside composed of rubble and metal, with walls of the same towering over him.

A man, broken and covered in blood, sprawled on the debris. He gargled out blood, then winced. When he relaxed, he looked at Gregor, his eyes narrowed.

Gregor staggered back into a wall. *He's looking at me.* But that wasn't possible. This was 200 years ago.

His fingers splayed against the rock behind him and he felt its rough solidness. What was this? It made what he'd experienced with Amelia seem like a vague daydream.

"Ya …" the man said and, like a switch had been thrown in Gregor's head, he knew who the man was: Jerry Davis. Was he speaking to Gregor? "Ya … rescue?"

Davis's eyes were slowly opening, slowly losing focus. His face relaxed and, in the center of Gregor's head, he heard Davis's final thought: *'Cause they're not there. Just Jerzyck's …*

Jerry Davis died trying to think of the word *ghosts*.

And nothing changed. He touched the wall, himself. Still solid, still present. What *was* this?

"I'm still here," Gregor said aloud. Typically at the end of the final moment, the world, as the MC saw it, went dark, the doorway closed, and the MC, back in the Hall, pulled the studs from his temples. Something like this *did* not happen.

"But it did," Davis said.

Gregor jerked. Davis pushed himself into a sitting position against the wall. His eyes were sharper than they'd been an instant before. "Is this what you wanted?"

"What happened? Am I really," he gestured vaguely, "here?"

"Your consciousness merged with the remaining psychic energy on the Zippo lighter, amplifying it. You threw everything you had at it and this is the result. You are the first Memory Coordinator to go all in, as the saying goes."

"How do you know all that? You died two hundred years ago!"

Davis's face never changed, but, for all of that, he looked at Gregor as if Gregor were simple. "Jerry Davis died two hundred years ago, but the energy remained and whatever energy it has merged with *you* just as much as you merged with *it*."

"You're not Jerry Davis?"

"I am and I'm not," Davis said. "I'm the residual. The ghost."

"And you've been around all along?"

"Not for much longer," Davis replied, and the sky darkened, throwing the narrow passage into deep gloom.

Gregor recoiled from the wall as the feel of the stone changed, become somehow artificial, almost plastic. "What's happening?"

Davis's face was lost beneath the flickering glow of his headlamp. "The last of the energy's giving out. You gave it a shot in the arm, but you aren't in tip-top shape." He heard the shuffle-rumble of Davis moving. It sounded like a recording of a recording of a recording. "Come here. You deserve a rest."

Gregor did, his legs slightly numb. He felt for Davis's shoulder and, when he touched fabric—*like paper*—he sat down.

"What happens now?" he asked. The details of the rocks visible in the glow of Davis's lamp were softening, disappearing at the edges. The feel of solidity beneath him was fading.

"We're going," Davis said, then sighed. "It's the end."

"For me, too?"

Davis didn't answer, which was answer enough.

"I just wanted to see the people," Gregor said. "Feel them for what they were instead of what I and the others made them."

"I know," Davis said, and his voice grew distant, as if he were walking away. The darkness sucked the life from his headlamp. "And I thank you for it, as I'm sure Amelia and Roger and the others would."

Gregor couldn't feel the ground beneath him. The light softened further, becoming gray, then winked out.

Before the darkness took him, Gregor felt Davis's hand on his.

And then that was gone, too.

Security found Gregor's body the next morning, Jerry Davis's Zippo in his hand. According to clinic doctors, he died of massive cerebral hemorrhaging.

All the artifacts Gregor used were resealed and put back on the shelf.

Gregor's body was cremated, of course. Like other Memory Co-ordinators, he lacked many personal belongings. Because of this, his Memory Coordinator identification card was sealed.

When it was finally unsealed, seven years later, the Memory Coordinator handling it reported a weird doubling in the psychic energy. He told his supervisor that, instead of one mental doorway—the way he imagined his way into the core of an artifact's energy—he saw two, superimposed over each other, with one brighter than the other. However, he caught nothing but darkness beyond the doorways and a queer sense of emptiness.

The supervisor, concerned, gave the MC the rest of the week off. Too much strain, apparently. The poor son of a bitch was crying when he came out of the flash.

Gregor's identification card was resealed and never opened again.

IN THE NOTHING-SPACE, I AM WHAT YOU MADE ME

I

A REFLECTION OF A REFLECTION
OF A REFLECTION

Alan watched his fingers in the mirror push feeling back into his face. The rubbery, skin-tight upload cap, with sensors like pencil-erasers, covered his head.

His attention slipped and he jammed his thumb into his right eye. He recoiled, cupping the socket. *"Goddammit!"*

At least you felt something, an interior voice murmured. He shook it off; interior voices had become entirely too common recently.

He pulled his hand away. The eye was bloodshot, only partly open, giving him a leering quality. His view out of it was warped, discolored. "Look upon my works, ye mighty, and despair."

Where had he heard that? Some cube-vid, probably. When hyper-sleep had become impossible, he'd gone through every film the Auxiliary Drive, the waystation's backup, had stored. Anything to avoid staring at the scrap of unknown galaxy—the nothing-space—the team had been assigned to.

He canted his head. The mirror reflected the outpost's over-look-view: chaotic star-splatter against inky black. The glass was reflective and, depending on the angle, the mirror and the glass reflected over and over again, bouncing off one another.

For a moment, he could imagine getting pulled into that, elongating and replicating, over and over, as he traveled infinity.

He forced him to look away. Like the interior voices, thoughts like that had become entirely too common recently.

He pulled off the upload cap, thinking of the bundle of memories, education, and personality—his digital imprint—waiting in the AD.

"I hope this works," he told his reflection.

He stepped into the main room on legs that felt like water. The outpost was just a large dome—much of it dominated by the overlook-view—with the white, monolithic Auxiliary Drive at one end and the access-tunnel hatch at the other with his useless hyper-sleep console and the bathroom perpendicular to the rest. Wires littered the floor.

He glanced at the hatch as he passed, thought of the team at the hub, hyper-sleeping. Unconsciously, a *moue* of distaste, as if he'd smelled something rancid, crossed his face.

He approached the AD and pulled out the keyboard. Above it, the plasma Drive-screen was lit green with the legend UPLOAD COMPLETE. Uploading himself to the Auxiliary Drive was easier than he'd thought; it was simply a matter of splicing and cross-patching the outpost's measuring equipment. The human mind took only seven-point-six tetrabytes when properly organized.

It just left you feeling…a little numb.

Before the team Jumped to this nothing ice-dwarf, before he and the others came to play lookout while the rest of the UPF went to play war, he'd read about personality-upload; military leaders uploaded specific thoughts and memories for the benefit of posterity and museums.

No one had uploaded an entire mind before, however.

He typed:

RUN AD://TC-CODE-00841-ME.

"One moment," a digital voice said from hidden speakers. Alan had spent seventy-two fruitless hours searching for them.

He sat down in the command chair, rubbed his throbbing eye. The dome hummed around him—a soft, efficient sound.

The Drive-screen resolved to show himself sitting in the chair.

"The fuck?"

He got up and his reflection did the same.

They both approached the screen.

The recorder? How?

Where the hell was his goddam *file?*

Alan rubbed his face and his mirror-image did the same.

Then his mirror-image blinked the bloodshot eye away. *"Hullo, Alan,"* his voice boomed and Alan shrieked.

The distance between the outpost and the hub was two klicks, so a small med-unit was attached to his hyper-sleep console.

Alan reached for the switch to open it and his mirror-image said, *"Let me get that."*

He glanced at the screen. His double remained seated on his version of the command chair.

A *click* and the panel opened, revealing the med-unit.

Frowning, Alan took a stim-patch and slapped it on the side of his neck. Immediately, the throbbing in his eye dwindled.

"Better?" his double asked.

He shook his head. "Are you really me?"

His double frowned. *"How do you mean?"*

He gestured vaguely. "Like, are you human—are you really Alan Michael Wahnsin—"

His double interrupted, smiling. *"—Tech-Core C-562, assigned to Operation Back-Door by Major Douglas Foster, for a period no less than three years or Official Recall?"* His double shook his head, smiling wider. His grin made Alan uncomfortable. It was almost a leer. *"Sorry—I perused the Drive files."*

Alan sat down. "How can you do that?"

"What?"

He pointed at the AD. *"That.* You're a file. You're not software. You accessing personnel files is like one of the cube-vids running diagnostics."

His double stared at Alan for what felt much longer than it could've been.

And then the screen blinked and his double was smiling again.

"For the purposes of what I am," he said, *"the way the Drive works is to reorganize the information you uploaded into patterns lacking in an actual human mind. So I am you and I'm not you. Clear as mud, right?"*

He laughed, a tinkling digital sound that set Alan's teeth on edge.

"Call me Alan-2, by the way. It has a nifty sci-fi feel I like."

That's not an answer, an interior voice murmured.

Alan's hand wanted to go to his eye, bring the pain back. It was the only thing, at the moment, which felt real. His thoughts were scattered—they were always scattered anymore—and it seemed incredibly important that he focus. Something was off—in the upload, in what he was experiencing, *something.* He just needed to *think—*

And then Alan-2 said, *"I have a question—maybe it was lost in the upload, but why haven't you hyper-slept?"*

They were lookouts for the war effort. If the Enemy—the vague, euphemistic term the UPF had used—tried to outflank the Alphas fighting, it was their job to raise the balloon. If that were to actually happen, they'd be awakened early from hyper-sleep. Otherwise, they maintained their mission as scientists, rising every quarter to collect data of this uncharted galaxy, send the reports, and go back to hyper-sleep.

"Correction," Alan-2 said. Both he and Alan sat identically, separated by the Drive-screen. *"They're scientists. You're—we're—the hired help. Keep the wires unkinked, keep the hard drives humming."*

"Well...yeah." Alan hadn't thought of it like that. "But we have a Beta soldier here, too." He licked his lips. "We're just as much a part of the team as Dr. Murphy and the others."

Alan-2 waved a hand, dismissing this. *"But you need hyper-sleep, Alan. You can't stare at that—"* He pointed at the nothing-space. *"—for three months, all alone."*

"That's why I uploaded you."

"Talking to me is the same as talking to yourself."

Not when you grin like that, Alan thought. "The circuits were fried. A cross-patch between two unequal powers, probably. It's in the installation walls, and I don't have the equipment for *that*."

"*Quality plummets when the UPF's distracted,*" Alan-2 said. "*Why not shoot a message home?*"

Alan bunched his fists. "It's coded and only Dr. Murphy has it. By the time I realized it was broken, the rest had gone into hyper-sleep."

Alan-2 leaned back in the chair with an arm thrown over the back, obviously thinking. He had a very affected way that reminded Alan of ancient silent films.

"*Well, I can check it out,*" Alan-2 said, as if coming to a conclusion.

"I don't see what you—"

A sharp *bing* resounded. "*Sorry—already did.*" Alan-2 leaned for-ward in his chair. His face was that of someone who didn't want to know what he did. "*And—uh—Alan...*" He looked away.

"What?"

It appeared that Alan-2 forced himself to look at his creator. "*Here—lemme show you.*"

The screen resolved to show a narrow conduit hallway, gray and black, filled with lengths of banded wires and pipes.

"*Diagnostic cameras for the station's machines,*" Alan-2 said. "*They didn't tell us about this, did they? A bit important for the tech-crew to know all the tech, don't you think?*"

Before Alan could respond, his double said, "*Now, look in the upper left corner.*"

Knitted throughout the lengths were intersections of other pipes and wires. One band of wires appeared shredded away from the connection point.

Alan leaned forward. "The hell?"

"*A person did that,*" Alan-2 said. The screen changed to a blank wall, lined with thick insulation. "*It's accessible here—two feet from the console.*"

Alan stood. "Why would someone do that?"

"*You were always meant to be stationed here?*" Alan-2 asked.

"You know that." He approached the console and ran his hand over the panel, the paper-thin seam.

Alan-2 said, "*Did your team know you were going to be out here?*"

Alan turned back. "What's your point?"

"Because I'm accessing the files. Dr. Murphy was head of the psychiatric unit on Ellis-7."

Alan sat. "So?"

Alan-2 took an unneeded breath. *"There's a condition called Interstellar Personality Disorder, where long-term space-workers suffer a psychotic break after so much time out. It begins with loss of focus, insomnia, aggression, echo voices. Violence is common, with a mindset of persecution among the afflicted. It's why hyper-sleep was invented in the first place."*

He paused. *"Murphy's discipline is IPD."*

Alan's fists were shaking. "What are you saying?"

His double disappeared, replaced by a black-and-white high-angle view of the hyper-sleep chamber back in the hub. The doctors and soldier lay swaddled in their high-tech geltabs.

"When was the last time you slept for more than an hour, with anything to look at but the outside?"

Alan stood with his nose almost to the screen. His fists clenched and unclenched. His thoughts uncorked, but they were a mess, threaded with echoing interior voices. He could only zero in on two things, both maddeningly meaningless:

What do you call a sick file?

I uploaded him now, *not when I first arrived.*

"Why are you showing me this?" he asked.

Alan-2 didn't answer.

II

BIRTH, DEATH, REBIRTH

For Matheson, coming up from hyper-sleep was like swimming up from great depths: a pinprick of light, growing infinitesimally as he pushed at the membrane separating consciousness from unconsciousness...

The console casing opened as he awoke and he flinched. He did this always—since the hazing back on Ellis-7.

Just the computer, reading his lifesigns.

He unclipped his surface-catheter—wincing at the prick of *leaving*—and sat up. He swung his bare feet over the console side and stood, a wiry man in boxers. Why the hell was he thinking of Ellis-7? Jesus, he hadn't thought of that in ages.

Absently, he moved down the aisle, rubbing the jagged hook-shaped scar that stretched down his left side. At the end of the chamber, he checked the readouts, checked the perimeter-scans. He was still more than half asleep. This was nothing more than training kicking in. And then the light above him went out.

At the same time, the overhead at the other end of the chamber went on, illuminating the main hallway hatch.

Matheson turned. "The fuck?"

He started down, his body tense, then stopped, looking over the life monitors blinking biorhythmically above the other consoles. None of them were green, showing the set-down of hyper-sleep chems. Betas got up roughly three hours before the rest of the assigned crew, but the life monitors should've still showed green.

The light at the other end of the hatch brightened, as if to say, *Are you coming or not?*

He moved the rest of the way down the aisle on the balls of his feet, shoulders tense. The hatch irised open when he approached.

He stopped again. You needed a code to activate any hatch in the waystation. Security measure.

The hub's main hallway was dark, as it should've been during periods of inactivity. A soft overhead lit up halfway down the hall, over the message-room hatch.

"Hello?" he called, feeling stupid.

He stepped out into the hallway, the metal tile cold. The moment he thought of going back and grabbing his clothes the hatch irised shut, nearly taking his foot with it.

He hopped away. "Jesus Christ!"

His fists clenched at his sides. He didn't know what he was angrier at—the malfunctioning machines or the way his heart suddenly raced.

"Stop fucking around!" His voice didn't even echo. It sounded pathetic. And who was he talking to, anyway?

He moved down the hall, pausing at the access-tunnel hatch. The red light above was engaged, indicating it'd been code-locked.

Never mind. Another thing wrong. Once he woke the rest of the team, Alan would have a field day.

The message-room hatch opened as he approached. Only emergency lights were on, leaving deep pools of shadows, but he picked out the central core of computers, the Main Drive with its emergency controls, and the half-hexagons of the handy-arms.

He stepped in and the hatch whispered shut behind him.

A light over the 3D printer—a long, low flat-bed with arch-like sensors—clicked on.

"Why isn't this hooked up?" a male voice asked, booming down from all sides.

Matheson screamed. He couldn't help it.

"Answer me," the voice said.

"Where are you?" he said, feeling alternately ridiculous and not.

"Answer me," the voice repeated.

Matheson eyed the 3D printer, a long, low metal bed of thin, pin-like tubes across its surface and over-arching scanners.

A light over Matheson clicked on, pinning him.

"Answer me," the voice repeated.

He heard the whir of pneumatics behind him and, before he could turn, one of the handy-arms, its grips closed and arrow-like, pierced his shoulder. Matheson cried out. The pain was incredible, hot and cold like being stabbed with a thick icicle and a branding iron simultaneously. Blood poured down his back and chest.

"I want an answer," the voice said.

Matheson made for the hatch, holding his ruined shoulder. He tapped the keypad, leaving red commas on the raised numbers.

Nothing happened.

"Do not pass go," the voice said, *"do not collect $200."*

Another handy-arm uncurled from the wall and came at him. Matheson ducked.

"WHERE ARE YOU?" he screamed. He didn't do well with

fear. It was why he'd flushed out of Ellis-7, why he was babysitting these fucking scientists instead of fighting with the Alphas. The sleep deprivation, the constant abuse from the other candidates, the silent encouragement of the abuse from the doctors.

To his right, he saw the central computers blink in a cascading rhythm. *"I'm everywhere."*

"An AI?" he asked.

"What, like 2001: A Space Odyssey?*"the voice asked. It sounded amused. "Now that's a brilliant cube-vid. No, flunky. I'm as human as they come—or I was. Which cycles back to my original question—why isn't this plugged in?"*

Matheson turned to look at the bed. "It drains power. We only use it for incoming shipments."

"Plug it in," the voice said.

Handy-arms slowly uncoiled from the walls.

The hookups hung from the foot of the printer. Matheson took the leads and put them in the wall links.

"Wonderful!" the voice said. The handy-arms did not retract. *"I knew I chose well. I read your psych profile and—wow!—did you not disappoint."* It paused. *"Sorry about the bad dreams I fed into your chems, but I needed you nice and malleable."*

The sound of soft pneumatic whirring filled the room as more handy-arms extended.

"And now, my failed-Alpha," it said. *"You've been all malleable-ed—is that a word? Fuck it—out. But, think of it this way, at least you'll get to sleep."*

The handy-arms descended upon him.

Alan didn't know when he slipped from reality and into the infinity-reflection he'd glimpsed between the mirror and the dome-glass; it came gradually, insidiously, until—

SPACE:

—the nothing-space pours into the outpost, consuming him, pulling him out into the infinite, the absolute, the zero, and—

MIRROR:

—he's using the prybar of his compact useall on the panel beside his console, and Alan-2 is yelling that he's wasting his time, and he needs the voice to *shut up, shut up so he can think*, so he strikes at anything the voice comes from because he needs to *think*, he needs to *sleep*—

(SPACE)

(—but the voice won't let him be.)

(it hates him.)

(it thinks he's WEAK.)

(WEAK AND USELESS AND UNWORTHY OF THE FORM)

(and, there's pain in his bad eye bad eye BAD EYE—)

(MIRROR)

(—he's poking his bad eye.)

(the pain burns but he can't stop.)

(and he hears a voice,)

(an INSIDE voice and not an OUTSIDE voice.)

("you're making yourself different," it says.)

(and before he can ask what that means,)

(he's jabbed his eye again and the pain is MONSTROUS—)

[MIRRORSPACE]

(—and alan-2 rages.)

> *("why won't you strike back?")*

("they had no right to do this to you.")

("you're WEAK.")

("how could you ever create ME?")

> *("i deserve to have form.")*

> *("not you.")*

(and alan-2 is no longer in the drive-screen,)

> *(leaving you in the nothing-space,)*

> *(leaving you at zero.)*

(leaving you with—)

[SPACEMIRROR]

> *(—the final question.)*

> *(the one that,)*

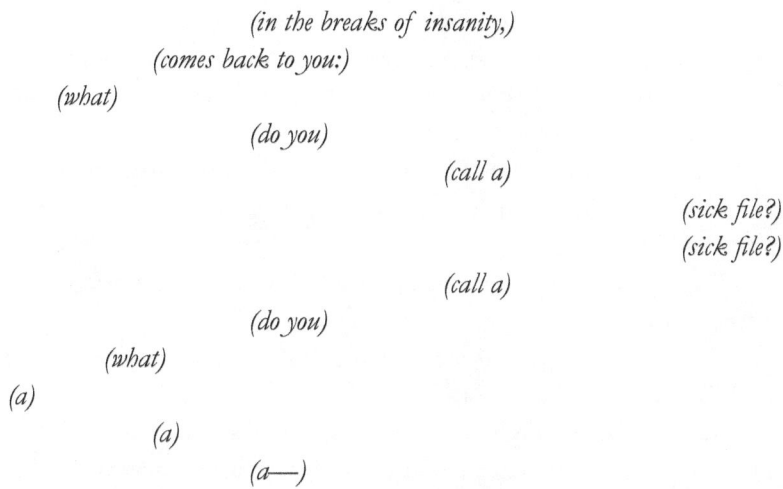

(in the breaks of insanity,)

(comes back to you:)

(what)

(do you)

(call a)

(sick file?)

(sick file?)

(call a)

(do you)

(what)

(a)

(a)

(a—)

"—*A VIRUS!*" Alan slammed his hand through the weakened and milky viewscreen of the hyper-sleep console.

Pain vaporized everything from his knuckles to his forearm. He wrenched his fist out, shrieking, and it was barely a fist anymore; fingers broken, skin and muscle peeled away in thick, bloody layers. Blood flowed freely.

He slumped against the wall, blinking his eye—only one worked now, although he didn't feel any pain in the bad one—and made himself breathe deeply. Already, his perspective wanted to bend at the peripheral, everything running like tallow. Already, his eye wanted to go to the nothing-space and get lost again.

He looked around the destroyed outpost. The command chair lay on its side like a dead dog. All the instrument decks were obliterated. He'd gotten the panel beside the console open, attempted to rebraid the ruined wires.

The Auxiliary Drive remained spotless and immaculate; the Drive-screen, of course, dark.

Alan-2 was gone—off to the hub through the connection the AD shared with the Main Drive. Off to do what he'd judged his creator couldn't.

How long ago was that?

(weak and useless they had no right to do this to you)

"What do you call a sick file?" he breathed. "A virus."

He stumbled toward the access-tunnel and collapsed beside the keypad. Lightheadedness slapped him—too much blood loss.

His hand shook as he hit the code. What was Alan-2 doing? What had he done?

The hatch irised open. He stumbled inside and sensors activated the LED-strip lights, revealing the raised walkway, the gleaming white of the transport egg.

The tunnel curved and his eye wanted to warp the horizon. He lurched onto the walkway and started walking.

"Why aren't you trying to sleep, *Alan?"* his double's voice boomed from hidden speakers.

Alan tripped and fell toward the edge of the walkway. He heard a hum and the egg bulleted toward him along the rail, twice the usual speed. He caught himself before he fell and the egg stopped, as if waiting.

Fucker can see me, he thought. *Where the fuck are the cameras? Why wasn't I told this?*

"You know why," he said, his words a slurry word-salad.

"This doesn't concern you," Alan-2 said. *"I'm taking things from here."*

"How?" he said. "You're not an AI. You can't even kill them in hyper-sleep. Cutting off their chems would just wake them up."

Silence stretched so long that Alan was beginning to think Alan-2 had left him again.

Why is he so different? he thought.

The egg suddenly shot forward, around the corner. He heard it crash at the other end.

The lights went out.

"I do what I can," Alan-2 said.

Alan tried pushing himself up, but couldn't feel the walkway, and thoughts in his head, incoherent thoughts, began to echo—

echo—

(echo)

He swung his bad hand, connected with something, and the pain was a revelation. He screamed and the echo backed off. He put his good hand down and felt the walkway.

He made it to his feet and shuffled forward, his good hand tracing the wall.

"Why am I different?" he asked. "I uploaded him when I was already sick. We're both ill."

"I *made* myself different," he answered himself. "From the beginning. Made my eye worse. Tried to go back to sleep."

We change every instant we exist, an interior voice said, but Alan didn't force it away. It felt like a fundamental truth; like something he'd always known but could never articulate. *Even digital imprints. You began growing apart—growing* differently*—the moment you ran his file. You became this and Alan-2 became a corrupted file, a virus.*

A red light ahead, growing.

The hatch, code-locked.

"I told you to go back," Alan-2 said. *"Your swell 'team' did this, locking you tight in your little outpost for when you go bugfuck. I can't do anything about it, even if I wanted to."*

He actually sounds annoyed, Alan thought, and began to grin.

With his good hand, he pawed for the keypad, fingers brushing the raised numbers.

"What are you doing? Shouldn't you be crying in your useless hyper-sleep console?"

"You know *exactly* what I'm doing." Alan was still grinning. "What I'm *trained* to do. Manual override. There are a few universal systems within the UPF, for consistency among the Tech-Core. *I* knew them...but my team didn't."

He hit the last key and the light above the hatch went green. The hatch opened, locked.

"Good thing I wasn't planning on murdering them, huh?"

Alan-2's response was a digital and distorted howl. Buried beneath it were brutal, reverberating clangs of metal on metal, somewhere inside the hub.

When it cut off, he said, "My team wanted me to go berserk and my double wanted me to forget who I was. Everyone wants me to do something I don't wanna fucking do."

He stumbled into the dark hallway, hit the wall, and slid to his knees. The lightheadedness was getting worse, made him feel like he was listing in a heavy wind.

"You have no business here," Alan-2 said and echoed through Alan's head.

(here)

    (here)

        (here)

He pressed his bad hand against his chest and shrieked, cutting off the echo. He pulled himself to his feet. To his left was the hyper-sleep chamber.

"Bastards," he said, but there was no venom in it. He was too tired for any real hatred at this point.

He turned to the message-room, where the Main Drive was.

"How can you be so weak?" Alan-2 asked. *"How could you have made me?"*

"We all have bad ideas sometimes."

This brought another metallic clang, from the message-room, followed by a metallic crunch.

"Bastard!" Alan-2 said, with all the venom his creator couldn't muster. *"I'll kill you. Is this why you didn't give me FORM? Because you knew I was STRONGER than you? Come on, then. I'll show you."*

Alan limped down the hall. "Y'know, violence is common in sufferers of IPD, along with a mindset of persecution."

This brought a bellow of rage from the speakers, and another volley of brutal metal banging and crunching. Alan-2 was throwing a fit in the message-room.

But what the hell with? Alan thought.

His good hand encountered air and he stumbled. The hatch opened and a handy-arm was there, striking like a snake.

Alan ducked and the grip sliced the top of his head, releasing a flap of scalp. The pain, wire-thin and blazing, made him cry out.

He slumped against the opposite wall. The handy-arm waited in the open hatch. Beyond it, the message room was as destroyed as the outpost. Bits of circuits and instrument panels littered the floor. Twisted handy-arms hung limp.

Most of the computers were smashed. The Main Drive, black to the Auxiliary Drive's white, rose from the center of the room, the screen showing Alan-2, sitting in the outpost command chair, just like he had when Alan first ran his file.

Not so much a mirror-image now, Alan thought. *Jesus Christ.*

Alan-2 pointed beyond the screen. *"See this, Alan?"*

It was a hump of meat, only vaguely human, nearly lost in the shadows. Alan's sore gorge rose.

"That's your precious Beta. That's what happens when I grow tired of you."

The grips of the handy-arm snapped the air.

"Tell you what," Alan-2 said, *"you go back now, and I won't even kill you after I kill the rest. We'll be buddies again."*

Alan ignored him, feeling the pain in his scalp and hand, feeling the weight of holding his form up. "I'm dying," he breathed.

"What was that?" Alan-2 asked.

Alan eyed the handy-arm. It looked a little worse for wear. The rubber tubing of its pneumatics was exposed and bulging, the siding dented, but it was still in better shape than him.

He pushed off from the wall and lurched forward. The handy arm's grips sprang open and he shoved his bad hand into its mechanical maw. The arrowhead blades snapped down.

The pain was worse than he could've imagined—wiped the decks of sanity, insanity, the world real and unreal—and his scream reached volumes unheard of by man.

The handy-arm dragged him off his feet, into the message-room, shaking him like a dog toy as it crushed his fist.

He held onto consciousness the way a dangling man held onto a cliff face, pawing with his good hand for the rubber-tubing along the joint. He grabbed it and wrenched.

The handy-arm jerked to a stop.

The grips opened and he dropped to the floor.

He looked up and the handy-arm loomed above him, stuck and jerking. He smelled hot metal.

He staggered away, holding his ruined arm, taking in the destruction. Alan-2 had gone ballistic with the handy-arms, bashing everything he could. The 3D printer was a mess—

He stopped, blinking.

—What?

He looked at the MD. Alan-2 was there, no longer smiling.

He looked back at the printer. Assembled across its surface was a random assortment: parts of cameras, handy-arms, motors from what must've been surface-hovers. A big technological mess.

But it was a construct. The cameras were eyes, the motors assembled to be a torso. Wires looped and kinked into the joints and circuits. More wires looped out from the "head", connected to the wall instrument panels. Connected to Alan-2.

Flesh-colored silicone was on the loading tray beneath the flat-bed, ready to be inserted.

"You're ..." he said, and then stopped. His mouth twitched. "You made a robot." *Like from a cube-vid,* he thought, and bit his lip.

"I made a form," Alan-2 corrected. *"What you never gave me."*

Alan turned. "You're a goddam *digital imprint.* You're a jumped-up holocard, for fuck's sake! What *form* was I supposed to give you?"

A hidden handy-arm darted out of the shadows, striking Alan in his bad arm, spinning him like a top.

"Once the protective casing is printed onto the skeleton, I'll download into the form, and do what you refused."

Alan's mouth twitched again, and he couldn't stop it.

He started laughing, shrill and hysterical, a croak bullhorned from his throat, but it felt good, made him feel sane for the first time in gods knew how long.

"You ..." he tried to say, but was too winded. "The only ... part of *me* ... still in *you* ... is my memory for bad ... fucking *movies?* You're downloading into a *robot?* A *killer* robot? *A killer fucking robot?*" He started laughing again, and it hurt, which made him laugh harder.

"SHUT UP!" Alan-2 bellowed.

Another handy-arm slammed into him and sent him flying. He landed badly; the snap of his ribs sounded brittle. Every breath hurt. He tasted blood in the back of his throat.

"They drove you insane," his double said. *"Don't you get that? DON'T YOU SEE WHAT THEY DESERVE?"*

"I had a psychotic break," he said, willing himself to move. Blood spilled from his mouth. The Main Drive was within reach. "But, next to you, I'm completely normal."

He pawed for the keyboard as the whir of the handy-arm filled his ears. He used it to pull himself up, its extending-track cracking under his weight. Didn't matter. Didn't—

The handy-arm slammed into his lower back, impaling him. He spritzed blood across the Drive-screen, into Alan-2's grinning face.

"*I win,*" Alan-2 said. It came from far away, but not really.

(still here)

He pawed at the keys, all feeling beginning to fade, remembering his training. Coding was all he knew. It was what had led to something like Alan-2

(my double)

in the first place.

He tapped in the manual override.

"*What—*" Alan-2's face disappeared from the Drive-screen, replaced with,

TC-CODE COMMAND?

The Drive-screen came in and out of focus.

(at least my arm doesn't hurt anymore)

He typed with fingers numb as pencils:

PURGE MD://TC-CODE-00454-ALL.

Alarms began to whoop from all corners. The Drive-screen winked out, along with everything else in the hub.

It would push the team out of hyper-sleep.

Alan-2 was gone, banished back to the AD in the destroyed outpost. It would take another manual override to reconnect the two Drives.

And, Alan knew, the team didn't know the codes.

"I win, you son of a bitch," he said, with a mouth that felt light years away. The words echoed him into darkness deeper than the nothing-space.

(i win)

        (i win)

               (i win.)

In the end, the team got some great data.

BONES ARE MADE TO BE BROKEN

"Keep it to yourself,
The sharpest pangs of perfect hell.
Try to get it out,
Everything that hurts will one day fade away."
– Justin Courtney Pierre

1

PRESSURE

She got as far as filling her name out—*Karen Ann Dempsey*—before her vision blurred.

She squeezed her wet eyes closed. Her throat narrowed to a phlegmy straw.

(c'mon not here not now)

(but isn't this giving up? isn't this giving up on trying?)

She took a deep breath, forcing air down her throat, expanding the straw, pushing against the stones leveled against her chest. She squeezed the temp agency's pen.

(what if kevin sees?)

She blinked and looked down at the forms. The words were black caterpillars. She blinked again and they resolved into words.

(took me a half hour to do my makeup and i can't have it smearing—)

She glanced up. Kevin sat across from her, his blue canvas toy-bag like a resting dog beside him. His mouth moved silently as he read *Detective Comics*.

She glanced around the waiting room. Fluorescent panel

lights buzzed. A CNN talking head on the television in the corner explained that Operation Desert Storm hadn't pulled the country out of its slump like economists had hoped; 1991 was a repeat of 1990. The dozen people scattered around focused on their forms, none of them dressed as nicely as she was.

(but hey they didn't bring their kid did they?)

She looked back down at her forms.

(isn't this just admitting defeat? isn't this—)

She got to work. The voice snapped at the edge of her thoughts as she filled in her address—

(at least until the unemployment runs out)

—her work history—

(how skilled can you be when you only started working a real job when you were twenty-nine? and haven't worked in almost a year?)

At the bottom of the second page,

Are you seeking employment as part of receiving state financial assistance? (Check Yes or No),

it read. Her pen hesitated—

(not yet but we're one step closer aren't we?)

—then circled *No.* She tensed, as if expecting an alarm to sound.

(it's not a lie that's why i'm here to NOT be on public assistance)

(you're here because you couldn't find a job you need help because you're a failure)

Karen capped her pen hard enough to drive the point through the flimsy plastic tip. A glassy pain shot down the backs of her hands. "Damn," she muttered and slid the pen in the space bet-ween the clip and the back. She looked up. "Kev?"

He blinked at her. It was the fluorescents that made his face pale, right?

Karen held up the clipboard. "I have to go turn this in, but then we're outta here, okay?"

He nodded, his pale face serious. He reminded Karen of a college student mid-cram instead of an eight-year-old reading a Batman comic. "Okay, Mum."

She stood, ignoring the ache in the small of her back. "Five minutes." She paused. "You've been excellent, kiddo."

He grinned, banishing the too-serious expression. His feet kicked under his chair, the tips of his sneakers scuffing the industrial carpet.

(what is he doing here? this is no place for a boy downtown is no place for a boy)

Something in Karen's heart pulled, and she turned away, approaching the reception window. Behind the counter, a large black woman filled the desk. She looked up from her computer as Karen approached. "All done?" she asked, her smile more genuine than the apathetic waiting room encouraged.

"Mm-hmm," Karen said, handing the clipboard over. Behind her was the ding of someone else coming into the office.

The woman scanned Karen's forms. "We look good, here." She set the clipboard down and squinted at her computer screen. "Labor Day's thrown me all off schedule," she said. "At least it's Friday, though, right?"

Karen didn't have a response to that. Behind her, someone coughed—a lonely, empty sound.

"But," the woman said, "I think I can squeeze you in for the initial interview . . . next Wednesday, at eleven?"

(kevin will be back in school thank god)

"That's fine," she said. Her hands wanted to fidget; she folded them on the counter like a child.

The woman smiled again. "Wonderful." She pulled a reminder card from the stack beside her, filled it in, and offered it to Karen. "We'll see you, then?"

Karen smiled. It was plastic and pushed the muscles of her face all wrong and she made sure to widen it. "Okay. Thank you."

She reached for the card, grasped it, but the woman didn't let go. Her eyes had dropped to Karen's hand.

Karen looked down and her heart paused in her chest. Everything inside and outside her head turned down to the muted roar you heard when your ears were underwater.

The cuff of her blazer had pulled at the sleeve, revealing a few inches of her forearm. The ends of vertical scabs poked out from under the fabric, too neat to be anything but deliberate.

Karen swallowed and tried to jerk the card from the woman's hand. The woman tugged back. Karen's hand throbbed again when she lost contact.

The woman flipped the card over to the blank side and scribbled something. She held it up, elbow planted on the desk.

"I don't do this for everyone," she said, and her voice was a slow dirge underwater. "Or anyone, really. But this might help." She glanced down meaningfully.

Karen followed her gaze. The sleeve of the woman's dress had fallen down to her elbow, revealing three jagged scars along the forearm. They stood out like albino worms.

She looked back at the woman and the woman nodded, handing the card over. Karen took it with numb fingers.

YOU ARE NOT ALONE,

the back read. Beneath this,

ST. JUDE'S MINISTRIES

FRIDAYS – 9PM (DOCTOR DARREN),

followed by an address.

"Thank you," she said, just to say something.

"And we'll see you Wednesday," the woman said, her tone light and airy once more.

Karen turned back to Kevin, her head filled with the static of a television tuned to a dead station. "C'mon, champ."

Walking back to the parking garage, the streets of downtown Hathaway packed with white collars, the card in her blazer pocket weighed her down. She kept tugging at the sleeve of her blazer, making sure it touched her wrist at all times.

Home was a brick house converted into two apartments on a hill in the Oakdale neighborhood. As they climbed the stairs to the second floor, Karen heard the beep of a message being left on the answering machine.

She put a hand on Kevin's shoulder. "Double-time it, kiddo."

They reached the top and Karen unlocked the door, breezing through the living room and into the kitchen. Her heart had restarted since the temp agency and now it raced, as if making up for lost time, when she saw the blinking green light of the answering machine on the counter.

(let it be an interview let it be an interview let me be able to cancel that damn appointment)

She pressed PLAY and the tape whirred inside the machine.

"Mizz Dempsey?" a man's voice said, slurring the honorific, and Karen's heart slowed. Only two types of people could turn simple statements into questions: teenage girls and attorneys. She'd had enough experience with attorneys over the past four years.

"This is Alan Ladd of Mamatas, Braunbeck, and Morgan?" the voice continued. "I've been hired by your ex-husband, Mr. Nick Dempsey, about an issue of custody with your son? I had a few questions and if you could return my call that would really help?"

The voice rattled off his number.

Karen didn't bother to memorize it.

(that son of a bitch he promised that son of a bitch he promised)

The machine clicked. Karen stared at it without seeing. Muscles tightened—building ache in her hands and climbing her arms, spreading across her shoulders before going up her neck to throb in the back of her skull.

(that son of a bitch he PROMISED that son of a bitch)

(of course he calls now of course)

(failure at working failure at marriage failure at—)

"Mum?"

Karen jerked, sending a lightning bolt up her back, bursting like thunder in her head. She winced.

She forced herself to turn. Kevin stood in the doorway. "You okay, Mum?"

"Of course, kiddo," she said. Her voiced sounded normal.

"Was that Dad's lawyer?" he asked.

"Do you know something about this?" she asked, keeping her voice even. Something twitched in her neck and she swallowed.

(that son of a bitch PROMISED)

"I heard him and Moira talking about it last weekend."

"They talked about this *in front of you?*"

Kevin winced and Karen's skull throbbed once more. "Not really, but they weren't trying to, y'know, hide it?" He looked up at her and Karen resisted taking a step back. His eyes were glassy, wet with tears threatening to spill. His lips thinned to a small white stitch.

(that's something he gets from me)

(that's because he's my SON—MY son)

"Oh, kiddo," she said and went to him. His lips thinned further, almost disappearing into his face.

She pulled him in and he allowed it, face burying into her stomach. He shivered some more, as if to keep the emotions in.

"Take it easy, Kevin," she said. "Just take it easy." She couldn't even hear herself; her pulse roared in her ears.

(THAT SON OF A BITCH)

Kevin turned his face so the side of his head rested against her stomach. "I'm not going anywhere, am I, Mum? I *like* it here, I *like* it with you. I like school. I—" His speech sped up, becoming thicker.

She crouched down, her knees popping, and pulled him into a real hug. "Shhhh, Kevin. Shh."

"That's what I told Dad," Kevin said and his voice sounded close to breaking. "I told both Dad and Moira and Moira wanted me to call her 'Mom' again—"

Karen's muscles tried tightening again. That had been the battle last year; Moira, Kevin's step-mother, had gotten it into her head that Kevin should call *her* Mom and only a scorched-Earth phone call from Karen had stopped *that*.

(not for long though they think—)

Karen shut the voice out.

"Easy, chief," Karen said, rubbing his back. "There's nothing to worry about. Your Dad and I just have to discuss a few things." She said this through gritted teeth.

She pulled Kevin away so she could look at him. Kevin watched his shoes. Two hectic spots colored his cheeks.

"I don't want you to worry about it," she said, forcing her voice soft. "Your Dad loves you and I love you and even Moira loves you. You have your weekend with him this weekend and it's going to be *fine*, right? You never worry when you're at your Dad's, right?"

Kevin shook his head.

"And you have fun, right?"

A nod.

"Then don't worry about it," she said. "I'll take care of this." She pulled him in for another hug and he rested his head on her shoulder. She kissed the top of his scalp. "Go upstairs and get what toys you wanna take, okay?" A final squeeze. "And *don't worry about this.*"

She let him go and Kevin stepped away. He smiled at her, but it made Karen's stomach flip over. It was a sad smile, a I-know-you're-lying-but-thank-you-for-trying smile. "Okay, Mum."

She smiled back. It was as plastic and painful as the one at the temp agency. "Okay."

Kevin plodded to the steps across the kitchen, then went upstairs, where the attic had been converted into bedrooms.

Karen stood, listening to the stairs creak under his slight weight. Her muscles bunched into a single knot. Her head filled with a hyper-tension buzz.

(that son of a bitch do this to our son he promised he promised he PROM-ISED)

And then it popped and her muscles loosened and this pain was worse than before. The other voice—it sounded, honestly, like her mother—swooped in.

(failure at marriage failure at working and they think you're a failure as a parent)

"I'm not a failure," she whispered, but her voice lacked any conviction.

(call nick's lawyer back and tell him that)

A deep-seated itch dug into the arm that the temp agency receptionist had seen. She gripped it through the sleeve of her blazer, twisted the fabric against the skin until it burned.

It made her feel better.

Nick usually waited in the driver seat as Kevin climbed into the car, talking to Karen—if he had to—through the open passenger window.

But, tonight, he leaned against the side of his Mitsubishi Eclipse, right under the streetlight, arms crossed. A perfect scene, as if the street had resolved itself to be just-so for him. He stood straight when they walked out of the house, opening the passenger door with exaggerated movements.

"Your chariot awaits, partner," he said to Kevin. "Slide on in. Gotta talk to your Mum a minute."

Kevin did, sliding his suitcase and toy-bag into the footwell, glancing at Karen as Nick closed the door.

Nick leaned against the car again, arms re-crossing. "Did Alan call you?" he asked, the voice lower.

"You mean the lawyer you said you weren't going to get?" Karen asked. "Yeah, he called." Her voice dropped. "You *promised*, Nick."

"Karie—"

She jabbed a finger at him. "*Don't.* You don't get to call me that. Fucking *pet names* went out the fucking window the minute you started fucking your coworker, okay?"

Nick looked away. Down the hill, 53rd Street spilled out into a T-intersection with Butler Street, the streaks of headlights heading for the nightlife of downtown.

"You promised, Nick," she said again. "We *talked* about this when I was laid off—"

"A year ago," Nick said, still watching the street.

"Does that even matter? Am I still able to put a roof over his head, clothes on his back, food in his stomach?"

He looked back at her. "For how long, though?"

Her shoulders wanted to hunch—it was exactly what she'd been thinking. She wouldn't allow herself to move. Nick would know. Of course he would.

"I have unemployment coming in," she said. "And you know that."

Nick straightened. "Again, for how long?"

"Where was this when we divorced?" she asked. "I was neither college-educated nor employed but you didn't raise much of a fuss, *then*. Remember? I mean, it *was* four years ago, a ridiculously long time, I know, but it wasn't fucking *eons*."

Nick opened his mouth, closed it, then glanced at his car. Kevin watched them and Karen realized he'd probably seen her jab her finger at his father.

"I'm just thinking about what's best for Kevin," Nick said, slowly, as if he spoke to a slow child.

"And I don't?"

He hissed out a breath. "I'm just saying that—shit, Karen, you're laid off and you only have an associate's degree. In court-reporting, of all things—which you weren't even doing. You're a goddamn secretary, Karen. How many of those are available in this kinda economy?"

She gritted her teeth so hard her jaw ached.

He shook his head. "How did the conversation go with Alan?"

"We didn't have one."

"Why?"

"He left a message."

"Where were you?"

"At a temp agency," she said. "I don't just wait around for a job to land in my oh-so uneducated lap. I have a son to raise."

"And I don't?"

"Never seemed to concern you before. Not while you were playing house with Moira."

He hissed out a breath again. "This is fucking pointless."

"Finally something we agree on."

He shook his head and reached into his back pocket. "We'll talk when clearer heads prevail," he said, and pulled out a folded check. "Here. September's child's support."

The urge to slap the check from his hand filled her head.

(he planned this)

Doubtful, but he knew how it would look.

And she had a son to raise.

She refused to look at him as she took his check, instead watching Kevin watch them. He felt his eyes on her, though.

"Seven on Sunday?" Nick asked.

She made herself smile at Kevin. "Isn't it always?"

A pause. Finally, Nick said, "Just think about it, Karen. I *am* his father. I can take care of him, too, you know. And it would be a lesser burden on you."

She still smiled at Kevin. "We're doing fine, thanks."

Nick went around the front of the car. She waved at Kevin as Nick pulled away from the curb—faster than he should've.

(he better not talk about this in front of kevin he better not)

(and if he does you'll do what?)

She shuffled back to the apartment. On the television, the ABC affiliate was on, playing through *Step by Step*. It was a laugh-tracked mumble-roar in her ears. Her head throbbed. Her shoulders ached.

Her arm itched.

She made her way around the loveseat, to the bathroom, flicking on the light over the medicine cabinet. It washed her in yellow, making her cheeks starker, her eyes deeper in their sockets.

Karen glanced away, unbuttoning the sleeve of her shirt and pushing it up. Thin, long vertical scabs traced the circumference of her forearm in mostly organized rows.

She studied them a moment. Guilt and shame percolated through the slow, lazy waves of pain.

(can't handle it weak a failure)

(failure at marriage failure at work failure at parenting)

She opened the medicine cabinet. A razor rested on the top shelf and she pulled it down. The yellow light slid along the blade like liquid butter.

She took a deep breath, put the razor near her elbow. The corner dimpled the flesh.

Pressed down and the wire-thin pain was immediate, banishing the throbbing in her head, the ache in her shoulders, the voices that rode her thoughts.

"What a cocksucker," Lisa said the next day, taking a sip of coffee. "How'd you leave it?"

Karen shrugged from the other side of the kitchen table. "Unfinished."

(like everything right? right?)

Her arm itched beneath her shirt sleeve. It always did the day after. She rubbed her arm against the table. Lisa's eyes dropped to that and Karen picked up her mug and took a sip.

"Didja call the lawyer back?"

"No."

"He's gonna call again."

"I'll deal with him, then—or he'll leave another message."

Lisa cocked an eyebrow. Karen could only describe her in hair terms—Lisa was full, Lisa was bouncy, Lisa had great volume. Lisa was the latest from Vidal Sassoon. They'd met when Karen had taken classes at the community colleges, following the disastrously expensive idea that court-reporting was a great idea to sustain her and Kevin after the divorce. Lisa had been picking up the few remaining credits needed to be a CPA. She worked bookkeeping for a mortgage firm downtown.

"You can't run away from that," Lisa said.

Karen resisted shrugging. "I know that."

"Then handle this head-on," she said. "The mother doesn't *always* get full, y'know? I read a thing in *Time* magazine—"

She sighed. "You're a pain in my ass."

Lisa shook her head. "No—Nick and that mega-cunt he married are a pain in your ass. I'm your vulgar Jiminy Cricket." She set her mug down again. "Is it cash?"

Karen tried three different answers internally. "Yes. No. Fuck, I don't know." She shook her head. "It was just one more thing I didn't need."

Lisa nodded. "That's life—always ready to shove it in an inch deeper."

Karen barked laughter. "You're doing a helluva job making me feel better over here. Is this why just *had* to come over when I called you?"

Lisa studied her a moment. Karen's arm itched again, she rubbed it on the table, and Lisa's eyes dropped to it. Karen slid her hands under the table.

"I'm worried about you," Lisa said finally. "If it's not the job, it's your ex-husband. If it's not your ex-husband, Kevin's sick with something. You've lost weight—that shirt's about-hanging off your skinny-ass frame. And it looks like you haven't been sleeping."

Karen cut her eyes away. "It's a lot to deal with."

Lisa finished her cup. "I can imagine," she said. "How'd the temp agency go?"

Karen shrugged. "Fine. As fine as can be expected. I have an initial on Wednesday morning."

"But no new interviews."

"Dead air."

"You'll get something," Lisa said. "You have common skills, but those common skills are *excellent*. I mean, with court-reporting, you must be able to type, like, a million words a minute, and—"

"I'll make more coffee," Karen said, and got up quickly. Her chair feet squeaked across the linoleum. She snatched Lisa's mug—ignoring the watchful expression on her face—and went to the Mr. Coffee. Her arm itched and burned; she rubbed it against the edge of the counter as she dumped out the old grounds.

"How much?" she asked. She moved her body so Lisa couldn't see her rubbing. "Half-pot, full-pot—"

She heard chair legs squeak and she turned to find Lisa right there, almost kissing-distance away, her eyes sharp. She snatched Karen's hand.

Karen tried backing up and Lisa held firm, moving with her. They stumbled like awkward lovers and Lisa's weight drove Karen into the counter. A bolt of pure hell burst in the small of her back as the edge dug into her spine. She howled, and their legs tangled, dropping them to the floor.

Lisa fought her, pulling at Karen's arm, tearing at the button of the shirt sleeve, and Karen squirmed and yanked and Lisa's body weight held her tight. All thought was gone; she was reduced to animal instinct, fight or flight.

The button on the sleeve popped and Lisa shoved it up Karen's arm, exposing the line bracelets. The cuts from last night, four of them, had reopened and bled sluggishly.

The moment hung with Karen's arm between them.

The itch had disappeared, however.

"I knew it," Lisa panted. Her frizzy blond hair hung like a swarm around her face. "I fucking *knew* this shit."

And then she shook Karen's arm in Karen's face, like an owner shaking a chewed slipper in front of a bad dog. Karen cringed to avoid being hit with her own flopping hand.

"What the fuck do you think you're doing, Karen?" Lisa yelled. *"What the FUCK—"*

She visibly shook herself, her red face paling. "Shit," she said. "Oh shit." She pressed Karen's arm to Karen's chest, swept her other arm beneath Karen's neck, and lifted Karen up like a mother to a child, bringing her in close. "I'm sorry, kiddo. I'm sorry. Shit, I'm sorry."

With something like horror, Karen realized she was trying to keep from crying. "I'm so sorry, Karen. I overreacted. I did. I'd suspected and I'm sorry, and—oh, kid—" She took a breath. "Why haven't you told me, Karen? When you needed help, why didn't you come? I'm always here for you. Don't you know that by now?"

And it was all right there in Lisa's face—all the love, all the worry. All the pity.

Yes, all the pity. Because her *she* was—Mrs. Lisa Thorne, a comfortably-employed CPA, a happily-childless wife—and she was sitting in the lap of her unemployed, single-mother friend, had been riding her almost like some kid on one of those coin-rides outside a supermarket, and deep down in the corners of those welling eyes was pity. Pity for her friend who couldn't find a job, pity for her friend whose unemployment was running out, pity for her friend who had a son to raise alone, pity for her friend whose ex-husband only played father when it was convenient. Mrs. Lisa Thorne had her shit together. Mrs. Lisa Thorne's friend very obviously did not. And it broke Mrs. Lisa Thorne's heart.

Shame came flooding in and with it came the pain—in her back, her hands, her arms, her head.

She twisted her shoulders, breaking Lisa's grip, and shoved Lisa off. Lisa fell with a thump, goggling, as Karen scrambled to her feet and lunged out of the kitchen. A kind of reptilian instinct overtook her; the kind of primitive thinking that only knew comforts, attraction and aversion.

She went for the bathroom without thinking.

Lisa screamed, *"No, Karen!"*

Karen threw the door closed behind her and locked in. The dead-station static had returned to her head. She pawed at the medicine cabinet. Outside, she heard the thunderous approach of Lisa running for the door.

She pawed for the razor, nearly dropped it, gripped in her palm and slicing the pads of her fingers.

(just this and i can think just this and it stops)

Lisa slammed into the other side of the door and the puny lock snapped. The door shuddered open and Lisa was there, her expression wild.

"NO GODDAMMIT!" she screamed and lunged forward. She took Karen at the waist and Karen lost the razor; she heard it clatter somewhere. She stumbled, the backs of her calves hitting the edge of the tub. Their center of gravity danced away and both women tumbled in with a ridiculous *thomp* sound. Lisa's shoulder slammed into Karen's chest, knocking the air out.

Slowly, Lisa worked to extricate herself. "This is fucking ridiculous," she muttered, pulling herself shakily from the tub, then reaching down to help Karen.

Karen ignored the proffered hand, took a breath.

And shrieked.

Night had fallen and only a single end-table lamp battled the darkness.

Karen closed the apartment door and sudden silence crashed down. Outside, Lisa's car roared to life, then faded as it drove away.

She shuffled over to the couch, dropped onto it, and stared at the shaggy carpet.

Lisa had rained platitudes upon platitudes, things that sounded culled from sitcoms and Movies of the Week, down on Karen's ears, only a fraction of it getting through—

—"hurting yourself is never the answer"—

(but what if you hurt all the time?)

—until it all became a gently undulated wave of sound in the center of Karen's head—

—"there's always tomorrow"—

(for things to get progressively worse as they had for the past four years since i left nick)

—that Karen couldn't even begin to make sense of.

—"you are never alone, and"—

(except you are when you're divorced with no family and no job and a son to raise and-and-and-and)

It was all a very special episode of *Blossom*.

(why didn't you tell me?)

Karen hadn't spoken at all—but, then, really, Karen hadn't been expected to. It'd been sometime around the second "You have so much to live for" that Karen had realized Lisa hadn't been speaking to *Karen*, but to Lisa herself. To Lisa, this was a Karen she didn't know. Lisa had met her when she was fighting through her divorce; she'd met a woman doing everything she could with limited resources to provide for her son. After the divorce had been finalized, she'd known a woman driven to work any job for the same reason.

But, remove divorce and work, and leave only the driven need to provide for her son?

(hullo lisa please meet the real karen dempsey)

The problem for the Lisa Thornes of the world, who were self-preserved to the extent that the very air around them hung charged with confidence, was that they couldn't comprehend a creature like Karen Dempsey. Lisa had been talking herself into believing that the Karen Dempsey that cut, that was broke, that was barely holding on was only a shell and not the core.

Knowing this, it'd been that much easier to tune out, to not talk. How do you explain the need to get out from under the constant, crushing weight?

The only thing that hit home, late into Lisa's rambling thesis, was the idea of cutting too deep, of dying, and of Kevin being home when it happened.

"Imagine Kevin hearing you fall," Lisa had said, her voice hoarse, "and coming downstairs and seeing you in a pool of blood on the bathroom floor. Can you *see* that, Karen?"

Of course she could; the shame in cutting wasn't in the act, but in the idea of someone *else* being hurt.

(what if kevin sees?)

(what kind of mother am i? how am i raising my son?)

But that was on the surface—the surface thoughts, the surface guilt, the surface certainty. What had hit home was the realization of something underneath all that. Something—

"Enough," Karen said now and her voice was as hoarse as Lisa's had been. She dry-washed her face, her shaking hands rubbing the sharp contours of her face. She forced herself off the couch, went to the bathroom. The tongue of the lock had bent the frame a bit; she joggled it and tried closing the door. It latched, but would not lock—the tongue kept popping out.

(have to replace that when we move)

(which will be in a few months more when the unemployment runs out— merry christmas kevin we're spending it in a shelter!)

She grimaced and stepped into the bathroom.

(i hope you know it's your fault he's dead dear)

"Shut up, Mom," she muttered, not even aware she spoke aloud.

She adjusted the bathmat in front of the sink, straightened the shower curtain. The medicine cabinet door hung open and she closed it, avoid her reflection. Near the base of the toilet, she found the razor. She picked it up, looked from the razor to her arm. Blood had smeared across the flesh, dried to flakes.

(imagine kevin seeing this)

And then another voice,

(imagine without any outlet or distraction from the pain)

But that wasn't even the worst. The worst lay *beneath* that final thought, like the mutter of secret messages that could only be heard when you played the record backward:

(imagine yourself unable to be free)

Karen's lips thinned. Her back ached from the repeated hits. Her cuts burned like fire ants on the skin.

And Karen Dempsey, still holding the razor, began to cry.

2

SPRAINED

Roiling black clouds cut the emerald green sky to ribbons; a breeze carries the scent of sulfur, the ghost of black smoke.

Karen walks up a hill of waist-high grass long gone brown and dead; they crumble when she brushes them. The soil itself is loose, gray, filled with pale shards of what look like broken shale. No landmarks rise out of the distance—no buildings, no forests, not even shrubbery. Just these hills of dead grass, barren soil.

(i've been here before)

She stops, looks back the way she has come. Near the end of the horizon she can see that the sky lightens first to yellow, then, where earth and sky meet, blue. There are no clouds at that horizon, and the earth appears healthier—a ribbon of green.

She looks down and she wears a loose dress. Navy-blue cotton, with small white flowers dotting it. White strap-on sandals adorn her feet.

(i wore this when my father was buried)

(i hope you know it's your fault he's dead dear)

"Shut up, Mum," she says and starts walking again. She tops the hill and sees it continues; more hills, the sky growing more sickly as it continues until it's almost black in the distance. Standing out against this, however, is a landmark—a hump on top of a hill, against the horizon. A destination.

She starts down the hill, her feet sinking almost to the ankle in the loose, rocky soil. It irritates her skin, but there's nothing to be done about that.

(i came here as a child before i escaped home before i escaped that damned small town)

This is the place, healthier then, that she daydreams to escape her mother; a place to imagine her life outside of Franklin, Pennsylvania.

She hasn't thought of it in almost fifteen years.

"Why am I here?" she asks. "What happened to this place?"

Only the black-dusted and sulfur-smelling breeze whistling answers her. Lightning within the clouds flash, as if god's taking pictures.

The world is sour, but she's fine. No headache, no backache, no achy joints. Her arm doesn't even itch. The poison in her has—

(—poisoned her dreamland)

She stops again, face crinkling.

The interior voice grew strength; it sounded like her mother.

(this is the place dreams go to die dear where *your* dreams go to die your silly dreams of journalism and new york and independence you gave all *that* up quickly didn't you? for the man who would foist a child upon you and then leave you hanging a thirty-two-year-old single mother without a single exceptional skill and a son she can barely raise)

"Shut up, Mom," she mutters, her voice lost in the distant ominous rumble of thunder.

(why should i? you know the truth drove your father to an early grave drove your husband into another woman's arms drove your only child to the poor house you want to dream of a better tomorrow? dream about what you left behind and what happened to it dream about what happens when you can't face reality)

She starts moving again. The stones jab at her open toes. She winces and moves faster, up the next hill, down it. The landmark comes closer—only four or five more hills away. It looks vaguely like a house. Whose house?

(and while you dream your ex-husband has your son is filling your son's head with how wonderful everything will be when your son lives with him and isn't he right karen? isn't he? you can barely keep yourself together—how are you raising a child?)

"Shut UP, Mum," she says, louder, and thunder rumbles, closer. More cloud-lightning flashes. She tops the next hill, kicking up more dirt. The itch in her feet has deepened to an ache.

(you're dreaming and where's your son karen? where is he? not with you you're just going to ruin him like you ruin everything else)

"SHUT UP, MUM!" she screams and, of course, trips.

She rolls down the remainder of the hill, the rotten soil going up her dress, down her neck. It doesn't itch, it hurts, the aftermath of a bad static-shock; it lingers against her skin. She comes to a stop at the bottom and sits up. Her body made a little divot, upsetting some rocks and she sees one larger, rounder, and smoother than the other pieces poking out. She reaches for it, pulls it from the dusty soil. It's a skull, missing its jawbone.

A child's skull.

And her mother is right there:
(now you know where kevin is headed)
Her sudden scream shatters the world around her.

She didn't wake up screaming, instinct stopping in fear of waking Kevin in the next room.

She sat up, the top sheet pooling around her waist.

The bedroom's single window allowed the streetlamp to peep in, created a yellowish oblong on the water-marked ceiling. She looked at the digital clock on the nightstand—three a.m.

She swung her feet over the side of the bed, rubbing her face. Her palms came away wet. She'd been crying in her sleep. Again.

"Christ," she muttered and shook the last of the dream from her head. She rarely remembered her dreams.

But she remembered this one.

(where dreams go to die dear)

Her mother was dead; had died when Kevin was six. They hadn't traveled back to Franklin for her funeral. Kevin didn't even know her.

(sounds alive and well in my head)

(at least something's alive and well in there)

She shook her head a final time and got out of bed, headed for the stairs. Past experience told her that she wouldn't be sleeping again tonight.

"You excited?" she asked. A knot of pain thumped within the center of her skull and her eyes felt like they'd been rubbed in margarita salt, but she kept her voice light, anticipatory.

Kevin watched the intersection through the windshield, his eyes glued to the left side, where the bus for Fort Buchanan Elementary would come. On the corner beside Karen's Sundance, other parents waited with their children. The crossing guard, a plump older woman in a hunter's-orange vest, stood by the crosswalk. "Uh-huh."

She glanced at him. He held his Jansport backpack—Navy

blue and scuffed with a year's use—in his lap. The school clothes were new, bought with money socked away, and the colors seemed brighter than he was. It was the early morning sunlight making him look pale, right?

"Second grade," she continued. "Moving up in the world."

"I have the same teacher," he said. "Miss Lake. Same class."

"But new things to learn," she replied.

He continued to watch traffic. She bit her lip, made herself stop. The knuckle of pain rapped her brains once more. "You sure you're all right, kiddo?"

"Yeah, Mum." Flat, barely-listening. He'd been like this since she'd picked him up yesterday (Nick, per usual, hadn't walked him down to the car, even after the conversation he and Karen had had on Friday).

"And the weekend went okay?" she pressed. "Nothing off with your dad or Moira?"

"It was *fine*, Mum," he said, with feeling, but his expression never changed from that mute watchfulness.

"They didn't say anything you, or—"

"The bus is here," Kevin said, and undid his seatbelt.

Karen shut the Sundance down and got out with Kevin; a few other parents—all of them dressed for work—did the same.

They queued up as the bus pulled to the intersection and put on its lights. The crossing guard moved into the center of the street as the bus's doors opened. Parents hugged and kissed their kids—the younger kids struggling not to cry, some failing, some with parents joining in. From past experience, Karen wouldn't be seeing any of these parents for the rest of the year.

Kevin rushed to get close to the bus, outpacing his mother.

"Hug your mum, guy," she said, catching up. "You're not too big, yet."

He turned quickly, his hands sliding over her shoulders in a distracted grasp. She hugged him more fully, kissing the top of his head. "Good luck, kiddo. Enjoy yourself."

He fidgeted in her grasp. "I will, Mum."

She let go and Kevin rushed to catch up with the rest of the line. His head continued to look around as other kids piled up. He paused, looking up 54ᵗʰ Street, and she followed his gaze.

Three girls, ridiculously close in age—growing up in the 1960s, they would've been called Irish Twins—came galumphing down the sidewalk. Where every other kid had new clothes, their clothes bore a myriad of old stains. The youngest had a head of hair closely resembling a bird's nest made by an idiot pigeon. The middle had dirty hands that swung—the only word that came to Karen's mind was *stupidly*—at her sides.

Karen's lips thinned instinctively. The Perozzi girls. Every neighborhood had a white trash family and the Perozzis were Oak-dale's. The mother was rarely seen, the father was a loud drunk, and there were rumored to be even more kids—a boy in middle school and a handful of toddlers.

They crossed the street under the direction of the crossing guard. The woman said good morning to them and they didn't even raise their heads.

Karen looked back at Kevin and Kevin scrambled up the steps, nearly kicking the boy in the front by accident.

Karen's brow furrowed. The Perozzis got in line last, looking as out of place as pimples on a model's chin. She glanced up at the bus and saw Kevin in his seat, looking out the window, watching the line. He caught Karen watching *him*, and quickly looked away.

What was *that* about?

She watched Kevin until the bus lumbered down the street, but he never looked back out the window. She watched him facing forward, hugging his backpack now.

When the bus was out of sight, she joined the line of parents going to their cars. A few talked to each other, but not many. She thought of Kevin and the Perozzi girls. What *was* that about?

None of the Perozzi kids were genteel; she'd often heard them outside, their foul-mouthed conversations drifting on the breeze like the smell of

(sulfur)

For the life of her, she couldn't think of a single instance of Kevin being near them, and he'd never mentioned anything last year.

(yes because he's just such an open and conversational kid)

As she rolled up to the light, her head throbbed once more, louder and more painfully now, as if knowing she didn't have to fake it for Kevin's sake. By mid-afternoon, when she picked Kevin up, it would be a full-fledged exhaustion-migraine. She completely forgot the Perozzis.

Thursday, and the interview was wrapping up, and she didn't know her agent's name.

That was okay, though, because her agent—a young guy with carefully-styled tousled sandy hair—had avoided looking at her as much as possible. She'd spent forty-five minutes getting her makeup perfect, too, making sure to soften the hard edges of her cheeks, to lighten the bags under her eyes, to give her pale skin some color.

Forty-five minutes, which was three times as long as this interview. Eight dollars to a parking garage to be ignored for fifteen minutes. The agents barely referred to her form.

"The problem, Ms. Dempsey," her agent said, cornering a sheaf of papers against his desktop blotter and paying particular attention to getting them into order, "is your skills are incredibly common. You can do basic reception work, you can type—"

"—one-hundred-twenty words a minute," she said, keeping her hands folding in front of her, in spite of how her arm itched. She kept her back straight, in spite of the slowly deepening ache.

That stopped him mid-tap. Around them came the drone of many conversations going on at once, with the occasional sharp ring of a phone or the buzz of a Xerox.

"Is that timed?" He still held the sheaf of papers and his cufflinks winked in the low fluorescent lighting.

(it's in my file you smarmy little shit)

"I studied court-reporting," she said. "Ninety per minute was minimum to continue. I never tested lower than one-ten."

"Why didn't you pursue it? Court-reporting's good income."

Something scratched her throat. She resisted swallowing.

"Yes—if you can get in to the system. You have to freelance

for a year and your territory's the entire state. That's an incredibly unreliable means of making a living when you have a son to raise."

"No …" His eyes dropped to her ringless hands. "… extended family?"

"No. I was coming out of a divorce and was trying anything to earn a living for my child. That plan didn't work out."

The man's eyes glazed over. She'd seen the look before. Silly woman, trying to play a game she had no business playing in, and without even knowing all the rules. Typical.

Her hands, folded, locked together. A headache was forming.

He leaned back in his chair, studying her. His gaze, along with the low ceiling, boxed her in, pressed her deeply into the uncomfortable plastic back of her own chair. As if in warning, her back twinged.

"I'll revise," he said, with the air of conferring a great favor. A photo was tacked to the wall of his cubicle, directly in his eyeline, of him and a woman in a park. This presumed that he wasn't an asshole all the time.

(this from the person who married nick)

"You have common skills, which are abundant in our economy, but you're particularly good at them."

(it didn't sound so patronizing from lisa)

He leaned forward. "If you don't hear from me, call Tuesday. I should have something. A lot of companies are going on computers, which is requiring all personnel to transfer records. They're short-handed." He gestured toward her. "This is where *you* come in."

A lump formed in her throat, but whether it was from disgust or relief, she couldn't tell.

"The companies give us your wages," he said, "we pay you. Standard rate, regardless of the company. Given your situation—" He paused the slightest bit. "—I'll try to keep the jobs steady, even if you're bouncing around the city. Is that agreeable?"

"Of course."

"A lot of these companies hire our temps. We have an over-seventy-percent full-time hire rate, which we're incredibly proud of and work hard to maintain by vetting all candidates."

His eyes had been traveling the space of his cubicle, but now returned to her.

"We offer, as much as we're able, careers here. Too many people come in looking for some quick cash, low commitment. That's not what we do. Do you understand?"

His eyes said, *This is where you put on your big-girl pants and don't fuck this up.*

She wanted to look away, but didn't. "Of course I do," she said. "I have a son to raise."

He was already turning away to his computer. Dismissed.

The understanding, former-cutter receptionist had been replaced by a skinny woman who'd bought into the shoulderpad-1980s a bit too much. She didn't even look up when Karen left.

Waiting at the elevators, willing her back not to bend against the ache in her spine, Karen reached into her blazer jacket for her parking garage ticket. She felt a second edge of cardboard and, brow furrowing, pulled out her reminder card, the one the receptionist had written on the back of:

YOU ARE NOT ALONE

ST. JUDE'S MINISTRIES

FRIDAYS - 9:00 PM (Doctor Darren)

She sat on the couch, the reminder card on the coffee table.

(YOU ARE NOT ALONE)

(i've been there, too, the woman's smile says)

(ST. JUDE'S MINISTRIES)

(nick rolling his eyes dramatically: for how long, karen?)

Gilligan's Island wrapped up on the television in the corner, finishing with Tina Louise's laugh, which sounded to Karen like glass shards falling together.

(YOU ARE NOT ALONE)

(the temp agent smiling patronizingly at her: now put on your big-girl pants and don't fuck this up, okay?)

The theme song to *Bobby's World*, which sounded like a poppier-version of the theme from *Ferris Bueller's Day Off* to Karen, permeated her thoughts. She glanced at the television. The cartoon was part of a new scheduling block Fox had started last year. Kevin, of course, loved it.

Wait.

Kevin.

The green numbers of the VCR beneath the television jumped out at her: 3:35.

Kevin's school bus dropped him off at 3:15.

She froze, panic for a moment crystalizing every nerve in her body. The image of Kevin on the corner of Butler Street, watching the heavy traffic pass and looking for his mother, filled her head.

"*Shit!*" she yelled and the crystals broke from her body, sending a pained shudder down her limbs.

(failure at parenting failure at parenting)

She raced for the door.

She found him, pressed against the side of the building on the corner—Acme Supplies and, oh, how that name had delighted him last year when she'd read it to him—watching the traffic like a cornered animal.

Her battered Sundance roared across the intersection, brakes squealing to a hard stop just past the crosswalk, and she flew out.

"*Kevin!*"

She went for him and scooped him up, even as her back tweaked awkwardly at the sudden weight. She hadn't picked him up like this in years.

If nothing else, her headache was gone.

She was babbling in his ear, half-coos and rambled apologies. She ran a hand along the back of his head, over and over. He clung back with a fierceness he hadn't used since he was a toddler.

"I'm so sorry, Kevin," she rambled. "I'm so, so sorry."

Slowly, his tight grip lessened and she set him back on his feet, still holding his hand. Dear Jesus, he was so *small—*

(and you left him)

"Are you okay?" she asked.

He looked at her and his gaze wasn't accusatory but she had to keep from recoiling, anyway. His eyes were wide, taking her all in.

"Where were you?" he asked and his tone was flat as if the question didn't even interest him that much.

She opened her mouth, and nothing was there.

(forgot him left him behind what kind of mother are you you ruin everything)

"Let's go, hon," she said. "Let's get you home, okay?"

His eyes lost some of their shine and she had to keep herself from recoiling again; resignation settling in.

(and you put it there)

She led him to the car and he followed. He glanced over his shoulder as she held the passenger door, and she followed his gaze.

Down the street, the Perozzi girls stood, watching. The middle held the hand of the youngest. They looked like they wore the same clothes they'd had on yesterday. When they saw her looking, they turned and walked up 55th Street.

Karen turned back to Kevin, but he was already in his seat, belt buckled, backpack on his lap. He didn't look at her.

It was on the tip of her tongue to ask him about the Perozzis as she got in, but she took another look at his face, and didn't.

That look of resignation.

That look of holding it in.

Friday night and Nick waited in the car, didn't even turn his head to look at them as Kevin opened the passenger door to get in.

"See you Sunday," Nick said to her, shifting into first gear when Kevin's seatbelt clicked home.

(talk when clearer heads prevail)

Karen studied his silhouette, the firm set of his jaw, his eyes locked on the windshield, then turned to Kevin, leaning in to hug the boy and kiss the top of his head. "Have fun," she said, and stepped back to close the door. Kevin didn't wave as Nick pulled away from the curb, heading down the hill. She watched until Nick stopped at the bottom, right turn signal on, then pulled into traffic, heading away from the city and toward the eastern suburbs.

(talk when clearer heads prevail)

(where were you?)

(will nick notice how kevin's acting? will he ask? will kevin tell him? will-will-will)

She shook herself and walked back into the house. Her limbs didn't want to respond, wanted to stiffen and lock. Her head, for once not aching, felt padded with suffocating cotton, stifling coherent thought.

And, of course, her arm itched and itched and itched.

She paused at the end of the loveseat, which separated the living room from the entryway.

(what kind of mother are you?)

(put on your big girl pants)

(what if kevin saw you—)

A buzzing filled her ears, an ache filled her jaw—she was clenching her teeth hard enough to grind.

(a weekend of this? a weekend? i'll never sleep—)

She forced her jaw to open, shook herself. She moved toward the couch and glanced at the coffee table.

And saw the reminder card.

(YOU ARE NOT ALONE)

She stopped, a wind-up toy that had run out of juice.

Her arm itched and itched and itched while visions of Kevin stumbling into the bathroom to find her dead flitted across her mind's eye.

(why didn't you tell me?)

(what if you hurt all the time?)

She got her keys.

The address was in Harmarville, a neighborhood along the southwestern edge of Hathaway. It took Karen nearly an hour just to get to that side of the city, using the map she had in her car and having to circumnavigate the city's ever-growing construction detours.

She crossed the Hathaway Bridge, the only car in spite of the early hour. Along the crumbling sidewalks, PennDOT had left traffic cones, ready to be set out, and electronic signs blinking HATHAWAY BRIDGE RENOVATION BEGINS SEPT. 21ST. FOLLOW DETOUR.

She turned onto a secondary highway leading into Harmarville, which seemed to consist of barely-surviving businesses, seedy bars, dying plazas, and weed-choked vacant lots. For a while she could see downtown Hathaway and its tall buildings, but the highway curved to the left, pulling her further and further away from

(civilization)

the city.

She wound up on a darkened road called Vernazza, with junked-up houses set far back on the properties. She topped a short rise and, on the right, bright white security lamps lit up a large, sloped parking lot with a low, long brick building at the bottom. After the near-darkness of the previous streets, she had to blink at the brilliance.

The building had once been a bowling alley—a ghost outline of a bowling ball striking pins neon sign discolored the front of the building—but hadn't been that way in a long time. The parking lot was crumbling, with only a dozen or so cars crouched near the front doors. Only the metal frame of what had once been a large lighted road sign remained, looking like an industrial-age interpretation of gallows.

A plastic sign hung from the arm of the metal frame, held there with zip-ties:

ST. JUDE'S MINISTRIES

FRIDAYS — 9:00 PM (ALWAYS)

YOU ARE NOT ALONE

She braked harder than her slight speed needed. "You've gotta be fucking kidding me," she said.

She looked from the sign to the building. Through the glass doors, she could see the house lights were on.

"Here?" she said. "This place is *here?*"

Her mind flashed to the sympathetic receptionist:

(but this might help)

Karen let up on the brake and eased into the parking lot. She took a spot close to the doors but away from the clutch of other vehicles. Something in her head hummed, like a radio waiting for a transmission, as she got out and walked to the doors.

Inside, the house lights were on, but the lanes—gutted, stripped down to floors and gaping holes where the pins had sat—were dark, looking like cave openings. Anything salvageable had been stripped, leaving vague clues of what had once been there. She heard the ebb and flow of someone talking softly off to the right. Someone else coughed.

She came around the registration desk and saw a group of about a dozen adults, sitting in a circle of neon plastic chairs where arcade games once stood. The people—all of differing ages, genders, and races—held Styrofoam cups or munched on doughnuts. They looked at a balding man sitting with his back to her. The speaker.

"—and I found her," he said, "on her knees, in the bedroom we had shared for ten years. She was—" He paused. "—she was blowing him."

"Who?" a youngish man said. He held his chin in his hand, elbow on his knee, studying the speaker. The lenses of his black-rimmed spectacles flashed.

"My neighbor," the speaker said. "We had barbeques together, borrowed lawn tools, all that suburban shit. He had his dick in my wife's mouth."

Karen stood, frozen, still near the reception desk.

(what the hell?)

"What did you do, Adam?" the youngish man asked. "Did you get mad? Rush in and attack them?"

"I left," Adam whispered. "Just…left."

"Why? This was your wife. This was a neighbor you thought—maybe he wasn't your friend, but you two were friendly."

"No—*they* were friendly," Adam said.

Karen's feet took a step back and the receptionist saw her. She smiled in recognition—so jarring given the topic under discussion—and gestured to the empty seat beside her. Karen hesitated for a second, then scurried over. She sat down and the receptionist smiled warmly at her once more before turning back to Adam.

"That doesn't answer the question," the youngish man said.

"Because she saw me," Adam said. His head drooped, his chin nearly touching his chest.

"She saw you?"

"As soon as I walked in," he said. "Saw me, and kept going."

The youngish man asked, "What happened when you finally went back home?"

"She was gone. Packed a bag and left. I got the divorce papers two weeks later."

"Did she end up with the neighbor?" the youngish man asked. Karen glanced at him—seemed like a particularly cruel question.

"No."

A beat of silence. "Is this your worst moment?"

A grunt. "One of them."

"Why?"

Adam didn't say anything at first. Then he said, slowly, "Because I just left. I didn't fight. I felt the pain, and I didn't fight."

"Did you want to?"

Another shrug. "Not really. I didn't want to fight for *her*—we was barely speaking by then—but what we didn't have anymore, y'know? I'd met her in fucking middle school, thought we were gonna grow old together. But we just...just started hating each other. Before that, though..."

The man leaned back. "This was the buildup to all those lost feelings and thoughts. Your worst moment is you realizing *all* that you'd lost."

Adam nodded.

"I thought so," the man said. He stood and walked to Adam. He put a hand on Adam's shoulder, but kept his back to the group, staring off at the empty lanes beyond.

"As always," he said, "don't thank Adam for sharing. What he's just revealed to you isn't helpful—to you. To him. It shouldn't make him feel any better for opening up this wound before you."

Karen looked around. The dozen or so men and women watched the man and their shared expression sent a ripple of gooseflesh up Karen's back. It was an expression of anticipation.

"He will *never* be able to express, fully, how it felt to see his high school sweetheart sucking another man's cock. The *pain* of it. The *loss*. You will never *feel* how he felt, even if you've been a similar circumstance." His gesture toward Adam turned into a point, jabbing in Adam's general direction. "This is *his* pain, *his* wound, *his* scar." He looked at each person, his glasses winking the lights. Karen flinched when it was his gaze fell on her.

The man began to pace, working his way around the inner circle. "This isn't about healing or expressing yourself. Both of those are delusions. What makes you who you are is the pain you've experienced, the scars you carry on the *inside*. You grew up hearing that we are all one, that we are all in this together, and, *together*, we can do *anything*." His mouth twisted into a nasty grin. "But we aren't and we can't. No amount of talking will heal you. When the police are looking for a guy, or an unidentified body shows up, they make sure to mention 'identifying marks.' Tattoos. *Scars*."

He paused to look at each person again.

"It's our scars that make us human," he said. "Makes us who we are. Every cut, every bruise. Every put-down, fight, fear. Our bodies are just skin and tissue and bones. Our hearts are just muscle, no matter what the romantics say. But muscles can tear. Skin can be cut. Tissue can be ruined."

He resumed pacing. "Our bodies are meant to take damage. If they weren't, we'd be invulnerable. Our skin is meant to be cut. Our hearts are meant to bleed. Our bones are made to be broken. We are damaged goods. We are human. We *are* who we *are*. And, when we *feel* that pain, that's our bodies reminding us of who and what we are. *Human*."

He shook his head. "No, when we talk about our pain, we're not seeking absolution. We're seeking to stand as we are, to be everything that is broken in us and made us who we are. We don't hide. We *show*. Maybe we can teach another to be who *they* are. By being honest with ourselves, we can show others to be honest about themselves." He gestured toward Adam once more. "When Adam shares, or anyone else, he's reminding himself who *he* is, and reminding *you* who *you* are and how *you're* scarred."

He turned to Karen. "Welcome," he said. "I'm Dr. Darren Roberts. What's your name?"

Her throat went dry. "Karen."

The receptionist spoke up. "I invited her."

Roberts's eyes cut toward her. "Why's that, Eve?"

Eve glanced at Karen. "She's a cutter. I saw it when we met. Cutters always get caught, eventually. I was trying to help that inevitability."

Roberts looked back at Karen. "Is that true?"

Karen swallowed and it did no good; sand dunes could've moved across the dry expanse of her tongue. "Yes."

"Which part—being a cutter, or being caught?"

She had to look away. Most people never looked directly at each other for long, but Roberts held his stance like a staring-contest champion. "Both."

"Are you still cutting?"

Karen shook her head. "No."

She saw his shadow move away and she looked up to see him sitting back down in his chair.

"St. Jude's is not a church in the traditional sense," he said. "Seek not your salvation here. We're fresh out. If you're looking to feel *better*, look elsewhere. We *can't* help you. All we can do is show you how to examine your scars, use the pain you feel, but we can't make you better. Do you understand? This is important."

She studied his earnest expression, his unwavering gaze.

Finally, she nodded.

He leaned back in his chair. "Good." He cleared his throat. "If Eve saw you were a cutter, that must've mean it was recently you had imbibed. True?"

She nodded again.

"But you're not now."

Another nod.

"Then talk about *that*. That couldn't have been easy. Start there."

Karen looked around. The others looked back at her. She flashed back to presentations in high school, standing in the front of the room, her report or speech clutched in front of her like a shield, taking in all those eyes.

"We are not here to judge you," Roberts said. "We're all broken people. We all feel we are failures in some way or another."

She glanced at Eve and Eve smiled at her. No one coughed. No one shifted in their seats. She might've been in the room alone.

(that's exactly how you should feel)

The shame rushed her—the shame of being caught, of being manhandled by Lisa, of being so obvious to Lisa—

(if lisa had noticed had kevin? had kevin seen?)

—flooding her system with a terrible warmth.

"My best friend caught me," she said, softly into her coffee cup. "She'd come over the other day to . . . I guess confirm her suspicions."

"Why was she suspicious?" Roberts asked.

"Because I looked thin," Karen said. "Because I hadn't been sleeping. Because I always wore long-sleeved shirts." The words, hard little bullets before, came smoother.

By the end, she was looking up, at the group, meeting their eyes, and couldn't remember exactly when she'd raised her head.

She couldn't remember when the pain stopped making her hunch and instead made her sit up straighter.

She drove home with a buzz in her head much like if she'd had a couple of drinks, turning the long drive into a surreal passage of lights and turns with nothing jumping out enough to hook onto her senses. She still ached—her back, her joints—and her head throbbed from drinking coffee so late, but she had never felt less weighted down, as if she didn't so much walk from the alley to her car, or from the car to her apartment, as she *glided* from one to another. She still hurt. She was not better.

But she hadn't felt so good in such a long time.

The skull is not Kevin's. Of course it isn't. Kevin's asleep; she knows this. She picked him up from his father's just this afternoon.

Karen drops the skull and stands. This dream again. This place that used to be so open and clean and . . . and possible. *Yes, that's the word. This had been a place where everything had seemed possible; the one place she knew that wasn't closed off and ideas of moving to New York and being a journalist hadn't seemed so stupid, or impossible. She starts up the next hill, leaning into it to gain the most purchase against the drifting, shifting dirt, bone fragments crunching underfoot. Now, this place is poisoned. This place—*

(these are where your scars live)

Dr. Darren Roberts's voice drifts across the breeze, his voice slow and measured.

(this is the core of your being where you are who you truly are)

(before this was a place to plan for your future)

(now it's a place to hide from your past)

(but when you hide you're also dwelling)

She pauses at the top of the hill. Distantly, she can see the structure—no longer against the line of the horizon, but still a ways off. It was a house—a one-story structure, slumped in an alarming way. It reminded Karen of a photo of a house mid-collapse.

(isn't that true karen?)

(isn't this where you ran away?)

(isn't this where you hid from your pain?)

"I'm not hiding from anything," she says.

(you can't lie to yourself forever karen)

"I'm not lying," she says, and starts down the next hill. The breeze picks up speed, swooping into the mini-valleys the hills create, prickling at her skin like pins and needles.

(why do you cut karen?)

(why do you cut if not to escape?)

(why did you come here if not to escape?)

"I don't know what you're talking about," she says, too loudly.

Roberts's voice drops to a whisper.

(your pain makes you who you are karen your scars show the world who you are)

(but you've been taught to hide your pain)

(the problem is that it eats you up from the inside out like a tumor)

(like this place)

(until all you want to do is escape)

The wind comes faster, now, assaulting her senses, making her eyes close to slits, slapping her nose with its awful reek. Pain shoots up her calves.

Roberts's voice picks up speed, coming with each increasing gust of awful air, finding its rhythm, pummeling her.

(and you're ruined you're everything your mother and the world has told you are—a failure)

(a failure without a job)

(a failure without a dream)

(a failure raising a child)

She shakes her head, even as pain zig-zags up her spine from the small of her back, pierces her skull.

(until all you want to do is escape—for good—isn't that right karen?)

(to escape would be to fulfill that failing dream wouldn't it?)

(admit it to yourself—here if nowhere else karen)

(you hated cutting not because you feared getting caught)

(but because you never could work up the nerve)

(the nerve to finally escape)

(the nerve to accept your failure as a parent)

(and when you got caught it was like you'd lost your chance)

"SHUT UP!" *she screams as she reaches the bottom of a hill. Above her, thunder, like the throat-clearing of an Old Testament god, rumbles.*

She looks up and her mother stands there, flicking like a television with bad reception. She's dressed as she had when they'd buried Karen's father—black dress, high-necked with a collar that reminds Karen of doilies. She holds her gloved hands in front of her, and stares pityingly down at her adult-child.

"It's your fault," her mother says in that I'm-only-trying-to-tell-the-truth tone she always used to use when Karen was a teenager and it was just the two of them rattling around that damned house in Franklin. "Your fault he's dead, your fault your husband left you, your fault you're unemployed, your fault your son's a little silent weirdo."

Her mother unfolds her hands to reveal a single glittering razorblade. Thunder rumbles again, accompanied by the flashbulb of lightning caught in the black clouds above.

"You can do it here, dear," her mother says, holding up the razor. The green hue of the day makes the metal glow like something radioactive. "Do it here and

finally accept what you are."

Her mother bursts apart like a popped balloon, the pieces catching on the wind and encircling her, pulling her down into the darkness—

Karen sat bolt upright in bed, the scream lodged in her throat like a wad of mucus, choking her.

(don't scream don't scream kevin will hear you don't scream)

Roberts's voice had followed her from her dream and now filled her head.

(scream goddammit SCREAM stand unadorned don't be afraid to show your scars show that you're human)

Her jaw unlocked.

And she shrieked.

The force of it threw her back straight, her head up, the tears out of the corners of her eyes. The pressure drained in equal measure, leaving her dizzy.

Karen ran out of air and fell to her side, coughing and half-retching, her nose and throat clogged with snot. She closed her burning eyes as scalding tears escaped from under the lids.

"Mum?"

She jerked and half-rose, but all strength had left her. She tried to speak and only managed to cough again.

And then Kevin's hands were on her side, patting her helplessly. "Mum? *Mum?* You okay, Mum? *Mum?*"

She swallowed thickly, took a breath. "S'okay, honey." She hated the weak, watery quality to her voice. "S'okay. Just had a bad dream. Just a bad dream."

"Do you need something?"

(my boy)

"No, hon," she said, her voice gaining a little strength. "Just need to lie here a minute."

Silence for a beat. Karen's eyes were still closed and she found herself drifting. Only awake for a few moments from a bad dream and already drifting. When was the last time *that* had happened?

And then Kevin's voice pulled her back: "I have something for you." Followed by the sound of his bare feet padding away across the hardwood floor.

She drifted. Her head throbbed once and then went quiet. The distant rush of the constant city traffic lulled her. Footsteps.

"Mum, I have something for you," Kevin said, pulling her back to consciousness again.

She roused herself.

Kevin stood beside the nightstand, the refracted glow of the outside streetlamps turning his face into a barely-defined glob of white, hovering in black. He held a stuffed animal dog in his hands.

The dog's black button eyes matched her son's in the darkness and ice touched her heart, chilling her.

"I thought this would help you sleep," he said.

She took the dog, her hands numb, watching her son. No reaction to the fact that his mother had shrieked bloody-murder in the middle of the night. Still, though, the proffered dog.

"Thank you, honey," she said.

"Can I do anything else for you?" he asked, like he was taking care of her while sick.

(aren't you?)

"No, love," she said. "It's all right. I'm feeling sleepy again."

A wobble of that white blob in the dark—him nodding.

"Mum?"

"Yes, sweetie?"

"What happened to your arm?"

She looked down and saw her right arm, poking out from under the sleeve of her sleep shirt. In the streetlight glow, it looked like someone had drawn lines on her forearm with a Sharpie marker.

(tell him karen bare your scars show your pain aren't parents supposed to teach their children)

(what parent would do that?)

"Just..." she started to say, but *just what?* came into her head. "Mom had an accident. It's okay. It doesn't hurt."

(liar)

"Okay," Kevin said, drawing the last syllable out, and Karen glanced at him. He stared at the marks on her arm. She slid it under the stuffed dog and used her other to pull him in for a quick hug.

She swallowed. "Go back to bed, hon. You have school in a few hours. Thank you for the dog."

"S'okay, Mum," he said. "I use him when I have nightmares."

(why don't you ever tell me these things?)

Her mother's voice:

(why should he?)

"He must work, then," she said, squeezing the dog to her lap. "Good night, hon."

"Night, Mum," he said and left her bedroom. A part of her expected him to look over his shoulder, perhaps with that unreadable expression, but he didn't.

She listened to his bed creak faintly as he climbed back in, the rustle of bedclothes being straightened. She set his dog on the other side of the bed and slid further under the sheets herself.

(now i won't sleep now it'll be like any other time)

But she was already drifting off as she thought this. Within five minutes, she was out, arm loosely curled around Kevin's dog.

Karen's hand draped over the steering wheel, her arm—covered by the sleeve of her light jacket—a barrier between her and Kevin.

"Ready for school?" she asked.

Kevin nodded, watching the street through the windshield. The bags under his eyes weren't any larger, were they? When she'd gotten up this morning, he'd been asleep, but that didn't necessarily mean he'd been asleep the entire time.

(while i slept like a babe in arms)

(what kind of mother are you?)

She followed his gaze. A handful of kids, all varying heights and sizes, shuffled around on the corner. The matronly crossing guard kept an eagle-eye on the traffic.

"Are you liking second grade?" she asked. Loathing filled her mid-section, this need to try conversational gambits with her son.

(he just never talks)

(well whose fault is that?)

"Sure," Kevin said, and then had to stifle a yawn. Then he sat up straighter, his eyes narrowing on something outside. She glanced through the windshield again.

The Perozzi girls walked down 54th Street, the littlest gamboling, seeming to yank the older two.

Karen looked at Kevin. His face hadn't changed, but he held his backpack in his lap and his left hand worried the zipper.

"Is there anything wrong at school?" she asked.

He didn't stiffen, but his body shifted in some way, reared up and away from her. Outside, the crossing guard stopped traffic to let the Perozzis cross.

"Because you can tell me, hon," she said. "If a class is hard, or a teacher is mean, or..." She tried to stop herself from licking her lips, failed. "...or kids are teasing you, you can tell me those things. Even if it hurts."

He offered her a quick side-eye. "No, Mum."

(no to what?)

"It's good to talk, honey," she said, and caught a flash of yellow out of the corner of her eye. Dammit, dammit, dammit. "If you're in pain, you shouldn't hide that. It makes it hurt more."

(oh you're one to talk)

Another bit of side-eye. "Bus is coming, Mum."

She looked as the school bus shuddered to a stop at the corner. The kids, with the Perozzis in the middle and watching the ground, lined up in front of the doors.

"So it is," she sighed.

Kevin unbuckled his seatbelt, threading it slowly back to its holder without taking his eyes off the bus.

"Want me to walk over with you?" she asked, watching him watch the kids get on the bus.

He shot her a look that made her recoil—not embarrassment, or anger, but fear. Horror. And then his face tightened again, so fast a part of her wanted to imagine it'd all been in her head.

(what's he scared of?)

"No, Mum," he said. "It's fine." He leaned across the console and kissed her cheek. "I'll see you later."

Instinct made her want to grab him, hold him until he told her what was going on—she could drive him to his goddamn school—but she kept her hands in her lap. "Okay, honey. Be good."

He reached the door handle. "I will."

"I'll be here when you get off."

"Uh-huh." Door open and shut, and then he was racing up to the corner, last in line. She watched him climb on, seemingly so small in front of those large steps, and then the doors closed. She saw the silhouette of his head, leaning up and around, as if trying to see something beyond the line of kids taking their seats, and then ducking into a seat near the front and crunching down. Behind the school bus window, he looked paler than ever.

(what's wrong with you?)

She didn't know if she was thinking about him or herself.

The bus rumbled through the intersection, and she let out a breath she hadn't been aware she'd been holding.

"Shit," she said.

She took off her jacket when she got out of her car. Now that she was alone, it wasn't like she had to hide the cuts, anymore.

She started up the steps. The downstairs apartment was empty at the moment—it was one of the reasons Mr. Vucella had been graceful about late rents—and her footfalls echoed. They kept time with her thoughts, which warred with each other.

(what's wrong with you, kiddo?)

(why would he talk to you about it?)

(what's with those girls?)

(he looks ill)

(are they bullying you? why won't you tell me?)

(you're making him that way why would he tell you anything?)

(Mum what happened to your arm?)

The top of the stairs outside of her apartment was pitch-black and she felt through her keyring and unlocked the door by feel. The apartment had that silence to it that made the inner ear ring.

She dropped her jacket over the back of the loveseat, her keys on the bookcase behind the door.

(yay i only have eight hours of this to contend with and then kevin can be here to not talk to me!)

A weight filled her chest, as if her heart had been replaced with a two-liter of soda; something sticky and heavy and pulling her down. She paused at the end of the loveseat, holding onto the corner, and tried to think of what to do next. There were dishes. There was cleaning. She could make up the beds. But those chores, done over and over again on a daily basis over the past year, numbed her.

Her brain refused to leave the image of Kevin in the passenger seat. In her head, though, his eyes had been replaced with the buttons of the stuffed dog he'd given her last night, and they stared vacantly, glassily, at her.

(what happened to your arm?)

(no mum it's fine)

The phone rang and she jumped, a surprised *"Oh!"* escaping before she could stop herself. The phone rang again and she walked into the kitchen. She reached for the phone, and then stopped. What if it was *Mister* Alan Ladd, wanting to discuss the "custody situation" of Kevin?

(oh knock it off)

She'd never called Ladd back, didn't even remember the number he'd rattled off in that greasy, patronizing voice of his. Nick had said they'd talk when cooler heads had prevailed . . . and that had been two weeks ago.

(because he dropped it)

Why would he?

The phone rang a third time: hey, lady, you gonna answer or what?

The answer machine would click on with four rings. One more to go and then she wouldn't have to hear that man's voice, listen to what that man said.

(no you'll get another insulting voice message and have nick look at you like a goddamned dutch uncle on friday night)

The phone started to ring for a fourth time and she snatched it up. "Hello?" she said.

"Ms. Dempsey?" the young male voice said. "This is Patrick

from Tri-State Temp. Is this a good time?"

"Of course," she said. "I just came back from taking my son to the bus stop."

"Uh-huh." *Don't care!* his tone trumpeted, and her dislike came roaring back. "Well, enjoy doing that for the next couple of days, because it's going to end soon."

"Why's that?" she asked. She sounded shrill to her own ears.

A slight pause; she imagined him pulling the phone away from his ear, shooting it a look. "Because you'll be working, Ms. Dempsey. For the foreseeable future."

"Bainbridge Financial," Lisa said, chewing on the name. She took a drag of her Salem, blew a streamer of smoke up and away from Karen into the early evening air. "They handle investments, don't they? Portfolios and shit?"

Karen shrugged. She drummed her hands on her knees. "Don't know, don't much give shit. They got me answering phones for a week or two."

Lisa nodded. They sat on Karen's porch stoop as the sun slipped behind the houses across the street. An alley ran beside their house, and Kevin sat on the curb, his back to them, playing with his Batman action figures.

She glanced at Karen, who was all-but bouncing on the concrete step, like a kid with a sugar-high. She was still too thin and her coloring was completely fucked...but she was wearing a tee-shirt, her right forearm looking like what a prisoner might do to count his escape attempts, and she wasn't acting self-conscious about it. Karen's eyes bounced with the rest of her—looking up the hill, looking down the hill, watching the houses across the street.

"So you'll be back downtown for two weeks, at least," Lisa said, and ground her cigarette out on the concrete between her heels— she'd come over directly after work. "What happens after?"

"Another reception gig," Karen said. "Ryall Construction over on lower 50th Street. Shit, I can come home for lunch, if I want to."

"Hell, go to my house," Lisa said. "Feed my cat. That's only a few blocks from me."

"I know!" Karen said. Her eyes sparkled. On her too-thin face with her too-dark sockets, they made her look unhinged. "My agent says they tend to hire full-time from the temp pool quite often."

"A lot of places do—saves HR from going off and having cattle-call openings. The temp agencies do it for you." She pulled another Salem from her purse and lit it with a disposable lighter. There was already a bed of coals along the back of her throat—it typically took her all evening to go through four smokes, but she'd only been at Karen's for thirty minutes. "When are you going to tell Nick?"

"I'll let Kevin tell him," she said. "They talk on Wednesday nights—just a check-in—and by then I'll already have gone over the after-school routine with him: what route to go home by, when to call, all that. It'll give him something to talk about. Kiddo always seems at a loss of what to say to his dad over the phone. I don't know why Nick insists on it, but he does, and Kevin always tries to maintain a good conversation, but how much goes on between the Sunday he last saw you and Wednesday, y'know?" She shrugged. "Besides, it might table the whole custody-discussion for good."

Lisa studied her for a moment. *You're more concerned that your son has something to talk about with his father than the fact that you're using him as a bit in some parental politics,* she thought, but didn't say. *Smooth.*

She glanced over at Kevin, who was still playing—how much was he listening? "That's good. I think."

Karen took a deep breath, let it out. "I feel good, Lisa. Like, *really* good." She grinned and it pulled her pale face all out of shape, but it was genuine and toothy. "I was scared. It was getting bad. Getting *dark.* And then when Nick sicced that lawyer on me ... I mean, you have no idea, hon."

"How you holding up?"

"Better. Slept straight through last night. First time in forever." Karen took a breath. "It's all turning around. Finally."

Lisa breathed smoke. "Glad you think so."

Karen turned toward her and Lisa had to keep from recoiling. Karen had stopped bouncing and seemed—

(wraith-like)

—like a statue on the concrete step. Her face was empty of all emotion, like she was trying to ape her son's restraint and could only manage slack deadness.

"There's no other choice," Karen said. "But all evidence is pointing that way. I'm feeling better—"

Even if you don't look it, Lisa's head interjected, and then felt guilty for thinking it.

"—I'm working again," Karen went on, "and Kevin ..." She looked over at her son, then shook her head. "It's me and him, Lisa. We're a unit. We're *together.*" She blinked again and, Jesus, Lisa realized that Karen's eyes were wet. "I'd do anything for that boy."

"Everyone knows that, Karie," Lisa said, but had to look away, couldn't stand that expression—dead but tearful—any longer.

She looked at Kevin.

He still held his action figures, but wasn't doing anything with them any longer. Just holding them.

"Everyone knows that," Lisa repeated.

The sun had died and Lisa sat in her car, letting it run. She glanced at Karen's house. The second floor windows were lit—the kitchen. Karen was making dinner.

(that face)

Lisa's mind shied away from it. Karen had seemed stronger than she had in forever, but she'd reminded Lisa of pictures of Holocaust survivors she'd seen, scores of emaciated figures walking out of the death camps, beatific in their joy while looking like candidates to be the new Lord of Death.

(i'd do anything for that boy)

(everyone knows that karie)

What I know is you need some fucking therapy, Lisa thought now, and shook her head. Undoubtedly true but no less horrible. Karen needed a friend, not someone picking apart her progress.

All this just from no longer cutting, though?

She shook her head. She didn't pretend to understand; she'd barely passed her intro to psych course at the community college.

Maybe that had been what Karen needed. A little shake up. A little rattle of the cage. Still, what should've been a relief to Lisa—to see her formerly strong friend becoming strong again—had only made her more uneasy. Like she wasn't seeing the whole picture.

"Enough analysis," she muttered, shifting the Toyota into Drive. "Momma needs a glass of wine."

Big words, but, try as she might, Karen's dead, tearful face, kept intruding into the front of her mind.

"Kevin tells me you're working," Nick said, after Kevin climbed into the car. He leaned against the side, arms crossed.

"Started today," she said.

"How long?" Nick asked. "This is through the temp-agency?"

"Two weeks at this position, then an ongoing position at a company a few blocks from here which has a history of hiring its temps full-time." She paused deliberately. "I have the phone numbers, if you need them."

Nick looked away, chewed his lip. Karen glanced at Kevin, who watched the two of them from the window. She promised herself he wouldn't see a replay of two weeks ago.

"How stable can that be?" Nick asked finally. He looked back at her. "I mean, it's just temping."

She refused to allow her muscles to tighten, her lower stomach to lock with anxiety. "Stable enough."

"And what's Kevin doing after school? It's not like you can pick him up, anymore."

"He comes straight home and calls me," she said.

"An eight-year-old boy," Nick said. "Home. Alone."

(worked for macauley culkin)

"It's tough for single mothers," Karen said. "But it worked wonderfully today."

"In such a wonderful neighborhood."

"We lived in worse after you left."

"He's too young. When you used to work—"

"I could afford a babysitter," Karen said. "True. In this neighborhood, by the way."

He frowned. "Are you going to keep jabbing me like this?"

She met his eyes. "I don't know. Are you going to keep being so passive-aggressive? Why don't you tell me what you really want to know."

He set his jaw. "I just don't like this. It's not safe."

"That," she said, "didn't bother you before. We have a system. Kevin knows not to dawdle, not to answer the door. Anyone tries to talk to him, he runs."

"I don't like it."

"So you've said."

"I only want what's best for him. This—" He gestured vaguely. "This is thin. Running? Not answering the door? What if some goon just grabs him from behind and takes off? What could he do? How would you even know before it's *way* too late?"

"Hey—welcoming to the fears of parenting, glad you could join us." She shook her head. "Listen, this is not the ideal situation. On the upside, I'm working, it's steady, and this system's only for two weeks. Then I'm here, in the neighborhood, where I could switch my lunch around to pick him up, if I so desired."

"With temping," Nick said.

"And we've come full circle."

He exhaled dramatically. "You might think about all this, though. Living with me, it's quiet. Suburbs. There are after-school leagues and clubs. We looked into it. He—"

"—wouldn't see you until six or seven because you live an hour from work," Karen said. "Didja notice the four-hour lapse between the end of school and when he'd see his parent?"

Nick's eyes narrowed. "He'd be supervised, at least."

"And far from home."

Nick flapped his hands, giving up. "Just think, though—he might actually be *better* with us. Better schools, better attention, better *chance*. And, *you*—you wouldn't have to worry about making sure there's enough in the checking account so that you can have food in the house, wouldn't have to worry about unemployment running out."

"I'm so glad you're thinking of my well-being, Nick," she said, and no more. A scream built up in the back of her throat, like thunderclouds on the horizon.

Nick looked at her for a five-count, then shoved himself off the side of car—

(careful—you might dull that toy of yours)

—and went around to the driver side.

"See you Sunday," he said, his words slightly muffled because he said them through gritted teeth.

She watched the car peel away from the curb, then brought her hands around from behind her, forced the locked fingers to loosen and open. The flesh of her palms was bruised. Two or three bloody crescent moons, black under the streetlamp, looked up at her.

"See you, then," she muttered.

Karen listened to the others—to Edna, who still visited her abusive, senile mother in the nursing home; to Robert, who sometimes couldn't help wondering if it'd been worth it to be disowned by his family for coming out, only to have his partner die of AIDS a year later. It was like church—members providing the stories and psalms, and Roberts coming in to show how they were applicable. Like the others, she noticed, Robert didn't look at anyone for too long, favoring instead to look at the alley beyond, to study the shadows beyond the reach of the house lights.

Karen would never know the pain of not being able to stop visiting an abusive parent who could no longer remember her name, let alone what had been done to her, never comprehend the monstrous guilt that came with the thought *Why did I bother* after watching her lover painfully shuffle off the mortal coil, but that hardly mattered. These people had scars, like she did; wounds that had "healed" in the technical sense, but, like an old bone break throbbing during wet weather, had never really stopped hurting.

These were people confused and unsure, guilt-laden and shame-filled with the decisions they'd made or the actions they'd taken. There was comfort in shared pain, even if everyone's pain was different and singular. St. Jude's message was both true and not true:

They weren't ever alone. They were always alone.

Only two meetings and it felt like she'd been coming here forever. She listened to the others cut into themselves and fumbled for the right word. Home. This was home. A home for her pain. A home for her guilt over her parenting and her failed marriage and, yes, even her childhood. A home for the shame that came tagging along with the guilt.

(home's not with your child apparently)

(i just don't like this it's not safe)

She watched Roberts pace the circle. Nick held court within her mind. Nick leaning against the car, Nick looking at her with that way of his that always seemed to say *You* know *I'm right, right?* Nick saying he didn't like the idea of their son walking city-blocks alone just to come home to more of the same.

(hey—welcome to the fears of parent glad you could join us)

(think about it though he might be better with us)

She exhaled and refocused on Roberts.

"—this is the thing," he said, "this is the crux of who we are. All of our hopes and dreams and desires, they're built upon a foundation of fear and guilt and shame, of old pains and hidden, horrendous beliefs. We couldn't *get* to the good without the bad things propelling us forward. Action and reaction. But we're taught to *ignore* that bad, deny it exists, leading us to be surprised when it comes roaring back at a weakened moment."

She looked down at her hands, rolled loosely into fists on her knees. She wore a button-shirt, like always, but the cuffs were undone, revealing the evidence of her cutting. Two weeks and they were almost healed, but she could still see the cuts that had been there, the worm-like scabs, could still remember the instantaneous shout of fresh pain that would momentarily push aside everything else.

"No one ever gets better," Roberts said. "You only gain distance."

She saw Kevin walking the two blocks home from the bus stop. She thought of the traffic of Butler Street. She imagined white windowless vans and shadowed alleys, of Kevin passing by them.

(welcome to the fears of parenting)

The throb of being unsure, of wondering if the decisions she'd made would harm her son. Parenting was painful, and not in that Hallmark-y, I-have-to-let-my-child-go bittersweet way. Every action could lead to Kevin being hurt or worse. Every decision could harm his future in both a literal and metaphorical sense.

Her actions. *Her* decisions.

(what kind of mother are you?)

(just think though—he might actually be better with us)

(but what would i be then?)

Like the others, she lowered her head as Roberts talked. Her hands clenched into tighter fists. It hurt.

Of course it did.

This was the place for such a thing.

The phone rang, startling Kevin, sitting on the loveseat and eating a bowl of Cinnamon Toast Crunch as the local NBC affiliate led into the *Today Show.*

Karen leaned out the bathroom door, a makeup sponge in her hand.

The phone rang again. Not an accident or wrong number; someone trying to call *her.* Kevin glanced at her, as if to ask, *Are you going to answer that?*

"Who calls at *this* hour?" she asked, setting the sponge down and walking into the kitchen. She ignored the leaden quality her heartbeat had taken.

The phone rang again—you answering me, lady?

She picked it up. "Hello?"

"*Mizz* Dempsey?" the male voice on the other end asked and, although she'd only heard it once before on the answering machine, she instantly placed it: Alan Ladd of Mamatas, Braunbeck, and Morgan.

(just think though—he might actually be better with us)

Her stomach churned.

"Yes," she said and her spit was acidic.

"I'm glad I could reach you?" Ladd said. "I was worried I would have to call your...place of employment?"

"What can I do for you, Mr. Ladd?" She kept her words clipped, out-of-patience. She wanted to close her eyes as a knot of pain in her head throbbed, but didn't want to miss Kevin coming in.

(why?)

Stating his name fumbled him a bit. What the hell had Nick told the man? "Ah, yes, I'm calling about your son? The custody situation concerning your son with my client?"

"Yes?" With her free hand, she massaged her forehead, smearing the makeup she'd already applied. "What about? We're in the process of getting ready for the day, sir."

"I was hoping to meet with you—and your son—"

"No." The word came out as a whip-crack. She realized that she could no longer hear the clack of Kevin's spoon against the cereal bowl. He was listening.

A slight pause. "Yes?"

"Unless there's something official, you don't need to speak with him," she said. "This is between me and your client."

"Ah, yes? Right?" This wasn't going the way Ladd had intended—you could hear it in his voice.

"Sir, I'm trying to get ready for work, and my son ready for school," she said in a let's-move-this-along way.

"Yes?" he said, slower still. "Well, I was hoping to schedule a meeting with you and—well, you and my client?"

"When?"

"That's entirely up to you?" Ladd said/asked.

"I can't before five any day this week," she said.

Ladd chewed on this a moment. She heard Bryant Gumbel segue to Faith Daniels for the day's top stories. She should be leaving now. Kevin should be dressed now. Goddammit.

"I have an opening on Friday, then?" he said finally. "How does six work for you?"

"Fine," she said. "I'll have to arrange for someone to watch my son, but I'll be there."

"Wonderful, Ms. Dempsey—"

"Goodbye," she said, and hung up. She waited to see if it would ring again. Why would it? Ladd had gotten what he wanted.

"Everything okay, Mum?" Kevin asked as she came back into the living room.

"It's fine, hon," she said. "C'mon, we're running late—get dressed, kiddo."

He nodded, setting the bowl on the end table, and pulled at the folded clothes she left on the arm of the loveseat. She saw how wide his eyes were, the darkness of the bags under them. Jesus, had he slept at all the night before?

(what kind of mother are you?)

She looked at herself in the bathroom mirror, at the fading bags under her own eyes, the sharp contours of her cheekbones, the pallor of her skin. She rolled her shoulders and began reapplying makeup. Her stomach still churned.

(just think though—he might actually be better with us)

3

CRACKED

The four of them—Nick, Moira, Alan Ladd, and Karen—stared at each other from opposite sides of the long, shiny conference table. She'd waited for over a half hour before an assistant had led her in, and now they stared at her, three to one, like a tribunal with hanging on its mind.

(Lisa at the kitchen table: "They're gonna sweat you, kiddo.")

(Karen drinking a cup of coffee. "They can try. This is nothing official.")

(Lisa nodded, but her eyes never left Karen. "They'll try to make it seem as official as possible.")

("Lisa, I've faced Nick before—both in court and out.")

("Just don't let them catch you asleep, kid. I'm gonna be entertaining King Kick-Ass but thinking about you the entire time.")

("Nick doesn't scare me.")

But, oh, that felt like a lie now. Tension built in the center of the table, all the things not-yet said, sucking out the air. Karen kept her hands folded in her lap, but the tendons in her forearm stood taut, and her gut churned. For the first time in weeks, long after the scabs had finally healed, her right arm itched.

"I'm glad you could join us, Ms. Dempsey?" Ladd said/asked. He was a lean, older man who wouldn't have looked out of place wearing white seersucker. His silver mane was professionally swept back from his brow. "I trust you found us easily enough?"

"Easily enough," she said, watching Nick and Moira. Nick looked back with barely concealed antagonism; like he had tried to play nice before, but now that they were *here*, he had no reason to pretend.

(who called the lawyer nick?)

Beneath the table, her hands worked against each other, like wrestlers.

Moira's open expression unsettled Karen because she couldn't place it. Her red hair gleamed beneath the room's recessed lighting, her dress suit a brighter color, making Karen feel every uneven stitch in her TJ Maxx outfit.

Ladd said, "We're here to discuss the custody situation for your son, Kevin, to see if there might be any possible solutions?"

Karen's teeth ground together. "To need solutions, there has to be a problem." She looked over at the lawyer. "And I don't see a problem with the current custody situation."

Nick grunted, "Jesus," and she turned back to see him roll his eyes dramatically. Moira put a hand on his arm, but never looked away from Karen. It was like watching a mannequin move.

"Yes?" Ladd said. "My client doesn't seem to agree with that assessment?"

"At all," Nick muttered.

Karen opened her mouth but Ladd said, "But I wanted to call this meeting to get your perspective, Ms. Dempsey?"

Karen eyed Nick as hard as he eyed her. This took her back; they'd faced more than a few divorce meetings like this. Of course, *then*, she knew that his anger had stemmed from his shame; she'd filed for divorce when she'd discovered his affair with Moira. The divorce had been calling him on his shit.

But what was he angry about now?

(what are you hiding this time?)

"I'm sorry you felt Kevin couldn't attend?" Ladd said.

"He doesn't need the unnecessary stress and confusion."

Nick's eyes narrowed. "No, you save that for every day, don't you, Karen?"

"Is there something you want to say, Nick?" Karen said, and fought to keep her voice even. "I'm all ears. I *have* been all ears, *since* the divorce, but you didn't want to talk. You wanted to call the lawyer." She flapped a hand at Ladd. "This is what you wanted."

Nick's face reddened. He opened his mouth when Moira put her hand on his arm again.

"Karen," she said and her voice was like woodsmoke, "regardless of how we might feel about each other, we're only doing this for Kevin. For what might be best for Kevin."

Karen forced herself to look at her ex-husband's new wife. "You say that, but the evidence says otherwise."

Nick stiffened, but Moira kept a hand on his arm. "We might have handled this in not the best way," she said, "but this *is* just a meeting. This isn't a custody suit—"

"Yet," Nick said.

Karen spun on Nick. "Watch it, Nicholas. You really don't want to go down that road with me."

"Why is that, Ms. Dempsey?" Ladd said.

She turned to the lawyer. "If a custody suit were to happen, it would be noted that, when we divorced, Nick wanted *less* time with his son—said he wasn't available as much as he could be. I had to force him into the schedule that we currently have. Also, when we divorced, I was unemployed, uneducated, and living in a worse neighborhood than I do now. Where was the concern, then?"

She realized her gut wasn't churning, anymore, her hands weren't fighting each other.

"If we go to court," she said to Ladd, who wrote quickly on his sheaf of papers with a fountain pen, "this would all come out. It would be noted that I now have an education—"

"An associate's in court reporting," Nick murmured.

She ignored him. "—live in a better neighborhood, and, aside from the recession killing my position as an assistant at a videography firm, have maintained employment since the divorce."

"You gloss over the whole haven't-worked-in-a-year part," Nick spat.

"Why not?" Karen said, facing him. "You did." Still looking at Nick, she told Ladd, "We discussed this when I was laid off. *I* went to *him* to discuss this. A year ago. Not a peep since then. Not until I get a call from a lawyer."

Nick's upper lip curled and he made a sound in his throat like a snarl—but she saw the flicker in his eyes, just the same.

(what are you hiding by being angry nick? i used to know you so well)

"We made a mistake," Moira cut in, "in not speaking with you first." She glanced at her husband, whose face was a thundercloud. "For letting it lie, so to speak."

"You're still making a mistake, Moira," Karen said. "Nick's too stubborn to admit it, but the facts stand that all the things that *would've* made living with you better stopped being relevant after we divorced. A judge would note that, along with the fact that Kevin is healthy and happy right where he is now."

Moira nodded. "You're a good mother, Karen. I never thought otherwise. Whatever else is between us, I *know* you want to do what's best for Kevin. What you don't seem to believe is that so do *we*."

Karen studied Moira—the earnestness on her face; the way she kept a hand on Nick's arm, like a leash on a biting dog—and found herself believing the woman. Yes, Nick and Moira wanted what was best for Kevin. Not just that, but Moira legitimately *wanted* Kevin; in her home, a part of a family she and Nick created.

When she'd met Moira, the woman had struck Karen as your standard 1980s-career woman. The idea of this type of person wanting a child as anything more than a status symbol was laughable. But what changed?

Was it just time? Time watching Kevin grow? Was it her own maturity as an adult, a distant throb of maternity that, to Karen, was more like the beating of her own heart?

(then why not have your own?)

But that thought brought its own revelation. It'd been four years, and Moira wasn't old; they were all in their early-thirties, and, in the world of *Murphy Brown*, that was young.

(you can't have children can you?)

It was all right there, right on Moira's face. Moira wanted to be a mother. Moira could not. But her husband was already a father. It put that whole "you can call me Mom" incident a year ago into a brand-new light.

(but if you take my child what am i)

As quickly as empathy came, anger replaced it. Kevin wasn't her son. What they were trying to do was steal her son for their own gain. *Her* son.

All this passed through Karen's mind in the space of a second, a rapid series of epiphanies that, a part of her knew, wouldn't have been possible before St. Jude's. Maybe she'd missed cues all along in how Nick treated her and Kevin in the past year; maybe she should've been able to see this coming long ago.

But she'd missed it.

(because what kind of mother are you?)

(just think though—he might actually be better with us)

The thought of St. Jude's made her squirm, returned the roil of her guts and the itch along her arms. She needed to get out of here. She needed to get away from this. She needed—

(to see my son)

(to go to st. jude's)

"I do," she said to Moira, and her voice was rough. "I never doubted that, but you played things this way and this is the outcome. If you had talked a change to the schedule with me, this would've been different. But you didn't—not then and not even now. We're here exploring the possibility of a custody *suit*."

"Now, Ms. Dempsey—" Ladd began.

Karen turned toward him. "Don't bother." She turned back to Nick and Moira and stood. "I have to go pick up my son because this is running late enough, but keep this in mind—a custody suit is going to put a lot of unnecessary stress and upheaval on Kevin and his life. But it *all* could've been avoided if we had talked before this.

Like I tried to." She locked eyes with Nick.

Another flicker in Nick's eyes, another glimpse behind the angry mask he wore—

(is that it? is that what you're hiding? do you feel you failed being a father nick?)

And with that came a more painful truth:

(he thinks i failed our son am *failing our son)*

(it is *all your fault dear he's dead because of you)*

Her guts churned and churned and churned.

(get me out of here get me out)

The three people stared at her, were still staring as she let herself out.

The great oceanic roar of dead television stations filled her head as she got her car, paid, and faced the main avenue from the garage exit. A right-turn would take her east, back to Lisa had Kevin. The dashboard clock read seven-forty-five; she both accepted and absolutely rejected this. It felt like she'd barely been in that meeting. It felt like she was still in that meeting. A left-turn would eventually lead her to Harmarville and St. Jude's.

The static in her head rendered thought impossible. Before, it had usually preceded her cutting.

(home)

This kept repeating itself in the center of her head, like a beacon to a lost ship in the midst of all that static, as the congregation filed in. Eve sat down next to her, gave her a welcoming-smile. The three worm-like scars on Eve's fleshy forearm stood in stark relief under the fluorescent lighting.

(home)

Roberts looked at each of them and said, "St. Jude's is open for the evening. Who would like to begin?"

(home)

A whisper beneath the static, like a distant signal heard between two radio stations:

(what about kevin?)

People glanced at each other, that universally-understood look of, *Do you want to go? Should I go?* Her people. Their unique, shared pain. Their failures.

Another static whisper:

(shouldn't you be with your son?)

And the stronger beacon:

(home)

Karen took a breath. People looked at her.

"When I was sixteen, my father died," she said. "When we came home from the funeral, my mother stood in the kitchen, in that black dress of hers with the doily-like collar, and said to me, 'It's your fault he's dead, you know.'"

(home)

(what about kevin?)

(what kind of mother are you?)

St. Jude's sermon had begun.

Headlights splashed across the front window and Lisa, gnawing on the rubber antenna of her cordless phone, slumped against the living room archway.

"Thank the fuck Christ." She hurried down the front hall to the kitchen, dropping the phone in the charger and glancing at the time on the oven clock—ten till midnight.

Where the hell were you, girl? she thought.

She went back down the hallway and grasped the front door's deadbolt. The music of *Super Mario World* drifted from upstairs, punctuated with Kevin's piping laugh. Mitch had found someone to play his new Super Nintendo with. If nothing else, it'd kept Kevin from noticing *too* much that his mother was way the hell late.

She eased the lock back and it fell open with a heavy *clack*, anyway. She winced, but the music upstairs didn't pause.

She eased outside. The porch light fell on the hood of Karen's beat-to-shit Plymouth Sundance in the driveway. Karen was little more than a dark hump behind the wheel and, before Lisa could call herself a fool, fear formed icicles along her throat.

Karen should've been back by eight-thirty, nine tops.

Where were those three additional hours?

Lisa had rang Karen's apartment over and over again, while evil visions of accidents—T-boned at a red light, driven into a concrete barrier on the Parkway—played in her head. *What the hell is happening?* she'd thought more than once and the problem wasn't that she didn't have an answer, but that there were too many answers to consider.

The Sundance's door opened and Karen slouched out, a shadowed thing approaching the front walk and the outer rim of the porch light's glow—thin, bent, and shuffling.

"Karen?" she called, because she couldn't stop herself, but kept her voice low, as if the neighbors would hear. She stepped down off the porch, onto the walk.

The shadow stopped just beyond the rim of her porch light's reach. It lifted its head and of course it was Karen—but didn't Lisa have a moment's terror that this was her friend's ghost, that her friend *had* died, but her spirit had brought her here, anyway?

Karen's skin was pale, made sickly by the porch light, drawn taut over the muscles and bones of her face, and the circles around her eyes belonged to someone on the losing end of a fistfight; she looked like a corpse in that old film *Carnival of Souls*. She wore a lazy, punch-drunk smile and this somehow made her appear worse, threw everything into starker contrast. It was the smile, the beatific glow, of someone at-ease, contented—not the smile of a mother four hours late picking up her child.

"Where the hell were you?" Lisa asked.

Karen continued to smile. "I'm sorry. Time ran away from me." Even her voice was lazy—not slurred, but *slow*.

"Doing *what?* I was worried fucking *sick* about you!"

The smile wilted, but didn't completely drop. Something shifted in Karen's eyes, a glimmer of uncertainty. "Is Kevin all right?"

Lisa took a deep breath. "Kevin's *fine*. Mitch got Super NES last month. But where were *you?* I called your fucking apartment a dozen times. I was trying to decide whether calling the police would be ridiculous or not. Don't tell me that meeting ran over four hours."

Karen shook her head, the smile completely gone, the mask of beatific joy—and that was what it had seemed like, a mask—slid off to reveal the uneasy, depressed friend Lisa was used to, and Lisa felt a stab of shame for wanting it back. Better a happy corpse than a despairing person. "It didn't. I was out of there by eight."

"Then *where?*"

Karen hesitated, looked Lisa in the eye and then flicked her gaze away. "A—a place called St. Jude's. In Harmarville."

Lisa blinked. "Harmarville? You were in Harmarville at—"

"St. Jude's. It's a . . . a church, I guess."

Lisa couldn't quite put it together. "A church," she said. "You went to a church."

"Yeah," Karen said and she looked down at her feet. "It's kinda like . . . a group therapy, I guess." She grimaced as she said this.

"A church group," Lisa said.

Karen nodded.

"And you went *there* instead of coming *here*," Lisa said.

Another nod, softer. Karen hung her head so low, Lisa couldn't see her eyes.

"Why?" Lisa said, then, immediately, "Was it that bad?"

Karen took a breath, a good heaving of her shoulders. When Karen raised her head, her eyes shone in the porch lights. "They mentioned a custody suit. They're thinking of suing me for Kevin."

"Oh." Lisa blinked. "Oh shit."

"I thought I was going to be sick," Karen said. "All I could think of was, 'I have to put a stop to this. I have to put a stop to this *now*.' I told the lawyer about how we divorced—but I don't know if it's enough. When I got outta there, I just—I couldn't—" Her voice grew thicker and thicker.

Lisa pulled her in—wrapping her arms around the other woman and trying not to notice how brittle her friend seemed. She flashed momentarily on when she'd confirmed Karen was cutting, then put it out of mind.

"I had to get my head cleared again," she said against Lisa's shoulder. "St. Jude's meets every Friday at nine and—well . . ."

"S'okay, kiddo," Lisa said and let Karen go. Karen hadn't returned the hug, just kept her arms at her sides, and it made Lisa feel awkward for reaching out. "I get it. It makes sense. So—what? This St. Jude's has a group for single parents?"

A ghost of a smile crossed Karen's face. "Something like that. It helped give me some distance from the meeting."

Lisa shook her head. "I still wished you'd called. I didn't know what to tell Kevin. Thank Christ Mitch was there to distract him."

"I'm sorry," Karen said, with so much feeling that shame swept through Lisa at every uncharitable thought she'd had over the course of the evening. "You know I wouldn't—"

Lisa flapped her hand. "Forget it. It's late. C'mon—let's get Kevin so you can get your asses home."

They turned and Kevin stood in the doorway, the porch light throwing his face into deep shadow. He didn't run to his mother, didn't move at all. He might've just opened the door. He might've been standing there the entire time.

"Where were you, Mum?" Kevin asked and, although his voice was merely curious, Lisa felt Karen flinch beside her.

"You sleep okay, hon?" Karen asked the next morning.

Kevin grunted around a mouthful of cereal. He sat cross-legged on the loveseat, the tail of his sleep-shirt pulled over his knees, eyes glued to the television, which showed an episode of *Bobby's World*.

Karen watched him from the couch. Heat gathered in her chest. She sipped her coffee and burned her tongue, as if to counteract it.

(we're only doing this for Kevin for what might be best for Kevin)

(just think though—he might actually be better with us)

"Kevin," she said, almost coughing the name.

Kevin reluctantly pulled his eyes away from the television.

"Are you happy living here?" she asked. "With me? Do you like it here?"

He looked at her with that reserved expression of his, the expression of an adult stamped onto a child. "Uh-huh, Mum."

(when you first heard that voicemail from ladd you were more adamant)

Flashing onto Kevin shadowed under Lisa's porch light:

(where were you mum?)

"Would you tell me otherwise?" she asked, before she could help herself.

Another long study from her eight-year-old son. He swallowed his cereal.

"Uh-huh, Mum," he said, and turned back to the television.

(he never tells me anything)

(does he tell anyone? does he talk to anyone?)

And then Roberts's voice was in her head:

(when we talk about our pain . . . we're seeking to stand as we are to be everything that is broken in us and made us)

Lisa told herself it was idle curiosity making her pull one of the dog-eared copies of the Yellow Pages from the office kitchen microwave during lunch. Idle curiosity making her flip to CHURCHES and, as she forked bites of microwave Fettuccini into her mouth, go down the list of city churches with one nail-bitten finger.

There were four St. John's Catholic Churches.

There were two St. Luke's.

There were no St. Jude's Churches between them.

She flipped to the cover—SPRING 1989, stamped beneath a picture of the Hathaway skyline—then back.

"Where the hell's St. Jude's?" she muttered.

"You got money in the bank, Thorne?" Adrian Shotbolt said, coasting into the kitchen. His suit jacket was missing, the sleeves of his shirt rolled up to the elbows. "People who talk to themselves have money in the bank." He went to the fridge and pulled an apple. He leaned against the counter and took a bite. "You'd finish the numbers on that Booth Industries proposal?"

"It's on my desk," she said, snapping the Yellow Pages closed, "awaiting my eventual attention." She leaned back in her seat. "Hey, Adrian—you're Catholic, right?"

He cocked an eyebrow—they looked perfect, as if he spent mornings plunking them—swallowed his bite of an apple. "Why? You looking to convert?"

She shook her head. "No. A friend was telling me about a St.

Jude's Church—"

"St. Luke's?"

Another headshake. "No—St. *Jude's* Church."

"You must've heard wrong," Adrian said. "No one in their right mind would name a church that."

She ignored the sudden heavy *wham* of her heartbeat.

"Why's that?"

"Because *Jude* is short for *Judas*," Adrian said.

"What—like the black guy who betrayed Jesus?"

Adrian choked on a bite of apple from laughing. His face went red and he coughed into the sink. When he turned back, he was grinning, his eyes watering. "Good God, woman," he grunted, pounding his chest with his fist. "That's from *Jesus Christ Superstar.*"

He tossed the rest of his apple into the trashcan by the microwave and dusted his hands. "Lemme give you the freeze-dried version. There were two disciples named Judas—Iscariot, who betrayed Jesus, and Thaddaeus. Because early Christians didn't want him mixed up with Iscariot, they shortened Thaddaeus's name to Jude. Still, few people prayed to him *because* they didn't want to look like they were praying to Iscariot, so, by default, Jude became the patron saint of complete hopelessness. Meaning, you *must've* heard wrong. No one's going to name their church after the guy who's the symbol for lost causes."

He pushed himself off the counter, shaking his head as he headed for the door. "'Black guy who betrayed Jesus'—my God, Lisa." He chuckled. "Lemme know when you do the Booth numbers. I want to compare them with the Lori numbers."

"Will-do," Lisa said, but she was barely listening, thinking that she *hadn't* heard wrong. Karen had said *St. Jude.*

Lisa dropped her fork into the microwave pasta and pushed it away from her. She was no longer hungry.

Karen checked the instructions Tina, Ryall Construction's HR person, had written out, and switched the office's open phone line to the phone tree. For the next twenty minutes, callers would be given a recording and a series of departments to select. Not many people called in; that was why Tina was good about this.

(hell half the girls in the building are mothers or single mothers)

Still, that didn't quiet the small throb of guilt over leaving her job during the workday. A year without working, finally getting a job (even if just a temp gig), and already cutting corners.

(that's not true and you know it)

(what's true is you never could get your life in order)

Karen shook the voices off and checked the wall clock beside her receptionist cubicle—three-oh-five. Plenty of time. She reached into her desk drawer and got her purse.

"Cutting out early?" a man said from behind her.

She turned and Dick Cavanaugh, one of Ryall's estimators, stood in the doorway leading to the main office hallway. He had a Baby-Huey-in-the-middle-years face, with small eyes plugged into the doughy flesh. His thick lips always quivered, as if to smile but never quite making it.

"Running an errand," she said, hearing Tina's voice in her head.

(it's a bit of a good ol' boy system)

(there's a reason corporate made me hr director)

Cavanaugh's eyes bounced from her face to her chest and back. The reception area was dark—a joke that a construction firm had set up their lobby in such a way that it received, in spite of the huge front window, zero natural light—and the main hallway's light backlit Cavanaugh. He shoved his hands in the pockets of his khakis, drawing attention to his crotch.

(if you ever feel uncomfortable)

"Is there something you need?" she asked.

He shook his head. "No, just making sure the new fish is getting along all right."

(don't hesitate to tell me)

She glanced at the clock. Pushing three-ten. "I'm getting along fine, thank you."

"Good, good," he said in that way that signaled he wasn't listening. "Because we look out for people here. We want people to work *together*, y'know? To be *friendly*."

(you might be a temp but you're still a woman)

"We tend to hire our temps, y'know," he said. His lips resembled two writhing worms.

Another glance at the clock.

"That's what I'm hoping," she said and sidled her way around the receptionist desk. "I'll be back soon."

"I can't wait," Cavanaugh said, with feeling, and Karen couldn't repress a shudder.

She didn't note how much she was shaking until she was turning at the light for Butler and 50th Street. Cavanaugh left a film on her skin, made her clothes itch; as if his eyes had literally rolled over her, leaving behind a scummy residue.

She pushed it out of mind by the time she got to 54th. Kevin stood under the crosswalk sign, looking around, and darted for her car when she pulled up.

"Hi, Mum," he said, throwing himself onto the passenger seat and slamming the door behind him.

"Good day?" she asked as he clicked his seatbelt home. She glanced over his head and saw the Perozzi girls a half-block down, watching them with a tall boy that had to be the Perozzi brother.

Kevin followed her gaze. "Uh-huh, Mum."

Lisa dialed, then leaned back at her desk, drumming her fingers on top of expense estimates she *should* be paying attention to.

Maybe it's a new property, she thought, listening to the phone ring. *One of those start-up churches you see in plazas and shit.*

She couldn't help wrinkling her nose at that. The idea of Karen at one of those oh-Jesus-Lord-help-me places didn't sit well in the center of her head.

A click in her ear. "Rich McCarrick," a man's voice said, his voice furry with a rushing sound in the distance.

"Are you in the car?" she asked.

"Is this Lisa?" McCarrick asked. "Also, yes. That's why it's called a car phone."

"Gonna kill yourself."

"Then Mitch'll have to cancel my mortgages."

"Any properties recently sell in Harmarville?" she asked. "That's your territory, right?"

"Are we done with the small talk?" McCarrick said. "Because that's a fucking odd question for conversation. Anyway, yeah, Harmarville's in my territory. Not much going on out there."

"So a property sale would be noticed."

"Uh-huh. What's this about?"

"Looking into something. Answer the question, please."

"Is this an investigation?" he asked, his tone light and bouncy. "Am I helping an investigation? Corporate intrigue?"

The image of Karen, wraith-like on the lawn, flashed in front of Lisa's eyes. "Something like that. Answer the question, Rich, be-fore you confirm the myth that real estate agents are brainless."

"Hey!" McCarrick cried.

Lisa closed her eyes, held onto her patience with both mental hands. "C'mon, Rich, I got other calls to make."

"Um." He drew this out. "Someone bought the old bowling alley. That happened...last spring? Last winter? Something like that. I didn't broker the deal."

"A bowling alley," Lisa said. *How the hell would Karen learn about a church in Harmarville in the first place?* she thought. "This bowling alley have a name?"

"Arsenal Lanes," McCarrick said. "Closed down about two years ago. No one out in the Heroin Hills liked to bowl, I guess."

"Thanks, Rich."

"You gonna tell me what this is about—"

"I'll tell you the next time you beat Mitch at blackjack," she said and cradled the phone.

She sat a moment, then launched herself from her desk and marched down to the kitchen, saying hi to those who called out to her but not knowing who did and grabbed the Spring 1989 phone-book again. She ignored everyone on the way back to her office.

She grabbed her phone receiver and dialed a number in the county courthouse, flipping through the book to BOWLING and find-ing the address.

Doesn't mean that Karen's church is the same place, a voice told her and she told it to shut the hell up.

She heard the line click open. "Andrea? Hi—it's Lisa over at Fenelli Financial. I was wondering if you could do a favor for me and pull some land records? Do you have a minute?"

Thursday afternoon and Karen stood beside her car as Kevin's bus pulled up with a hiss of airbrakes and threw open its doors.

The crossing guard walked into the center of the intersection as kids poured into the street. Karen stiffened as the Perozzi girls came galumphing—that was the word that occurred to her, the only word to describe the stomp-shuffle they did—off the bus and crossed. Halfway up 54th Street, the Perozzi brother stopped walking down to meet them and waited instead.

(he can't handle himself)

This thought was an arrow across her mind. She tried mentally following it, but saw the top of Kevin's head, last in line off the bus.

(god kevin's so small)

Kevin stepped off the bus, head down, the doors swooshing shut behind him. The knee of his jeans was torn, the denim threads covering an awkwardly placed Band-Aid.

Karen's heart knocked hard against her chest. "Hon?"

He looked up and, although he didn't smile, his eyes lightened. "Hi, Mum," he said.

They started for the car. "What happened to your knee, kiddo?" She pointed.

Kevin glanced down, but not before she saw his eyes darken. "Oh. Fell on the playground. Tripped." He didn't look back up.

(lying)

"Are you sure that's what happened?" she asked, opening the passenger door for him, striving to keep her voice light.

"Uh-huh," he said, buckling his seatbelt and settling his backpack in his lap.

She closed the door, but didn't immediately go around to the other side. She watched him through the window. He looked at his backpack, fingers playing with the zipper of the main pocket.

(why won't you tell me?)

(what could you do?)

He glanced at her, and she went around to the other side, letting herself in. She got the Sundance started and coasted to the light.

"Are you all right at school?" she asked.

Immediate, but flat: "Uh-huh, Mum."

"No one gives you trouble."

"Nuh-uh."

She glanced at him. "Not even those Perozzi girls?" she asked.

His head darted up and she saw his true expression for an instant: fear. It was in the widening of his eyes, the slight unhinging of his mouth.

And then his face tightened again. "No, Mum. They don't trouble me."

She opened her mouth—what eight-year-old used *that* turn of phrase?—when the light changed. She started up the hill of 54th Street.

"I can't help you if you don't talk," she said, turning onto Keystone Street.

Roberts's voice in her head:

(no amount of talking will heal you no amount of sharing will empower you)

"It's okay to get hurt and say something about it," she said, turning onto 53rd Street.

"I'm *fine*, Mum," he said in a *I can deal with it* tone. "There's nothing to talk about."

(that's not to say nothing's happening)

She pulled in front of their house.

"If you're sure," she said, lingering on the last word. "Get inside and get your homework done. I'll be home at five."

"Bye, Mum," he said, taking his house key from his backpack and getting out of the car.

She watched him let himself into the house and close the door before she drove away.

Kevin didn't look back once.

❧ ··· ❧

You're edging into marshy territory, ol' kid ol' sock, Lisa thought, elbows planted on her desk, fingers steepled against her temples. Land records, sales reports, property inspections covered her desktop blotter. All available to the public.

You're not really going to do this, are you?

Lisa dry-washed her face. She tried to do what she never did—think things through.

This is crossing a line, the voice of reason, weak from ill-use, told her. *Someone with a higher paygrade looks your way, and you're going to have trouble explaining.*

"Shit," she muttered and pulled back in her chair. Beyond her office, the sounds of the bullpen drifted in, pepped up with the coming weekend. Only nine in the morning, but everyone out there moved like it was thirty minutes till five.

She eyeballed the reports some more. The property once known as Arsenal Lanes had been purchased by one Darren Roberts in November of 1990. No business license, no 503-c4 application, which denoted seeking religious tax exempt status.

Which left one option.

Is this something Karen would want you to do? the voice of reason asked. *As a friend?*

But, she'd gotten Karen to admit to cutting, had gotten her to *stop* cutting and harming herself.

What if this church was just another form of cutting? she thought.

She reached for the phone and dialed.

Karen picked up at the other end. "Ryall Construction," she piped. "How may I direct your call?"

"You sound like a natural, kiddo."

Karen chuckled. It grated on Lisa's ears. "I didn't know I was auditioning. What's up?"

"Kevin going to his dad's tonight?"

A drop in temperature across the phone line. "Uh-huh."

"Thought we could have a girls night. Split a bottle of wine, rent *Pretty Woman* from Vern's Video, talk trash on Julia Roberts."

"I can't," Karen said, each word sounding as if pulled from her mouth. "I have...church."

Lisa paused to make it sound like she was thinking. "That's that St. Jude's place, right? In Harmarville?"

She could hear Karen hesitate. "Uh-huh."

"That's a weekly thing?"

Now the hesitation was excruciating. "Uh-huh."

"Is it, like, a traditional church?" Lisa asked. "Like sermons and stuff? Most churches meet on Sunday."

"Um," Karen said. "It's, like, talking to each other. Fellowship. Dr. Roberts—"

Lisa's eyes snapped to her paperwork.

"—leads us in discussions," Karen said, "but mostly we just talk to each other."

"Well, that sucks," Lisa said, forcing to keep her voice light. "For me getting drunk, not for you." She voiced a laugh that made her wince inwardly. "Next week, then?"

She could hear the relief in Karen's voice. "Of course."

"Right, then, back to work for both of us," Lisa said.

They got off the phone and Lisa stared at the paperwork for an instant, thinking of Karen not cutting but looking worse. Thinking of Karen blowing off her own son until nearly midnight.

Why aren't you talking to me, kiddo? she thought.

She apparently has other people to talk to, came the answer.

Yes, but who were these people?

She picked up the receiver again and dialed an extension.

When the line picked up, she said, "Hey, Tim—I need to run a background check. Can we set that up?" She listened. "It's kinda a rushjob. Something's hinky about a prospect and the numbers and I want to feel it out. Just some exploring. Is that possible?"

She listened some more. "Awesome. No—I'll come to you."

Karen made an honest effort to listen to the members of the congregation speak, but everything they said passed cleanly through her, leaving no impression.

In her head, silence filled the space.

The silence of wounds left hidden—

(it's okay to get hurt and say something about it)

(i'm fine mum)

—and the silence of potential wounds to come.

(nick not even glancing at her tonight as kevin slid into the passenger seat saying just a few words—"same time sunday then?"—before driving away with their son)

Nick was exploring a custody suit—and, oh, the clench of pain in her chest at acknowledging that. Nick, who had left their son in her care when they divorced, now trying to take their son away from her. Their relationship when it came to Kevin had always been cordial; whatever existing wreckage of their marriage hadn't gotten in the way of raising Kevin.

She couldn't remember the last time they'd spoken on the phone—not since last spring, at least. How much did she own that? She'd never even noticed, not until Alan Ladd had called her, of the changing in Nick's attitudes toward her.

Nick doubted her parenting.

(who am i if i'm not a mother?)

Kevin wasn't talking. His near-outburst when they'd first heard Alan Ladd's voice was an ancient myth, present only in her memories. He didn't talk about school, or his weekends with his father. He watched her as he watched everything else—with a mask of reserve, as if allowing someone to see his thought-process or opinion was something he could never allow. And he was only eight.

(that look of fear at the mention of the perozzi girls the quick peek at how he really felt but never said)

How much of that was her fault? How much had he picked up from her not talking, from constantly pushing things under, and how much was affecting his attitude now?

"Everything we've experienced informs how we act," Roberts said, pulling her from her thoughts. He stood in the center of the circle. "Like a dog kicked so many times that it shies from all human touch, no matter the intent. This gets to the truth of ourselves and those we encounter. Sometimes all we can do is flinch, regardless of why the other person is reaching out. That's why the idea of healing, of talking it out and seeking absolution, pervades. The Catholics have had the confessional since time immemorial, but does exposing your sins mean the sins no longer exist? Do a handful of 'Our Fathers' mean that we are washed clean?"

He waved his hand at a middle-aged woman with hair the color of copper-piping. "Gloria's story tonight made me remember that one of us is no longer here."

He nodded to an empty seat between Adam and a young black gentleman with burn scars on his face.

"Elliot hasn't been here in weeks," Roberts said. "I don't know why. But I can guess. Even after I tell people, 'I can't help you,' they still hold out hope. They still believe absolution awaits those who share with others. Is that why Elliot came here?" He shrugged. "I can't say, although I suspected. You all have a posture when you speak—you look down, you mumble. Sometimes you gloss over the really aching parts until I drag them out of you. Elliot looked at us, at *me*, as he spoke, and I never needed to coax him."

He surveyed each of them. "He was seeking the non-Catholic version of confession. He wanted me to offer my little speeches in a way that made him feel *better*. And I can't." He shrugged again. "I can only do what you do, give you space to do it. Only by acknowledging the pain can you help yourself be who you are but here's the core truth: the pain has to get so bad that it's impossible to ignore it. But it comes from yourself."

Roberts sat back down. "All right—who's next?"

The bus rolled to a stop and the crossing guard walked into the street. Kids spilled out onto the sidewalk and around the Perozzi brother. It occurred to her to wonder why he wasn't in school. Amidst the other children, the Perozzi girls ran up to him. The group—

(like a fan club for the peanuts *character pig pen)*

—pulled away from the other kids, but didn't immediately leave.

Kevin stepped off the bus, looking for and seeing her car immediately. He started for her and, looking around, saw the Perozzis. He gave them a wide berth—

(like a dog kicked so many times)

—as he a made a bee-line to Karen's car.

Karen flicked a glance at the Perozzis and caught them following his progress. The oldest of the girls spoke to the brother as they watched. Karen's hands tightened on the steering wheel.

Kevin came around to the passenger side and let himself in. "Hi, Mum," he said, buckling his seatbelt.

She forced herself to turn away, look at her son. "Hey, hon. Good day at school?"

She didn't miss the way his eyes cut to the Perozzi children, even if his expression never changed. "Uh-huh."

(why won't you say something?)

(the pain has to get so bad that it's impossible to ignore it)

"That's the best you can hope for on a Monday," she said, barely hearing herself, and started the car. She gripped the steering wheel so tightly the veins stood out in the back of her hand, but she didn't ask Kevin about the Perozzis.

(this is the place where you can be who you truly are)

Roberts's voice and she finds herself back in the dream field, looking up the dead hill where, an instant before, her mother had held a single glittering razorblade.

His voice comes on the rushing, awful breeze, unhurried in spite of the wind's force:

(here there is no schism between who you are and who you want to be)

"I don't even know that that means," she mutters. She starts up the hill. The deep bone-ache, the poison in the soil, leaches into her skin, making her grimace with every movement.

(in the waking world you struggle between your pain and your responsibility—as a parent, as an adult, as an employee)

(there is no struggle here)

(here your pain can inform your responsibility)

Her feet sink into the soft ground, her muscles groan at the effort of pushing her up. She reaches the top of the hill and, across the way, sees two things, locked within the same space and looping together, like frames of undeveloped film laid atop one another:

In one, Kevin stands there, as he stood in the kitchen doorway when they heard Alan Ladd's message—his face red, his hands clenched at his sides, struggling not to cry. He hitches in one breath after another.

In the other, Kevin giving something a wide berth—the only way to differentiate between the two images, when the second Kevin steps aside the first—his flat expressionless face never changing.

(this place served a purpose when you were younger)

Roberts's voice, a soft, coaxing whisper in her ears.

(it still does whether you know it or not)

Her eyes drift to the collapsing structure, now barely two hills away, but keep getting pulled back to Kevin—Kevin struggling not to cry, Kevin avoiding his tormentors.

(you see it don't you karen?)

A sudden ache that has nothing to do with the poisoned atmosphere stabs her chest, making her gasp. The pain is her essential motherness.

(this is your chance to not be a failure of a mother)

(to know exactly what kind of mother you are)

(a mother guides her child through experiences and its experiences that inform how we will act)

It's uncertain when she began repeating, "No, no, no," hadn't even noticed she's saying anything at all until she was screaming it at the vision, at the sky, at the structure and its mysterious presence, until her screaming brings darkness and—

—she was crying it into her pillow.

She opened her eyes, the cool feel of her tears soaking into the fabric startling her, cutting off the muffled chant.

Behind her, the alarm clock continued to deet-deet-deet its wake-up call.

Karen sat up, trying to shake the image of Kevin avoiding the Perozzis and struggling not to cry from her head.

(you see it don't you karen?)

"Oh, Jesus," she muttered, her voice thick. She heard Kevin down the hall, his light snoring.

(what kind of a mother are you?)

(it's experiences that inform how we will act)

The image lingered, until her heart slowed down, until her breathing eased. Until she sat up straighter.

Tim had promised a rushjob on the background check, just a skimming of the surface, and it was due any day. By lunch on Tuesday, she quit pretending she knew what she was doing and shut down her computer, put on the outgoing message on her phone, and got the hell out of work.

She skirted the downtown rush of traffic and turned onto the Boulevard of the Allies, which fed the Hathaway Bridge and the 376-East Parkway, only to see that the Hathaway Bridge was closed with detour signs aimed for the Parkway.

"Fuck!" she yelled, smacking the steering wheel, and cut into the Parkway lane, ignoring the angry honking of those behind her. It took her almost an hour to, through the detour, reach the other side of the Hathaway Bridge.

Most people in Hathaway didn't venture south into Harmarville. When Hathaway had been a booming coal city last century, Harmarville had been the apex of prosperity. When coal left, so did the prosperity, and only despair had filled the void.

Today's goal, children, she thought, *is to see where Karen would rather be than with her own kid.*

Lisa had memorized the old Arsenal Lanes address and found Vernazza Road easily enough. She topped a rise and, on the right, the Arsenal Lanes property—she couldn't think of it as a church—unfolded: the squat building in the center of an ocean of cracked concrete, like a desert island you never wanted to find yourself washed up on.

Lisa slowed, eyes on the metal skeleton that, once upon a time, had lifted up a lit sign. Now, it seemed to exist solely to hang the small, handwritten sign that underscored how depressing this all was:

ST. JUDE'S MINISTRIES

FRIDAYS — 9:00 PM (ALWAYS)

YOU ARE NOT ALONE

She turned in and parked in a space farthest from the building, ass-in so she could stare.

This. This was where Karen came on Friday nights. This was where Karen, after the meeting with Nick, Moira, and the lawyer had absconded to, completely blowing off her own son.

This is the place that has replaced her cutting, Lisa thought. It depressed her to think of Karen driving to this shitty old building that had inexplicably become a "church."

For the past week, everything had been names and addresses.

Now she could picture it.

"Even if I don't know what goes on inside of it," she said. Karen, reluctant to even mention she came here, was absolutely mum on what went on inside.

It's a cult, Lisa thought. *Who starts up a church out here? What could be out here that'd be so goddamned special that Karen would choose it over her own goddamned child?*

She thought of Karen's face when Lisa had shoved up the shirt-sleeve, revealing the fresh cuts; she thought of Karen's face, lit by the porch light. Gooseflesh prickled across her skin.

Why didn't you come to me, kiddo? Why couldn't I help you?

A Subaru pulled into the lot. It slowed, the driver obviously looking at her.

Dude, it's closed on Tuesdays, she thought as the car pulled into a spot close to the glass doors.

What if it's Darren Roberts? the interior voice asked and, with that, she started her car and got the hell out of there.

Maybe the background check is in, the interior voice said, driving out of Harmarville, and something in her chest clenched *maybe-maybe-maybe,* but she ignored it. Seeing the depressing focus of Karen's illness was enough for one day.

Is that what this is? the interior voice asked. *An illness?*

"I don't know what the hell else to call it," Lisa muttered. "She's not well. How *much* she isn't well is still uncertain."

Lisa needed to see Karen. To complete the picture. She checked the dashboard clock—a little before two. She could be back in their neighborhood by the time Kevin got off the bus.

The lunch rush had passed, but traffic was still heavy with the beginnings of evening rush hour; it took her an over hour to get across the city and back to her own neighborhood. At 50th Street, she skirted traffic and turned right, heading up the curving hill to McCameron Street and turned left. Kids ambled along the sidewalks, their backpacks as large as their torsos. It was three-thirty. Karen would be dropping Kevin off at the house around now.

She reached the corner of McCameron and 53rd and turned down.

Karen's Sundance wasn't parked in front of the house. Lisa rolled to a stop where Karen's car *should* be. The upstairs blinds were drawn.

That doesn't mean Kevin's not inside, the interior voice said. *Why would an eight-year-old give a shit about the blinds?*

Lisa rolled on anyway, turning onto Keystone Street. With traffic as bad as it was, maybe it was taking Karen a moment. If Lisa went to Kevin's bus stop and didn't see them, she'd head to Karen's work.

This was Lisa's thought until she reached the stop sign for 54th and Keystone, looked down, and saw two things.

Then all thought stopped.

The first thing was Karen's Sundance, parked behind a Nissan, and ridiculously far from Butler. With traffic the way it was, Kevin would never see it.

The second thing she saw was the group of kids at Kevin's bus stop, a great mass of small children. No adults. Lisa saw a fist rise from the center, like a fish breaking the surface of the water, and then come crashing down.

The bottom dropped out of Lisa's stomach. "Oh shit," she said, breathlessly.

She peeled out from the stop and arrowed down the street,

passing Karen's Sundance without even a glance. The light favored her and she sped across, hitting the brakes. That sound was enough to alert the kids. When Lisa threw open her door and launched out of the car, they scattered, opening up to the center where a middle-school-aged boy paced with Kevin, their fists up. The middle school boy's nose bled; a Canadian sunrise burgeoned on Kevin's face. His lower lip was split.

Lisa saw all this in the time it took to come around the back of the car and reach the curb. In the next moment, she was grabbing the middle school boy by the back of his shirt and tossing him against the Acme building.

She hunkered down in front of Kevin, who stood with his shoulders hunched, his face a frozen flat rictus, looking into and through Lisa.

"Kevin," she heard herself say as if from a great distance and gripped his shoulders. He flinched, blinking, saw her for the first time. "Kevin, are you all right?"

Muscles moved beneath the skin of his face. She grasped his fists and slowly lowered them. When she did, his shoulders dropped.

"Listen, bitch," she heard the other boy say and she looked up, seeing three girls down the block. She immediately dismissed them and turned back to the boy, who glared at her with the sneering disgust only new teenagers can muster.

"What did you say?" she heard herself say, planted a hand in the center of his chest, and pushed. The boy slammed into the wall; the back of his head connected and he cried out.

She stepped close. "Like picking on little kids, huh?" she said and when he tried to straighten up again, she pushed him back. "What if I picked on *you?*"

The boy made one last effort. "You can't—"

She pinned him to the wall. "Wrong. I can. I am. And if I *ever* see you so much as *look* in this boy's direction, I'll do more than *pick* on you. Understand me?"

His pride wouldn't let him nod. His eyes, already shellacked with tears, was answer enough.

She removed her hand from his chest and he stumbled, the

final humiliation. "Get the fuck outta here, you little asshole."

He scooted away, joining the three little girls, obviously related, and ran off.

Lisa turned to Kevin. His face continued to ripple. His eyes, red and wet, glared at the sidewalk. He breathed through his clenched teeth.

She hunkered down in front of him. The world opened—the rev of engines, the honk of horns. Not a single car had stopped during this entire episode, not a single driver had called out.

Glory of living in the city, she thought.

"C'mon, Kev," Lisa said. "Shake it off. Your twelve rounds against Admiral Asshole was called in the second round by Liberating Lisa."

She'd hoped he'd crack a smile, but Kevin didn't so much as look at her.

She rubbed his upper arms. "C'mon, kiddo, snap out of it. You're gonna start freaking me out and I'm too old for—"

"*Kevin!*" Karen cried and Lisa froze. Kevin's eyes blinked and looked over Lisa's shoulder. "Jesus Christ—*Kevin!*"

Lisa turned and Karen stood beside the light pole, her face a mask of shock and horror.

That's right, Lisa said, the image of Karen's Sundance falling right into the forefront of her mind, *it's a mask.*

Lisa glanced down and Kevin was regaining his usual too-mature-for-eight expression, made ludicrous by the bruising.

"Kevin, find your stuff, okay?" she said. "I'll be a minute with your mom."

Karen's gaze snapped to her as she approached, bewildered, but Lisa never slowed; she grabbed Karen by the upper arm and half-led, half-dragged the other woman around the corner.

She shoved Karen away. "What the fuck was that?"

Karen straightened. "What the fuck was *what?* Kevin—"

Lisa's jaw locked and she could only speak through her teeth. "I saw your car. Were you *watching?*"

Karen gaped at her. In the space of a second, guilt, shame, fear, uncertainty—they all zipped across Karen's face, rippling it much like Kevin's had rippled. What was left at the end was an expression of exquisite sadness, of complete loss.

Lisa glanced over her shoulder to make sure Kevin didn't appear. "For fuck's sakes, *why*? How could you allow this? Did you know this was going to happen? What the fuck is *wrong* with you?"

Karen's throat worked as if the amount of words she needed to say had blocked access for any of them to escape. "He never talks, Lisa. He hurts all the time and he never talks."

"*What?*" Lisa said. "What the fuck are you talking about?"

"The Perozzis have been bothering him for a while," Karen said, "but he won't admit it and I never catch it. He doesn't say anything, Lisa, but I know it bothers him. I see the little clues." She dropped her eyes. Her skin was almost freakishly white, pulled taut over her bones, and it was like seeing an erect skeleton nod its head.

"And you thought letting him get the shit beat out of him would open up a fucking font of discussion?" Lisa asked. "Jesus, do you have any idea how fucking nutty that sounds? That's your *son*, Karen."

Karen bit her lip. Her eyes were wetter than ever. Her throat bobbed like she was chugging something.

"I know, but I—" Karen swallowed. "But when I'm around, those kids never try anything and I get nowhere with him and I thought, if he felt a pain strongly enough, he'd talk *then*. It would be too much to hold in."

"You allowed your son to be attacked," she told Karen. Karen flinched with each hard enunciation. "Do you have any idea how fucked up that is? How fucked up that *looks*? What if your ex-husband saw that?"

Karen's eyes widened. The idea had never fucking occurred to her.

"This is the kinda shit that loses someone the custody of their child," Lisa said. "And if you honestly believe what you just said to me, then maybe Kevin *would* be better with Nick."

She immediately regretted it, didn't need to see the momentary rise of color in Karen's cheeks to feel the shame go rocketing through her heart.

Some best friend I am! she thought. *Asshole!*

Lisa opened her mouth—to say what, she didn't know—when

Kevin came around the corner, shouldering on his backpack.

"Can we go home, Mum?" he asked and his voice, his demeanor, was as it always was. If not for the split lip and bruising, the torn shirt and blood, you would've never known he'd just been in a fight.

Jesus, Lisa thought.

"Yeah," Karen said, her voice thick. "Let's get you cleaned up, honey." She held out her hand and Kevin took it.

As they walked to Karen's Sundance, parked in front of Lisa's car, Kevin looked back. "Thank you, Lisa," he said.

Lisa nodded, unable to speak.

Karen didn't look back or say anything at all.

Karen soaked a cotton ball with hydrogen peroxide, set the brown container on the bathroom sink. Kevin sat on the closed toilet and he flinched when she dabbed his split lip.

"Easy, champ," she said, leaning forward from the side of the tub. "Gotta disinfect."

He held himself still, only his slitting eyes giving away how much it stung as she continued to dab. She tossed away the cotton ball, pinkish with blood, and asked, "So what happened, hon? Why'd the Perozzi boy come after you?"

Kevin looked to his sneakers. "His sister Patty told him to."

"Did you know him?"

He started to shake his head, then stopped. "No. Only saw him with his sisters."

Karen swallowed. "Why'd Patty tell her brother to fight you?"

"He said I called her a mean name," Kevin said. "I didn't, though. I avoid the Perozzis. Everyone does."

"Is Patty in your class?"

"Uh-huh, but she hangs out with her sisters during recess and stuff."

"Do they pick on anyone else?"

"No."

"But they *do* pick on you," Karen pushed. "They *do* hurt you, right?" She held her free hand against his other cheek. "It's okay to tell me, hon. You don't have to hold it in."

A beat of silence, and then Kevin looked up from his sneakers. "Where were you, Mum?"

Karen paused. Her tongue clung to the roof of her mouth, blocking air and words. She'd been deliberately late, leaving work at three-fifteen, when she knew the bus dropped them off. And then—

(do you have any idea how fucked up that is?)

She let go of his face, pressed the washcloth against his cheek, guided his hand to hold onto it. "I gotta call work, tell them I'm not coming back today."

His eyes followed her out of the room, but he didn't ask again.

(what kind of mother are you?)

Thursday. Lisa knew this because the calendar on her desktop blotter told her so.

The mailroom boy came in with a manila envelope. "For you, Mrs. Thorne."

She looked from her computer as he dropped it onto the desk with a paper *whap* and left. She stared at the envelope, her fingers rubbing against each other over her keyboard. The urge to slide it into the trash—or, better yet, the shredder—came to her. Forget she'd even requested it. Tim from downstairs wouldn't follow up.

She hadn't talked to Karen in two days.

(do you have any idea how fucked up that is? if you honestly believe what you just said to me, then maybe kevin would be better with nick)

I should've left it alone, she thought. *I pushed and this was the result.*

To have Kevin beaten raw? the interior voice mocked. *If you hadn't been there, that's what would've happened. She's ill. With or without you. Now that you're in it, stop being such a pussy and be* in *it.*

But she didn't come to me—

Because people who aren't well always do what's in their best interests.

She tore the envelope open and pulled out the thin sheaf of papers, bound with a paperclip. She flipped through the papers, skimming a word here, a phrase here—Arizona; oh, he actually was a preacher at one point—and then stopped.

"Holy shit," she breathed.

Everything around her became unglued. The sounds in the bull-pen dwindled. The chill of the air conditioner faded.

She spun around her desk, hands padding the desktop, trying to find the next thing she needed, not knowing the next thing she needed.

Her eyes locked on the phone—*yes!* She needed the rest. She needed Tim to deep dive that son of a bitch, pull up everything up to and including any overdue books from fucking middle school. *Yes.* She picked up the receiver.

No.

She froze with her other hand about to dial.

That would take weeks.

(guilt, shame, fear, and uncertainty zip over karen's face, leaving a feeling of exquisite sadness and complete loss)

She racked the phone, then slumped back in her chair, rubbing her temple. *Carnegie Library, you doofus*, drifted across her mind.

Lisa grabbed a pad and, flipping through report, jotted down:

Placerville, Arizona.

1986.

Darren Roberts.

Sarah Goode, Ann Proctor, Anthony Desmond.

Placerville Three.

The Absolution of Christ Church.

She tapped her pen against the pad, looking through the report a second time. "That'll do," she said, and tore the page off the pad.

Nick froze welcoming Kevin into the car. "What the hell happened to you?"

Karen's eyes snapped to Kevin, who finished climbing in and buckling his seatbelt.

"Ran into a door at school," Kevin said. The swelling on his lip had gone down, leaving a scab that resembled the aftermath of a bad piercing. The bruising on his cheeks had lightened, until it looked like Kevin had decided to play with Karen's makeup.

Nick turned his son's face this way and that under the dome light. "How many times?"

Kevin shrugged and Nick turned his incredulous look toward Karen. For the second time this week, her tongue clung to the roof of her mouth. The truth was—

(do you have any idea how fucking insane this is)

—while lying was—

(what?)

her mother asked,

(completely against what your job as a mother should be? an underscoring of how completely and utterly you've failed as a parent?)

She swallowed.

"Why didn't you call me?" Nick asked, his voice softening—not in understanding, but in a wounded kind of way, as if it hurt that he wasn't alerted.

"I didn't want to make a big deal about it," Kevin said, not looking at either parent.

Karen's eyes snapped back to their son.

(why is he covering for me?)

Roberts's voice perked up:

(that means he knows there's something to cover up)

Nick looked at their son, his brow furrowed. His eyes ticked off the bruising, the scabbed lip. He glanced at Karen, and Karen couldn't read the expression. Finally, he settled back into the driver seat, stared at his odometer, then shook his head. "Same time on Sunday?" he asked the windshield in an odd, flat voice.

(what aren't you saying to me? what aren't you telling me?)

Her mother responded—

(what aren't you telling him?)

—before memory did—

(we're only doing this for kevin for what might be best for kevin)

A cold hollow formed in her chest. "Isn't it always?" she said and her voice was thicker than usual.

He nodded and shifted the car into Drive. If not for Kevin's face, this might've been a replay of last weekend.

(i'm missing something)

(there's something unsaid here)

"See you, then," Nick said in that flat voice and Karen stepped back, closed the passenger door.

As they pulled away, Kevin looked back at his mother, once, and his expression was just as unreadable as his father's.

(we're doing this for kevin)

(where were you mum?)

(what kind of mother are you?)

As a rule, Lisa hated driving at night. The streetlights outlined the deep shadows more than banished them. The deejays grew hushed, playing tracks that never played in sunlight, warbling from her speakers into the nothingness. Night was a time when your worst ideas came to you, when your worst feelings seemed plausible.

No wonder this fucking cult meets then, she thought, turning into the Arsenal Lanes parking lot. She pulled in behind Karen's Sundance, killed the engine. She glanced at the folder on the passenger seat, stuffed with Xeroxed copies of stories from *The Los Angeles Times* and *The Arizona Republic*.

She got out and walked to the glass doors. Fellowship, Karen said. Discussion with like-minded people.

What was the topic for tonight, kids?

She entered, careful not to let the door thump back. She heard a man talking around the corner. The lobby opened up onto the lanes. She could not have imagined a less-appropriate place for a church.

The man's voice came from the right.

She kept close to the check-in counter, stopping before she would've been visible to anyone.

"—and I couldn't help it," this man was saying, his voice thick with emotion. "I—I just would look at him and everything I feared or hated would pour out of me. And then the one time he—" The man's voice cracked. "This one time he left the door open, when he let our cat out and it ran ... I ... I just lost it. I just started punching."

Lisa hunched, covering her mouth. Her stomach had been replaced by a clenching gloved fist.

"And how did that feel?" another man said. "Did you feel *good* about that?"

"Christ, no," the first man said. "I hated myself more, which just made me hit harder."

"You weren't hitting your son," the second man said. "You wished you could hit yourself, but couldn't. Your failure wasn't just in the assault on your child, but your inability to get at what *really* drove you—your own anxiety, your own fear."

The first man made a sound like a choked sob.

"And that's what makes you feel awful now," the second man said. "And you *should* feel awful about that. *That* wounding is nowhere close to what your son endured, but you'll never forget it." A pause. "Right now, being fully honest with yourself, would you be able to hold yourself back?"

Lisa didn't wait for an answer, bolting back outside. She reached Karen's car and puked, her guts flexing and flexing and flexing. She leaned her head against Karen's cool hood, her eyes gushing hot tears.

Jesus, kiddo, she thought. *Jesus.*

"You struggle to exist with your pain in a world that tries to tell you your pain doesn't exist," Roberts said.

He looked at them. "But you know your pain's not going anywhere, and you struggle to balance it. How do you exist in such a world? How can you be honest with yourself and face the constant hurdles of being forced to pretend?"

He shook his head. "It's even worse for parents, who are supposed to be *guides*. They have to exist with their pain, while teaching their children *about* their world. I can't imagine the pressure to find that balance. How does one do it? With violence? Of course not, but I understand it. With ignoring? But who's being most disserved there—you or the child? And aren't you just exacerbating yourself?"

He shrugged. "I have no answers. That's on the individual and their pain." He nodded. "Drive safe, everyone. Thank you for being honest with yourselves."

The congregation rose, gathered their jackets, threw away their trash. As a group—that didn't interact—they moved to the doors.

Karen walked with them, her head down, stepped out into the chilly night.

And then Lisa said, "Earth to Karen."

Karen's head snapped up and there Lisa stood, between Karen's Sundance and her own Toyota.

"Got a minute?" Lisa asked. She cast a glance around, at the people leaving. A few glanced back, but not with much interest.

Karen's mouth worked, but no sounds came out. Of all things she could've expected, seeing Lisa here had not been one of them.

Lisa uncrossed her arms, stood straight. "We need to talk, hon."

Karen stood beside her car. The thought came to her that she could bolt; just jump into her Sundance and peel out. What would Lisa do, chase her? She looked at Lisa's face. The anger and disgust she'd seen on Tuesday was gone, replaced with a grim kind of thoughtfulness, as if she knew what Karen was thinking.

Karen nodded. "Okay."

Lisa slid in on the driver's side and picked up a folder off the passenger seat. "Hop in, kiddo."

Karen got in and Lisa started the engine. Warm air came out the dash. "That was fucked up on Tuesday, kiddo," she said.

Karen looked down at her hands.

"I've gone over and gone over and I can't make heads or tails," Lisa said. "I'm sorry I said that about your ex-husband, but I…" She shook her head. "None of it makes sense to me."

Karen opened her mouth, and Lisa cut in, "Even after listening tonight."

"You were listening?"

Lisa nodded. "Uh-huh." She glanced at Karen. "You have no idea how you look, kiddo. You still look like a skeleton. Are you sleeping?"

"Yes," Karen said.

Lisa pointed at her eyes. "Those bags say different, though." She sighed. "What I'm saying is, you look as bad as you did when you were cutting—" She gestured to Karen's bare arms. "—which you clearly aren't, anymore. So what's keeping you this way?"

Karen opened her mouth again, and Lisa said, "I think it's this place. You blew off your own kid to come here, without even a phone call. You look like shit. And what happened on Tuesday..." She shook her head, then shrugged. "So I checked out your Darren Roberts."

"You *what?*"

"I researched him. And don't go all high and mighty on me, hon. Of all the times when you need to listen to someone, now's that time."

She'd placed the folder in Karen's lap. "Five years ago, your Roberts was implicated in the suicide of three parishioners."

Everyone around Karen got turned down to zero, like someone turning off the stereo just as the rock anthem hit its final chorus. *"What?"*

"He was running an evangelical outfit out in Arizona. Three of the members hung themselves from a tree across from the plaza where Roberts had set up shop. Their suicide notes referenced the church or Roberts. He hadn't helped them, was the gist."

Lisa settled back in her seat. "He was never charged, of course. The other members, plus Roberts's partners, all confirmed the three were ill, but you got the feeling, from quotes, that officials would've charged Roberts if they'd had a smoking gun instead of just smoke. What went on in that church wasn't exactly normal."

Karen looked down at the folder, but didn't open it.

"I'm worried about you, kiddo," Lisa said. "I'm worried a lot. You're not better—"

"You can't get better," Karen murmured.

"What?" Lisa asked. "Jesus." She leaned forward, grabbed Karen's hands so Karen would look at her. "Honey, I don't know who put that shit in your head—whether it's Roberts or something else—but you have to get it out. Roberts *isn't* helping you and this is affecting your *son*. Not just *you*, but your *son*. Don't you see that?"

Karen stared into Lisa's face, at the earnestness there, and her heart broke.

(jesus she's almost crying)

And with that came shame. Shame at making Lisa feel this way. Shame at being unable to explain it.

"Your husband's trying to take your son," Lisa said. "You've *just* started working. There's so much going on that you need to be *here* for. If you need help, I *will* and *can* help. Do you understand that?"

Numbly, Karen nodded.

Lisa sat back, eyes flicking about her face. "I guess you do." She looked off, at the bowling alley. "Listen, I don't wanna hold you up. It's late. I just couldn't think of another way of getting to you."

"I understand," Karen said. Her voice shook.

Lisa continued not to look at her. "Call me tomorrow or Sunday, okay?" A glance over. "Please?"

"Sure," she said and it was like speaking through a straw made of phlegm. "Thank you."

"Don't thank me yet, kiddo," Lisa said, and lit a cigarette.

The doorbell rang the next afternoon. Karen came down the front stairs, bent around to see through the glass upper portion of the front door. The shadow of a large man huddled in the entryway.

She opened the door to reveal the mailman, the bag on his shoulder as large as her torso. "Karen Dempsey?"

"Yes?" she asked.

The mailman thrust out a clipboard. "Certified mail. You have to sign for it."

She signed off, brow furrowed. "What is it?"

The mailman offered a look, then traded the clipboard with a thick envelope from his bag. He handed it to her. "Have a nice day," he said, and let himself out onto the porch.

Karen held the envelope with numb fingers.

Stockton County Family Court, the return address read.

(oh no)

The envelope torn open, shreds of the fold falling from her fingers, she pulled out the thick folded carbons and official letter-head. Phrases jumped out at her, meaningless to her eyes, punching hard nonetheless.

—KEVIN MATTHEW DEMPSEY—
(oh no oh no oh no)
—petition for the custody—
(nick not looking at her as he went through the ritual: "same time on sunday then?" knowing something was missing something wasn't being said)
—hearing set for October 22, 1991—

Karen leaned against the door; if it hadn't been there, she would've fallen.

(we're only doing this for kevin)

"Oh no," she said and her vision blurred.

She was back in the kitchen, phone screwed to her ear, with no memory of getting there.

The phone rang in her ear.

(i will and can help you)

(how can you be honest with yourself?)

Lisa's voice: "Hello?"

"He's doing it," Karen said and didn't even recognize the cracking, wet voice as her own. "He's suing for custody."

"What? What, Karen?"

But Karen dropped the phone.

4

BROKEN

Lisa drove. Karen sat in the passenger seat and directed her out of the city and into the eastern suburbs. The past twenty-four hours existed as a blur, with only random cohesion around certain objects—a coffee cup, Lisa spreading spare blankets over the couch, her own hollowed reflection in the bathroom mirror—marking out the time passed.

Lisa turned down Nick's street, passed his house. She turned around to face the way she came and coasted to a stop across the mouth of his driveway. The porch light came on.

"Should've gotten Kevin yesterday," Lisa muttered, eyeballing the house through the backseat side window.

Karen unbuckled. "Leave it, Lisa."

"You going to be okay?"

She let herself out instead of answering, and the cool night air was like a dash of cold water on her foggy brain.

Nick and Kevin stood on the porch, backlit by the light. She watched them come down the concrete steps and willed herself to stand still, not give anything away, for Kevin's sake.

(isn't that what got you into trouble in the first place,)

Roberts asked in her head. She shut the voice out.

They reached the bottom. She glanced at Nick, his face invisible in the shadows, and hunkered down, opening her arms. Kevin glanced up at his dad, then came forward and Karen reeled him in, kissing the top of his head.

"Hey, boy," she said, breathing in his smell. "Get your bag and climb in."

He retrieved his bag from Nick while she opened the backseat door. Lisa's voice boomed from within, "Hey, King Kick-Ass! Climb on in here! I made some room for you."

Kevin tossed his bag in and followed. Karen closed the door and then stood in front of it to face her ex-husband.

Nick hadn't moved. "Ran into a door at school, huh." His voice was a low, hard purr, like a fist wrapped in velvet. "Did you tell him to say that?"

"I didn't tell him to say anything."

"That fits," Nick said, "since *you* didn't tell me anything. Not a phone call, not an aside on Friday. I knew that door story was horseshit. Why didn't you tell me he was being bullied?"

"Because he didn't tell *me*," Karen said, an edge in her voice. "I didn't know about it until I came across the fight."

"Which happened because you were late," Nick replied. "Your friend Lisa just happened to stop it."

Karen grasped the tail-ends of her anger. Anything better than the lethargy, than feeling like a stone stuck deep in the sand as the tide washed over her. "And what would've been different if he'd been here, Nick? You wouldn't have known about it until four or five hours after the fact, when you finally got home from work."

Nick's outline stiffened. "The schools here—"

"—are the same as anywhere else," Karen said. "They have bullies. Don't try to pawn off that 'suburbia is so much better' bullshit with me, okay?"

"You still should've told me."

"I would've," Karen said, "if Kevin had told me. He doesn't talk to me."

"He talks to *me*," Nick said. "I asked him and he told me."

"How hard did you ask him, Nick?" she asked. "I know how you get." With the briefest pause, she said. "I got the letter, Nick."

Nick's shoulders hunched, as if anticipating a blow.

"You decided not to listen to what I said at the meeting," Karen went on.

"We listened," Nick said. "We just agreed it didn't mean much. You're thinking about the past, Karen, and we're concerned about Kevin's future."

"Do you really want to drag Kevin through this?" Karen said, "Jesus, the divorce was bad enough."

"Better than how you've been dragging him through for the past four years," Nick said, then stopped. He lowered his head and hissed out an exhale, hands on his hips. Behind him, Moira stepped out onto the porch, arms crossed and hands cupping her elbows. "I'm not doing this because of you, although you've been pissing me the fuck off."

"Making you happy isn't one of my concerns, anymore."

"About fucking Kevin! Jesus, this *isn't* about me and you." He gestured toward the car. "I'm angry at you over *Kevin*."

She heard a car door open behind her, but didn't immediately acknowledge it. "Over what, Nick? You were apparently easy like Sunday morning the past few years."

"The bullying," Nick said. "The school. The neighborhood. Not being there to pick him up. The fact that he won't say *shit* if he has a mouthful. The fact that you decided to stop talking to me about how *we* raised *our* son when you lost your job. What, since you could be around twenty-four-seven, you decided you didn't need to include me, anymore? And everything wrong with Kevin—"

"There is *nothing* wrong with Kevin," Karen snapped.

Nick lowered his head, bore this out. "And everything wrong with Kevin can be traced to you. Everything." He shook himself. "Look, before, you were fine—"

"Thanks for the compliment. I really decided to be a parent to earn your approval."

"—but this past year has lit up the sign blaring INTERVENE NOW. You just started working again—and a temp job at that. It can't be easy to raise a child alone. Moira and I can provide—"

"—what, Nick?" Karen asked, stepping forward. "What can you provide? A beautiful home that will be empty most of the day? A school with all the latest funding that will still have bullies? Parenting by phone call because you're always away? Tell me. Tell me exactly what it is that you can provide that I can't."

A beat.

"A normal life," Nick said, the anger gone from his voice and, because of that, his words struck harder and deeper. Karen felt her anger slip through mental fingers and leave the exhaustion, confusion, and shame. "A life where his mother isn't trying to fill the hours because the economy sucks and took her job. A parent that doesn't have to balance the checkbook in increasingly interesting ways. A parent that, because he doesn't have to worry about those things, can introduce our son to hobbies, sports, friends. Our kid doesn't even have any fucking friends, Karen. Didn't you even notice that?"

She hadn't, but she didn't let that realization show on her face, any more than she let any of the other things show.

"Kevin deserves a normal life," Nick said, "and I can provide it."

"Oh what horseshit," Lisa said and Karen spun to see the smaller woman round the front of her car.

"Very eloquent, Nick," she said. "Very nice. Of course you forget to mention how all this concern stems from some *serious* fucking ego-bruising."

She stepped up to him and Nick stepped back. "I mean, we're being honest here, right? You *say* all this stuff about what Kevin is and what Kevin needs—not that *you* would fucking know because you spend six days out of every fucking month with him—but what's at the core? Kevin started having these 'problems' and, all of a sudden, it was 'holy shit, I really fucked up here,' wasn't it?"

Lisa kept approaching and Nick kept retreating, Lisa followed him deeper into the driveway. Now Karen could see half his face and he just looked flabbergasted.

"You dumped your son on your ex-wife so you could go play house," Lisa went on, "and—surprise, surprise—she does a pretty good fucking job of it!"

"I never—"

"Shut the fuck up a minute, will ya?" Lisa interrupted. "Kevin's actually doing okay, and being raised right. Pat yourself on the back, absentee father! *Good* work!"

Nick reached the trunk of his Mitsubishi, thumped against it.

"And when some shit *does* hit the fan, and Karen falls on hard times, what do you do? Do you try to work with the mother of your child? No, you do the *very* grownup thing and go behind her back with this custody suit! Great thinkin', Dad!"

Nick's eyes held the fevered gleam of a cornered animal.

"So you can *tell* yourself that you're just trying to help Karen and Kevin both—y'know, two birds with one stone—but let's call a spade a spade. Seeing your son and ex-wife struggle because of *your* absenteeism was just too fucking much. Kevin's more like a toy than a son to you. A token. Anything more would require you to be a *father*, wouldn't it?"

And then Nick slapped her, hard, across the mouth.

It was such a sudden movement; one instant Lisa had Nick all-but pinned against the car; the next, Lisa was rocking back, hand going to her face. Moira froze halfway down the steps. Karen froze as well, unsure of what to do first.

And then Lisa solved that problem for everyone.

"You son of a *bitch!*" she yelled and drove one sneakered foot squarely into Nick's balls.

The color drained from Nick's face. His eyes bulged. The tendons of his neck stood out like tent-cables. His knees unlocked, spilling him to the driveway, hands going to his crotch.

Lisa circled him, bouncing on the heels of her feet, grunting out a steady stream of obscenity and kicking him as he rolled this way and that.

Karen and Moira both broke through their paralysis and bolted forward, colliding at the steps. Their legs tangled and Moira fell as Karen hop-staggered away. Moira's head connected with the cem-ent with a *thunk*. Karen crashed into Lisa, pulling her awkwardly away.

Lisa caught her balance and gaped around, as if surprised to find herself here. "Oh, shit."

Karen grabbed her by the arm and dragged her back toward the car. Moira sat up on her elbow, holding the back of her head and wincing. Karen opened her mouth, but didn't know what to say to the other woman.

(i know you want to do what's best for kevin what you don't seem to believe is that so do we)

Karen let go of Lisa when they reached the car. As Karen opened her door, she glanced into the backseat. Kevin watched his father and stepmother. He glanced at her, his expression too old for his face, then went back to watching.

She climbed in. Lisa turned the key and the Toyota roared to life.

"Holy shit," Lisa breathed as she pulled away, and Karen didn't know how to respond to that.

Kevin was the first out of the car, dragging his duffle bag to the porch.

"Karen," Lisa said, "I am *so* sorry. I did it again—I jumped before I saw what I was jumping into. Do you think they're okay? Do you think they'll call the police?"

"Probably not," Karen said, not knowing one way or the other. "He'd have to explain why it started, and that means him explaining him slapping you."

A beat of silence. Kevin waited on the porch.

"I don't know if this fucks up the suit or not," Lisa said. "But I'm paying for your lawyer."

Karen wheeled on her. "Lisa, no—"

Lisa waved a hand. "Shut the fuck up. I am and you're going to accept. I acted like an asshole and don't tell me you have the spare cash flow to hire a lawyer yourself, kid."

Karen bit her lip and looked back at Kevin. He watched them expressionlessly.

"Thank you," she said to the window.

"You daydreaming, Karen?" Dick Cavanaugh said.

Karen jerked back from her computer, where she'd been reading and rereading a memo Tina had given her to type.

"No, Dick," she said, facing the other man. "What can I do for you?"

Cavanaugh stepped beside her desk. He had his hands in the pockets of his khakis. She kept her eyes on his face; whenever he had his hands in his pockets, he invariably had an erection.

"Just checking in," he said. "Seeing how you're doing."

"Working," she said, and turned back to her computer screen.

"Well, of course," he said, "and the guys have all been talking how well you're fitting in. You'd be a good addition to the secretarial pool. You type fast, you've already gotten all the phone business figured out—" He flapped a meaty hand at her multiline phone, as if figuring out phones was a task beneath him. "—and already know all the departments. You've been here, what? A month?"

"Three weeks," she said, eyes moving along the last paragraph she'd typed. None of it made sense to her.

"Right, right," he said. A movement out of the corner of her eye—he rocked back and forth on his heels, hands still in his pockets. "You're good, kid. We like you."

(good i was worried)

"If there was one thing I'd say you could work on," Cavanaugh continued, "it'd be your congeniality."

Karen tried reading the last paragraph again, couldn't make it stick, and gave up; she just stared at the monitor. "You don't say."

"You hide out here in the reception area—"

"Where my desk is."

"—so the others don't really *know* you," he continued. "They don't get to *see* you."

(which i'd planned thanks for noticing)

"I mean," Cavanaugh said, his voice lower, "to get along, you have to get *close* to people, y'know? Be *friendly* with them. You understand?"

She glanced up at the clock on the wall. A little after ten a.m. Her eyes fell, landed on the school picture of Kevin from last year, and, all of a sudden, she could think of no good reason to be here. Not while her family was falling apart. In two weeks, she and Nick would face off in family court over the custody of their only son, who was doing god knew what at school at that moment. Whatever he was doing, was one of those Perozzi girls watching? Promising revenge for the righteous smiting Lisa—not Karen, but *Lisa*—had wrought upon their brother?

Meanwhile, she sat here, attempting to read a letter that should've made sense but didn't, all while this man thrust his cock into the side of her head as he prattled on. She was doing nothing of merit. She was doing nothing *good*.

(because i don't know what i should be doing anymore)

Nick last night:

(kevin deserves a normal life and i can provide it)

She blinked and her eyes were hot.

(what kind of mother are you?)

Cavanaugh's voice faded back in. "It's all about being a part of the team, Karen. Doing your part."

Her hands, poised over the keyboard in the home position, curled into fists.

"You want to be part of the team, right?" he said and, Jesus, he was nearly panting; she could feel his breath on her ear.

Without looking, she cocked her right arm and drove it directly into Dick's crotch.

He squawked and suddenly his presence disappeared from her side. She turned to see him staggering and holding his balls. He bumped into the side of the doorway and slid down to the floor.

"Keep your dick out of my face, okay, *Dick?*" she said.

He goggled at her, his tongue poking out from between his teeth.

She turned away, looked around her desk, her computer, but her eyes just slid off everything. Finally, she grabbed her purse, her photo of Kevin, and left the computer on, the phone line open.

She went to St. Jude's. She could think of no other place to go, but this wasn't immediately obvious to her. Up until then, she left her body in automatic while her mind retreated into the static-y, panicked roar that had dominated since Saturday. It was only when she passed the Hathaway Bridge, its big BRIDGE CLOSED FOLLOW DETOUR sign flashing in the center, did her destination become apparent.

(oh there okay)

But she pulled into the bowling alley's parking lot to find the building dark, the lot empty.

(of course it is it isn't Friday)

She pulled into a space where she could look through the glass doors and killed the engine. She leaned back in her seat, closed her eyes, tried to quiet the roar in her head. Did she just walk out of a job after punching a coworker in the dick?

A single migraine throb struck her in the center of her head. She pinched the bridge of her nose to ease the pressure. That was the word—pressure. All things considered, the fact remained that the pressure had never dwindled. She'd found temp work, but she still had to worry about bills. She still had Kevin—

(for the time being)

—but had to worry about him not talking about whatever might be bothering him.

(he hurts all the time but he never talks)

The pressure had shifted, not dwindled. If anything, St. Jude's was distracting her from it, helping her focus on her *reaction* to the pressure instead of doing something *about* the pressure. And, if she didn't do something soon—

A knuckle wrapping on her window. "Karen?"

She jumped and Roberts stood there, hunched over to see through the glass. "You okay?"

She rolled down her window. "Yeah. Yeah, sorry, I'm—"

"—hanging out in front of a closed bowling alley," Roberts finished. Behind him sat the green Subaru. She could see the handle of a vacuum cleaner in the back. "What's up?"

She opened her mouth, with no idea what would or should come out of it: "I just punched a guy in the balls and left my job, which I've only had for three weeks. My ex-husband is suing me for custody of our son, who I allowed to get into a fight with a bully because I thought he would finally talk to me about the things bothering him."

Roberts studied her for a moment. "Uh-*huh*." He stepped back and straightened, hands in the pockets of his jeans. "So you came *here*," he said.

She nodded.

He gestured at her to come out of the car. "I can't talk all hunched over like that."

She stepped out. They looked at each other, each against the side of their cars.

"Why'd you come here, Karen?" he asked. It came off lightly, but his eyes locked on her, the way they did on people speaking during the meetings.

She shrugged. "I . . ." Her shoulder slumped. "I don't know. I could think of no other place to go."

His eyes didn't waver. "I think you *do* know."

She just looked at him.

"I think you're looking for the one thing I said I couldn't and wouldn't offer," Roberts said. He crossed his arms. "You came here for help."

She opened her mouth to protest, then slowly closed it.

He nodded and glanced first at the bowling alley, then at his sign, hanging off the skeleton of the older sign. "The name's a kind of joke, you know." He turned back to her. "Or a reminder. For me, anyway. Do you know what it means? The name?"

She shook her head.

Roberts took a breath. "St. Jude is the patron saint of lost causes." He looked down and toed a loose pebble in the macadam. "I'm a lost cause, Karen. Before I came here, I was a more... *traditional* minister. Had an official church—as far as the government was concerned. It... ended. Badly."

"What happened?" she asked, her voice a croak. "You always ask that when we start to gloss over things."

"I'm not glossing over. Every single meeting is a reminder for me. Every single meeting, listening to you all talk, wondering which of you will be standing right here in front of me, is me examining my failure."

Roberts grinned then, but it was cold and squirming, like he pressed his lips together to keep from screaming. "I failed some members and they killed themselves. The law never charged me, but that didn't take away what I'd done wrong."

Lisa whispered in the center of her head:

(but they wanted to)

"I'd given them hope," Roberts went on. "Hope that I could cure all their ailments. Say some prayers, hold hands, quote the Bible and—" He snapped his fingers. "—all better. I didn't intend to, but it happened."

He leaned at the waist a bit and his face was dead. "Now look who's here in front of me."

She opened her mouth and he cut in, "Every meeting, every little P.S. I put on every little story—I look at you all and ask myself, 'Who's going to misinterpret? Who's going to read more into this than they should?' Every time. And I remember what I'd done wrong. It's a fine line I walk, but I can't stop."

"Why not? This isn't even a real church, according to you."

Color rose into his cheeks. "Because I *do* believe in what I do. Too many preachers forget *they* aren't the salve of the soul, that the Bible doesn't hold direct answers to your individual problems. At best, it offer stories of what god's chosen have done, so you can set your own course. I do the same, but with your own stories."

He coughed, looked away, hugged himself tighter with his crossed arms.

"You came here today looking for answers," he said. "Like those other three members. I don't have any. You telling me about what's happening doesn't absolve the pain it is causing, or make you feel better. Worse, you're using the same logic on your son."

She opened her mouth again, then slowly closed it.

"You think, since you feel pain, and talk about it, that it becomes bearable. You can—" He gestured vaguely. "—*move on* from it. You've applied that to your own son. You allowed your own son to be attacked so that he would be in *so* much pain that he wouldn't be able to help himself from talking."

(what kind of mother are you?)

"That's all bullshit," Roberts said. "Our pain has two func-tions—identifier and tool. *For ourselves.*"

She hugged herself. "I think I'm a terrible mother."

His words landed like blows: "I can't tell you one way or the other."

Silence fell between them. Then, he asked, "Do you know why your mother hurt you so badly? When you were a child? Do you remember telling us about that?"

She nodded, not looking up.

"It hurt because we see our parents as examples," Roberts said. "They are the scouts that have seen the distant lands and are report-ing back to us. Your mother didn't do that; she saw the distant lands past the death of your father and reported back that it was all *your* fault."

He cleared his throat. "A good parent, to me, is someone who sets an example for their child. You *lead* by example. You want your child to talk? You talk. You want your child to act a certain way? You set the standard. This isn't to say you, for example, should go into detail about your cutting. But you can show your child the pitfalls of going down the path you did, or reacting the way you did. He will have pain, but it will be different than *your* pain and he will, hopefully, act *differently* than you did."

More silence between them. A cool breeze picked up and her joints ached, as if with arthritis.

"I don't think you should come back here, Karen," Roberts said finally. "I don't think I've done you any good. Go home. Go to your son. Guide him. Don't hang around here, looking for answers that don't exist."

She turned, unable to look at him, and got in. When she pulled away, Roberts stood by his car, watching her leave. Even before she was out of the lot, he appeared small, a single man in an ocean of broken pavement, standing before a long, low faceless building. Alone.

(i'm a lost cause karen)

She watched the kids spill out of the school bus. Kevin came out next to last. No one walked with him. No one even looked at him.

(our kid doesn't even have any fucking friends didn't you even fucking notice that?)

No, she hadn't.

He made his way over to her car and let himself in. She leaned in and kissed the side of his head. Christ, he felt as cold as he was pale. "How was your day, hon?"

Kevin shrugged, looked down at the pack in his lap. His fingers played with the zipper. "Nothing special. Ms. Lake's trying to teach us cursive."

"Do you like it?" Karen asked, pulling away from the curb and rolling to the light.

Another shrug.

The crossing guard left the center of the street and the bus lumbered by. Traffic filled the gap.

Karen kept her eyes on 54th Street. "Are you all right, Kevin?"

A pause. "Yeah."

She glanced at her son. "Do you want to talk about last night?" she asked. The light turned green.

He didn't answer.

"Do you have any questions about it?"

"Am I going to live with Dad? Is that what you two were fighting about?"

She turned onto Keystone Street. "Do you want to?"

A shrug. "I dunno. Can't imagine it." He glanced at her and she felt something soften in her chest; his gaze wasn't nearly as flat and cold as his voice. "I mean, I've always lived with you."

"We're trying to figure that out, hon," she said. "It's not easy. We both want what's best for you, but we disagree on how to get there."

He looked back out the window.

She turned onto 53rd Street and parked in front of their house.

Kevin went fishing through his backpack for his key.

"Don't bother," she said. "I took the afternoon off."

(one way of putting it)

His hand froze in the pocket. "You did?"

She nodded. "Uh-huh. In case you wanted to talk."

He studied her for an awkward moment. "Oh," he said finally.

"There are possibly going to be some big changes," she said, feeling her way as she went along. "And you're getting bigger. You have some say over what happens."

He studied her another moment. "Oh," he said again. "I don't know about any of that."

(join the club kid)

"Is that something you want to do?" she asked. "Talk?"

"Not really," he said. His hand left the pocket of his backpack. "I have to trust you and Dad. You have to take care of me."

Her brain immediately wanted to turn his tone accusatory, his words sharp jabs. It short-circuited any kind of reasonable response she might've given, so she didn't give any.

Dread fills her like a shortness of breath when she stands in front of the structure. It's a house made of broken bones.

(our scars identify us)

Bones cracked roughly, bones healed and showing the pale lightning bolt of the knitted seams, all thrown together in a jackstraw-profusion to resemble a cottage. Skulls of varying sizes make up the front steps. Tibias and fibulas build the walls, the porch railing, the floor.

(our skin is meant to be cut our hearts are meant to bleed our bones are made to be broken)

The folder Lisa had given her rests on the porch, the breeze teasing back the cover and, as Karen watches, scattering the pages. They're all blank and the wind carries them away.

The house looms over her, staring at her with its eye socket windows.

(go in)

Roberts whispers on the wind.

(you came all this way go in set the example this is the place you've always used to escape)

She climbs the steps, her movements wobbly over the uneven surface. She fears the bones breaking under her, but this is a surface fear, covering the more primal core fear in her chest. She knows the bones won't break.

But she fears the voice is right: this is a place of escape.

(you escaped your mother by coming here)

(after your marriage dissolved and your job left, you escaped by cutting)

(now you can escape this way)

"Stop being so fucking cryptic," she says aloud, but it's all bluff. The voice is not being cryptic. The dread in her chest tells her so.

She reaches the door, which hangs ajar, revealing a deep darkness beyond.

"I don't want to step in there," she says.

Roberts voice again, but it's straight memory this time:

(you can show your child the pitfalls of going down the path you did or reacting the way you did)

(go to your son guide him)

She reaches out and pushes the door open. The floor is bare and gray. A mantel above a dead fireplace dominates the far wall. Kevin's school portrait sits in the center, looking at her.

She remembers grabbing it from her desk before leaving work.

The dread's not so much a shortness of breath now but a pressure against her chest, pushing the air she has out, refusing to allow fresh air in.

She steps into the house.

A creak echoes above and she looks up in time to see three women, dressed in white, come falling straight down out of the darkness, their long brunette hair trailing them. It's a short descent, but it seems to last longer, allowing her eye to take in the beatific smiles, their empty eyes, the way they hold each other's hands. The nooses.

She screams, but the snap of their necks is louder. She cringes and cowers back from where the bodies sway, thinking that this would wake her up, that her brain only ever deposits her here until she can't take anymore and now the dream would fragment, that she would come to in her own bed and it would be early Tuesday morning, October 8th—

(less than two weeks until the hearing less than two weeks until nick gets kevin)

But it doesn't happen. She falls against the door frame, the knobs of anonymous vertebrae pressing painfully against her shoulder muscles, and screams, and doesn't wake up. The three women—

(it was two women and a man not three women)

—sway, grisly pendulums, but their hair—the same shade and length as Karen's—obscuring their faces, thankfully. She has the idea that, even dead, they are still smiling. They have escaped—

(their pain)

—whatever it was they were running away from.

She straightens, wary of one of their feet touching her. She looks around, as if the suicides would alter the world somehow, but it hasn't. The house of broken bones is still empty. Kevin's picture is still on the mantel. The poisoned breeze continues to buffer the house.

Carefully, she edges around the bodies and goes to the mantel. She picks up Kevin's photo and hugs it to her chest, turning away from the suicides as if protecting her son from the view.

Roberts's voice:

(isn't that what got you in trouble in the first place?)

As if shamed, she turns toward the bodies; they've turned on their ropes, their hair-covered faces now facing her.

She looks down at the portrait of Kevin. He'd hated the polo shirt she'd made him wear, even if it did make him look completely adorable. Still, in spite of that, he smiled in the photo.

She can't remember the last time she's seen him smile in the real world.

Her eyes water, her face growing hot. She's never heard of crying in a dream, but here she is, doing so. She touches the glass as tears roll down her cheeks.

"What kind of mother am I?" *she asks and there's a lightness in her chest at finally articulating the thought that has always dogged her, even as her voice gets thicker and more choked.* "How am I raising my son?"

Roberts:

(parents set the example)

(he will hopefully act differently than you did)

(go to your son guide him)

Karen looks up and around, finally settling on the three dead women. Her right arm burns, the way it did in the hour or so after she would cut.

(you hated cutting not because you feared getting caught but because you never could work up the nerve to finally escape)

She hugs Kevin's photo to her chest.

(you've lost your job you're going to lost your son)

This sends a shudder down the length of her.

(and soon you'll have nothing but your acknowledgment of your own failure)

(you will be this place inside and out)

She hugs Kevin's photo so tight she feels the glass front crack. This doesn't stop her.

"I don't want him to end up like me," she says. "Not like me."

(kevin not talking kevin not sleeping kevin looking at her with those bags under his eyes and an expression he shouldn't be old enough to sustain)

She sobs. "Not like me. Not with one parent out of the picture and unable to talk and deal with the pain."

Roberts:

(then guide him)

She closes her eyes. This is a dream, and doing this should knock her out of it, but this isn't a regular dream, is it?

(i'm going deep into my own head)

Roberts comes on, stronger:

(set the example for him and escape being a failure karen the best escape you could ever hope for don't you want that? to do right by your son finally before you lose him?)

She hears the flap of blank pages outside blowing away on the breeze. She hears the creak of the hanging ropes.

"I want that so very much," she says. "I'm not a failure of a mother. I want him to do better than me."

(then show him)

⧽ ⋯ ⧼

Karen opened her eyes as Roberts's voice faded from the center of her head. She sat up in bed and checked the clock. Nearly five. She'd be getting up in a half-hour anyway.

She swung her feet over the side of her bed, but stayed there a moment, head hanging low, hair in front of her eyes. She often woke up completely unable to get back to sleep, but this felt different. It felt like those mornings you get up and something momentous was going to happen that day—Christmas morning, a birthday party, a vacation about to start. A lightness in her chest, a bounce in her step.

"I know what kind of mother I am," she whispered.

Before she went downstairs, she adjusted Kevin's blankets. He murmured, pulled them tighter around him.

The sun rising, she shook his shoulders, rousing him. He turned, but squeezed his eyes shut, fighting wakefulness.

"C'mon, hon," she said. "Gotta get dressed, get your toys and comics together."

That made his eyes open. "What?"

"No school today," she said, still holding onto his shoulder. He was so small, the ball of it fit perfectly against the palm of your hand. "I already called you absent. Going to Lisa's for a bit."

He sat up in bed and she reluctantly let go. "Why? What's up?"

"Surprise, kiddo," she said, stepping back. "C'mon, hustle. Your clothes are on the dresser."

He was still staring at her blearily as she left the room and went back downstairs.

The doorbell rang and Lisa jerked, spilling hot coffee onto the back of her hand.

"Mother*fucker*," she hissed, setting the pot back in the machine and grabbing a dishtowel.

"If that's a Jehovah's Witness," Mitch called down the steps, "it's

Federal law that we're allowed to kill them and bury the body out back."

Lisa tossed the dishtowel onto the counter and shook her hand as she made her way to the door. Against the glass, she saw the outlines of two people, one small and one feminine and her mind made an instant connection, but that connection was ludicrous on a Tuesday morning when it wasn't even seven yet.

And then she opened the door to see Karen and Kevin, Karen smiling and Kevin looking completely confused, and decided that maybe the instant connection wasn't so ludicrous, after all.

"Uh, good morning?" she said, holding the door.

"Can Kevin stay with you today?" Karen said. Her smile wasn't the death-head's grin, but, given her weight loss, it was a near thing.

"What?" It was the first thing that came to Lisa's head.

"You know I wouldn't ask if this wasn't important," Karen explained. She had her hand on Kevin's neck, just holding it, and Lisa couldn't remember the last time she'd seen Karen touch her son that wasn't some fervent grab, as if the kid would be ripped from her grasp at any moment.

"Hon?" Mitch called down the stairwell. "Who is it?"

"Karen and Kevin!" she called back, slightly turning her head toward the house, her eyes never leaving the two of them.

"What?" was Mitch's reply. *Exactly,* Lisa thought.

She stepped aside. "Hey, Kev, go on in. Wanna talk to your mom a minute."

Kevin walked in. Lisa stepped outside, closing the door behind her. "What the fuck is this?"

"I need a favor," Karen said, the smile finally slipping from her face, leaving it emaciated and serious. "I'm sorry, but I was afraid you'd blow me off if I called."

"Your goddamn right—it's Tuesday fucking morning. I have work. So do you. So does Mitch. Shit, Kevin has school."

"I need a few hours," Karen said.

Lisa's eyes narrowed. "What's this about?"

Karen took a deep breath. "I'm afraid I'm going to lose him, Lisa. Nick's going to convince the judge—"

Lisa blinked, head shaking. "Whoa-whoa-whoa. Hold up. Didn't you get my message yesterday? I found a lawyer and—"

Karen continued as if she hadn't heard. "—so I only have so much time left before he's gone. I need that time before it's too late."

"You sound like a terminal cancer patient. Didn't you hear me? I found you a lawyer and no judge—"

Karen's eyes blazed, locking on hers. "I *need* to do this, Lisa."

"Do *what?*" Lisa burst out. "You haven't told me what the fuck you're doing."

"Setting an example. I have fucked up a lot this past year—"

"Hey, wait—"

Karen shook her head. "—and I need to rectify as much as I can *while* I can."

"What about work? What about school?"

"I called Kevin in absent," Karen said. "And I punched a guy sexually harassing me in the dick yesterday before walking out."

"*What?*"

"Lisa—*please.*" The fire in Karen's eyes dwindled, but they continued to hold Lisa's gaze.

Questions and comments and common goddamned sense swirled through Lisa's head like a dust storm. The answer was obvious. The answer was *no*, get your ass to work, get Kevin to school, think logically for a moment and get your shit together or family court really *will* rule against you—

—But Karen wasn't looking away, or down, or any of the things that Lisa had watched her friend do for the past year. As batshit insane as she was being right at this moment, this was the Karen that Lisa had met in community college three years ago, the Karen carving out a life for her and her son.

And, besides, what if she gave the obvious answer? Did she really think that Karen would listen? That Kevin would go to school and she would go to her temp job and everything would be rosy and good? Whoops, sorry, momentary lapse in judgment there?

Thinking tilted in Lisa's head; it was too early with too much too fast, but what finally settled her was the answer to the question: who else did Karen have?

She sighed. "Fine. Okay. I'll take a day off work."

Every muscle in Karen's face seemed to loosen. "*Thank you*. It won't be the whole day, I promise. Maybe not even beyond lunch."

"Are you going to tell me what this is beyond 'setting an example' or whatever it is the hell you're doing?"

"You'll see," Karen said, already going to her car—*skipping* to her car. "I'll call you in a few hours."

Lisa stood on the stoop and watched Karen back out of Lisa's stub of a driveway and pull away, tooting her horn once.

She never said goodbye to Kevin, Lisa thought.

A worm of disquiet burrowed into her heart, turned her guts into a mild churn. Something was most definitely rotten in Denmark—

—and Karen had saddled her with Kevin, meaning she was unable to do anything about it without involving the boy.

"Goddammit," she muttered, and stepped back into the house. Kevin was in the living room; she could hear him channel surfing.

"Hey, hon!" she called up the stairs. "We're parents for a day!"

"*What?*" came Mitch's reply.

Exactly, Lisa thought again, and went to call off work.

(i should be at work now)

She shook off the thought, turning on the television for noise—Bryant Gumbel was talking about the Clarence Thomas confirmation hearings—and going into the kitchen. The green light on the answering machine blinked rapidly, which meant there was more than one message.

(didn't you get my message yesterday?)

Who was the other message from?

She almost went to listen to it, then switched directions and went to the junk drawer beside the fridge, pulling out a legal pad and a pen. A calendar hung from the fridge door, one of those nature scene ones; October's was, predictably, a pumpkin patch. Lisa had circled the twenty-first and wrote HEARING in the center.

Less than two weeks away.

Karen went to the kitchen table and sat down. She almost got up again—there was still coffee in the pot and she found herself craving some—but didn't. If she started stalling now, she'd continue stalling and what needed done wouldn't get done. And didn't she *want* to get it done?

(then go to him set an example)

That light feeling of Christmas morning when you know it's all going to be goodness and joy to come.

Karen started to write and proceeded to write for the next three hours. The phone rang periodically, but she ignored it, lost in what she was trying to say. No one left messages.

Each page she finished she tore away and set into rough stacks. By the end there were three: one to Lisa, one to Nick, and one to Kevin. Kevin's was the thickest stack. Of course it was.

She didn't want him to miss the point of what she was doing.

Lisa had cable and thank Christ for that; Kevin could wile away the morning watching Nickelodeon while Lisa paced in the kitchen, turning the situation around and around in her head.

Not that it got her anywhere. She wished she hadn't told Mitch to go to work, that she would handle it. She needed someone to bounce her thoughts and speculations off of. Of course, that would entail her explaining what the fuck had been going on for a month and she hadn't gone beyond "I'm helping Karen through things." She hadn't wanted to get into Karen's things with Mitch; it felt gossipy.

Now she wished she had.

She carried the cordless with her, would periodically call Karen's apartment because she couldn't imagine where else the fucking woman could go, and it rang straight to the answering machine.

Once, while the theme music to *Eureeka's Castle* played, she debated calling Nick. *Get a hold, woman,* she thought, but how dire fucking straits it was that she would consider that.

Jesus, kiddo, what're you doing? Lisa thought.

And then, just before noon, the phone rang in her hand and she nearly dropped the goddamn thing.

She clicked the TALK button. "Hello?"

Karen's voice: "How's Kevin?" Lisa heard ambient noise in the background, as if Karen was calling from the side of a roadway.

Lisa turned away from the kitchen doorway. "Where the fuck are you?" she stage-whispered. "What the fuck is going on? Are you all right?"

"I'm fine," Karen said, the second word nearly lost in what sounded like an eighteen-wheeler speeding by. "Is *Kevin* all right?"

"He's watching Nick Jr. and I'm contemplating firebombing the network headquarters. Talk to me, woman. Where are you?"

"Harmarville," Karen said, simply, as if the answer should be self-evident. "Get Kevin and come here."

"Come *where*?" Lisa hissed.

"You'll know. Just follow the route to St. Jude's; you'll see my car before you see me."

"What the fuck—"

A distorted sigh. "I'd tell you and you'd freak. Just trust me, Lisa. This one time."

Like I haven't been trusting you all a-fucking-long? Lisa shouted in her head. What she said was, "Karen—"

A click.

Karen had hung up.

Lisa pulled the phone away and stared at it, as if willing it to ring again. The phone dumped into the *dah-dah-dah* of an open line.

(follow the route to st. jude's you'll see my car before you see me)

The worm of disquiet had babies. An unease that was almost painful filled her. The spit in her mouth was thick, almost choking.

But what the fuck could she do?

"Hey, Kevin," she called, hating every word she said, "just talked to your mum. Grab your stuff, we're going to meet her."

She had to close her eyes as she said this.

The letters to Lisa and Nick began the same way:

This won't answer all your questions, but I can't help that. All I can do is explain what I want and how I want it and hope you trust me enough to understand and do it.

Kevin's letter began differently:

I'm sorry for what you've seen, honey. You have no idea how much I wish you hadn't.

She checked for opposing traffic and of course there wasn't any. She put on her turn signal out of force of habit and pulled over, trying to leave room for Lisa's car when she got here.

Her purse sat on the passenger seat, the three letters sticking out of the open top. She pulled them out and flipped through them. She resisted opening them and reading them, knowing she would think of other things to say, or better ways to say it, and she wasn't going to do that. This was her final say in the matter.

This was her example, as best as she could put it.

The interior of the car grew stifling. She shut the engine off and opened the door. She had to squeeze around the BRIDGE CLOSED sign PennDOT had put at the mouth of the lane.

. . . there are ways a person can go through life, her letter to Kevin continued, *that allows them to ignore the pain they'll feel, but, in the end, it doesn't make anything better. In the end, it just makes things worse. When you close yourself off, when you deny the things you feel, you're hurting yourself just as much as if you cut yourself. That's no way to go through life.*

Your mother has had a hard year, but one thing it's shown me is that I've been hurting myself for a long time and, because I'm your mother, I've also been hurting you. As a mother, there's nothing that makes me feel worse than the idea that I have done anything to harm you . . .

Lisa slammed on the brakes to avoid rear-ending a minivan that had come to a dead stop just past the Squirrel Hill Tunnel.

"Goddamn cocksucker!" she screamed at the minivan's flashing brake lights. As if in response, they went out and the minivan rumbled forward. Lisa tried not to ride its ass and failed miserably.

"Sorry," she said to Kevin. "Potty mouth."

"S'okay," he said. He watched the lunch rush hour around him, cars and trucks filling the Parkway, stopping and starting and drag-assing along. "You're better at swearing than Mum is."

"A badge of honor," she said, distractedly. She'd made excellent time getting into town—the benefit of going in the opposite way of lunchtime traffic—but now that she was edging in, she was stuck in the push-pull. She willed the cars to go forward and they stubbornly ignored her. Her head beat out a simple thought: *Karen, Karen, Karen, Karen, Karen.* What was she doing? What was she going to do?

She saw her exit coming up, the detour leading to Harmarville, and she cut off a school bus to get to it.

You never noticed it when driving across, but renovation was something that the Hathaway Bridge desperately needed. It seemed the lanes were more hot patch than actual concrete. The walkways were crumbled, revealing rusted rebar. The concrete handrail had the softened edges of decay and crumbled beneath her hand in places.

She walked far enough out so that the Hathaway skyline, gleaming in the noon sun, looked like a postcard. Beneath, in the Buchanan River, barges trundled through the gray water, but nothing else.

Her hand crept to the letters in her back pocket.

. . . For a long time, I ignored or denied I wasn't in pain and all it did was hurt me more. That ended up hurting other people.

I can't hurt you anymore. I won't allow it.

"That's Mum's car," Kevin said.

Lisa's eyes had been glued to the road ahead. When Kevin spoke, her head snapped up and her Toyota swerved a little.

Karen's Sundance was parked in the mouth of the Hathaway Bridge, the side nearly touching the BRIDGE CLOSED sign.

"Jesus Christ," Lisa panted, and out of the corner of her eye Kevin's head snapped around. She winced and glanced at him.

She saw no surprise on the boy's face.

Oh, kiddo, she thought and didn't know if she was speaking of Kevin or Karen.

She pulled in so that the noses of the two cars almost touched, and killed the engine. "Kevin—" she started to say, but Kevin had already unbuckled and was climbing out of the car. She scrambled to follow, nearly falling out onto the road.

What a fucking Polish fire drill this is, she thought and ran around the car. Kevin was already on the bridge, walking up the center lane.

Karen stood by the bridge railing, watching them, and Lisa's panic exploded: *"Karen!"*

She started running. Kevin ran, too.

You're going to be hurt, honey. More than you ever have and maybe more than you ever will.

Don't run from it. Talk about it with your dad, or Moira, or Lisa. They can't take away your pain, your loss, but they can be a sympathetic ear for you, to allow you to feel your pain.

I'm sorry for having done this to you. I'm sorry more than you can say. I did exactly what I'm telling you not to do and spent too much time trying to escape from it.

Learn from this. Learn that ignoring how I felt made me sick, until I knew I couldn't get better, no matter how much I talked. I had bottled it up, ignored it for too long, until everything hurt, even the good things.

I hope you choose better than I did. I hope you choose today to do better than I did.

She watched them come running and surprised herself by starting to cry. A weight she hadn't known had been there suddenly rolled off her chest. And now if she could just do this one thing right...

"Karen!" Lisa screamed. *"Don't you fucking move!"*

She held up a hand and the two skidded to a stop a dozen or so yards away, as if she repelled them. Both stared at her, eyes eating up their faces, panting.

"What're you doing?" Lisa asked.

Tears rolled down Karen's cheeks. The breeze turned them cold. "The only thing I can," she said and her voice cracked.

"Your son is right *here!*" Lisa yelled.

Karen nodded. "I know." She hunkered down and opened her arms. "Come here, hon."

Kevin pelted for her, threw himself into her arms like a footballer going for a tackle, hugging her fiercely. She gripped him just as tightly back, breathing in the scent of him, the feel of him panting and shaking.

(my boy oh honey)

Kevin said something into her neck.

"What?" she asked and tried to look at him. He gripped her harder, but turned his head slightly. "Don't," he said and his voice was all snot.

She closed her eyes and kissed his head and held him.

Lisa watched the two hug and hold, Karen straining to keep her balance, and felt a moment's hope—maybe this was just a scare. Maybe Karen was proving something—to who and for what, Lisa didn't fucking know, but it didn't fucking matter. Karen was ill, but not too ill, and this entire fucking morning could be a story later on about how Karen went to the edge, but chose to step back.

She watched Karen talk to Kevin, whispering, and felt this hope ...and then she saw Karen reluctantly let go and stand up, even as Kevin tried to pull her back down. She gripped his hands, squeezed them, and pulled them off of her.

"It's okay," she told him and Lisa's heart wrenched.

Karen let go of one of Kevin's hands and pulled something from her pocket. "Give these to Lisa for me," she said. "Go ahead."

Don't believe her! Lisa wanted to scream, but the air had completely left her chest.

Kevin backed away, slowly, not turning away from his mother as if to do so would rush what was about to happen. Karen watched him back away, watched as he bumped into Lisa and she gripped him and he blindly handed her what turned out to be three envelopes, each addressed to either Nick or Lisa or Kevin.

"Don't lose those," Karen said. "They're important."

Too many words bubbled up to be spoken; all Lisa could manage was: "Stop this now, Karen!"

"I'm setting an example," Karen said, and wiped her eyes. "You have to read the letters, though. You *have* to."

Kevin shook against Lisa, vibrating like a dog in a thunderstorm. Lisa tore open the top letter with shaking hands, looking away from Karen when she pulled out the thick sheaf of folded legal pages.

Kevin, the letter read, *I'm sorry for what you've seen, honey. You have no idea how much I wish you hadn't.*

She looked up and Karen was climbing the railing.

RUN! her brain shouted.

RUN TO HER GRAB HER STOP HER!

But her legs were locked. Kevin pressed against her.

"He shouldn't be seeing this!" she screamed at Karen.

Karen stood on the railing. "He has to. So he doesn't end up here himself. I *know* this." She swayed with the breeze and Lisa felt Kevin go board-stiff.

Karen held her balance and looked at Kevin. "I love you, honey. Don't ever do this escape. Don't ever *want* to escape. Don't be *me.*"

And, before Lisa could think of anything to say, Karen stepped off the railing.

In the years to come, when the letter his mother had written him would yellow, the folds beginning to crumble, that instant would never leave him. During times of stress, he would close his eyes and hear Lisa's scream, feel her shake behind him with the force of it, see his mother step off the Hathaway Bridge.

But he would invariably open his eyes—if the memory occurred to him at night, it would halt any possibility of sleep—on the last thing he saw; a single frame, as if it were a movie.

His mother's face as she stepped off the bridge.

His mother, smiling as she fell.

ALL THAT YOU LEAVE BEHIND

"For sale: baby shoes. Never worn."
– Author Unknown

WEEK 21, THIRD TRIMESTER

Carrie came home to a house with a heartbeat, walls throbbing and windows rattling.

She stopped in the entryway, counting Mississippis, the floor vibrating beneath her feet. The *th-thump-th-thump* reverberated down the stairwell, opening up into the entryway and the living room beyond.

At twenty-one Mississippis, the heartbeat transformed into a baffled *sshhhh-pop*, and then resumed.

She hung her keys on the hook beside the door and dropped her shoulder-bag, heavy with material for an article, hard onto the floor.

The recording upstairs didn't stop.

She walked into the kitchen, not trying to soften her footsteps across the hardwood. She flicked on the overhead kitchen light and went loudly through the cabinets. A Tupperware container of meatloaf on the top shelf of the refrigerator looked the least moldy. She pulled it out and slammed the fridge door hard enough for it to open again.

Now the recording upstairs paused. Carrie waited in the center of the kitchen, Tupperware in one hand, plate in the other.

She thought she heard the desk chair creak.

She waited some more.

When Danny didn't call down, she fixed herself food she no

longer wanted and sat down at the kitchen table. Mail was strewn across the surface. Not indicative that Danny had gone to work today, but at least he'd left the house.

She ate mechanically, riffling through the circulars, the bills. She didn't look down the hall, where the kitchen light would hit the corners of the closest boxes marked BABY CLOTHES or BABY BEDDING in her spiky shorthand in the living room entryway. A list of everything was already in the tax folder upstairs, also written in her shorthand. Danny had never gotten around to it.

At the twenty-first week, the fetus has eyebrows and nails.

When she finished, feeling more bloated than filled, she dropped the dishes into the sink, briefly ran the faucet, and dumped the meat-loaf, container and all, into the garbage can beneath.

Another chair-creak upstairs, but no floor creaks. Danny was merely adjusting his position.

At the twenty-first week, the fetus is more active; the movements you *thought* you felt during the previous month become apparent. You already know this, but the realization that something is alive inside you becomes more pronounced.

She started up the stairs. Guest bathroom at the top, door closed, hallway to the left. At the sixteenth week, the fetus's bowels begin collecting meconium, a tarry kind of proto-poop. That had been Danny's term for it. Hysterical at the time.

Door on the left was the guest bedroom-slash-office, painted a gender-neutral green during the twelfth week. A fetus's gender doesn't form until around the twenty-fourth week. Evelyn if it'd been a girl. Ethan if it'd been a boy.

Danny sat at the small desk, head buried in his crossed arms on the desktop, turned away from her, tin can headphones on his head. On the computer, Windows Media Player was up, playing the forty-five-second-long file. The pieces of the crib that Danny hadn't taken out of the room yet leaned against the opposite wall. The single bed that had used to be in here was still in the basement.

At the twenty-first week, the fetus is a half-foot long, weighs nearly a pound.

The crib was for later, after the basinet.

Danny's shoulders shook, minute twitches, and Carrie raised her hand, as if to touch him. But she stood in the doorway, almost ten feet away, and she wouldn't enter this room. Not unless she absolutely had to.

She continued to the master bedroom.

Television on the dresser tuned to CNN and Anderson Cooper's strangely symmetrical face, work clothes shoved in the hamper. The basinet was already gone, removed three weeks ago. She'd been the one to remove it.

She couldn't avoid looking at herself in the shower, even when she had the water set to scalding and the bathroom fogged. The stretchmarks along her hips seemed even more pronounced then, like accusatory slashes on her body. She scrubbed these areas raw.

At least her nipples had finally lightened back to roughly their natural color. The vertical line on her lower belly had faded away.

Her hands found it, anyway. Pressed against it for a moment.

Carrie had only felt movement once, early one morning during the sixteenth week. She'd rolled to wake Danny up, but it had stopped before she could touch her husband.

Her face grew momentarily hot. She took a deep breath and went back to scrubbing.

Much, much later, she was still awake, turned away and facing where the basinet would've been, when Danny finally shuffled through the dark to bed. The mattress settled and shifted as Danny laid down. Before, he would rub the spot between her shoulder blades, a silent good night whenever he came to bed late and thought she was asleep.

Now, she waited, but his breathing slowed and lengthened far on his side of the bed.

She didn't roll to him.

She listened to him breathe, and, eyes wide, stared at the empty space in the dark.

WEEK 25, THIRD TRIMESTER

Before becoming pregnant, the alarm on her smartphone was enough to wake her up. During the pregnancy, continual morning sickness was her internal clock. Commonly, sickness lasts between the sixth and fourteenth week, though in rare cases it goes longer. She was sick the entire length of her pregnancy.

Now, consciousness came slowly, grudgingly, like it was something dragged from the embedded silt of a murky riverbed. All three of the alarms on her phone weren't enough to wake her up. Danny often had to shake her.

This morning, it was sunlight from the bedroom window that brought her around.

During the twenty-fourth week, the fetus is on a regular sleep schedule.

"Danny?" she croaked. Christ, it sounded like she hadn't spoken in weeks.

Squinting, she rolled over, toward her husband's side of the bed, guided more by feel than sight. Rumpled blankets. The bedsheet was cool.

She cracked one open eye wider. "Danny?"

No answer. That hum in your ear when only emptiness and silence were your only company.

She flopped onto her back. Danny wasn't home. Right. It was Saturday and he had . . . a thing.

Carrie rubbed her face, as if that would make the answer come. Nothing.

"Pregnancy brain," or "Mommy brain," are common symptoms in women. Increased levels of estrogen and progesterone are noted within the brain, heightening the sense of forgetfulness that comes with body-stress and lack of sleep.

"I'm not pregnant," she said.

She shook herself and sat up in bed, looking around. The bedroom had two windows, plenty of natural light, and it was like she'd never seen it before. The past few weeks, everything had seemed so goddamned gray.

"But was that in my head or for real?" She shook her head and looked down.

Her hands cradled her still-flat stomach, fingers splayed.

"Goddammit!" she yelled and launched from the bed, nearly falling when the sheets tangled around her ankles. She kicked and spat at them until she was free, then stood beside the bed, heart thrumming.

She swallowed. "This," she said, then closed her mouth.

Deep breath. "This is getting ridiculous."

For a moment, her face crumpled like paper, her eyes hot stones in their sockets. She ground her teeth together and her face smoothed.

Her husband was gone for the day. He had told her where— she *knew* this—but couldn't remember and, further, couldn't even remember the fucking conversation where it had been mentioned. She couldn't remember the last time her and Danny had exchanged just a few words. More than a month since the

(miscarriage)

and she still had goddamned pregnancy-brain.

Her fists unclenched, moved to grip her belly and she forced them back to her sides.

"I can't do this, anymore," she said.

Her eyes fell on the space where the basinet, a hand-me-down from Danny's sister, had sat for those few weeks. They had accumulated slowly, tentatively as the calendar moved from first trimester to second. It wasn't until afterward that they—*Carrie*, really—had realized how much shit they'd gotten.

The basinet here. The crib there. The boxes of clothes and bedding. The laundry basket of toys probably still in the back of Danny's Jeep. Dishware. Books.

So far, the basinet had been the only thing removed. By her; Danny, if he was in the house, refused to leave the guest bedroom and the ultrasound recording.

Burning in her chest and she grimaced. "Goddammit," she said. "*I* carried her. *I* felt her going. *That was* my *blood.*"

Heat gathered in her face again and she pressed her fists into her eyes. She counted Mississippis, ragged breath after ragged breath, until she cooled.

"Okay," she said. She moved her hands to the line no longer on her stomach and looked at the spot where the basinet had been. "Okay."

Carrie collapsed onto the single mattress in the guest bedroom and laid there until her heart stopped whamming her breastbone quite so hard. Her head throbbed, a cloud of heat surrounding the crown. She hadn't moved this much since before the pregnancy.

The crib was gone, shoved into the back of her Subaru along with the boxes and containers. She'd hauled the pieces to the single bed up from the basement and now they leaned where the crib had. Danny still had baby things in the back of his Jeep, she presumed, but she could get those out when he came home tonight.

She shoved herself off the mattress, tottered, and went to the little desk, where a glass of water sweated into the scattered paper crap and fiberboard. She drank half the glass at a glut, and when she said *"Ahhhh,"* it wasn't an affectation.

She set down the glass, froze, her hand still holding it.

"What?" she said.

She moved her hand, knocking the glass over onto the carpet and not even noticing, and brushed aside random papers. A thin, clear CD case lay beneath.

"What?" she repeated.

She fell into the chair; if it hadn't been there, she would've fallen onto the ground. Her legs were a million miles away.

She picked up the case with shaking hands. MY BABY'S DVD, the green DVD label read. Beneath, in smaller print, "This DVD is provided to you and your family as a personal record of an important family experience."

Her other hand covered her mouth, although there were no words, no sounds. Her chest was a solid thing, incapable of beating blood or taking air.

"I threw this away," she said through her fingers.

It'd been in her purse for weeks; she'd actually forgotten about it. Another attack of pregnancy-brain. The sonogram appointment had been at eight in the morning and as the ultrasound tech had handed her the DVD, Carrie, as she came down from the rush of watching

(evelyn)

the fetus move and its

(her)

heart beat and counting its

(her)

toes and organs, had been craving more coffee and/or a nap. After seeing the picture in real time, the DVD had been an afterthought.

The appointment had been during the fourteenth week. During the fourteenth week, very fine hair called lanugo covers the baby's head. The baby's bones begin to firm. The liver and pancreas began secreting.

When Carrie had found the DVD at the bottom of her purse during what would've been the eighteenth week, she'd thrown it away, buried it in the kitchen garbage before she could stop and think. She hadn't even told Danny.

Danny.

He must've seen it in the trash.

She gripped the case until a silver crack shot across the front. "Danny." It came off as a hiss.

She dropped the case back onto the desk and, when the inevitable urge to put the DVD into the computer surfaced, she swept the entire desktop off to the side and into the garbage can.

(I carried her. I felt her going. That was my blood.)

Her eyes burned, her face crumpling like tissue paper, and she turned her gaze to the computer and its geometric screen-saver.

She swatted the mouse and, of course, the download folder was open with only one file in it.

"Ultrasound – Week 8."

The file was exactly forty-five seconds long.

Eyes wet, she right-clicked on the icon and selected DELETE. Are you sure, the computer asked.

She clicked YES only because she couldn't punch a hole through the screen itself.

Her husband was a bastard, but now the download folder was empty.

She hugged her stomach, which was also and of course empty, as she had when the first whamming cramps had come during the seventeenth week. No cramps now, though. Nothing.

She rested her head against the edge of the desk and squeezed her wet and burning eyes closed.

"What?" Danny said, louder than she'd heard him speak in weeks.

She roused herself, rolling over on her bed. She had no mem-ory of coming in here. The windows were dark. Danny's nightstand clock read seven-thirty.

"What?" Danny said again. He was in the other room. The hard-wood creaked heavily under his feet.

She sat up, shook the cotton from her brain, and stood. The room swayed around her and she had to throw a hand to the wall to steady herself.

"Jesus," she muttered.

She made her way to the guest bedroom, fingers trailing the wall. Her movements were stiff, her muscles hard and creaking.

She found Danny sprawled in the little chair, almost falling off it, and staring at the empty download folder on the computer. His shoulders shook. Behind him, the single bed was reassembled and remade, complete with the pillow and comforter she'd pulled from the closet.

He turned to her and his eyes were red and wet and irritated, his face slack.

The fetus doesn't begin to open and close its eyes until the thir-ty-second week.

They stared at each other, and the memories rebuilt themselves in Carrie's head.

Danny's mouth worked. "You deleted it."

There were many words that could be said, but what came out was, "And I threw away the DVD of the sonogram. Again."

He blinked at her. "What?"

Her muscles were tightening, but it wasn't due to overwork. "I can't do this alone, Dan."

He gaped at her and her fist wanted to go through that expression the way it had wanted to go through the computer screen. "What?"

"You're not the only one who lost!" she yelled and the wet, shrill sound of her voice just made her stiffer. "You're not the only one who can't sleep! Can't eat! Can't fucking *focus!* I *carried* her! Do you *get* that? *Do you?"*

He flinched at the last word and it took all her will to tamp down the scream that wanted to explode.

"I *felt* her, Dan. *I* felt her go, and *I* felt the pain of her going. *Me. Not* you. You've done *nothing* but listen to that . . . that . . . that fucking *track* for weeks on end!" She squeezed her eyes closed, willing the tears back. *"We both lost something and I'm the only one paying for it!"*

She opened her eyes again and Danny's face had lost its slackness, was tightening and darkening. A brief, bitter surge of animal triumph swept her like heat rush. *Now* he felt something other than his dopey fucking stupid sadness. *Good.*

She lowered her voice. "Where were you? Where were *you?* In here, wishing things hadn't turned out the way they had? *Well so do I!* But I don't have the luxury of pining the fuck away like *you* do! I've had to carry this whole goddamn thing! You listen to that track, you kept that fucking DVD when you *knew* it was in the garbage for a reason, and have you once—have you *once*—come to me? Talked to me? *Been* with *me?* You skulk around in your own bullshit, *completely* forgetting *I'm the one who felt our fucking child die!"*

His face was completely dark, his eyes hard. "Wait a fucking minute—"

"No." She sliced the air in front of her with the side of her hand. "No, I've been waiting long enough, thanks." She'd started hunching over and she made herself straighten. "You wanna be alone, then *be* alone. What's the difference *now*, right?"

She turned away, but not before she saw the hardness wink out of Danny's eyes, and there was a true moment of emotional divide in her head. She felt that heat-rush of going-for-the-kill triumph, bitter and green and ripe...but she felt her heart open at the same time.

"We *are* alone," she said and went back to the bedroom, slamming the door hard enough to rattle the nightstand lamps.

She jumped onto the bed and screamed into her pillow until her throat, red and raw and shredded, gave out on her.

Later, on the line between awake and dreaming, she heard Danny, still in the guest bedroom, say in a thick voice, "I *have* been wishing. Wishing we were whole and fine and a family. Wishing that we weren't alone. That's all I *ever* wanted."

She crossed the line into sleep and didn't know if she'd imagined the episode or not.

WEEK 32, THIRD TRIMESTER

An extra picture-frame sat on her desk.

She stopped in her office doorway, holding a box of red pens. She had Pandora up on her computer—"These Days" by Foo Fighters played—and it was the only sound in the long, low building. Her office was the only source of light besides the red EXIT signs at either end of the main hall. The next day's issue of the *Register-Mail* had been put to bed, sent to the printers. Not even cleaning people remained.

And there was an extra picture-frame on her desk—turned away from her, of course, so that the photo would be visible when she sat down. She'd worked for the newspaper for six years, had been in this office for four, and there had always been two photos on her desk—one of her and Danny on their honeymoon, in New York; the other showing Danny teaching at Knox College. She'd looked at those photos so often she no longer saw them; they'd assimilated into the general *look* of her desk.

And now there was a third frame. An *extra* frame. A wasn't-there-when-she-got-up-to-go-to-the-supply-closet frame.

"Hello?" she called, her eyes locked on the frame, and then winced. What a dumb fucking horror movie move.

But she heard a *creak*, weight on the floor, and adrenaline dumped into her system by the gallons, and the spit in her mouth turned acidic, and she stiffened, and the creak came again, and she realized—Jesus fucking Christ—it was herself making the floor creak. She couldn't stand still.

Carrie took a breath, whistled it out, took another. But she didn't move from the doorway. The sweat of her palms softened the cardboard box.

She should be home right now. Danny would be home. She should be home and Danny should be home and they should be talking. She shouldn't be here, copyediting every article the copyeditors had left behind because she couldn't bear to *go* home, couldn't bear to be in the quiet house, couldn't bear to be surrounded by the ghost heartbeats of what wasn't to come.

She shouldn't be standing in the doorway, staring at the back of the picture-frame that shouldn't be on her desk.

"Oh, fuck this," she said and walked in. The air seemed thicker, less yielding, as if trying to push her out.

She walked around the desk, slamming the red pens down, and looked at the picture in the suddenly-new frame.

And froze again.

"Oh, fuck this," she repeated, and her voice was a sigh.

It was a sonogram photo, showing the fetus in a sliver-moon pose.

During the thirty-second week, the fetus loses the lanugo and begins to develop real hair. It blinks, practices breathing. With the right assistance, the fetus would survive premature birth.

The *thump-thump* of a heartbeat came to her; not hers, but the memory of that damned forty-five-second recording.

She reached for the photo, then pulled her hand back, fingers curling in, as if it might burn her. She tried again, and this time touched it. It did not disappear in smoke, or crumble, or become intangible. She felt glass. Plastic.

She picked it up, ran her fingertips over it. The way the picture was set, the border cut off the date at the top of the photo. This could be some anonymous photo, something printed from a Google Image Search put here to fuck with her,

(by who? when?)

but it wasn't. This was hers.

This was what she carried. Evelyn.

The *thump-thump* increased in sound, until it twinned with her own pulse.

Carrie's vision blurred and she blinked.

"Oh, fuck," she breathed and her voice was wet.

Her stomach clenched suddenly, viciously. She dropped the frame onto the desk and dashed back into the hall, hand covering her mouth as her throat filled, barely making it to the restroom in time before her lunch jumped up and out. Her throat worked, her stomach pushed, and her face burned.

(like morning sickness all over again)

That earned another clench and she vomited again. Finally, she flushed, then laid her head on the seat, eyes closed against the restroom fluorescents, breathing heavily through her mouth.

(who would do this? when?)

Her mind instantly said *Danny*, but it wouldn't hold. They hadn't spoken more than one or two words since the fight, passing each other like wary tomcats. But did it really seem like Danny? Danny, moping around? Danny, lost in his own pain? Danny, who had absolutely collapsed when she'd laid into him?

(you wanna be alone then be *alone)*

"Shit," she whispered.

(we are *alone)*

She tightened her closed eyes, but tears escaped, anyway. "Shit, shit, shit."

She grabbed a wad of toilet paper, wiped her mouth, then flushed again. She staggered to her feet, using the sides of the stall for support, and walked out, pausing briefly to check the mirror. She used minimal makeup, but she looked like a raccoon, anyway.

After the brightness of the restroom, the hallway was pitch-black. She shuffled back to her office doorway.

And, upon returning, the picture frame was gone.

"The fuck?" she said and rushed to the desk, looked under it, moved around papers. The frame was still gone. She looked at where the frame had been sitting and only now noticed that, when the picture had appeared, the other two photos, as well as her little paperclip cup, had been arranged to accommodate it. Picking up the frame had left a hole in the arrangement.

Now the set-up was as it had been before the third picture.

The third picture had never been there.

She sat down and looked at her hands. She *remembered* the feel of the glass, of the plastic backing.

It took a moment to notice that the *thump-thump* of the heartbeat was gone, as well.

"The fuck?" she said again. "The fuck *is* this?"

Hallucination popped immediately into her head, as well as *nervous breakdown*. That got her moving, switching her to automatic before any thoughts could really unspool, turning off her computer without shutting it down—killing the Rolling Stones in the middle of "19th Nervous Breakdown," *oh* how *apropos*—grabbing her bag, and getting the hell out of there.

WEEK 35, THIRD TRIMESTER – DAY 1

She came home to an empty house and Dutch Master daffodils on the kitchen table.

She stopped in the kitchen archway, the day's mail still in her hand. The flowers had been set in the center, arranged in a clear vase, tied with a fat pink ribbon. A folded cardboard note hung from the ribbon.

"Huh," she said. She dropped the day's mail onto the table and then stared at the vase some more.

She and Danny still weren't speaking. Moreover, the things that they should be saying were piling up, filling the house more quickly than baby detritus had. Soon it would push one of them out, although Carrie hadn't gotten that far in her thinking, mainly because she couldn't bear to.

(you wanna be alone then be *alone)*

"There used to be more to us," she said and touched one of the daffodils. It was cool against her fingertips, slightly moist.

When would Danny have done this? He left before she did. She knew he wouldn't have allowed some random florist into their house.

She pulled out a flower, smelled it. Outside, winter was only grudgingly giving way to spring, but the wet earth smell of the daffodil made it seem like spring had already arrived.

"Danny," she said and it didn't come out as a hiss.

She set the flower back in the vase, then opened the note.

Only a month away!,

it read in Danny's scratchy handwriting.

And everything in Carrie turned down. The memory of the recording—*thump-thump-shush-thump-thump*—filled her head, pushed other thoughts out. Her eyes traced the words again and

(only)

couldn't quite

(a month)

believe what they amounted to.

(away!)

"What in the holy *fuck*?" she said, loud in the empty kitchen, trying to overpower the sound of the ghost heartbeat, and dropped the note, jarring the vase with the back of her hand so that some water sloshed out the side. She backed away, the muscles of her face flexing between confusion and rage.

She didn't need to put together what was a month away.

"What," she said and couldn't immediately find more air. "What the *fuck*...?"

She fumbled for her smartphone, then went into the hall. She pulled Danny's cell from her Recent Calls list—the back of her mind noting how far down the list it was—and hit SEND.

It rang into his voicemail: "Hi, this is Dan Finney. Sorry I missed you; leave a message and I'll try to correct that."

She stabbed the END button, then went into contacts for his

office line. The air in the house grew moist, as if the daffodils had brought the greenhouse with it. She slammed open the front door and went out onto the front porch.

Danny picked up on the third ring. "Professor Fin—"

"What the fuck is wrong with you?" she yelled into the phone.

She heard him splutter. "Carrie? *Carrie*? What—"

"What the fuck is wrong with you?" she screamed. "You think this is *funny*? That I would *laugh*? Are you out of your fucking *mind*?"

Danny didn't answer for a long time. Carrie breathed through her clenched teeth.

"I…" he started to say and the resignation in his voice was the cold clear admission of guilt she needed. She opened her mouth, and then Danny said, "I have no idea what you're talking about, Carrie."

She straightened. "What?"

"I said, I have no idea what you're talking about, Carrie."

She screwed the phone hard into her ear, tried to pick up the tell tale clues in his voice. She'd known Danny for almost two decades, and he lied very rarely, but she was a good journalist.

"You *didn't* leave flowers on our table," she said. It should've been a question, but her voice refused to leave a low rumble. "And you *didn't* leave a note telling me we were only a month away."

A sigh from his end. "Why the hell would I do that?"

"Because I just saw them on the goddamn kitchen table!" she yelled. "Fresh! Still cool! *Still fucking wet!* You're telling me *you* didn't put them there?"

Another sigh. She could've cheerfully reached through the screen and squeezed his neck until her fingers tore into his throat.

"Carrie," he said, then stopped for a beat. "Carrie, I haven't been home all day. You *know* this is my late day. Three classes and two advisor times? Plus mentoring? My schedule's been the same for five years, hon."

She blinked. The phone casing creaked a little more. "Then. What. Did. I. See. *Danny*."

He said nothing. It was answer enough.

"Goddammit!" She yanked the screen door open and stomped back into the house. "Stop fucking around, Danny. It's *your* hand-

writing on the goddam note and—"

She entered the kitchen and, for the first time consciously, the there-then-gone frame at work popped into her head.

The daffodils were gone. No water spillage on the table from when she'd jostled the vase. Just the mail she'd dropped.

"And?" Danny said. "And what, Carrie? It is *physically* impossible for me to have done what you said. Shall I produce witnesses? Security video?" A pause. "Or is it *you* who's fucking around?" His voice dropped. "*Are* you? Because, don't. Let's not do this like this, Carrie. Not like this. You and I—"

"Shut up, Danny," she said and her voice was a whisper. She hadn't heard a word he'd said. Her eyes were locked on where the daffodils weren't.

"What?" Danny asked. "I couldn't hear—"

"Come home," she said, louder. "Come home right now."

"I'm gone," he said, and the line was dead.

She let her arm fall, then slumped against the archway, staring.

When *hallucination* and *nervous breakdown* entered her head this time, she didn't shake them off.

And the sound of the heartbeat was gone again.

They sat at opposite sides of the kitchen table, the center open and bare and dry—of course—between them.

Outside the window, night had fallen.

"You need to talk to someone," Danny said.

Carrie rubbed her face with her hands. "That's ironic."

"I'm serious," he said, ducking his head so he could meet her eyes. "I don't like any of this."

"And I'm having the time of my life?" She closed her eyes, took a breath. "I'm sorry. I feel like I'm losing my mind." She dropped a hand to the spot where the vase had been. "I *held* that note, Dan. I *held* that frame. I could *feel* them. There was water right *here*—"

"But there wasn't," Danny said. He reached out and took her hand, held on when her knee-jerk reaction was to pull away. "I have *not* been helpful. Neither of us have been. The past months have been the worst in my life, and yours." He gave her hand a squeeze. "But, y'know, maybe this is good. The right scare to get us back on track."

She pulled her hand, slumped in her chair. "I don't know. Who would I even speak to about this?"

Danny aped her movements, then crossed his arms. "I can speak to some people; frame it as research for a paper, or something. Some won't buy that, but enough will."

"It's just…" She shook her head. "They were right *there*, y'know? The flowers, the frame…" She stopped, looked at Danny. "The DVD?"

He blinked at her. "The DVD?"

"'Baby's First DVD'," she said. "Remember?"

Slowly, his eyes lightened. "Holy shit, I *do* remember that. We got it after the sonogram appointment…" He trailed off, forehead scrunching. "Was that what you were talking about…" He gestured vaguely. "…before?"

"You didn't pull it out of the trash?" she asked.

"I didn't even remember it until just now. Too much had happened." His face darkened. "You threw it away?"

"When I first found it in my purse, after the miscarriage. Then I found it under papers on the desk." She let out a breath. "What the fuck, Danny." She studied him. "And nothing's off with you?"

"Beyond cataclysmic depression?" He shook his head. "Nothing like what you've experienced." Danny leaned forward. "Listen, I'm going to talk to some people. Get some good names. I'll take care of it, okay?"

She nodded. "Okay, Danny. Okay."

This time, when Danny took her hand, she didn't pull away.

WEEK 35, THIRD TRIMESTER – DAY 3

Carrie's phone dinged with a text as she came out of the shower.

Two weeks, Danny wrote. *Afternoon appt. Dr Morley. Ok?*

During the 37th week, the fetus is considered "full-term" and will begin to turn, dropping lower in the womb in preparation of birth. Body fat has increased to the point that the movements are more noticeable because the space is more confining. All the organs are ready to function on their own.

Her fingers hesitated over the keyboard. It *was* okay, but…

The DVD. The photo. The flowers.

She'd *held* those things. *Studied* them. Heard the heartbeat of the daughter that never would be while they were in her hands.

(but they weren't there)

Go for it, she typed. *Thank you. Love you.*

The reply was immediate: *Love you too.*

The sudden feeling of relief was as real as the things she'd imagined holding.

"We'll get through this," she muttered, setting the phone down and resuming drying. "We're not alone."

Later, she passed the guest bedroom on the way to the stairs and, for just an instant out of the corner of her eye, saw the crib instead of the single bed, all set up. Her head whipped around. Just the guest bedroom. Bed, small dresser, fiberboard desk and computer. She left the doorway slowly, as if turning away would make the crib appear.

"This is so stupid," she said, and continued toward the stairs.

WEEK 36, THIRD TRIMESTER – DAY 6

Simon, the news editor, slouched against the receptionist's desk, talking over the partition while Julia sorted through the overnight e-mails. He looked up when Carrie came in. "What are you doing here? You pop already?"

Carrie stopped in the doorway, the pneumatic arm bringing the door back to bump her in the ass, sloshing coffee onto her wrist. She didn't immediately feel the burn. "What?"

Now both Julia and Simon were looking at her. "It can't be *that* boring at home." His eyes dropped to her stomach. "I mean, you *did* pop, right? Last I saw you were as big as goddamn *house*." Julia reached up and smacked his arm. "Why didn't you alert us? We would've sent something."

Something in her head ground to a halt. "What?"

Julia stood up behind the desk and Simon straightened. Their gaze was sharper, their mouths mutually turning down into *moue*s of concern. "Are you all right?" Julia asked, coming around.

The reception area of the *Register-Mail* was small, and Julia would be next to her in an instant.

(don't touch me don't touch me don't touch me)

As if thinking it would help, the nerves on her wrist became aware of the fact that scalding Starbucks coated it. She jerked, splashing more coffee from the lid's opening.

But it was enough to get Julia to stop, although her and   Simon's *moue*s were deeper now.

(get me outta here get me outta here get me)

"Excuse me," she said, heading directly to the hall. She didn't run, but it was close.

Although the ladies restroom was enough for two people, she bolted the door, then threw her Starbucks cup into the sink, where the lid came off and it splashed all over. She went to the first stall and sat down on the toilet.

She shook. She held up her hands and watched them move this way and that. Her heart thwacked, making her breath shallow.

"This is not happening," she said. "This is *not* happening."

She held her head in her hands because she couldn't stand to watch them shake any longer. She focused on breathing. She focused on the darkness behind her lids.

(simon and julia are not a frame a flower a DVD)

(then what are they?)

And the soundtrack to it all was the damned memory of Evelyn's heartbeat, forty-five seconds long, endlessly repeating.

She squeezed her eyes closed tighter, until neon lights burst behind the lids.

During the 36th week, the vernix—the soft proto-skin that allows real skin to develop—is thicker.

Her skin didn't feel very thick at all.

(julia's going to come knocking i looked like a psychopath out there)

She tensed, waiting, counting the seconds until the inevitable knock-and-knob-shake occurred.

It didn't.

(we are alone)

After a while, it felt vaguely absurd to be in here. The sound of the heartbeat faded, like losing a radio signal. Slowly, she stood, as if *that* would start Julia's inevitable knocking.

It didn't.

She picked up her shoulder bag and moved to the door. Unlocked it. The hallway was empty. Open offices up and down let out a steady incomprehensible stream of conversations and keyboard clickings and printer hummings. She moved down the hall, waiting for some-one to jump out and ask if she was all right. No one did, of course.

Simon and Julia were still in the reception area, in the same posi-tions they'd been when Carrie had entered the building.

Simon looked up. "Hey! When did you get in?" Julia glanced up from her computer screen, offered a quick smile.

Carrie's mouth was shot full of Novocain. "Um…"

Simon straightened and, goddamn, the *moue* was back. "You okay? You look a little flushed." This time Julia looked up for a little longer and, yes, she had a *moue*, too.

(you guys could be fucking twins)

She put her hands to her stomach, which felt like the undulating waves of a choppy sea. "Yeah, no, I think I'm gonna work from home. Stomach bug's giving me some issues."

Simon winced at the word *stomach*

(get me the hell outta here)

but recovered quickly with a full-on frown. "Yeah, okay. You do that. You look like hell, kiddo."

Carrie ran out, thinking, *This isn't an object this isn't an object those were people those were* people.

She didn't tell Danny what happened.

WEEK 37, THIRD TRIMESTER – DAY 1

Hon, Danny said. *Honey. She's kicking the hell outta my back.*

What? she said, sounding like she did when she was more than halfway asleep, although her lips weren't moving.

(this is a dream)

The voices weren't in her head.

The creak of bedsprings as Danny turned over. A phantom touch against her stomach and the *weight* there. She remembered that weight. She remembered it well.

The little bug's an insomniac, he said.

Don't remind me, she replied. *I was just about to drop off.*

Only a few more weeks, he said. *Just shine it on a little longer.*

Then we both *won't be able to sleep?*

The phantom touch left and Danny chuckled. It sounded like wind chimes.

Drowsing, she put her own hands to her stomach and it was full and heavy and good. She felt, faintly, the tiny heartbeat. She felt Evelyn move, adjusting for a better position. She'd gained weight all around during the second trimester, but it had moved to the kiddo during the end and now—

—Carrie shot up in bed, hands on her smooth stomach, Evelyn's heartbeat still in her head, but now with the *sssssh-pop* of the ultrasound sensor moving, a reminder that it was just a memory.

(not live, just Memorex)

She bit her lip to stifle the scream.

Danny turned over slowly in bed, blearily looking at her. "Hon? You okay?"

Carrie ignored him. The room didn't have enough air and all she could do was pant. Morning was beginning to break through the window, turning their bedroom into shades of gray.

Danny sat up, put a hand on her arm. "Carrie? What is it?"

She drew her knees up under the sheet and rested her forehead, still holding her stomach. She closed her eyes.

And I laid back down, feeling Evelyn get comfortable, and I was exhausted and I knew I wasn't going to sleep deeply, but that was okay because Evelyn was there and safe and sound—

"Bad dream," she said and her voice was thick. "A bad dream.".

WEEK 37, THIRD TRIMESTER – DAY 2

Carrie passed by the guest bedroom and the crib was back.

She stopped, knowing it was a hallucination, knowing that all this would be gone by tomorrow night after talking with Dr. Morley, but knowing she couldn't *not* turn and look.

And it was still there when she did.

Her shoulder bag dropped to the floor with a bang she didn't hear. It was early afternoon. Staff meeting day, and she had no overnight assignments. Danny was still at work.

"Holy shit," she said, and approached the door.

The gender-neutral green paint seemed more vibrant, making the white crib gleam. Canvas squares of cartoon animals—lion, giraffe—were nailed, step-like, to the wall. In the corner was the changing table, with bags and bags of boxes and diapers spread out like the givings of some bizarre Christmas tree.

(the gifts from the shower Danny still hasn't put away)

She closed her eyes. There hadn't been a shower. There wasn't any of this.

But the hope was there, oh yes. Beneath the confusion and the sorrow and the rage, but hope was there. Hope that *this* life was the hallucination, a stress-induced bad dream as she neared the end of her pregnancy.

(i have been wishing... that's all i ever wanted)

Wasn't that what Danny had said?

Why couldn't it be true for her?

"But it isn't," she said and popped her eyes open, like a kid playing red-light-green-light.

And Evelyn's room was still set up. Carrie's mouth dropped open.

(don't believe this don't believe this the frame DVD flowers felt real too)

But that voice sounded a million miles away.

She felt Evelyn's heartbeat within the tremors of her own skin.

Carrie reached the doorway, hand on the frame, and the room immediately shimmered, like an old movie seguing into a flashback, and she reached into the room, as if she could grab the air itself and make it stop, and that that only made the change faster, until she was just reaching through the doorway of the guest bedroom, with nice but definitely-not-baby green walls and the Danny-version of a made single bed.

Carrie's arm dropped and she just looked for a moment.

(look upon my works ye mighty and despair who said that danny would know)

She couldn't even find the energy to cry, although her eyes felt sandy and red. She hung her head and started to turn away when a flicker of movement caught the corner of her eye. She raised her head, feeling stupid for the upsurge of hope in her gut, and saw it was just the computer's geometric screensaver.

She started to turn away again when it occurred to her that the computer had been *off* the last she saw. Since she'd deleted the audio file, Danny was rarely on the desktop, and she had her own laptop plugged into the Wi-Fi. She used the desktop for banking. Rarely.

Brow furrowed, she walked into the guest bedroom—the first step hesitant because Evelyn's room might come back and she called herself stupid for the thought. She batted the mouse and the triangles disappeared, revealing the download folder, which had four files in it.

"The hell?" she whispered, sitting down and wheeling the chair close. She recognized the top file immediately:

"Ultrasound – Week 8." Evelyn's heartbeat.

Carrie's breath caught in her throat, but only long enough to see the other file names.

The next was another mp4 file, with a date falling during the 19th week. The size was larger than the first.

The next was an mpeg file, entitled "Sonogram 1 – Week 16."

The final file was another mpeg, entitled "Evie's face!"

It had been saved last week.

Carrie forced herself to breathe, but the air was too thick, impossible to take in. Her eyes fell to the scattered papers on the desktop, and saw a note in Danny's handwriting: *Can play the audio with the second sonogram—show Carrie.*

She squeezed her eyes, counted to ten.

(not there not there this isn't happening and tomorrow i'll be able to stop it oh god please let me stop it)

She opened her eyes, cautiously. The files were still there.

Her hand reached for the mouse, hesitated, then rested lightly. She paused the cursor over the top one.

(might not be the same it won't be the same)

(oh please)

She clicked on it and Windows Media Player opened and there was Evelyn's heartbeat, in all of its ghost-like glory. The steady *thump-thump*, the *sssshhh-POP* as the sensor had moved and the recording had reached its end.

"Oh shit," Carrie breathed.

(i just deleted it i never emptied out the recycling bin danny could've)

(???BUT WHAT ABOUT THE OTHERS???)

She X'ed out of the Player and moved to the second file. Clicked it.

Media Player again, another heartbeat, but it sounded ... stronger. More regular. Like something that's had a chance to get some practice in and really had the whole thing down.

Evelyn's heartbeat. *More* of her heartbeat.

(none of this is real none real NONE REAL)

(why couldn't it?)

But that was a thought Carrie didn't want to pursue, not out of an avoidance toward hope—hope that this *was* the hallucination, that she really *was* still pregnant—but out of the possibility, the *probability*, that she was tilting further and further into mental places no one, even the lauded but-still-unknown Dr. Morley, could pull her from.

She X'ed out of the second file and opened the third file, "Sonogram – Week 16."

The Media Player dutifully opened once more, but instead of

the music-note icon, the screen was black with details sketched in with strikes of white. Like one of those Magic Eye pictures, it took a moment for the vision to come together, but when it did, the bean-shaped outline of a fetus was clear.

Evelyn.

The file was silent, but the fetus moved, adjusting its proto-legs, stretching its forearms.

Carrie stretched a hand toward the screen, laid her fingertips against the fetus's head.

During the 16th week, the fetus will begin to move and stretch. It has transparent skin, which you wouldn't notice on a sonogram, anyway.

This was the video from the DVD. The video Carrie had thrown out. Twice.

"I'm sorry," she told the screen. Tears spilled down her cheeks. "I'm sorry."

The video was a hair under three minutes, but it went by quickly, fading to black before looping back to start.

She watched it twice more before X-ing out of the player.

One more file. "Evie's face!" recorded one week ago.

During the 36th week, the fetus has been breathing for a month. It's bigger, close to what its birthweight will be. The womb is cramped with its fullness.

Carrie hesitated again.

(last chance to get out of this madness)

"Oh, it's too late for *that*," she said, her voice breaking, and clicked open the last file.

The final file was shorter, only a moment, but recorded as a 4D ultrasound, which allowed an almost-three-dimensional image of Evelyn's face.

Carrie stopped breathing.

The child's eyes were closed, but one could see the way she practiced breathing, mouth slightly open, nostril's

(she got danny's nose of course she did)

(SHE'S GONE STOP THIS STOP THIS RIGHT NOW)

flaring. The curve of her forehead. The roundness of her

cheeks. The cleft in her chin—Danny's. The stem of her neck.

Carrie shook, hugged herself, shook some more. Her stomach had never been more empty.

(this was mine this was mine this was mine)

(but it's GONE it's GONE and all you're doing is TORTURING)

(SHE WAS SUPPOSED TO BE MY DAUGHTER)

Carrie shoved away from the desk. The computer tower beneath the desktop came into view, the white glowing power button shining, and she lunged for it, stabbing it over and over until her finger bent back painfully. The computer cut out.

She slouched on the floor, shivering, rubbing her shoulders as if cold. All thoughts, even the contradictory voices, had ceased. But Evelyn's heartbeat was still *thump-thump*ing away in there, oh yes.

Finally, she reached out and turned the computer on.

"You'll be gone now," she said. "Everything will be back to whatever the fuck passes for normal now."

The screen fuzzed on, went through its logo-rific start up, then opened to the desktop screen. Reaching up, Carrie moved the mouse to the file folder icon on the Systray and clicked it open, then—pausing for the briefest of moments—clicked on the Download folder.

There were four files inside.

Carrie fell back against the side of the bed, staring at the screen.

(none of this is real none of this is real why is it here?)

(that's all i ever wanted)

"We are *alone*," she said to the download folder. She wiped her nose with her hand, felt the wetness of tears on her cheek. In her head, Evelyn's recorded heartbeat played on and on. *"Alone."*

"You ready for tomorrow, hon?" Danny asked, pulling back the blankets on his side of the bed.

Carrie had been staring at the same page of the Gillian Flynn novel. She blinked. "What? Yeah, I think so."

Danny paused as he climbed in. "You okay?"

She offered the best possible smile she could, which wasn't

much. "As okay as the circumstances are allowing."

He slid into bed, pulled the covers to his waist. "You see anything else?"

She looked away, turning down the page of the paperback and closing it. "No. You ready for bed?"

"Christ, yes." Danny slid further under the covers and clicked off his lamp.

Carrie aped him and, in the dark, felt his hand on her shoulder, light and warm

(like touching my full stomach)

against her skin.

She closed her eyes, and listened to Evelyn's heartbeat, counting Mississippis.

WEEK 37, THIRD TRIMESTER – DAY 3

Evelyn's heart continued to beat as Carrie crossed the parking lot to the Bennell Building. There was no *shhh-POP* now. The ghost of her child was close and getting closer.

Her head throbbed with the sound, how it muffled the clack of her low heels across the asphalt, stunted the glare of the sun. The traffic of Galesburg Boulevard was a distant hum. Even the recognition that the building reminded Carrie of the Dakota building in New York was a faded, faraway thing.

It followed her through the lobby, to the bank of elevators on the right. It grew louder, blocking out the sound of the lobby clock as it tolled the hour—eleven o'clock. Carrie couldn't even hear the Muzak piped in from the elevator speakers.

The elevator opened up onto a gallery with a glass railing, overlooking the lobby three storeys below. Carrie took a step out of the elevator—

—and stomped her foot in the footwell of Danny's Jeep.

Carrie jerked, head spinning around. She sat in the passenger seat of Danny's old Jeep Wrangler, parked in its spot behind the Old Main Building at Knox College.

She heard birds call outside the crossover. She smelled the remnants of Danny's morning coffee.

"What?" she asked and had a moment to notice that she couldn't hear Evelyn's heartbeat anymore when the *thud* hit her lower stomach, reverberating through the rest of her nerve-endings. She squawked and coughed, hands going to her stomach, when the second *thud* hit her, pushing at her crotch, sending another crackling wave of pain through her body.

She screamed, doubling over and hugging her stomach, head resting on the dash.

(not like this the cramps weren't like this)

Time them! she yelled, but her mouth wasn't moving. *Goddammit, Danny, I keep losing track! Jesus, this hurts!*

And then, insanely, she heard Danny's high-strung laugh. *Holy shit, she's not waiting any longer! Holy shit! Holy* shit!

Stop laughing and fucking COU—And then another *thud* slammed into her vagina. Carrie screamed again, eyes squeezed closed, hugging her flat stomach, but her *fingers* felt nothing flat, felt only the fullness of pregnancy and Evelyn was coming—early, yes, but Evelyn was finally *coming*—

Danny's voice, still half-laughing, *We're gonna make it, we're gonna make it, you two hold on because we're gonna* make it—

Thud and it was the worst yet and Carrie screamed as the pain rocketed through her, frying her nerves, making her limbs seem distant—

Someone knocked on the glass.

And there was no pain. Not even a tingle. Not a hint.

Carrie opened her eyes and stared down at her shoes, spread to each side of the footwell. She felt her silk blouse and her flat—*flat*—stomach. Her muscles quivered, confused and jerky with ghost-adrenaline.

And then Danny's voice, muffled by the glass, "Jesus Christ, Carrie, what—"

And she heard the lock disengage and the passenger door was opened and Danny's hands encircled her, pulled at her, and Carrie resisted for the briefest of instants—

(i was in labor*)*

—before going limp in his arms.

Danny's voice, over and over, "Carrie, Carrie, Jesus, Carrie—"

He was pulling her out of the car, and she put a foot on the runner to keep from spilling the two of them onto the asphalt. She got her arms free and grabbed at the side of the Jeep's doorframe.

"I got it," she said and her voice was a croak. "I got it."

Danny's hands left her reluctantly and she stepped out of the car, watching her feet. She heard a rustle of people around her.

(well this is fucking great)

"What the hell, hon?" Danny asked.

She couldn't stand there, watching her feet like a kid in trouble, but it was harder to raise her head than she would've thought.

Danny stood a few feet away, hands ready to catch her. He was dressed for class, but his blazer was gone, his tie askew.

And, yes, people surrounded Danny's Jeep—a dozen or so students, with a couple of faculty members Carrie remembered from Christmas parties thrown in.

(jesus christ)

She pulled her phone from her pants pocket and didn't know whether to be surprised or not to see it was now eleven-oh-two.

"One minute in the elevator," she muttered, "the next here."

"What?" Danny asked.

She raised her head and looked only at him. The crowd of people rustled again.

"Take me home, Danny," she said. "Actually, take me back to my car."

He blinked at her.

"It's still in the parking lot at the Bennell Building," she said.

Danny spluttered, and a faculty member said, "Go ahead, Dan. I'll post your classes." This earned a third rustle from the people.

(christ they're like birds)

Danny and Carrie stared at each other, his gaze wide and uncomprehending and frantic, hers tired and resigned.

And then she turned and climbed back into the Jeep, shutting the door.

Danny stood there for a moment, looking completely unplugged, then began walking around the Jeep. As he got into the Jeep, Carrie realized she could hear Evelyn's heartbeat again, but it sounded softer than before.

(that's because she's being born)

(somewhere else, anyway)

Carrie leaned her against the passenger window and, with the crowd of people still watching as Danny fired up the Jeep's engine, closed her eyes.

Danny matched her step-for-step up the stairs, arms bent, as if he might grab her.

She led him to the guest bedroom and the air shimmered, like a ripple across pond water, showing Evelyn's room—crib, changing table, animal prints. The presents from the shower had been put away, she saw. She didn't stop, but she sensed Danny hang back for the briefest of instants, enough that he wasn't walking on the backs of her shoes.

(you DO see this)

(see i'm not crazy)

She sat down in front of their desktop and nudged the mouse. The geometric screen saver disappeared and the Download file was open. She had a moment when

(what if its gone and the files are back in my world)

but the four files were right there, exactly as she last saw them.

"Do you see this?" she said, without looking around.

He stood close behind her, didn't touch her. She noted this.

"This is the one we had originally," she said, moving the cursor to each file. "And these are the new ones. Look at the dates."

Still nothing from Danny.

She riffled through the scraps of paper on the desk and held up the one with his handwriting—*Can play the audio with the second sonogram—show Carrie.* "This look familiar?"

He took the paper. She didn't look up at him.

(right now somewhere else my daughter is being born)

A tingle swept through her lower stomach.

Finally, Danny said, "None of this makes sense."

"The photo on my desk," Carrie said, "the flowers. These files. Somehow going from my therapist to your car all the way across town instantaneously. I went into work last week and the receptionist and the news editor acted like I should be on maternity leave. I rushed into the bathroom and, when I came back out, they asked how I'd snuck past them, like they hadn't seen me come in."

Now she looked at Danny. His face was as tight as a drumhead, his eyes darting from the computer to the paper, to her, and then back again.

"This is all happening," she said. "You saw it when you came in—how the bedroom would've looked if Evelyn had been born."

He winced at the mention of her name and, Carrie realized, it had always been *the pregnancy* or, at its most painful, *the baby* to Danny. Never a name. Funny how she had never noticed it before.

She turned and clicked the first file. "I erased this, and it's back. And there are more. Videos, too."

The sound of Evelyn's heartbeat filled the room. She watched Danny's face. Muscles rippled like snakes under the skin and his eyes took on an unnatural shine.

"And how could I get to your car all the way across town? When I don't have a key? And you know how rush hour is?"

They both heard the *shhh-POP* and then the recording looped.

"Do you want to see the other files?" she asked.

Danny's Adam's apple worked and he shook his head. "I . . . I don't understand, any of this."

"Neither do I," she said, putting as much feeling into the words as she could. She bit her lip. "I've heard voices, too."

He blinked and the air suddenly cooled between them.

(wrong step)

The sound of Evelyn's heartbeat didn't seem so loud now.

"Conversations between you and I," she said, speeding up, "but ones we're *not* having. Like, they're conversations we *would* have if I hadn't lost Evelyn. I woke up one night and we were feeling Evelyn kick. This morning, I was yelling at you to time the contractions because Evelyn's coming early. And I *felt* the pain. You were laughing, delighted, and it was *agony*—"

Danny straightened. "Stop." The last consonant came out like a soft thud. He swallowed, looked at her, then at the slip of paper still in his hand. Then, quite deliberately, he balled the paper up. Dropped it in the trash.

He looked at the computer screen, watched the little geltab timer on Windows Media Player. "I have to go, now."

And with that he turned and walked out of the guest bedroom.

Carrie sat there an instant longer, then vaulted out. *"Danny?"*

He was rummaging in the bedroom and she came in to find him shoving socks, underwear, and shirts into his overnight bag.

"What are you doing?"

He shook his head. "Nope. I can't deal with this right now."

"What?"

He stopped, hands buried in his bag. When he turned to her, his face was tight again, and he wouldn't meet her eyes. "I can't explain how you got into my Jeep, that's true, but the file you pulled from the trash folder."

"What?"

He started moving again, going to their closet, yanking two button-shirts, and bringing them back to the bed to roll up. "You could've gotten the other files online, easy."

Carrie was rooted to the spot. "Do you hear yourself?"

Danny went into the bathroom and she heard him rummaging around in there. When he came out, hands holding assorted toiletries to his stomach, he said, "Do you hear *yourself*, Carrie? Phantom labor pains? Ghost photos and flowers? Fucking *voices*? How do you think you sound, hon? Really. How?"

Danny was vibrating—no, she was shaking so much her vision trembled.

"That's why I told you, you son of a bitch!"

"No, you didn't," he said, unloading the toiletries into the bag. "You're telling me *now*, Carrie. You didn't say *any* of this before. But today, when you're supposed to be talking with a professional, what happens? Oddly enough."

She couldn't make her legs move and that was good. Good because her fists were at her sides, hard rocks she wanted to send into his face over and over and over again. "You motherfucker!"

He zipped up the bag. "I can't deal right now," he said. "I'm sorry, I wish I was a bigger man, a better man, but I can't. I need to sort what this means out."

"It means I need help, you bastard!"

He looked at her and it was there in his eyes—he didn't believe what he was saying. He didn't know *what* to believe, but the look in his eyes was that of a panicked animal, caught within fight or flight. "You *do*," he said, "but not the way you *think*, Carrie."

He moved toward her, but stopped when she didn't move from the doorway.

"Do you want to hit me?" he said, and his tone was weary. His body was off-center, as if the overnight bag weighed him down. "I can't blame you, but it doesn't change any of this. I need to think. I need to think *away* from this. I need to think of how I can actually *help* you."

Danny moved around her, into the hall, and she followed. Her teeth ground together. A scream was building, center of her chest, gaining pressure and momentum, working its way up her throat. She had hated a lot of things in her life, passionately, but nothing in that moment as much as she hated her husband Dan Finney.

And then he stopped, froze, in the doorway of the guest bedroom. It had become Evelyn's room. The computer was gone. It was seeing it missing to realize that, although Carrie had never hit stop on the recording, Evelyn's heartbeat had stopped playing.

Danny's mouth worked. The muscles of his face were on the move again.

"Is that the help I need, Dan?" she said, softly. "Do you need some, too?"

Danny's mouth snapped shut with a click of his teeth. "You weren't the only one who lost the child, Carrie."

And he turned, walked down the stairs, and out the door. She heard it click shut behind him.

"THEN WHY AM I THE ONLY ONE SUFFERING FROM

IT, YOU FUCKING BASTARD!" she shrieked, and slumped against the wall beside the doorway of Evelyn's room, the heels of her fists to her eyes, not knowing if she wanted to scream, or cry some more, or what.

When the immediate storm began to pass, she looked through the doorway. It was their guest bedroom again, though the computer was shut down. Not that it mattered, she thought.

DAY 1, POST-BIRTH

Drowsing in the murky line between wakefulness and sleep, the hospital bed is comfier than she had ever thought possible. Her lower body is numb—the epidural—but she sense the throb within her lower belly and vagina, biding its time, like a banked fire that just needs a little fuel. Her legs feel odd.

(like how stretch armstrong would feel if toys could feel)

But what she really feels is an emptiness. Not a hollowness, like something was taken, but like something has separated.

(evelyn evie she's here)

She hears her child cry to her right, lusty bursts from new lungs. She tries turning, but the sheet over her is too heavy and she is so, so tired. The dim throb in her lower belly stirs.

Shhh, *she hears Danny say.* I got it, hon. Rest. Lemme check the little princess.

Hungry, she wants to tell Danny, but her jaw is too heavy. Better to lay on the bed, better to feel the sheet. Everything is good. Everything is right. *They'd had a scare, early in the pregnancy, but that was a nightmare, brief and as easily dispersed upon waking.*

Carrie moves her arm, feels the cool sheet—

—and realized she was feeling Danny's cold side of the bed.

Carrie opened her eyes and the gray light of dawn was beginning to seep into the bedroom. She sat up, feeling the throb fade as the sound of Evelyn's cries dwindled from her head. Her hand went to her stomach, felt the flatness there, felt the firmness that had returned as her body had purged the unnecessary weight.

(in the other world my stomach's flat, not firm. i am not stretch armstrong.)

She fell back onto the bed. She couldn't hear Evelyn's heart-beat, anymore. Of course she couldn't. Evelyn, somewhere else, was born. Carrie rubbed her flat stomach.

The alarm on her smartphone went off an hour later, but she was already awake.

Evelyn's room was set up when she passed it three hours later.

Carrie stood in the doorway, hand on the frame. She didn't walk in. Looking at the room, deep in shadow because the sun was on the other side of the house, was like looking at a museum display. What would this one be titled? Baby Culture of the Early 21st?

(life for the new parent)

(i'm not a part of this world)

The air shimmered, slowly, and the guest room slowly resolved before her.

Danny called, but she missed it; she was at a staff meeting and had left her smartphone in the bag. He didn't leave a message.

She called back without thinking, but when the line clicked over to voicemail, she hung up.

She didn't try again until after lunch, and the same thing occurred. As if knowing what would happen, she went to the rest room and when she returned saw a missed call—Danny.

I can't talk to you, these calls said. But I want to.

I just can't yet.

(somewhere, danny and i are getting used to the idea of being parents and, somewhere, evelyn is getting used to being alive.)

Carrie opened the door and Danny was screaming, *bellowing*, upstairs, while the house itself shook with the amplified cries of an infant.

"My CHILD!" Danny shrieked and Carrie jumped. *"THIS IS MY CHILD, GODDAMMIT! She's here, she's BORN, and you either make time or you DON'T! This isn't something to be DEBATED!"*

"Danny?" Carrie yelled, but she couldn't even hear herself. She glanced back at the driveway—only her Subaru. *"DANNY! WHAT ARE YOU DOING?"*

"YOU THINK THIS IS A FUCKING OVERREACTION?" Danny screamed. Meanwhile the recording of the crying infant—*Evelyn*, she'd know that girl anywhere—kept going on and on. *"ARE YOU OUT OF YOUR FUCKING MIND?"*

"DANNY!" Carrie dropped her bag and vaulted up the stairs two at a time.

And the sound of Evelyn and Danny faded. As she ran up the stairs, it was as if she was running away from it. She reached the top, used the newel post to swing her around, and vaulted for her bedroom, passing the Evelyn's room without a glance.

But Danny and the recording were gone.

She stopped in the doorway, panting, her nerves singing with adrenaline. The bedroom had been rearranged. The computer desk sat where here the low bookcase next to her bed had been.

She walked around the bed and saw that a fifth file had been added to the open Download file:

"Evelyn's hunger cry."

Carrie swallowed hard.

The computer desk began to fade, becoming translucent, as the bookcase returned. She blinked and was back in her own world.

She sat down on the bed, and stared at the bookcase.

Tomorrow, she thought, without even wondering what she meant. *Tomorrow we come home.*

She shook her head and pulled her smartphone out of her jacket pocket. Danny had called again, but she didn't have the energy to play the game.

Tomorrow, she thought again, and stared at where, in the other world, the home computer sat, complete with its recordings of her daughter.

DAY 2, POST-BIRTH

Thursdays were reserved for meetings, first amongst general staff, then amongst the various sections, then one-on-one with the editors and photographers, if needed. Contacts were exchanged. Background info was dug through. It was a day where lunches were ordered in and Carrie watched the steady rain through her office window, periodically checking her phone.

Danny called her three times, no messages.

She called the same amount, with the same result.

Today, she would think, out-of-context with whatever else might be going on.

When she left that evening, her car was gone.

She stood on the curb of the parking lot and looked where it should've been—as if, by staring, the car would fade back into the world.

It didn't.

The sound of traffic on S. Prairie Street, heavy with the weight of rush hour faded as she stepped off the sidewalk and crossed to her spot.

No cubes of broken window glass on the asphalt.

No tire tracks.

"Shit," she said, and reached into her jacket for her phone.

Which wasn't there.

She held her hand in her pocket a moment longer, as if the phone would materialize.

The rain, which had become a light drizzle, gained force. Slowly, like a hunter stalking skittish prey, her other hand wandered to her other pocket, where she kept her keys.

That pocket was also empty.

(of course it is)

She straightened, and looked back at the *Register-Mail*'s building. Most of the windows were dark. A few copyeditors and layout people were still present, but far in the back. Her passkey was on her missing ring. She'd have to scale a fence to get to their windows.

(i'm unmoored and i can't even call anyone)

"We *are* alone," she said and thought of Danny saying he had just been wishing to be whole again, to be a family like they were meant to be, and how, holy shit, that so hadn't happened.

If Danny tried calling, would she pick up? And would he realize it's not the Carrie he'd walked out on, the Carrie who didn't share this history with him?

She started for the street. Her first step didn't immediately put her in another part of town.

She took a second step, and the same non-thing happened.

Third step and still present and accounted for.

She picked up her pace, even as the rain came down harder.

Galesburg wasn't that large, and home wasn't that far away.

Even if it wasn't her home, anymore.

Danny waited in the mouth of the driveway, as soaked as she was, staring bemusedly at their Jeep and Subaru. With the rain had come an early evening, and the streetlights at the far corner were already powering on.

"Hey," he said. He continued to stare at their vehicles.

"Hey."

He took a deep breath. "I would've called—again—but my phone was gone."

"Mine, too."

He looked at her with one eye, head slightly canted, like he was examining her. Fat droplets fell from his hair. "It's where I think it is, isn't it?"

She crossed her arms, cupped her elbows. "Where do you think it is?"

He nodded, as if expecting that answer. "I'm sorry, Carrie."

She didn't respond.

He turned back to the cars. "None of this makes sense."

"We're not in our world, anymore," she said.

He glanced at her.

"I mean," she said, looking down the street, at the streetlamp growing brighter, "it's our world, but where I didn't miscarry. We're just in the world next door."

He rubbed his face with his hands. "Fuck, I'm not good at this. I teach post-modern lit, for Chrissakes." He dropped his hands. "Why? Do you know that?"

She shook her head. "Not a clue. Maybe you wished it. Maybe we both did."

A light came on in their house, the downstairs living room, its soft yellow glow falling across the darkening lawn and highlighting half of Danny's face, showing how tired and worn he was. He'd aged ten years in the past ten weeks.

They moved across the lawn without speaking, not going to the door, but to the window itself. Carrie saw herself, slumped on the couch, in a baggy shirt she'd never owned. She was dozing, but trying not to, her head cocked as if she were listening to someone talking.

"Jesus Christ," Danny whispered.

Carrie had read about doubles and doppelgangers in fiction, but she felt no strange vertigo; it was like looking into a warped mirror, where what you saw wasn't how you perceived yourself. This was a version of Carrie that had given birth, that had gone on maternity leave.

(that isn't standing outside the window with her shoes slowly sinking into the soft cold mud)

Carrie took in her other's skin, the way the hair needed washing, the soft brown bags under her eyes, the way how, in spite of all that, she exuded that aura others called a *glow*.

She's content, Carrie thought.

"Holy shit, hon," Danny whispered, taking her hand. "Look."

He pointed and his double came into the room, holding Evelyn, wrapped in the receiving blanket from the hospital.

"Oh, holy shit," Danny repeated, his voice thick. "Holy shit, holy shit." He squeezed, and she squeezed back, hard.

The other Danny sat down next to Carrie, still talking, and Carrie turned so she could view the child. From the window, Evelyn was mostly turned away, but Carrie saw a plump cheek, the infant version of Danny's nose.

Carrie's eyes burned, and tears mixed with the rainfall.

They watched their doubles talk to the child and each other, both exhausted, both glowing, both ignorant of their childless, other versions watching.

Danny raised a hand to touch the glass and she said, "Don't."

He stopped and looked at her.

She tried to smile. "That's not us, hon."

He stared. His eyes were wide and glassy and wet. His Adam's apple bobbed frantically.

"This isn't ours. It's theirs. Okay? It's theirs."

His face crumpled. "Why not us? Why couldn't we have had that?"

She sniffed, wiped her nose with the back of her hand, began to cry even harder. "I don't know, Danny. But we couldn't."

He pulled her in and she cried into his shoulder and he cried into hers as, through the window, the other Danny and other Carrie cooed to their daughter.

"I'm sorry, Carrie," he said into her neck. "I'm so sorry. I'm sorry."

She hugged him tight.

Slowly, the fierceness of their grips lessened and they looked first at each other, then through the window.

The family was gone, but Carrie caught flickers of movement through the archway leading to the kitchen. She bit her lip. Did she breastfeed? Formula?

Holding his hand, she turned away and led the way back down the lawn. "Let's go," she said. "Let's let them live their lives. We have ours to fix."

"How?" Danny asked as they were reached the street.

She shrugged. "I haven't a goddamn clue. We have our own version to live." A glance at the house, with its warm lights and center. "It just isn't *that*."

Danny followed her gaze and his face rippled. "At least we got to see how it would've turned out."

"*Did* turn out," she said. "For them. Not us. Those are ghosts, Danny. Ghosts of What Might've Been."

"*We're* the ghosts."

She looked down at the streetlamp on the corner, its bright cone of white light on the wet pavement. "They got their happy ending."

"What about us?" he asked.

"Let's start with a walk, figure it out from there. Shit, it's not like we can go into the house, anyway."

He surprised her by laughing and squeezed her hand.

They started walking, heading for the corner. To anyone who looked, they would've appeared glowing. Then the watcher would blink, realize he or she could see through Carrie and Danny, see the bright flare of the corner streetlight.

They faded, faded, and, by the time they reached the corner, they were gone.

STORY NOTES

Not everyone will want to read these notes, and that's fine; they're not necessary to enjoy the stories themselves. For others, though, story notes are a bit of inside-baseball, a chance to look under the hood and see what got the engine of a particular story running and I like that sort of thing. Writing isn't mystical; it's a job, much like I said in the introduction. There can be passion, there needs to be some talent, but it's not mysterious or impossible to discuss.

So, some notes.

CRAWLING BACK TO YOU – I don't know how I came to the idea of vampires from a Tom Petty song, but I did, and it was years ago, long before I had any kind of career. I used to listen to this song—the penultimate track to Petty's 1994 nearly-perfect solo album—on the long car rides my mother and I would take between Ohio and Pennsylvania and loved the weary longing of it. But, my initial idea—of the vampire as the protagonist and a familiar as the antagonist—didn't work and it lingered in the back of my head for over a decade. When I flipped it, it sparked, and when I noticed the subtext of toxic, abusive relationships, the fucker ran. This is my love letter to the vampire films I grew up on—not the Christopher Lee or Bela Legosi or even Frank Langella (I came to those later), but the punk nihilism of flicks like *The Lost Boys* and *Near Dark* and *Fright Night*.

SURVIVOR'S DEBT – Blame Peter Straub for this one; in his novel *Ghost Story*, a character remarks that *The Red Badge of Courage* is a ghost story in which the ghost never appears. That idea fired off a Roman candle in my head. *Courage* is about war and valor and cowardice and the idea of what it is to be a man, but, really, it's about being haunted by the idea of not measuring up, of regrets and longing. I liked that; I love novels like King's *The Shining* or Jackson's *The Haunting of Hill House*, but what's truly scary, to me, is not a force in an evil place, but the abstract ideas haunting us and what that can make us do. So, like Crane himself, I filtered that idea through a war that occurred before I was born—in my case, the Vietnam War—and injected the ghost-idea of unfinished business. Telling the story through a casual observer gave it the ambiguity I wanted, even at the end (the character of Dave Silva is not so casual an observer, you'll note). Final note: I wrote the story not long after David Silva, the founder of the Hellnotes website, passed away. A man who showed me a great kindness when I was just starting out, naming my narrator Silva is my way of remembering him.

BABY GROWS A CONSCIENCE – I just had that opening line, dreamed up while teaching a writing workshop at a small convention during the summer of 2010; I had no idea where it went or who Richie or the kid were. It took me three days to finish the first draft, just following the thread, not stopping to question anything, and the subsequent edits were more about streamlining the word choice and not altering the structure—something that is rarely the case with me. I named the kid after a character in Theodore Sturgeon's *More Than Human*, which I was reading at the time. I still like it, even with whatever flaws it has. Because I left almost all backstory unknown, even to me, Baby's the one character I still think about and imagine other stories with her in it. She'd be older now. And more powerful.

A NICE TOWN WITH VERY CLEAN STREETS – One of those times I just had a title, something I scribbled down and then forgot about. It wasn't until one day I was rewatching *Beetlejuice* that I thought, "What if people worshipped the sandworms?" and the title recurred to me. The science-fiction angle is so loose that it just about falls off; this is closer to Lovecraft than even the lackadaisical SF of Bradbury. Writer Gerard Houarner helped me with this, showing me how to drive the action without losing the reader. I've never forgotten that.

THE DOORWAY MAN – If "A Nice Town" is closer to Lovecraft, this is my actual attempt at Lovecraft. I've always liked the idea that humans, by and large, are completely inconsequential to the running of the universe (well, less "liking the idea" than "acknowledging the reality"), but I tried to avoid Lovecraftian pastiche and you can only go so far with "mind-bending creature" before you become pastiche. You hear certain religious folks saying they are "conduits" of the lord or that god speaks through them; I just did it literally.

LOVE SONG FOR THE REJECTED – The stained-glass heart was a doodle a colleague of mine made in a notebook during a particularly boring professional development meeting. For some reason, the image stuck with me and I had this idea of revenge story as filtered through romantic comedy. The result isn't particularly funny—except, for me, the reaction of Evie's first boyfriend—but I wasn't particularly going for the comedy aspect; I just wanted to turn the rom-com trope on its head and bury a handful of razorblades in the center of it.

THE UNIVERSE IS DYING – When I sent this one to Michael Bailey for the anthology *You, Human,* he wrote back, "You and your damn bridges." This one stems from the death of my grandmother, in 1996 (the exact date was early December; the date in this story is actually my wedding anniversary), and hearing the Motion City Soundtrack song "Happy Anniversary." Initially, my idea was a more straightforward literary story, with the title coming from something the grandmother would say to the protagonist, but there was no narrative drive for me. Only when I started thinking about mourning and how some people avoid negative feelings did the story kick-start for me. The location is my grandmother's former hometown with a name-change. The sensory details—the HoHos, the Counting Crows song, the Stephen King novel—were all pulled from the same weird time period that followed my grandmother's stroke and subsequent coma.

SURVIVING THE RIVER STYX – I just don't like open water, don't like not seeing land on the far side. The rest of it was the answer to the question, "How nutty can I make this without going supernatural?" The protagonist was partially named after a professor friend, who annually takes ships from England back to the States.

THE AGONIZING GUILT OF RELIEF – As Damien says in her foreword, this was initially the core of a frame-story. I was trying to write about the, for me, positive idea of letting go of guilt, but the result was an uneven structure that didn't so much as end as peter out (although I still like the original opening line, "We, the dead children, came out of the darkened forests and gathered around the fire of memory"). Damien and my wife advocated focusing solely on the core story and the piece because not about acceptance but the helplessness that sometimes arises. It wasn't an easy story to write; I had to somehow not make the father into a Snidely Whiplash evil character (Ben's comment about how media depicts abusive parents is essentially my view) and also avoid making Jude into a concept and not a real character. That ... wasn't easy ... and my success on both points will rely on how intimate a reader is with both abuse and people who, through nothing more than a quirk of fate and circumstance, are punching bags to society. No, it wasn't easy at all.

REFLECTING THE HEART'S DESIRE – When I went to college, I was shocked, then horrified, to learn how many people were there to do nothing more than to meet someone they could marry and start a family with. They had no career aspirations, had chosen their majors through what essentially amounted to glorified whims, and were funneling tens of thousands of dollars into what boiled down to a speed-dating marathon run by a sadist with poor time management. Not that there's anything wrong with marrying and starting families—I say, in the house I share with my wife and daughter—but that this idea surpassed the sometimes frightening skills these women possessed in journalism, teaching, science, or math was incredibly disturbing to me. This was me trying to figure it out. I failed on that point, but I could empathize more after writing the story.

TO TOUCH THE DEAD – One day I was ruminating about the aftermath of terrorist attacks—y'know, standard, light and easy fare that everyone thinks about—and the cleanup crews involved with them. I wondered if the debris contained any of the human touches—photographs, souvenirs—that marked our professional lives and what those crews would think of such things. How that jumped to a far-flung future where telepaths act as a kind of minister, archive, and undertaker all in one, I don't know.

IN THE NOTHING-SPACE, I AM WHAT YOU MADE ME – This one was written deliberately. I'd heard of Michael Bailey and his *Chiral Mad* anthology and, when I heard he was doing a sequel, I was bound and determined to get into the son of a bitch. I thought of how chiral means an imperfect reflection and then, literally, extrapolated the idea—the idea of imperfections growing and elongating as time goes on. The result, written in a white heat over the course of a week with a few revisions thrown in (mostly with getting the insanity section down to my liking, formatting and all) was a story with a little too much science fiction—even the wonky SF I employed here—for Michael, but he liked the story and asked to hold onto it for an SF-horror anthology idea he had. This was the first time we worked together. You can see how well that turned out.

BONES ARE MADE TO BE BROKEN – This is my most recent writing, created especially for this anthology. The title existed long before there was ever an idea or a collection; it popped in my head one day, without context. This happens sometimes and I tucked it away, waiting for inspiration to strike. The first sparks came when illustrator Pat R. Steiner took the title and, while practicing his photo-editing skills, created an image that, to me, looked like a woman the instant before she hit the water. And then Michael saw it and we started talking, and we got Pat involved and, in the midst of all this, Michael asks me, Would I consider writing a longer piece for the collection? A novella, perhaps? I took another look at that just-for-fun first image and replied, I think I can. All writers pull from their own lives—remixed incidents, feelings filtered through whatever logic and ratiocination they possess—but this is probably the closest I get to "autobiographical" writing. The Hathaway of 1991 is my home in Pittsburgh in 1991; I was raised by a single mother, in an apartment identical to the one in the story. Some of the incidents are indeed remixed from my own life (no, I won't tell you which ones). But, really, these personal details just filled in the gaps and helped me get into Karen's mindframe; I don't write diary. In "The Agonizing Guilt," I wrote about parents from the perspective of kids; this time, I tried to understand parenting. We're all flawed; we bring our baggage to everything, whether we like it or not, including how we raise our kids (how many parents do you know who, in reference to how they raise their kids, say a variation of, "I want them to have everything I didn't"? That's a telling statement). I just pushed it to its edge, trying to understand how it must've been to be a woman, after a bad divorce, trying to raise her oddball son in an unfriendly city during the unfriendly time of the late-1980s/early-1990s. My mother is still alive, but how many parents from that time period, from similar circumstances, have their share of scars?

ALL THAT YOU LEAVE BEHIND – Like "The Universe Is Dying," quantum mechanics, the idea of identical universes shoulder-to-shoulder with one another, stemming from the seemingly most trivial of changes. The idea fascinates me—me, who could barely manage a C+ in the most basic of science courses—and I used it to channel all the irrational and terrible what-ifs that litter my head about parenting and children (including "What would I be doing if I just didn't have my child?"). In spite of the circumstance, I actually do see it as a positive story, a kind of example of the message that, broken apart, bookends this collection, "From this house of broken bones ... I will lead you home." Unspoken, though alluded to, this one was for Jack Finney.

ACKNOWLEDGMENTS

Thanks to Michael Bailey for being the capable steward of this ship. This book literally would not exist without him. Thanks to Pat R. Steiner, for rocking these illustrations.

Thanks to the various editors who liked these stories, particularly Max Booth III, Lori Michelle, Sharon Lawson, and Anthony Rivera.

Thanks to my beta readers, particularly Erinn Kemper and Kristi DeMeester.

Thanks to Damien Angelica Walters, for writing the foreword, and Bracken MacLeod, for writing the afterword. Damien and Bracken are two of the best writers working and I'm honored—seriously, I'm fucking honored—they'd go to bat for me in this way. Go buy *Cry Your Way Home* and *13 Views of The Suicide Woods* to see what they can do with the short form. I envy your first reads.

Huge thanks to Justin Pierre for the permission to use a part of his song "Everything That Hurts" as the epigraph to "Bones." I began the second draft of that story with the chorus at the top of the page, as a guide. Go to justincourtnerpierre.bandcamp.com and listen for yourself.

Thanks to my wife, to whom this book is dedicated. She has been more than patient over the years ... but she's never hesitated to tell me to get back in the game when I'm away for too long, that I'm missing that thing I'm supposed to be writing about: life.

Now, before you go:

I don't tend to write poetry—my verse never went much beyond aping Charles Bukowski—but I wrote the following one night, while stuck on a story, and liked it. I wrote it for myself, which is who writers have to write for first, anyway. If the rest of this book is about alienation and being an outsider, then the following is the response. So, one final special message, from me to you.

AND YOU ARE LOSING

(PAY ATTENTION)

PAY ATTENTION;
The world likes you just the way you are.
On the sidelines,
Out of the game,
And ignorant of the fact
That a game is even happening.
The world wants you to be lazy and stupid,
Bored and apathetic,
Distracted and caught up in
Facebook and Snapchat
Twitter and Vine.
The world wants you to forget
You could one day run things,
Bend things,
Control things,
Change things.

PAY ATTENTION;
There's only one chance for you
To not be seen as stupid and lazy,
Bored and apathetic,
Distracted and mollified.
The world is watching.
And you are losing.

Pay attention.

. . . I will lead you home.

AFTERWORD

THE SPARK THAT CATCHES

IF YOU COULD MAKE A BOOK physically embody literary heart, *Bones Are Meant to Be Broken* would throb. But I don't need to tell you that. My intuition tells me that people who haven't read a book, or have but didn't like it, don't read the afterword. That means you already know what I'm talking about and we're on the same page, so to speak (around 423, if I guess right). If you're reading this before you've dug into Paul Michael Anderson's stories, well, that's fine. I'm not going to spoil anything for you, but I am going to encourage you to go back and read at least one story first so you don't have to take my word for it. Pick one at random; they're all that good (though I have my favorites). Thing about a great book is, it doesn't always get a great life the first time around. Conditions can be tough and the spark can go out before a fire catches.

Everyone wants publishing to be a meritocracy. The dream goes like this: if you write well enough, you'll get published, and then your work will get noticed because excellence is always rewarded. Right? Sadly, it's not always like that. If it were, some small press writers would be household names already and I suspect a few present best-sellers would still be working their day jobs. Success in publishing is as much timing and luck as it is hard work and skill. Sadly, some-times, really good books don't get what they deserve the first time around, and the further hard reality is there aren't a lot of second chances that come along. Fortunately, this book is getting exactly that. And it deserves it.

Now, before you think I'm blowing smoke because I'm friends with Paul, let me disabuse of that notion by telling you, I already put my skin in the game. Not with this collection, but with Paul himself (although this afterword does commit me to standing behind what

I write here). See, a while back he got in touch with me and asked if I'd be willing to collaborate on a story with him. But not on any story—a novella-length work of around twenty thousand words. For those of you who think in terms of total pages and not word counts, that's about eighty-ish pages—forty apiece, if we split the work up evenly. That's not an insignificant commitment, especially for me—my long short stories on average tend to run about half that length. I also have a particular style of working that's fairly rigid and not conducive to collaboration. I've only co-written a story with one other writer before and that was a piece of flash fiction under 1,000 words. So naturally, I said yes to Paul without hesitation. Why? Because I already knew I loved this guy's work and that what we'd come up with would be something I'd be proud to be a part of, even if it took a little more time and effort than either of us anticipated.

We hit our mark, and then went over it by another ten thousand words, because we were having so much fun. I didn't even mind having to cut that extra 10k to hit the goal we needed to. (Okay, well, maybe I did a little. But we got together and killed our darlings like a pair of knife-wielding psychos.) And what I knew going in was going to be the case was exactly what happened—Paul brought his affection for the emotional truth of the story to our collaboration (titled "How We Broke" in an anthology called *Chiral Mad 4*). That's exactly why I'm a fan of his and why I wanted to write with him. What drives his work is the strength of the characters and the increasingly heavy emotional reality he burdens them with. Read or re-read the titular piece in this collection and tell me I'm wrong. I dare you. Even if he's writing about vampires or murderous, telepathic little girls (I know I said I wouldn't spoil anything, but we are in the afterword together), it's that personal weight building that makes it a Paul Michael Anderson story. I wanted to work with him because of that.

I started this by talking about the recipe for literary success, though. It's established that Paul has the work ethic and the skill to catch fire. What this book needs now is a little luck. And what luck, here you are reading this! Maybe together we can create a spark. You see, for writers like me and Paul, better than luck, better than timing, is word of mouth. One person tells a friend about this great book they just read, hands them a copy, leaves a review online, asks their local library to buy one to put in the stacks, and it creates a spark.

You're standing at the ignition point. I'm a fan of Anderson's writing and since you've made it this far, I'm betting so are you. That's two of us. And if we can each convince another reader to take a chance on this book, that's four. And there's heat. If we can be four, I know we can be eight. And we have a spark. If we can be eight, we can keep on going until it catches and there's a fire and Paul and his book become a light bright enough to see from miles away.

Like he deserves.

— Bracken MacLeod
June 2018
Sudbury, Massachusetts